THE YEARS BETWEEN

Further Titles by Margaret Bacon

Fiction

KITTY
THE EPISODE
GOING DOWN
THE PACKAGE
THE UNENTITLED
HOME TRUTHS
THE SERPENT'S TOOTH
SNOW IN WINTER
THE KINGDOM OF THE ROSE
OTHER WOMEN
FRIENDS AND RELATIONS
THE EWE LAMB *
MOTHER NATURE *
NORTHROP HALL *

Non-Fiction

JOURNEY TO GUYANA

For Children

A PACKETFUL OF TROUBLE

* *available from Severn House*

THE YEARS BETWEEN

Margaret Bacon

This first world edition published in Great Britain 2003 by
SEVERN HOUSE PUBLISHERS LTD of
9–15 High Street, Sutton, Surrey SM1 1DF.
This first world edition published in the USA 2004 by
SEVERN HOUSE PUBLISHERS INC of
595 Madison Avenue, New York, N.Y. 10022.

British Library Cataloguing in Publication Data

Bacon, Margaret
The years between
1. Upper class families - England - Fiction
2. Domestic fiction
I. Title
823.9'14 [F]

ISBN 0-7278-5967-6

Except where actual historical events and characters are being described for the storyline of this novel, all situations in this publication are fictitious and any resemblance to living persons is purely coincidental.

Typeset by Palimpsest Book Production Ltd.,
Polmont, Stirlingshire, Scotland.
Printed and bound in Great Britain by
MPG Books Ltd., Bodmin, Cornwall.

For Becky and Alex

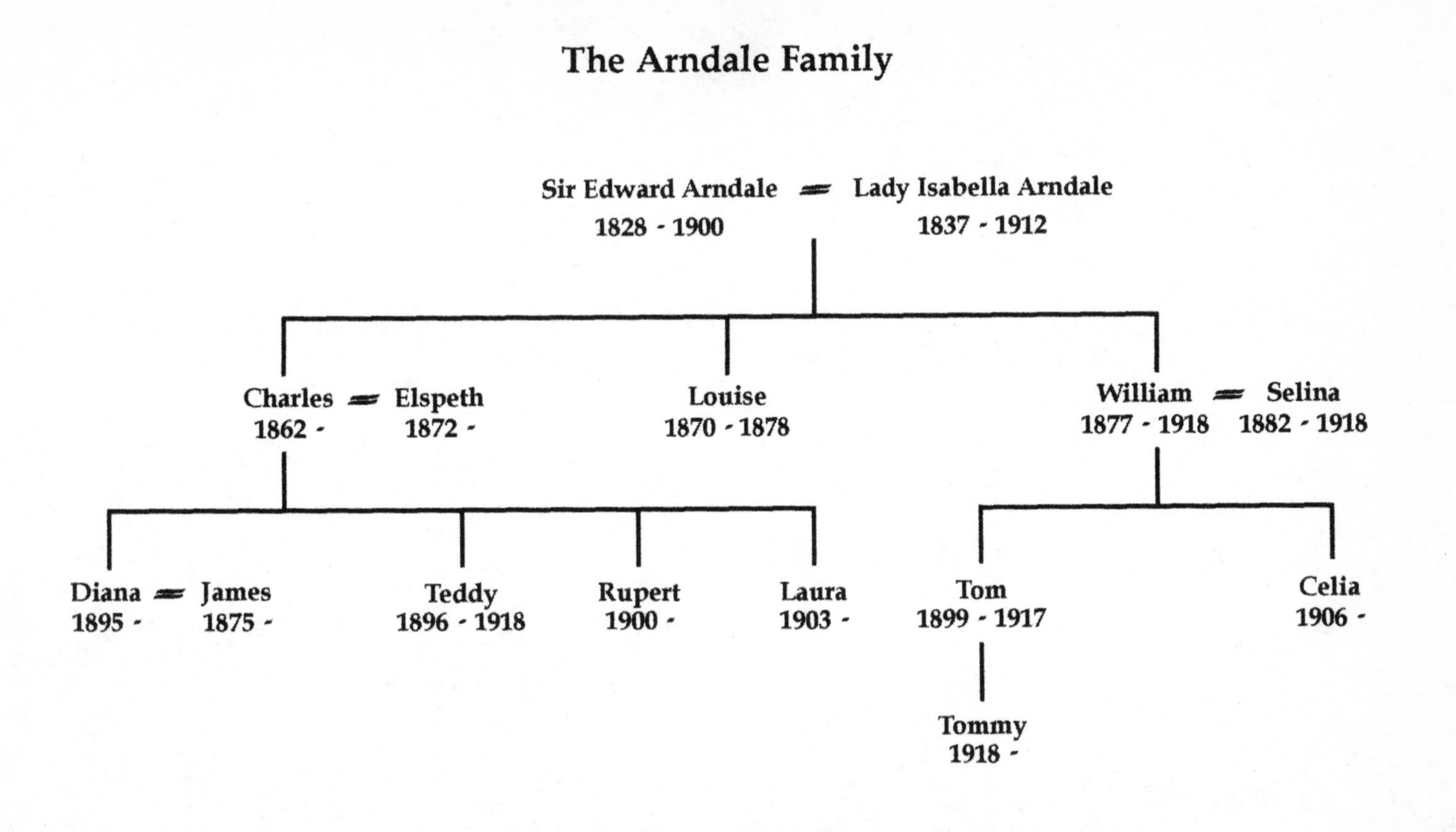
The Arndale Family
Sir Edward Arndale = Lady Isabella Arndale
1828 - 1900
1837 - 1912
Charles = Elspeth
1862 -
1872 -
Louise
1870 - 1878
William = Selina
1877 - 1918
1882 - 1918
Diana = James
1895 -
1875 -
Teddy
1896 - 1918
Rupert
1900 -
Laura
1903 -
Tom
1899 - 1917
Celia
1906 -
Tommy
1918 -

One

James came into breakfast carrying a large envelope.
'This was pushed through the letter box, Diana,' he said, handing it to her. 'It's addressed to both of us.'

She knew what it was; her mother never forgot an anniversary and this was their fifth and therefore special.

Five years had passed since that quiet wedding in the registry office; five useful years in which James had transformed the lives of so many men and hadn't once remembered his own wedding anniversary.

She hadn't given him a card herself, not wanting to draw attention to his forgetfulness on this day which was so important to him for quite different reasons. Tonight he was to speak at a dinner in London; all the ex-servicemen's organizations, all the fund-raisers in the land were to be represented there and he was the guest of honour.

'Oh, my dear,' he exclaimed when he saw the card. 'I am so sorry; I forgot all about it. Happy anniversary, dear girl. Well, well, you and I must just do our celebrating together this evening. You'll enjoy staying overnight at the Imperial Hotel. I'm told it's very luxurious.'

He sounded like a kindly father offering a little girl a treat. It irritated her. She didn't need luxury – just attention, just to be noticed, she thought with sudden savagery. Stop it, Diana. He's a great and good man and you're being silly and ungrateful.

'And you'll enjoy the drive up to London this evening,' the great and good man said, patting her head as he got up to go. 'The country roads are very beautiful at this time of the year.'

She didn't reply.

'Well, I must be off,' he told her. 'A meeting with the councillors in Littleton and then off to Oxford, but I'll be back in good time to pick you up.'

She nodded, raised her face towards him; a perfunctory peck on her cheek and he was gone.

She walked over to the window and watched as he crossed the courtyard to the car. He climbed in rather awkwardly, she noticed. Still strong and well built, he was less agile than he had been, moved less freely. Of course, he worked too hard, often putting in a sixteen-hour day. If she said anything, he just reminded her that it was nothing to the hours they'd worked during the war, when he'd operated for days on end with just occasional catnaps. But that was different and besides he was older now. He was in his late forties, exactly twenty years older than she was.

A thick mist was swirling across the garden, but even as she watched, it began to lift; it was not exactly sunshine yet, but a kind of diffused brightness in the eastern sky.

Now she could hear sounds of the men moving about the building. Doors slammed, feet shuffled, sticks tapped, men laughed, trolleys rattled, nurses' voices scolded and encouraged. A bell rang. Then silence as they all settled down in the dining room.

It was like getting up at boarding school, one of the men had once told her, and it was, in a way, a kind of grown-up boarding school for the disabled, the paralysed, the limbless. '*Les blessés de guerre*,' as the French called them.

The mist had cleared as she made her way over to the dower house for her morning visit to her parents. Shafts of sunlight caught a myriad spiders' webs that stretched from stem to stem, from leaf to leaf and twig to twig, vibrating like gauze in the light breeze. Was it just that they showed up more, or did spiders really make many more webs in the autumn? And, if so, why?

Her parents were still at the breakfast table.

'Here's Diana,' her mother said in the special bright voice she used to her husband nowadays. 'Diana's come to see us.'

Her father rose and held out his hand.

'I don't think we've . . .' he began. 'How do you do?' he added courteously.

'I'm well, thank you, Papa,' Diana assured him.

'And you are?'

'Your daughter, Papa.'

'Of course, of course, but don't let that worry you, my dear.' And he gave her his sweet smile and patted her hand.

'Do sit down, Diana,' her mother said. 'Have some coffee, dear?'

'No, thank you, I mustn't stay long. I've really just come to tell you that we're staying overnight in London, so I won't be in tomorrow morning. I'll call when we get back. But I must hurry back now – there's a pile of post waiting to be dealt with before I go off this evening.'

'It's too bad, the way you have to work over there. It worries me.'

'I enjoy it, Mamma.'

'I'd much rather you busied yourself providing me with grandchildren.'

Diana didn't reply.

'Have you heard from Laura?' she asked instead.

'No. I'm worried about her too, being away from us.'

'Well, she wanted to train as a doctor, Mamma, and when she found she couldn't, she thought this biology course was the next best thing.'

'Why couldn't she? She did tell me.'

'They required Latin.'

'I can't imagine why a doctor should need Latin. Not that I approved of her doing that anyway. This business of women doing men's work is all wrong. I can't imagine what the old queen would have made of it.'

It occurred to Diana to point out that the old queen had done precisely that, but she knew better than to say so. Besides, her mother had adapted so much better than she'd expected to all the changes which had been wrought in Northrop. She'd even accepted that her maid, Mary-Ann, should live nearby with her love child, little Tommy, sharing Nanny Stone's respectable cottage; in the old days the girl would have been shown the door, ordered off the estate without a reference. Oh yes, her mother had accepted so many changes that it would be churlish to argue about the few that she couldn't accept.

'And I'm worried about Rupert too,' her mother was saying.

'But he's on the mend, isn't he?'

'Yes, but what will he do now that he can't fly any more? Of course this is his home, I mean Northrop Hall *was* his home. He was born and brought up here, but now, it's well, it's an *institution*, isn't it?'

It cost her a lot to bring out the hated word, Diana knew that. It wasn't that Elspeth Arndale was against the rehabilitation centre, she supported it, but what she sometimes couldn't accept was that it had replaced her family home. This was one of those times.

'I cannot but blame myself, Diana, when I think that after Teddy was killed, Rupert should have inherited. And I have been instrumental in depriving him of his inheritance.'

'No, Mamma, there was no other way. All the estates are being put to other uses, divided up, sold off. There aren't the staff any more and for so many there are no sons left to inherit.'

'Rupert was left. He was spared.'

'Remember, Mamma,' Diana said gently, 'that Rupert was never interested in running the estate. He knew it wasn't something he'd be any good at. He has other talents. He'll find his own way in the end.'

Her father got up and began to wander about the room.

'Have you lost something, Papa?'

He shook his head. 'I can't remember where I put it,' he said.

'What was it, Papa?'

'I can't remember what it was.'

She glanced at her mother who was always so calm, so able to accept her husband's return to childhood, his escape into his own, strange little world. She herself found it much harder. She didn't know why, just knew it was so. Maybe you can accept the child who was once your husband more easily than you can accept the child who was once your father.

He had always been so powerful, so strong. People ran to his command. Papa could put anything right. She remembered how years ago, before the war, he had divined her unhappiness about Sebastian Crawley and helped her back to normal, everyday life on the estate.

Better not to think about Sebastian.

As she left the dower house and walked back to the hall, the men were beginning to drift out into the garden, well wrapped up against the cold. The fitter ones were planting out winter vegetables and bulbs; others, supervised by Adam, the head gardener, were tidying up the herbaceous beds, cutting back dead stems, mulching the earth between plants. The men in wheelchairs were in the conservatory, some mixing sand and compost which Adam's son, Jack, barrowed round to them, others using the mixture to repot flowering plants and tamp down into seedboxes.

They all waved and called out greetings. Smiling, she waved back, and thought how good was this use of the their old home. To her, who had nursed throughout the war, it seemed a continuation of that care. It was different for her parents' generation. They had stayed at home, sure that the old ways would return when the war was over. Timeless and changeless their old world had seemed and it was now suddenly gone. The buildings at Northrop were the same, but oh, how different was the life within them! There were no footmen now, no ladies' maids, no awe-inspiring butler. The great staircase was still there but no glittering guests glided gracefully down it in evening dress; young men now struggled, holding on to the bannisters or supported by a nurse or orderly. No wonder her mother could sometimes scarcely believe it. And it had confused her father beyond curing; he was another kind of *blessé de guerre*.

As she settled herself at her desk, she could hear thumping sounds coming from the nearby gymnasium, which was James' latest brainchild and the result of four years' cajoling, fund-raising, argument and discussion. And now it was finished and the men were exercising under young Peter who had been training to teach gym at a boys' school before the war, before he had had an arm blown off and both his legs smashed at Paschendaele.

All this James has achieved, she thought humbly, and I should count myself privileged to have played a part in it; I should not mind that he forgets wedding anniversaries, nor should I resent being patted on the head and told how much I'll enjoy a car ride to London.

In fact she did enjoy the drive. The Gloucestershire countryside was at its most lovely on this calm October afternoon. They drove through avenues of trees whose leaves, golden, red and brown, had not yet fallen, but still twisted and turned on thin autumnal stems. The sky was opalescent, turning imperceptibly dimmer as evening approached, but still aglow even as the earth darkened. Then they reached the bright lights of London and all that was natural was left behind.

The hotel was luxurious, as James had promised. Their bedroom had a carpet that reached all the way to the walls and their bed was huge and draped like a four-poster. The commodes on each side of it, as well as the wardrobe, the chest of drawers and the little writing desk, were all imitation antiques, as was the long looking glass which was tilted in a dark frame near the window. There were electric lights on the walls and lamps with silk shades by the bed and on the desk. There was even a basin in the corner of the bedroom, with hot and cold taps and a wooden surround. The maid showed them the way to the bathroom, down the corridor.

Diana prowled around their bedroom, opening cupboards and drawers, a little bemused by all this luxury. Then suddenly, as she stood there, a sharp picture came into her mind; a very clear vision of her little hut in Etaples, her tiny, mud-encircled hut, cold and dingy in contrast to all this illuminated spaciousness. Ten of us could have shared this room, she thought.

She said so to James, when he returned from his bath.

'A different world, my dear, a different world,' he said.

'Well, for some of us anyway. I'm hoping to have a few words tonight with some of these housing people. Perhaps, yes, I should say something about it in my speech,' and he settled down at the writing desk with his papers.

She would so have liked to talk more to him about this strange vision she'd had, the clarity of it, how it had flashed unbidden into her mind. In a curious way, she knew that she dwelt more on the past than he did, yet he was the one who was working tirelessly for the men who had suffered in that past. He was so much more practical than she was, altogether more admirable. She began to dress.

The blue chiffon she had bought especially for the occasion, for it was a rare event for her to come to a celebration such as this, was pale blue and gauzy, and looked, she thought, a little drab hanging there on its coathanger. Slowly and carefully she drew on her pure silk stockings, fastening them to the suspenders of the little corset, blessing the fact that stays were now something which only old ladies persisted in wearing. Boyish figures were all the rage now, so she tied herself into the breast flattening bust bodice and looked at the consequent result with satisfaction in the long mirror.

The dress *did* look better on than off; she hardly recognized herself and was pleased for James' sake that she wouldn't let him down as she stood beside him to welcome all these important guests.

'Will I do?' she asked him, for once coquettish, as they stood by the door, ready to go down.

He glanced at her.

'Very nice,' he said.

'Is that all?'

'You always look very nice, my dear. You know you do,' he admonished, patting her gently on the back, then opening the door and leading the way out into the corridor.

But I don't really believe it, she thought, unless you tell me so; it's not reasonable of me but that is how I am.

They were to stand in a line alongside several others – mayors, chairmen of various committees, representatives of the fighting services and their wives – to welcome the guests. She and James were at the far end; after shaking hands with them, the guests were to move through wide open doors into the reception. All this was briefly explained to her as the first guests were announced.

She felt nervous as they moved slowly along the line towards her for she had never done anything like this before, but she found it was easy; James seemed to know them all, repeated their names to her and they were all very friendly, these strangers, and obviously pleased to meet James' wife.

After that they crowded in, so many of them that there was scarcely time to do more than smile and shake hands. Then she heard a familiar name being announced.

'Sir Arthur and Lady Crawley. And Mr Sebastian Crawley,' the major domo's sonorous voice rang out loud and clear.

She felt herself go very hot, she gasped and paused mid-sentence. The little red-haired lady she was talking to looked at her, surprised; it was a look that made her get a grip on herself. This little woman, with her hennaed hair and rouged cheeks, had come all the way from Lancashire for the occasion; she had raised a great deal of money for the disabled men who had come back from the war, having lost her husband and her only son on the Somme. This widow was far more important, Diana told herself, than the young man she had met before the war and seen only once since.

She saw his parents approaching.

'How do you do, Lady Crawley?' she heard herself say with perfect calmness.

'What a lovely surprise, Diana!' Sebastian's mother said, kissing her. 'I'd no idea that you were now married to Dr Bramley, of whom we've heard so much.' And, turning to her husband, she said, 'You remember Diana, don't you, dear? She stayed with poor Selina before the war.'

'Of course,' he said, adding jovially, 'you were the lovely girl who turned all the boys' heads,' and they smiled at her and moved on, into the reception.

Sebastian didn't follow them in the line, as she'd expected. Perhaps he'd seen her and managed to dodge the queue and go straight into the reception. She'd been horrified at the prospect of meeting him here in this public place, but somehow the idea that he might have avoided her was even more painful.

Suddenly he was in front of her. She couldn't think of, much less utter, any of the usual polite phrases; silently she held out her hand. Sebastian, who had been practising his lines as he made his way towards her, couldn't remember them. He took her hand. He seemed to hold it for a long time and then, without speaking a word to each other, they parted, he to the reception, she to talk to a little, bald-headed man, bespectacled and gnomish, whose spiky fringe of hair, which stood up around his shiny pate in defiance of the laws of gravity, gave him a somewhat ridiculous look, an impression immediately contradicted when he spoke to her in a beautiful, deep and serious voice, of work that he and James had done together.

'A great man,' he concluded, nodding towards James. 'I am glad for him that he has such a lovely wife.'

She did not see Sebastian at the reception, but when they moved into dinner, he was seated so that from her place at the top table, she looked directly down at him. He looked older, she thought, than when he had come to Northrop, much older than the boy she had danced with before the war.

After that first long look, she concentrated on the man at her side, who turned out to be the spiky-haired gnome with the beautiful voice who told her at length about the way he had worked with James since the war. She interested herself entirely in what he had to say and managed to put Sebastian out of her mind.

'You will be full of wifely fears when your husband gets up to speak,' he foretold. 'There is no need of course because he is a great speaker, but that is how it is with wives.'

He was right, she *was* nervous for James. Something unexpected might happen to upset him, his notes might get jumbled up, or even dropped, he might get hiccups or develop a cough, he might dry up.

None of this happened; he was a passionate as well as an informative speaker and the audience listened with rapt attention. It wouldn't matter if he'd lost his notes, for he never looked at them. Afterwards they gave him a standing ovation, crowded round him eager to talk. She stood a little apart, but when it was announced that there would be dancing, and she was told that she and James should lead the way, she took his hand and together they went towards the dance floor.

Just as the band struck up with a waltz, he saw someone he recognized nearby.

'Oh, there's Dr Sykes,' he exclaimed. 'The eye specialist, doing great work among the blind and partially blind ex-soldiers. How did we miss him? He wasn't at the reception. Must have arrived late. Excuse me, won't you?' And he turned abruptly away, leaving her alone on the dance floor.

Sebastian, watchful, saw it all.

'Perhaps, sir, I might dance with Mrs Bramley?' he asked, hurrying towards them.

'Oh, would you, my dear fellow? How kind. Excuse me, Diana my dear,' and he hurried away to talk to his specialist colleague.

They didn't speak, just moved to the music, both remembering the last time they had waltzed together. Should she feel guilty? No, not when James had virtually pushed them together. Besides, there was nothing wrong in dancing, they weren't even conspicuous now, joined as they soon were on the dance floor by so many other couples.

James was still talking to the eye specialist when the music stopped.

'Let's sit this one out,' Sebastian said and led her to one of the many couches that lined the ballroom.

'Why are you here?' she asked as they sat down.

'I think I probably wouldn't have come if I'd known you'd be here,' Sebastian said. 'I wouldn't have wanted to embarrass you. I'd no idea when you said, on that awful day, that you were married, that you'd married Dr Bramley.'

'Of course not. But I didn't mean that. I meant why are you here as a guest?'

'It's because of the work I do connected with housing.'

'Oh, of course, I remember you were going to be an architect.'

'Yes, and I have become one, Diana, despite all.'

He smiled at her sadly.

'Despite all what?'

He shook his head.

'And then,' he went on, ignoring her question, 'I became involved in plans to house the disabled. You know how they said they'd come home to houses fit for heroes—'

'Oh, yes. And James says they've come home to houses only heroes *could* live in.'

'That's why I'm involved,' he said. 'We need good, cheap houses for renting, not by swindling landlords, but by trusts who'll see the houses are well kept and the rent's fair.'

'Where will the money come from in the first place?'

'The trusts would have to borrow money to build them but once the rents come in, they'll pay for themselves and won't need to make a profit anyway, just cover their costs. I've been working to get the Houses for the Disabled Committee to fund the initial expenditure. In fact one of the reasons I came tonight was that I knew that some of their members would be here and I thought I could do some canvassing.'

'Then shouldn't you go and talk to them?' she asked.

'No,' he said firmly. 'I'd rather talk to you.'

She didn't know how to answer that, so resorted to the safe topic of his home-building scheme.

'Where will you build these houses?' she asked. 'I mean, there's been so much criticism of all this ribbon development going on along the main roads out of towns.'

'Oh, it's dreadful. No, the men need to be in the towns, close to shops and cinemas and so on. Of course, it's more difficult to find the space to build in towns.'

'Couldn't you convert some of the existing houses? They say there are an awful lot on the market now that people can't sell.'

He turned to her, surprised.

'That's exactly what I've started to think. In fact, I'm going to see if my firm would consider helping us do it.'

'Your firm?' she repeated. 'Do you have your own firm?'

'No, nothing so grand,' he told her, laughing. 'I work up north for a firm called Booth and Samson, one of the oldest in the town. It started as a letting agency and then developed a building branch which in turn made them start to employ architects. Then they dropped the building side altogether and for the last twenty years it's been a firm of architects, though Mr Samson still sees to the agency, more or less as a sideline.'

They were talking so easily now, so naturally. Perhaps, Diana thought, we can become friends, just ordinary friends. Not have to part as we thought we must three years ago. Just go on like this.

'That's enough about me,' Sebastian said. 'Let's dance.'

As they danced again, she knew it wouldn't be possible just to be friends. They must not meet again. Must not. But don't think about it now, just live this blissful moment.

She danced with other people too, and once or twice with James, but she was always aware of Sebastian watching her. She seemed to feel his presence, feel a little lost without him and then, when she was again dancing in his arms, she felt safely at home again. It was unexpected this feeling, it was inexplicable, but real, so real.

She and James stayed, of course, to the end, bidding farewell to the departing guests, some of whom were journeying home, others staying in the hotel.

'Well, I'm thankful we're staying here,' James said as they went up to their bedroom. 'I don't think I'd have stayed awake long enough to drive home tonight.'

'I'm not a bit sleepy,' she told him. 'Only my feet are a bit tired.'

'A good soak is what they need. Run along and have a bath. I'll put the shoes outside the door for cleaning, then I'm into bed.'

He was asleep by the time she had undressed.

He had this amazing gift for accepting sleep the moment the chance of it was offered, she thought, looking down at him. She herself was wideawake, as she put on her dressing gown, gathered up towel, sponge bag and nightdress, pushed her feet into slippers and set off down the corridor.

The bathroom was locked. Somebody in there already. She remembered there was another bathroom in the other direction; she'd noticed it as they'd walked down the corridor to the lift. She had turned to go when, hearing the door being unlocked, she turned back.

A man was standing opposite her in the doorway, a man in a green silk dressing gown, below which a few inches of naked leg protruded and then carpet slippers. She raised her eyes and took in the astonished face, the wet and tousled hair. It was Sebastian.

She seemed unable to move, just stood there like a statue, then she heard him say her name, felt his arms drawing her into the room behind him. Heard him turn the key in the door.

'Now we can talk, Diana,' he said.

The bathroom was still warm and steamy. She noticed the brown linoleum on the floor, the striped blind at the window, the white wooden chair with a cork seat by the bath. Then all these things were blanked out because she was in Sebastian's arms, he was kissing her and then her head was resting against the green silk dressing gown. And again she had that feeling of having come home, safely into harbour, where she belonged.

He moved her over to the little wooden chair, sat down and held her on his knee. His dressing gown was wide open now. And so was hers. He cupped her breasts in his hands.

'They're so much better without those awful flatteners,' he said.

'It's the fashion,' she told him.

'My mother doesn't approve of them. Her doctor said they were bad for women.'

'Why?'

'I can't remember.'

What was she doing? she asked herself in disbelief, sitting in this bathroom, half naked, discussing bust bodices with Sebastian, while her husband slept in a room just a few yards down the corridor? How had it happened, when she hadn't planned any of it and nor had Sebastian? Yesterday neither of them had even known they would see each other ever again.

'I don't know why or how we're here like this,' Sebastian said, as if echoing her thoughts, 'but oh, my darling Diana, it's wonderful that we are.'

He had moved so that her body was stretched across his knees, her head and legs supported by his arms. Leaning over her he kissed those breasts about which they'd just had that curious discussion and she raised her hands to hold his head more closely against her flesh and he responded by kissing her stomach, kissing her all over, nuzzling and kissing until she wanted nothing but him, longed for nothing but him, could be satisfied with nothing less.

'Come, let's go to my room,' he whispered.

It broke the spell. She could not go to another man's room, she Diana, James' wife. She could not do this wicked thing.

'We can't, Sebastian, we can't,' she said, standing up abruptly, trying not to see his face, which had been so full of love and joy and was now shocked, crestfallen. She had done this to him, she had inflicted this awful pain. But what else could she do? She had to choose the lesser of two evils, didn't she? Except that she was no longer sure of the meaning of that word evil. What did it mean, that word? When something felt so right, could it be so utterly wrong? Yes, it could.

Miserably, he helped her to stand up, pulled his dressing gown together, tied the cord, watched as she did the same.

'I'll leave you,' he said, 'to have your bath,' but he began kissing her again until, gently, she pushed him away.

'Goodbye, Sebastian,' she said, as he opened the door.

'Goodbye, my love,' he said and left her.

She looked around the room as if it had been the scene of a crime. Too sad and weary to bath now, she made her way back to the bedroom and climbed into bed beside the sleeping James. But she lay awake for a long time reliving what had happened and wondering how it would have been if Sebastian hadn't invited her back to his room, but had let nature take its course uninterrupted. And she wondered if he, lying awake in his room down the corridor, was thinking the same.

Two

'We missed you at breakfast, dear,' Sebastian's mother gently reproached him as he came down late the next morning.

'I wasn't very hungry.'

'You look wretched, darling. Didn't you sleep well?'

'Not much. You know how it is after these occasions.'

'No, I don't. Your father and I slept like logs. Such a comfortable bed and a lovely room. This really is a beautiful hotel. But come along, your father is waiting in the hall with the cases.'

He hesitated, fearful of whom he might meet in the hall. To his relief he heard his father say, 'We said goodbye to Dr Bramley on your behalf, Sebastian. They've only just left.'

'Yes,' his mother said, laughing. 'I think the dear man would have been here all day talking to everybody, but Diana seemed in a hurry to be off.'

Of course she was, in case she saw me, Sebastian thought as they left the hotel. She's as relieved as I am that we haven't met this morning. Yet at the same time he was despondent at not seeing her again.

As he drove his parents home, he felt again the shame he had felt in bed last night, the shame of his behaviour. She would think him an unspeakable cad, all hope of keeping up that old trusting friendship was destroyed. He'd wrecked it with his beastliness.

'You'll stay over tonight?' his mother said, noticing, when they arrived, that he didn't take his case out of the car. 'You surely won't drive up north today?'

'Yes, I must. I've work to prepare for Monday.'

'Then we'll have an early lunch before you go.'

'I'd rather just have some coffee and be on my way,' he told her.

He knew that he couldn't bear to hear them going through the events of the previous evening, praising Dr Bramley, speculating, as his mother had done in the car, about whether the Bramleys had any children.

He needed to be alone with his thoughts. But as he drove faster than he should have done up the Great North Road, his thoughts were as confused as ever. He'd wrecked everything; he felt the shame of it intensely, yet a part of him refused to have regrets and would have given much to have Diana naked in his arms again, even if it was only for a few minutes on a wobbly bathroom chair.

'Now tell us all about last night,' Elspeth Arndale instructed her daughter, handing her a cup of tea.

Diana looked at her mother, sitting there, so composed as she wielded the silver teapot at this beautifully laid table with its delicately embroidered cloth and fine bone china, and wondered what would happen if she really did tell her mother all about last night. Surely the very Crown Derby would rise up in horror?

'It all went off very well, thank you,' she said instead. 'James made a very good speech. In fact, he was so good that everybody stood up and clapped afterwards.'

'And so they should. He works tirelessly for these men. I think he deserves more recognition. I always look for him in the honours list and I think it very unfair that his name is never mentioned. He ought to have an OBE at least.'

Diana laughed.

'Oh, I don't think James would be a tiny bit bothered about an honour. Getting a better artificial limb for some poor amputee would be much more important to him.'

Her father, who had been cutting a cucumber sandwich into tiny pieces, suddenly said, 'You are the lady who usually comes at breakfast time. Of course you are! I knew it.'

He nodded and smiled, pleased that she was there and pleased with himself for remembering that she usually came earlier.

'That's right, Papa. I usually come to see you after breakfast but I went to London and stayed the night. We didn't get back here until nearly lunch time.'

'Isn't it wonderful,' her mother said, looking at him fondly, 'how he remembers such details, like the time you usually come to see us? He still has such an orderly mind and likes routine. James says it's remarkable the way he remembers the pattern of the days.'

What struck Diana as remarkable was that her mother found comfort – pride even – in the fact that her husband, who didn't even know his own daughter, had some vague idea that a woman visited them every morning at breakfast. He who used to organize a whole estate and never forgot an employee's name.

'I'll just go and make sure they've locked the door,' he said now.

'There's no need, Papa,' Diana began, but her mother signalled her to let him go.

'He likes to perform these little duties,' she explained. 'And it does no harm.'

Diana shook her head, not in disagreement but because she was always amazed at the way her mother, who could still be sharp with others, was always gentle with her husband, endlessly understanding and patient. The only other person who could soothe him, smooth away his childish fears, was Nanny Stone, familiar to him since babyhood, once his nanny and then nanny to his children. He turned to her now, in his second childhood, with the same trust and affection as he had done in his first.

How calmly her mother accepted this great disaster! She who worried endlessly about trifles.

'You've heard about Laura?' she asked now.

'Yes, we got the message that she's gone to Edinburgh.'

'But weren't you and James horrified? I mean, to go off by herself, just like that!'

'She always was impetuous, Mamma, but she would never do anything really foolish.'

'But it's so extraordinary! Surely it was enough that we allowed her to go to that college to study science? What more could she want?'

'She always wanted to study medicine, Mamma, you know that. But she needed Latin and now she heard of this one university where she could study medicine without it, so she just went straight away. You have to admire her courage – and she seems to have been very lucky.'

'But think of what might have happened to her on that dreadful journey! Just going off *on a train* unchaperoned like that, whatever was she thinking of?'

'Girls do go about unchaperoned now, Mamma.'

'Not well brought up girls. And one hears terrible tales of girls being kidnapped into white slavery by those dreadful foreign people. Whatever was Laura thinking of, to go and stay with a stranger, a woman who had picked her up on a train?'

'She was a very kind lady, Mamma, who offered her accommodation.'

'But that's what they do,' her mother persisted. 'They use these sweet old ladies to decoy girls, then they sell them into slavery.' She dropped her voice and whispered, 'And they use them in harems.'

'But it didn't happen, Mamma. Mrs MacFadzean had been a wonderful landlady. It all ended happily for Laura.'

'But I can't help worrying about how it *might* have ended,' her mother told her.

She saw that her mother was in one of her worrying moods; with genteel persistence the words would flow. She knew that it was no good trying to stop her mother worrying, once she had made up her mind.

'And I worry about Celia,' she was saying now.

'Celia? But she's been settled for years with those relations of her mother's.'

'Of course, I know that. In Bradford or Leeds or one of those northern places, but she is nonetheless your father's niece. His dead brother's only surviving child. I cannot but feel we should have done something for her, brought her here, oh I don't know what, but done *something* anyway.'

She shook her head and added, 'The war seems to have turned all our lives upside down.'

It turned my life upside down too, Diana thought, remembering last night, thinking of what might have been, as she watched her father undoing all the bolts and locks to let her out. She kissed him goodbye and stood for a moment by the door, listening to all the bolts and locks being put back in place.

As she walked back to the house, the men greeted her: 'Good afternoon, Mrs Bramley; pleasant day, Mrs Bramley; do you think the doctor could spare me a few minutes to look at these new exercise frames, Mrs Bramley, and that wheelchair isn't as good as the last one.'

Tell me all about last night. What would her mother have said if she had told her? She wouldn't have believed it, of course. Unthinkable that a daughter of hers could behave wantonly. And somehow, back here in Northrop, she could hardly believe it herself.

Oh, yes, of course I'll tell him about the wheelchair and ask him about the exercise frames. That's what I'm for. I am his helpmeet, I am his secretary, his go-between, his receptionist, his protector against too many interruptions.

Last, and most certainly least, I am his wife.

Don't be bitter, she told herself. Don't think of what might have been. Don't make comparisons. Forget last night. Bury the memory of it. Bury it, bury it, bury it.

Three

'What we need to do, sir,' Sebastian explained to the Senior Partner of Booth and Samson, sometimes still known as Old Mr Samson as he had once been called to distinguish him from his son, who would have succeeded him, if the war hadn't intervened, 'is to sell some of these properties that we are unable to let.'

Old Samson regarded him with shrewd, hooded eyes. It was a world-weary face; he'd seen so many young men in his time, listened to so many modern ideas that somehow never worked out, never became current, never matured into old ideas. Just fizzled out. But he liked this young man, all the same. The most hard-working he'd ever had in the firm, certainly more of a worker than young Booth, son of the man with whom he'd set up the firm forty years ago. There was a time, he remembered, when he used to pity Robert Booth and his wife for their childlessness. Now he envied them; the son who was born to them in their middle age had only been twelve years old when the war broke out.

This young Sebastian Crawley seemed to work hard during the day at the drawing board in his office and then, he gathered, spent evenings and weekends working on this project for getting homes for the disabled soldiers.

'You see, sir,' he was saying now, 'they're looked after as well as can be by these rehab places but afterwards, they need a decent, manageable place of their own.'

'There's plenty to rent. And rents are low nowadays.'

'But with respect, sir—'

'Which usually means without any,' the old man put in drily.

Sebastian smiled and nodded.

'But this time it's meant,' he said. Then he went on, 'Living in a rented house wouldn't give them security. And we couldn't be expected to make expensive adaptations to a house that might later be let to an able-bodied family.'

The old man nodded.

'And I reckon it makes business sense. We can't let these houses now in the slump. It's a good time to sell.'

'Except that I'm told you can't sell a house either. There's no money around.'

'But you see, sir, we have funds, limited admittedly, but enough to put down a deposit on a mortgage.'

Mr Samson pulled a face, turning down the corners of his long, thin mouth.

'Mortgage,' he repeated with distaste. 'I don't like that word.'

'But why not? People can't afford to buy a home now, but when this new building society movement really takes off, people *will* be able to buy homes, paying for it over the years.'

Old Samson shook his head.

'I don't think building societies will ever become common,' he said. 'It was a nice idea and did well for a while, but it'll never catch on.'

'Why not?'

'Because British people don't like borrowing. "Neither a borrower nor a lender be", as the bard said. A decent man doesn't want to live in a borrowed house any more than in borrowed clothes.'

He looked at Sebastian's downcast face and his own expression softened.

'Well, you had a try, lad,' he said. 'Nothing's lost by that.' And then he added casually, 'You could always try another firm that's not ruled by an old codger like me.'

It was only after he'd left the old man and gone back to the drawings he was working on for a new town hall, the old one having been the recipient of the only bomb that fell on the city centre, that the significance of these words struck him.

Of course there were other firms he could approach. There were all sorts of businesses that dealt with houses; solicitors winding up estates might be interested, other renting concerns, builders possibly though there was little building going on now that the post-war boom had collapsed. Still there was no harm in touting round them all. Nothing lost and maybe something gained. And if it meant that he filled every hour of the working day and half the night, so much the better. When you need to blot something out of your mind, keep your imagination from straying, you must leave no vacuum for nature to abhor and fill. You must fill it yourself with work.

And so the winter passed, his first winter up here in the north. His parents had demurred when he showed them the notice of the job in Gradby and told them he was applying for it. He knew that they were surprised that he had settled in so well. The truth was that he liked it up here, liked the people, liked their dry humour, the directness of them.

He loved the countryside which waited for you just on the edge of the town. He had even grown to like this grimy city, with its soot-encrusted buildings, its blackened trees, its grinding trams. There was a homeliness about it. Homely too was his landlady, Mrs Jordan, whose lavish cooking had resulted in his putting on a stone, to his mother's delight. He was sure that it was that, more than his success at work, which had reconciled her to his moving away to the north.

Fog had lain in a thick pall over the city for most of the winter as he worked on the drawings for the town hall and went the rounds of companies who might be interested in his housing scheme. But spring was coming, the fog lightened to a mere misty drizzle, when Mr Samson called him into his office one morning and asked him how he was getting on.

'Not much luck so far, sir,' he told him.

'Might be worth trying Nathan and Braithwaite. They say that young Braithwaite's in charge nowadays. He might be better suited to your ideas than some of the others.'

'Thank you, sir. I'll write to him straight away with details, then follow that up with a telephone call and maybe he'll agree to see me.'

'That's a good plan,' Old Samson said, nodding approval. 'Not that I'm saying it'll work, mind,' he added, always afraid of sounding too encouraging.

'As I see it,' Matthew Braithwaite of the firm Nathan and Braithwaite, said to Sebastian, 'you're suggesting that we offer some of these houses to the trust on mortgage for the war disabled.'

'Exactly.'

'And then we're to throw good money after bad by adapting them.'

'No, I am raising funds for that. And I will give my own services free to draw up plans and supervise all the alterations.'

Matthew Braithwaite was about his own age and had just become the junior partner in the firm, his father having died the previous year. He too had served in the war. He was sympathetic to Sebastian's cause. But northern shrewdness held him back.

'You won't find it easy in these hard times to raise funds.'

'Not easy, but possible,' Sebastian told him. 'Not everyone has forgotten what we owe these men.'

'Well, how about coming and telling me about it over lunch?'

Sebastian was delighted. This was the most encouraging response he'd had in the few weeks he'd been touting his scheme.

On the stairs they met Joshua Nathan. Matthew Braithwaite introduced him to his senior partner.

'We have a scheme to discuss over lunch, Mr Nathan,' he told him, 'which I will of course come to talk over with you afterwards.' Then he added, 'Mr Crawley's from the south, Mr Nathan, but he's settled up here now.'

The old man offered Sebastian a hand which was frail but had a surprisingly firm grip, as he said, 'We won't hold that against you, Mr Crawley. A man can't help where he's born.'

But his eyes were kindly and he smiled as he spoke the words. He seemed to Sebastian a sad and weary man; he sensed that most decisions in this firm would now be left to this Matthew Braithwaite who was taking him out to lunch.

Old Mr Nathan stood for a moment watching them go. It should have done his heart good, he thought, to see those two: his late partner's son, a tall, fair, good-looking lad with something carefree about him and that other young chap, equally well set-up, though dark and more serious looking. It should have done his heart good, he knew that, to see there were still some strong young men left to take up the burden that was now too heavy for their elders' shoulders. But all he could think of was that other young man, that young Nathan, who should have succeeded him in the firm but was buried far away in Flanders.

Four

It was a lovely morning as Diana walked over to the dower house; winter had at last given way to spring, the birds were singing, daffodils that had been successively frozen by frost, bent under a weight of snow and battered by rain, now raised to the sunshine flowers that might have been newly unfurled, so fresh and bright they seemed.

Everything in the garden looked clean and well cared for. The men were busy everywhere; she could see some of them in the greenhouses repotting plants under Adam's instruction. Others were outside working on the beds, surrounding the herbaceous plants with compost to keep the soil moist this summer and breaking down the roughly dug vegetable plot to a fine tilth ready for planting.

It's a wonderful thing which James has done here, she thought. She always knew it, of course, but sometimes it struck her suddenly like this, when she saw the men working. How he had transformed their lives! Nothing could give them back the strong young bodies that the war had destroyed, but James had given them courage to make the best of what they had been left with. Others had just accepted their sacrifice and forgotten them. James would never allow them to be forgotten; their needs had taken over his life and she was privileged to be allowed to share in his schemes, she knew that. She must cling to that knowledge, she thought as she made her way slowly over to the dower house.

'Oh, I thought you were never coming,' her mother said as she opened the door. 'I've had such a time stopping your father locking you out. And I've such news!'

'I can see you're excited about something,' Diana said, laughing as she kissed her mother. 'So what is it?'

'I found an address for Celia! I think it may be a later one than we tried before.'

'Where did you find it?'

'You know how I've been hunting for your father's old address book? I came across it quite by chance when I was looking for something else among his bank papers. And there was Celia's address! He hadn't written down the name of Selina's relations – the ones she'd sent Celia to, I mean – but it does have an address in a place called Gradby and he'd written *Celia* in brackets after it.'

'And it's not the same as the one you wrote to before?'

'Really and truly, I can't remember but I do know I didn't get an answer, so it must have been the wrong one or Celia would certainly have replied.'

She went over to her desk and took an envelope from it.

'Look, I've written to her telling her how we've tried to make contact in the past. Would you put it in the pillar box for me? I've put a stamp on it. Oh, dear, it would be so helpful if we'd known the name of the poor girl's relations on her mother's side. Of course, normally we should have been in touch, but the war, well . . .' She shrugged and didn't complete the sentence.

'Do you think they've adopted her by now?' Diana asked, as she took the letter.

'I've no idea. It's dreadful that we don't even know such a thing about our own niece. I do feel we've let her poor parents down, especially after all the sacrifices Selina made.'

Diana didn't reply. The Selina she had known, unpredictable and treacherous, bore little relation to the heroine of her mother's invention.

'Poor little Celia!' her mother went on. 'It would all have been so different if your father . . . but still, it's no good thinking about that.'

'She's probably perfectly happy, Mamma,' Diana said gently, taking her mother's hand.

'Yes, yes, I suppose you're right. Dear Selina would never

have sent her away to anyone unsuitable. But all the same I'm very relieved to have found this address. Wouldn't it be wonderful to hear from her after all these years?'

'I hope we do, Mamma.'

'And I must write to tell Laura all about it. She'll be so pleased. They used to play together when they were little.'

Then her face clouded over, as Diana knew it would, as she said, 'Oh, it's *dreadful* to think of Laura so far away!'

'She's happy there, Mamma, and doing well.'

'But she's so thoughtless, one never knows what she might do next.'

'Yes, we do. She'll work hard and do well. She won't let anything distract her from her studies. She's very determined, you know.'

'I don't doubt that, she was always headstrong. But what class of person will she be associating with? We know nothing of these students, no introductions to their parents, nothing.'

'They're all working hard to become doctors, as James did, Mamma.'

Her mother's face softened, as she knew it would. As far as Elspeth was concerned, her son-in-law could do no wrong.

Then she sighed and said, 'But *Scotland*. To go all the way to *Scotland*. How can I not be anxious about her?'

'I don't think you need to be anxious about Laura,' Diana told her firmly. 'She's always wanted to be a doctor and she's done very well. You should be proud of her.'

'Of course, dear, of course I'm proud that she's done well. But I can't help wishing that she'd done well somewhere nearer home.'

Her daughter laughed and shook her head, knowing her mother would not change.

'Give her my love when you write, Mamma. And now I'll take this letter to Celia straight up to the pillar box, if Papa will let me out of his fortress.'

He did so unwillingly. Perhaps he doesn't want me to leave, she thought, or perhaps he just feels insecure if doors are unbolted. She reached up to kiss him and he looked down at her with his old fond smile and held her close for a moment so that she had a sudden wild hope that he truly was her father once more, that he'd magically re-entered her father's body. But, when he released her, she saw that he had forgotten who she was. He thanked her for coming, as he would have thanked a chance acquaintance, and asked her to call again if she was passing.

Sadly she made her way back to the hall, thinking of the damage the war had done to so many lives, not just the dead and wounded soldiers but their elders who had broken under the strain and loss, and the childless widows and the orphaned children.

She thought about the orphaned Celia, little Celia who had come to stay in Northrop in those old pre-war days which now seemed so long ago. She used to come with Aunt Selina and Uncle William and one of those young nursemaids whom Nanny Stone despised for their slapdash ways. She remembered that last picnic by the stream when the boys had built a dam and they'd played hide-and-seek and Celia had nearly fallen over in the water and Tom had sat in Cook's special custard pie. What an innocent world it now seemed, before the war which left Tom and Teddy both dead and Celia orphaned, her parents buried in a great pile of rubble which had once been their home.

She thought about her Aunt Selina, who had so nobly stayed in London to comfort the soldiers, so her mother said. All she herself could remember about her aunt was that she had lied to Sebastian, not given him that vital letter, told him that she, Diana, was engaged. How could she? *Why* should she? It made no sense – unless her aunt was one of those people who sought to augment their own happiness by diminishing that of others. She didn't look that sort of person, her lovely face gave no sign of it. Could that beautiful exterior really have been clothing something evil within, like a perfect-looking peach, rotten at the core?

Despite all her good resolutions, she couldn't help imagining how different her life would have been if that note had been delivered: a life shared with Sebastian. Of course, she would still have worked with James in the war. He would have remained her mentor, her deeply respected guide and friend, never her lover.

This won't do, she told herself: I must recapture that earlier mood, acknowledge my pride in James and the work he does, which I am privileged to share, which I should be happy to share with him. Most of the time I am. I must ban memories of Sebastian; he belongs in the world of long ago.

Thus determined, she walked up the drive and out into the road where the pillar box stood at the corner. It was still painted VR, Victoria Regina. It too is a relic of a bygone age, she thought, as she posted her mother's letter to the orphaned Celia.

Five

'If your aunt says black is white, then black is white,' Celia's uncle often told her.

He wasn't really her uncle, Celia knew, any more than her Aunt Ethel was really her aunt. The Grimsdykes were distant cousins of her dead mother, Selina, who had died in the war when the house fell on her, killing not only her but also her husband, just home on leave, and an American soldier who must have been visiting and whose body was found completely naked, his clothes having been blown off by the blast. These bombs did extraordinary things, the newspaper article said.

She hadn't been particularly upset when her uncle showed her that piece out of the paper. She didn't miss her parents; she hadn't seen much of them even before the war, her mother being too beautiful and sociable to have much time for children. Sometimes her brother Tom had bothered to play with her in a rather rough, big-brotherly sort of way, but he had been killed in the war and she had only the vaguest memories of him and of going to stay somewhere in the country where they played by a stream. But that was a very long time ago, when she was only about seven or eight, just before her mother sent her to Aunt and Uncle so that she would be safely away from London and the bombs.

Her parents and brother were never mentioned thereafter by Aunt Ethel and Uncle Arthur, who had taken her out of charity, as Aunt Ethel often pointed out, when nobody else wanted her. They alone had kept, clothed and fed her when the money her mother used to send stopped with her death.

They had done their duty by her. Duty was a word frequently on her aunt's thin lips.

Duty ruled the household; it was her duty now to take up her aunt's breakfast tray. Her aunt always had her breakfast in bed ever since her Big Operation twenty years ago. Long before Celia was born it had taken place, in her aunt's bedroom where two doctors, a nurse and a surgeon had anaesthetized her aunt and removed some recalcitrant part of her body. Celia knew no more than that, just that her aunt had been in bed for six months and had decreed that thereafter she must have breakfast in bed and a long rest in the afternoon. As far as Celia was concerned, The War and The Big Operation were great and equally important events of the twentieth century, both scarcely understood and clouded in mystery.

Dutifully now she put the toast in the little silver toast rack and checked that everything was on the tray that should be on the tray. Sarah, the maid, should have finished blackleading the kitchen range by now, but she was still polishing up the brass knobs as Celia picked up the tray.

'Hurry up with that, Sarah,' she said in a voice which already resembled her aunt's. 'I want to see all that put away and the hearth washed before I come down. And put the kettle on the fire, will you?'

'Yes, Miss Celia,' Sarah said, hastily finishing the polishing, then gathering together her brushes and cloths in the hearth box and carrying it out into the scullery. Sometimes she could hardly tell if it was Miss Celia or her mistress speaking, they could sound that alike. The mistress had the sort of voice that went with her face, but Miss Celia was beautiful to look at with her fair hair and fine skin and somehow you wouldn't expect her to sound so hard. It was puzzlesome, she thought, as she filled up the kettle at the sink and carried it back into the kitchen and set it to boil on the fire, thrusting it firmly back into the embers. Then, pushing her hair back and thereby adding another black smudge to her pale little face, she set about washing the hearth.

Upstairs Celia balanced the heavy tray on one knee as

she tapped at her aunt's bedroom door. The stern voice bade her enter.

Aunt Ethel was sitting very upright in bed, supported by three hard pillows. Everything about the room was hard; the dark furniture had no softening curves, the linoleum on the floor was cold and hard, the lamp that hung from the ceiling gave out a harsh, cold glare of light. But none of this was as hard as the face of the woman sitting up in bed. Her mouth was set in a hard, unforgiving line, her sharp little eyes were as hard as two chips of grey slate, her nose, like her chin, was sharp and pointed, her hair was drawn back into a tight little bun.

'Well,' she said, as Celia came into the room with the tray, 'how's that girl getting on downstairs?'

'She's nearly finished the range, Aunt.'

'About time too. It's gone eight o'clock.'

Actually it wasn't yet five to eight, but of course if Aunt said black was white, then black was white.

'There are some letters this morning,' Celia said, settling the tray down on the table by the bed.

'Then why ever didn't you bring them up, child?' her aunt demanded, exasperated. 'Let your head save your heels.'

'Uncle was still busy with them, but I'll go and ask if he's finished with them.'

'No, tell him to bring them himself when he comes up. You go and get on with your work. You've to finish spring cleaning the dining room today. Were there enough tea leaves to clean the carpet?'

'Yes, I'd been saving them for a while.'

'And mind you keep the shutters closed in case the sun comes out.'

'Yes, Aunt.'

Her uncle was coming up the stairs as she crossed the landing. He was dressed in his office clothes because, although retired now, he still went into his old firm, Nathan and Braithwaite, every Friday to help with the accounts. She didn't know why, but he always looked younger and happier on the day when he wore his office clothes.

'Good morning, dear,' he said to his wife as he sat down on the hard wooden chair by the bed. 'Is everything all right?' he asked, his voice hesitant, eager to please.

She looked at him sharply.

'Is there any reason to suppose it shouldn't be?' she asked.

'No, I just wanted to be sure,' he explained with a placatory smile.

He paused. She waited. He went on, 'She's had a letter from those Arndale relations of hers. It seems,' he explained, glancing down at the envelope, 'that it has been forwarded, after some delay, from our old address in Cross Street. They've suggested that Celia might visit them. I don't know how you feel about that?'

'Of course she can't go. She's needed here.'

'The decision must be yours, my dear.'

'Her duty is to those who took her in.'

'So should I reply – or will you?'

'Neither of us,' she told him. 'It will only cause trouble. They're not to know we ever got their letter. Burn it.'

'As you wish.'

The word burning reminded him of something.

'It's cold in here, dear. Don't you want the fire lit?'

'No. April has come and we never light fires upstairs after April.'

'Of course. I just thought you might feel the cold. The doctor said you must keep warm after your big operation.'

'It's warm enough. I'm not soft like some.'

'As you wish. I must be away now. Or shall I wait and take your tray down?'

'No, one of the girls can fetch it.' She paused. 'I've been thinking, Arthur.'

'Yes?'

'Now that Celia is nearly eighteen and quite strong . . .'

'Yes, she's a good strong healthy girl.'

'Due to the way we've done our duty by her.'

'Quite.'

'I've been thinking that we might do without Sarah.

Celia could manage her work and we'd save ten shillings a week.'

Ten shillings a week! He did a quick calculation: twenty-six pounds a year. What an addition that would be to their savings! They had already built up a substantial amount out of the lavish sums which Selina had, up to the time of her death, sent them each month for having Celia – far too much to spend on the child, Ethel had said, for it was their duty to see that she didn't grow up spoilt, worldly and idle like her mother.

He repeated these thoughts and figures to his wife, adding, 'And even if Celia leaves us to get married in, say, five years' time, there would still be a saving of –' he made another quick calculation – '£130 in total.'

'Marry?' she said. 'Who'd she marry? Tell me that.'

'It's true she doesn't go out much, but you never know. The new curate pays her some attention. She's a good-looking girl.'

'So was her mother and look where it got her,' his wife pointed out sharply. 'I'll tell you where it got her. It got her in with those Arndales, getting ideas above her station. Celia will be safer with us, kept well away from them.'

Her husband nodded. Of course, if preserving Celia from harm was the reason for not acknowledging the letter, then it was the right and proper course to take. He could see that.

'And if the work is too much for her,' his wife went on, 'we can always hire an hourly help at times like spring cleaning. It would still be much cheaper than keeping Sarah. She's a poor bit of a thing anyway. We could get a good strong woman for a few hours when we needed it – there are plenty of strong young widows about now, grateful for any work they can get.'

He nodded again, glad to agree to this scheme which would help some poor war widow. How wise his wife was, he thought, as he watched her scraping butter on to toast, how right about these things!

Sarah was sweeping the tiles in the hall when her master

came downstairs and told her she could go and fetch her mistress's tray.

She went upstairs slowly. Her mistress's bedroom was a place of terror to her. The thought of going into that cold, dark interior, the sight of that old lady sitting up in bed with her eyes sharp and glassy as a parrot's made her clumsy and stupid with fear. And if she said anything in that terrifying, cold voice, Sarah could hardly manage any kind of sense in her reply.

But this morning her mistress said nothing, just nodded towards the tray to indicate it was finished with.

'Make a good job of the dining room,' she said as the girl stood by the door, balancing the tray on one knee as she opened it. Her voice was so sudden and so harsh that Sarah nearly let the tray fall from her knee.

There were two pieces of toast on the tray and a little piece of butter on a dish and a spoonful of marmalade in a little pot, which was always measured out carefully from the two-pound jam jar which had to last a month.

She put the tray down on the kitchen table. The toast mesmerized her. So did the shiny slice of butter, the glossy little hillock of marmalade. She yearned for them. She looked about her. The master was out, the mistress wouldn't be down for a while, Miss Celia had just gone up to tidy her own bedroom. It would be wicked. She mustn't do it. But she was so hungry. She had had her breakfast of two mugs of tea and piece of bread at six o'clock before she did the kitchen range, but it had inexplicably worn off.

It was a wicked thing to do, stealing from her employers, she knew that, but suddenly the temptation was too much, the craving of her empty stomach spoke more loudly than her conscience. She snatched up the knife, smeared all the butter on to the toast and dolloped the marmalade on top, gazed at it for a brief delicious moment of anticipation and then stuffed it into her mouth.

She stood by the kitchen range, with this wonderful taste in her mouth and the fire warming her bare legs; she chewed slowly, savouring every delicious morsel. She thought she'd swallowed the last crumb and then discovered yet another lodged behind a tooth. Carefully, delicately, she probed it out with her tongue, chased it round her mouth and then let it rest there for a moment before allowing herself to swallow. She stood by the stove a little longer and then began slowly to lick every finger in turn.

At last she sighed a deep sigh of satisfaction and carried the trayful of dirty dishes into the scullery. But before plunging the little butter dish and marmalade pot into the hot water, she rubbed her red and workworn fingers around them to extract any last trace of greasy stickiness that might remain. Only then, having licked her fingers once again, did she surrender the dishes to the sink, scouring them thoroughly as if to wash away her guilt.

Celia had donned a coarse apron in readiness to do battle with spring cleaning the dining room. They had already moved as much of the furniture as possible into the hall and brushed down the ceiling and walls. Now they dragged the big square of carpet, which they'd left rolled up in the hall, out into the garden and managed to heave it up over the clothes line for Sarah to beat. She enjoyed doing this. It was pleasant outside now that the sun had got a bit of life in it and she whacked enthusiastically at the carpet with the wicker mat beater as if her recent illicit meal had given her joy as well as energy.

'You can leave it hanging there,' Celia called out to her. 'You get on with scrubbing the floor while I wipe down the pictures.'

The floorboards were stained dark brown all round the edges, but the centre of the floor was pale, where the carpet would cover it. She took her two buckets, one with sudsy water and one with clear, and, tucking her sackcloth apron between her legs, knelt down. She enjoyed scrubbing, rhythmically moving the hard brush up and down, up and down until a square of the floor in front of her was covered with a dirty grey scum which she wiped clean with the big coarse floorcloth, dipping it into the clear water. It didn't stay clear long: every few minutes she had to carry the buckets out to the scullery, tip them into the shallow stone sink, swill them round and refill them, adding hot water from the big kettle which she kept boiling on the kitchen fire.

Miss Celia meanwhile was washing the pictures, polishing the glass, wiping the back of them. They mostly portrayed dead animals, or bowls of fruit or barren landscapes with foreign-looking mountains and waterfalls. There was only one that Sarah liked, much prettier than the others with a big blue bowl of bright pink flowers. She'd heard that the mistress had painted it when she was young, but it didn't seem the sort of thing the mistress would ever have given time to, even when she was a girl. Not that she could believe the mistress ever had been a girl. Not really believe it.

'I think it's going to rain,' Miss Celia said at the end of the morning. 'We'd better bring the carpet in. Is the floor dry?'

'Yes, Miss Celia, I've wiped it over with dry cloths like you said.'

'Good, then come and help me with the carpet.'

They replaced the carpet on the floor and hung the pictures up.

'We'll have a rest for half an hour,' Celia told her, 'then this afternoon we'll wash the furniture with vinegar water, polish it and put it back in place. And we'll need the steps to rehang the curtains. You could get them now in readiness.'

At the end of the morning they always had a cup of tea and some bread, the mistress thinking it bad for the digestion to work on a full stomach.

Sarah was crossing the hall to get the steps from under the stairs when Ethel Grimsdyke called to her from the drawing room.

'A word, Sarah,' she said.

She was sitting very upright on the horsehair couch, her needlework beside her.

'I fancied a little toast for my lunch, Sarah,' she said. 'But my niece tells me it has gone. Where is the toast left from my breakfast, Sarah?'

Sarah blushed crimson. Her hands flew to her face and

then dropped and lay limply against the coarse sacking of her apron.

'I don't know, m'm,' she said. 'Perhaps it got thrown out.'

'Things don't *get thrown out*, Sarah. *People* throw them out. So where did you throw the toast?'

Sarah shook her head, too terrified to think.

'And there was some butter left on the tray, Sarah. I saw that it was not put back with the pat of butter when I inspected the larder.'

It was all too much for Sarah. She'd been wicked and she'd been found out.

'I ate it, m'm, with the toast, m'm,' she said and burst into tears.

Her mistress watched her with cold hard eyes.

'So you lied to me when you said you'd thrown it out?'

'Yes, m'm, I'm sorry, m'm. I don't know what come over me. It was wicked. It won't happen again, m'm.'

'No, it won't, not in this house, it won't.'

Sarah was not a quick thinker. It took a little while for the meaning of the words to sink in. She stared, horror-stricken, at her employer.

'If you had told me the truth from the start, Sarah, I should have overlooked your fault. But you lied, you tried to deceive and I cannot have a liar in my house. I will be more lenient than you deserve, you may work and be paid for another month, but after that you must go.'

She could have given the girl a week's notice and so saved herself having to pay three weeks' wages, saved one pound and ten shillings, but she resolved to be fair and, anyway, a month would see all the spring cleaning finished.

Sarah was still crying, but she saw that she should be grateful, for was she not being allowed to have a whole month's work and time to look for another post, even though she had been so greedy and told lies as well?

'Thank you, m'm,' she managed to say through her tears.

Six

It was Saturday; Sebastian lay in bed and, still only half awake, daydreamed about Diana. During the day he kept all thoughts of her out of his mind by concentrating on work, but in those early hours when sleep has just given way to semi-consciousness, when the imagination is free and takes off and lands where it will, before full awareness takes control, that was the time when Diana occupied his mind. He thought about her when she was a girl, remembering the dances in London, and he thought about her when she was the woman who had walked with him on a beautiful, crisp winter's morning down to the lake and kissed him and he had known, known with certainty, that she loved him. And, most persistently of all, he remembered her three years later as she lay naked in his arms. Then the awful longing started, the fruitless longing for her to be there with him again.

Soon, as he grew more wakeful, reality reasserted itself. It was a terrible thing that had happened; whatever would his parents have thought, as they chatted happily in the car that next day, while he, silent, drove them home, if they had known he had behaved so dishonourably? They wouldn't have believed it, of course. Their son to have behaved like that with a married woman? Never! And furthermore with the wife of that great and good doctor – but somehow he couldn't even bear to think the name, the name that was now shared with Diana.

And yet amid all the shame and humiliation, he could still think of her, long for her, shamelessly. How could it sometimes feel so right, and yet be so wrong?

He was aware that such fruitless speculation did him no

good at all, aware that if he had a friend who confessed such things to him, he would say, 'Put it behind you, dear fellow, she's beyond your reach now, forget the longing and then the shame will cease to plague you.' No doubt a good friend would say the same to him; sometimes he found himself on the point of telling Matthew, but he knew that a decent chap like Matthew would be bound to think worse of him for it; their friendship would never be the same again.

Of course, some men would just laugh and think it naive to have such misgivings, would try to ease his mind with tales of harmless affairs with married women, with stories of how some women had behaved in the war when their husbands were abroad and so on. But such men could never be his real friends, their words would be meaningless to him. No, he must keep this to himself.

Fully awake now, he turned his mind to today's business. Work was a far more worthy subject for his mind, he told himself, altogether more wholesome than dwelling on the past. He devoted his weekends – except for the rare occasions when he went down south to his parents – to the Homes for the Disabled campaign. He only worked at Booth and Samson until midday on Saturdays, so this afternoon he was going over to see Matthew to discuss with him the agenda for the first meeting of the trust in a month's time.

Matthew shared his enthusiasm, they'd got on like a house on fire ever since their first meeting. And it was so good to have someone to discuss things with. It had been Matthew's idea that they might buy some of the big houses that were up for sale but nobody wanted nowadays because they couldn't get the servants to run them. Then they could divide them into flats or bedsitters, and let them to ex-soldiers with varying disabilities, so that the fitter ones could keep an eye on their fellows. They'd all cared for their mates so well in the war, Matthew said, and would have the same spirit if they were together again in peacetime. A lot of them said how they missed the camaraderie that had helped them to bear even the worst conditions in the trenches.

Of course, Matthew knew everything about this town and

everybody in it – or at least anybody who would be likely to help them. He had been unerringly right; every person to whom they'd written, businessmen and officials alike, had responded warmly.

The smell of frying bacon drifted into his room and reminded him that it was time to be up and about. He was lucky in his landlady, he thought, as he shaved; some of his bachelor colleagues told fearsome tales of the gruesome harpies they lodged with.

Comfortable was the word that came to mind when he thought of Mrs Jordan. She had a round, cheerful face with pink cheeks and clear blue eyes that only looked anxious when she was trying to please and wasn't sure how to go about it.

'Good morning,' she greeted him cheerfully, as he came downstairs. 'A lovely summer morning. Everything all right?'

He assured her that it was as he sat down at the round table with its spotless white cloth and shining cutlery, tipped himself some Force out of the packet, poured creamy milk on it from the blue and white willow pattern jug and scattered castor sugar over it from the silver dredger.

In the kitchen Mrs Jordan mashed the tea, covered the pot with the cosy and put it on the tray with the plate of bacon and eggs, sausages, fried bread and tomatoes. Her lodger liked to wait for his tea and have it with his main course, she'd noticed that. She'd make him another cup when he was ready for his toast. Her daughter, married and away down south, said that she spoiled her lodger, but why shouldn't a man have things the way he liked them? It was just as easy to do things right as wrong and anyway he was such a nice, appreciative gentleman, thoughtful, with something of the dreamer about him, artistic maybe, so that's why he'd be good with all those drawings of houses he brought home with him. He was considerate to her, so why shouldn't she be the same to him? Besides she enjoyed indulging men.

That was really the reason why she'd taken in a lodger when she didn't need to, being comfortably off. She'd always enjoyed keeping a good house for her husband who'd died before the war and then for her son who had been killed on the Somme. She tried not to think of them during the day. Any tears she shed, were shed in the early hours of the morning before her defences were up; they were wiped away when she rose and put on her cheerful face to greet the day.

'I think,' Matthew Braithwaite said, as they sat in his office in their shirtsleeves, for the town was airless and sticky this July afternoon, 'that we'll call Arthur Grimsdyke in for discussion before the first meeting of the trust. He was our accountant for so long. He's retired now but still comes in to help out on Fridays.'

'But Travers is the man in charge?' Sebastian queried.

'Oh, yes, he's very capable, young Travers,' Matthew agreed.

Travers was only a few years younger than they were, but anyone who had still been at school when the war ended seemed young to those who had fought their way through it.

'It's just that he lacks the kind of experience which Arthur's built up over the years. Besides,' he added, smiling, 'between you and me, Mr Nathan will find it reassuring to think that Arthur was in on these negotiations. After all, our firm will be quite involved in all this. He trusts Arthur. If he can't get to this meeting himself, he'll be glad to know that Arthur was there.'

'He's no better then?'

Matthew shook his head.

'Not really. The bronchitis persists and there is always the danger of pneumonia. Very dangerous at his age.'

'Or any age.'

Matthew nodded. He was very fond of the old man, knew how deeply, silently, he grieved for his dead son.

'Sometimes when I look at him,' he said, thinking aloud, 'I feel guilty for surviving.'

Sebastian looked up, surprised, then briefly touched his hand.

'Oh, I know that feeling so well,' he said. 'I had a friend – but let's not dwell on it. Let's give all our thoughts to doing what we can for those others who've survived, but not unmaimed as we are.'

Matthew nodded, then looked up smiling as if with renewed determination.

'Absolutely. And we're taking the first step at this meeting.'

But on Friday the meeting had to be postponed; old Mr Nathan died that morning.

'The funeral is to be next Wednesday, Ethel,' Arthur Grimsdyke said, as he sat there by her bedside, grief-stricken, the letter still in his hand.

He looked at her apprehensively and then added, 'I think it would be appreciated if we both went to the funeral.'

'Of course,' she agreed. 'I hope I never shrink from my duty, Arthur,' she said, thinking that she would be able to wear her funeral bonnet. It had lasted well, that hat wrapped in black tissue paper in a black box. Oh yes, it had earned its keep, had that hat. 'You must go and I shall be at your side in the pew.'

He smiled, relieved.

'We'll just sit near the back,' he said.

Showing her into her pew the following Wednesday, the usher thought that she would not have been out of place at a funeral a hundred years ago. Ethel Grimsdyke in full mourning was a formidable sight. Her dress, her coat, her stockings, her shoes, were all black. A black scarf entwined her thin neck, she carried a black umbrella with an ebony handle and wore a jet brooch and beads. All this blackness was topped with the black bonnet of antique make, adorned with black ribbons and black veil. Even her hard eyes seemed to have darkened to reflect the blackness and, like two black buttons, kept company with the jet beads and brooch.

The church was crowded with Mr Nathan's family and friends and many business associates, for most of the firms in the town had sent representatives. Oh, yes, he was well thought of, was our Mr Nathan, Arthur reflected sadly to himself, grieving not just for the old man, though that was grief enough, but also for his dead son and all of that lost generation; that's the tragedy of war, Arthur thought as he struggled to join in the singing of 'Abide with Me'.

Everybody was invited back to the house for refreshments after the funeral.

'We won't go, of course,' Ethel said as they left the church.

For once he was firm.

'Yes, we shall,' he told her. 'Mr Nathan would have wished it and young Mr Braithwaite most particularly asked me.'

Motor cars were provided to take them from the church to the house. Ethel had never travelled in one before and didn't enjoy it. It was a senseless extravagance, she thought, with the tramline so near, and would have said so had there not been a couple of friends of the family in the same vehicle.

Mr Nathan's sad little widow greeted them in the hall, flanked by various nephews and nieces. Arthur's heart ached for her. Her son should have been standing by her side, ready to shoulder all the responsibility for her and for the company. He had been such a good lad, so keen, so kind. Oh, the waste of it, the waste of it.

Two elderly maids served the tea, their habitual black uniforms altered only by the addition of black armbands. Ethel looked at the array of sandwiches and cakes with disapproval: a decent burial was all that was needed, not all this fuss and carry on.

Young Mr Braithwaite made much of Arthur, introducing him as an old servant of the firm and a trusted friend of Mr Nathan for many years. Arthur's eyes filled with tears at these kindly words. Mr Nathan – he never thought of him by his Christian name – had been his guide and mentor since he'd joined the firm as not much more than a lad. They'd always thought the same about all business matters, mistrusted change, helped each other adapt to it when it was inevitable, supported each other in opposing it if it seemed preventable.

Young Mr Braithwaite put a kindly arm around his shoulders and led him to meet Mr Crawley, the gentleman interested in housing the soldiers.

'Tell Arthur about your plans, Sebastian,' he said, knowing the older man needed some distraction.

So Sebastian told them all about his housing scheme and Arthur listened and tried to imagine what Mr Nathan would have thought of it. He'd have approved, he decided, because of his lost son and because, despite the asperity of his manner, he was a kind-hearted man. Yes, he could imagine him nodding his head in the approving way he had and saying, 'We've got to do the best we can for the lads, when you think what they did for us.'

Ethel did not join in the conversation. Despite her disapproval of funeral sweetmeats, she allowed her cup to be refilled and her plate replenished, telling herself it would save the expense of supper tonight.

She mentioned this thought to Arthur as they sat on the tram going home. He nodded, but his mind was still on that scheme of Sebastian's.

'He wants to give the disabled men a decent home, which they deserve,' he told her.

'I heard him,' she said.

She sniffed, tossed her head so that the black ribbons shook on her bonnet.

'Some of them never had a decent home in the first place and their wives wouldn't know how to keep it decent if they did,' she said. 'Wherever has that conductor got to?'

The tram was crowded and the conductor was slow in getting round to them.

'He's got a limp,' Arthur said. 'Possibly the result of war.'

'Then he's lucky to have a job and should look sharp if he doesn't want to lose it,' she told him.

'Two to Bartholomew Church corner,' Arthur requested, holding out fourpence, when the conductor finally reached them.

'From Wellington Crescent?'

'That's right.'

'That's just over the tuppenny fare. It'll be threepence each.'

Arthur was searching for a sixpenny piece, when Ethel said, 'Just over? What difference does that make?'

'Well, if you get off at the stop before Bartholomew's Church, it's still only tuppence.'

'Then we'll do that,' she said, getting up. 'It's no distance to walk. You put that sixpence away, Arthur, and give the man fourpence.'

'But it's raining,' Arthur pointed out.

It was too late; she was pushing past him into the aisle, making her way down the tram.

He got up and followed her.

'Hurry up, it's this stop,' she called back to him.

'Too late, lady,' the conductor called out.

She ignored the warning and jumped off as the tram was moving away.

The motorist had no time to stop. One minute, as he explained at the inquest and many times later, he was driving along and the next thing there was this tall figure falling apparently out of nowhere, sprawled across the bonnet of his car like a spiky puppet and the worst part was that she landed with her feet sticking out behind her and her head with those terrifying eyes glaring at him, only a few inches away on the other side of the windscreen.

Seven

Celia watched as her uncle grew day by day more morose. She could tell by the dark circles under his eyes that he wasn't sleeping and he blamed himself continually, day and night.

'Oh, Celia,' he would say. 'All for the saving of tuppence! That's all it was, you know. Just a penny each. I should have prevented her. The best wife in the world, the best wife a man could wish for, and I lost her *for tuppence*.'

'But it seems, Uncle,' Celia would say, trying to console him, 'that it was her wish.'

'Oh yes, she was a woman who kept to her principles. Look after the pennies and the pounds will look after themselves: that was her motto. And she was right, of course. They do, they do. But oh, to lose her for *tuppence*!'

He would be silent for a while and then start blaming himself again for letting the accident happen, blaming himself also for her funeral being so delayed.

'That's not your fault, Uncle. It's because of the inquest. If it's anyone's fault, it's the coroner's for being so slow, not yours.'

'My last duty to her should have been to give her a decent and a prompt burial,' he would say, tears filling his eyes from a mixture of grief and frustration. 'And I've failed to do that. Failed most dreadfully. Your poor aunt, how she would have hated the thought of lying there all these days. She never could abide being kept waiting.'

The least miserable one in the household was Sarah; nothing further had been said about her dismissal, so she went on working and asked no questions. She didn't even know if the mistress had told the master or Miss Celia. If she hadn't, then things might go on like this for ever.

Nonetheless she crept nervously about the house for her mistress's presence seemed to be everywhere now that she was no longer fixed in one place, now that she might be watching from up above. Sometimes she'd come into a room and maybe it would just be a shadow or she'd blink and out of the corner of her eye would seem to see someone standing there and she'd have to rush out again, almost unable to stop herself screaming, and pretend she'd forgotten her duster or something, because she knew it was all really just her silliness. The dark curtain on the landing sometimes moved as she went up to bed and she'd scuttle past thinking it was her mistress moving behind there, but really it was only the draught moving the curtains. The house was full of draughts and dark curtains.

The worst thing was, of course, having to go in every day and clean her bedroom; it was an even more frightening place than it had been when her mistress was alive. As Sarah crept guiltily into the room, first knocking from force of habit, even the squeak of the door made her jump. She felt like a thief coming in alone like this; the dark furniture seemed to bear witness to her crime and she found herself apologizing under her breath to the very drawers and cupboards.

Polishing the dressing table mirror terrified her because she knew that she might see that familiar, forbidding visage suddenly appear in the glass behind her own, accusing her with angry, snake-like eyes. So she had to contrive to keep her own eyes lowered so that she couldn't see either reflection, as her arm moved the duster blindly across the glass.

Worst of all was being expected to help Miss Celia with the clothes. Oh, what a liberty to take! To open the mistress's cupboards! The horror of opening the wardrobe and seeing all those dark skirts hanging there like dead bodies! Sometimes, as they took them out and folded them up, she'd groan and say, 'Oh, I can't, miss, I can't,' and Miss Celia would say, 'Come along, Sarah. It has to be done.' Cool as a cucumber, Miss Celia was.

Once that dread task was completed, she began to get more used to the house without her mistress. It had been miserably cold when she died, more like winter than summer, but now there was a warm spell and the house seemed brighter and, best of all, the mistress's bedroom was allowed to remain untouched. She felt almost cheerful as she prepared the tea trolley one Sunday afternoon. She had to tell herself not to be smiling as she pushed it across the hall; it wouldn't be right to look cheerful with the master still so very sad.

He wasn't in the drawing room; he must be writing letters in the dining room. He seemed to be writing so many letters nowadays; she took no end of them up to the pillar box at the end of the road, for he seemed too sad to go out himself now, even that short way. It was a pity: a bit of fresh air would do him good. She'd heard Miss Celia tell him so, but he took no notice even of her.

The trolley bumped as she pushed it across the floorboards and then ran more smoothly over the carpet. She parked it in the usual place by the empty hearth. She saw that the clock on the mantelpiece said it was four o'clock; she nodded at it, pleased with herself for keeping to the exact time the mistress had ordained for tea, which was still strictly adhered to even though the master hardly touched anything. It was dreadful to see him looking so pale and thin, his clothes seemed too big for him now. In a minute she would go and call him and Miss Celia. 'Four o'clock,' she'd tell them, 'and the tea is in the drawing room.' They'd surely never dismiss a maid who was as punctual as that with their tea?

She went to get the cake stand from its place near the piano that was kept well polished but never played. And then she saw them: two feet, feet with black shoes on, the soles turned towards her. She wasn't imagining it this time. She couldn't move. She stood there and screamed. And screamed. And screamed.

'He's had a massive seizure, Miss Grimsdyke,' the doctor told her, as they stood in the drawing room after he had come downstairs from examining her uncle. 'I'm afraid I can't be too hopeful about the outcome.'

Celia nodded.

'I shall arrange to have a nurse sent to look after him.'

Celia shook her head.

'If you give me instructions,' she said, 'I shall nurse him myself.'

She knew that her aunt and uncle would have considered it profligate to employ a nurse. It was her duty to care for him herself.

The doctor looked doubtful.

'It will be heavy work, Miss Grimsdyke,' he warned. 'And there will be tasks to be done which are more suitable for a nurse to carry out than a young girl like yourself.'

'I understand that,' she said. 'And if I find I cannot look after him properly, then I will ask for a nurse to be sent.'

Reluctantly the doctor agreed, promising to call in each day. At least, he thought, it can't go on for long.

In fact, Arthur lingered longer than he had expected, his niece tending him day and night, sponging him, turning him, feeding him liquids which were all he could swallow. He tried again to persuade her to employ a nurse, but she just replied, 'I am only doing my duty.'

One morning, three weeks after he had been struck down, he turned to her and tried to raise his head to speak. She bent over him, her ear to his lips, desperately trying to make out the words. 'All for tuppence,' he said, then he seemed to shake his head in bewilderment, and fell back on the pillow.

He died a few hours later, on the same day as his wife's death certificate was finally signed.

'A double funeral,' Matthew Braithwaite told Sebastian. 'I've heard of double weddings, but never heard of a double funeral before.'

Then he stopped and they both knew that he was thinking of the mass burials of their dead comrades after funeral services hastily read against a background of gunfire. The war, the war, it was always there just below the surface, suddenly intruding into your thoughts, catching you unawares when you were thinking of something quite different, like this sad business of Arthur and his wife.

'You'll come with me, Sebastian?'

'Of course, if you think it will help.'

'Thank you, it will. I know how Arthur enjoyed your talk with him at Mr Nathan's funeral. And I can't think who else might come. Travers is away on holiday and scarcely knew him anyway. Mrs Nathan got to know him quite well over the years, but we can't subject *her* to another funeral.'

'Mr Grimsdyke had no children?'

'Not that we know of. He never mentioned any. Just a niece who lived with them. I imagine she's a middle-aged lady who perhaps helped to keep house.'

Two days later, standing in St Bartholomew's church, they both remembered this conversation as they watched a young girl follow the coffins up the aisle. So much for the middle-aged niece.

Neither of them could help thinking how different this funeral was from the last one they had attended together. There were so few people here; just the two of them from the firm, the couple's young niece and a few elderly neighbours. The vicar spoke of the Grimsdykes' regular attendance at this church, but they seemed to have made few friends among its congregation.

It was a miserable day as they followed the coffins out to the graveyard; a grey dampness hung in the air, turning to steady rain as the last remains of Arthur and Ethel Grimsdyke were lowered into the earth.

Their niece, Sebastian observed, stood still and impassive and even when the vicar told her the time had come to throw a handful of earth on to the coffins, her face showed no emotion and she shed not a tear.

As they turned away, the vicar conveyed a message to them that they were all invited back to the house.

'What do you think?' Matthew whispered to Sebastian. 'I mean we don't want to intrude, do we?'

'I think we should go. Otherwise there will be hardly anyone there to support that poor girl.'

It wasn't far to the house; they walked slowly to make sure she would get there first.

It was a depressing road that the Grimsdykes lived in, darkened by the overhanging branches of trees whose leaves were already dirty with soot and dripping now from the recent rain, which had given way to a steady drizzle.

There was a high privet hedge in front of the house and, as if that might not give privacy enough, the garden was thick with vegetation and the front windows shrouded in laurels.

A nervous little maid answered the door and showed them into the drawing room, where Celia stood with the elderly neighbours and the curate from the church, to whom they were introduced.

Conversation wasn't easy: Matthew did his best, chatting to the curate about his work in the parish while Sebastian talked to the niece.

She was very composed, this Celia. And very pretty, slightly built, fine-boned. He didn't know much about women's clothes but could see that her high-necked blouse and long black skirt were old-fashioned. She didn't wear her hair up as the fashion of yesteryear would have dictated, nor was it shingled in today's fashion. It fell loosely on her shoulders, very fair, very fine, neither straight nor curly, just falling in gentle waves.

She looked so young, he thought, could still have been a schoolchild. She looked so alone too; he pitied her deeply.

'I don't wish to seem to intrude,' he heard himself say, 'but do you have any other relations to help you?'

'I don't think so,' she said. 'My aunt and uncle never mentioned anyone.'

'Perhaps you have an old family friend? Or a solicitor perhaps?'

She shook her head.

'I once heard my aunt saying solicitors weren't necessary. She said they took money for doing what you could do for nothing yourself.'

She tried to remember when it was. 'I think it was to do with making a will,' she added.

'Well, as I say, I don't want to intrude, but I'm sure that your uncle's former employers at Nathan and Braithwaite will be very pleased to help you in any way they can.'

'Thank you, I should be grateful for that,' and she looked up and smiled and he saw the relief in her eyes; clearly she must have been worried about it.

As they walked back to the office, he repeated this conversation to Matthew.

'I don't think she even knows if they've made a proper will,' he ended.

'How dreadful,' Matthew exclaimed. 'We just don't realize, do we, what goes on. I mean Arthur has had a good job with us for years. He was the methodical sort of man you'd think would see to everything like that.'

'Maybe he was a different man at home.'

Matthew nodded and they walked in silence for a while, both remembering Arthur's wife at old Nathan's funeral.

'A formidable woman, that wife of his,' Sebastian said.

They relapsed into silence again, until Sebastian suddenly said, 'If there isn't a will the poor girl probably doesn't even know if she owns the house or not.'

'Well, there doesn't seem anyone else to claim it.'

'Not as far as we know. I mean there might be some estranged son or – oh, I don't know, but I think it's a lawyer's job to find out.'

'And we're not lawyers, so there isn't much we can do about it.'

'But, Matthew,' Sebastian reproached him, 'her uncle worked for your family for years.'

'Yes, I'm sorry, I didn't mean we'd wash our hands of it, just that we can't give the legal advice she needs. We could perhaps write and ask if she would like us to introduce her to a trustworthy solicitor.'

'Oh, good. I'm so glad you feel that. I think she's going to need all the help she can get. I mean it could be that she has no income at all.'

'Arthur had a pension.'

'Could she claim that?'

'Oh, no,' Matthew said, surprised at the other man's ignorance. 'That dies with him. The Grimsdykes may have had the state pension as well, the one the Liberals introduced before the war. They'd get 7/6d a week from that.'

'And she couldn't claim that either, I suppose?'

'No, but of course they may have saved it. They did have a reputation for frugality, I believe. But that's only gossip – though I can't imagine Arthur lived extravagantly. We can only hope they've left her enough savings to give her an income sufficient to keep the house going.'

'Of course she may not want to stay in that house . . .'

'It's awfully gloomy, isn't it? I wouldn't want to live in it. I suppose you could clear away all those awful bushes and trees, but it's still pretty miserable inside.'

'Yes, but that's just the gloomy way it's furnished. I mean everything has the stamp of Mrs Grimsdyke on it, doesn't it? The building itself looks sound enough.'

'You're the architect, you should know.'

'Oh, I think it would sell well, a solid Victorian house like that. It would be a sound investment for anyone; she'd get enough for it to get herself some decent lodgings.'

'Except that people aren't buying houses at the moment and . . .'

He stopped and stood still. Sebastian stopped too and they looked at each other, the same thought in both their minds.

'Just the sort of place we're looking for. Near to the centre of town . . .'

'So the men can get to the cinemas and the shops even on crutches and . . .'

'A pretty big garden at the back, I imagine.'

'Yes, I've been in a similar house further down Waterloo Road and they all have land that goes right down to the canal and . . .'

'Big rooms if that drawing room's anything to go by.'

They were so excited that they were standing on the pavement, facing each other, both talking at once.

'We've got to stop this,' Matthew said suddenly, taking Sebastian's arm. 'We've got to get back to the office and think it all out properly. And before we can do anything we have to know what the niece's plans are about the house. She might want to go on living there herself,' he added gloomily. 'We must be realistic.'

'She might not even *own* the house,' Sebastian said, not to be outdone in gloomy realism.

Eight

'Good morning, Mr Crawley,' Mrs Jordan greeted him cheerfully. 'Though it's not a very good one, I'm afraid, misty outside and there'll be fog later, I daresay. I'll bring your tea in a minute.'

She had lit the gasfire in the dining room and turned on the lamps, so the breakfast table looked warm and welcoming. Whatever the weather was doing outside, Sebastian reflected as he looked appreciatively around the dining room, she always managed to create an atmosphere indoors that was bright and cheerful. She had the knack of making things look cosy. Yes, cosy was the word. She made things look cosy.

The house that he was going to visit this morning would be anything but cosy, he thought, remembering the Grimsdyke homestead. Of course, he told himself, he had only been there on the day of the funeral when it probably wasn't looking its best, but he had a feeling that it would look just as dreary this morning when he went to inspect it to see how it could be converted into suitable accommodation for the disabled.

It was now a month since Arthur Grimsdyke had died. How well Nathan and Braithwaite had looked after the affairs of their late employee, he thought as, bacon and eggs demolished, he helped himself to more tea. It had always been Mr Nathan's policy, Matthew had told him, to give immediate financial help to the family of any of his staff who died in service. Take money to the widow, in cash, he'd instructed Matthew, before you do anything else. That's what they need, and *cash* it must be for they'll not be having a mind to go worrying about taking a cheque to the bank.

So Matthew had seen that this Miss Celia had everything

she needed in those first few weeks, though she seemed to manage on very little. Then he had helped her in her dealings with the solicitor over the handwritten will which had been found among her uncle's papers.

So at least they knew that the house was hers and they could put to her the proposal that they should buy and convert it, if she didn't want to go on living there. But what puzzled both Matthew and Sebastian was that Arthur had so few savings.

'Arthur was the sort of man you'd expect to have a savings account at the bank or government stock, you know, something solid,' Matthew said, puzzled.

'Or money invested in the building society. I know some of the older people don't trust them but surely Arthur would have realized that getting interest tax free now that income tax is six shillings in the pound would have been a good place to put his savings?'

But there was nothing like that and so it had become apparent that the niece would need to sell the house and go into lodgings. There was no rush, they assured her; they could always get on with some preliminary planning after Sebastian had given a report on the suitability of the house for conversion. To this Miss Grimsdyke had consented, although, as Matthew said, it was hard to know what she was really feeling – or even if she was feeling anything at all.

Mrs Jordan had been right about the weather, Sebastian observed as he took his hat and coat off the hallstand, opened the front door and set off for the tram stop. The mist was thickening; it lay greasily on the pavement, felt damp and cold against his face, gathered in droplets on his coat. People hurried by, muffled up against the cold, motors moved slowly in the road, the tramlines gleamed.

The tram, when at last it came, was crowded and smelled of bodies and wet clothing. He had to stand, hanging on to his leather strap, as the tram rattled and swayed towards the city centre.

Here he changed to a tram which took him the much shorter journey out to Bartholomew Church corner. The mist was denser as he walked along the road to the Grimsdykes' house; thousands of fires had been lit in the city by now and thousands of chimneys were pouring out their soot and smoke to thicken the mist into fog.

The first thing he noticed when the frightened little maid showed him into the house was that it was as cold inside as out. He let the girl take his hat but kept his coat on. She had been sweeping the hall as he arrived and he saw that the tiles were chill and damp so that there was a pattern of smeary moisture where she had swept.

'I'll tell Miss Celia,' she said, leaving him alone in the drawing room.

A small, economical fire smoked grudgingly in the far wall, warming perhaps a few inches of the chimney but having no effect on the temperature of the rest of the room.

Celia Grimsdyke came into the room and they shook hands. Her little hand, he realized with compassion, was even colder than his own.

'I see that Sarah hasn't taken your coat, Mr Crawley,' she said. 'I'll call her.'

'Oh, no, please. I'm keeping it on in case I need to go out into the garden,' he lied.

She nodded and led him to the dining room. If the drawing room had been cold, this room was a morgue. The cold struck even as he opened the door. There was no fire here; only a fan of paper graced the empty hearth.

The room was decorated in the same way as all the others: brown paintwork and thick dark wallpaper.

He nodded, murmured something noncommital and followed her to the next room, the morning room. Like the other two rooms it was gloomy but of a good size which was, for his purposes, much more important. Each of these rooms would make a splendid bedsitter for men who couldn't manage the stairs.

'That is a very nice carpet,' he said, at a loss for anything to say about the furnishings.

'Yes, my aunt was always very careful of the carpets. We

kept all the curtains drawn in the summer – to protect their colours, you know.'

He nodded. So even the cheerfulness of sunlight had been banned in this forbidding house.

The last of the downstairs rooms was her uncle's study, much smaller than the others, though no less gloomy. Now this could be made into a nice little snuggery for the men, he thought, mentally furnishing it with easy chairs, a roaring fire, books and magazines.

At the back of the hall a baize door led to the domestic quarters. He entered a very large kitchen with a huge range at one end. What a devil it must be to clean, he thought. We'll have that out and get a decent modern cooker. The stone floor showed signs of having recently been scrubbed, as did the big wooden table in the centre of the room. He stood for a while envisaging what might be done: a much smaller, more manageable kitchen, then put in a partition wall with a hatch through to what would become the men's dining room, to which he'd make an access door from the hall.

There was a door at the far end of the kitchen into the scullery, another large room, stone-flagged like the kitchen. Shut the door off, turn it into a bathroom, make a doorway through from the hall. He was really beginning to see how ideal this place was for converting to a home.

Did one need a scullery, he wondered. What exactly was a scullery *for*?

'What do you use the scullery for?' he asked.

Celia Grimsdyke looked towards Sarah who blushed at thus having attention drawn to herself. She knew something was going on about the house, but she'd been told nothing and just hoped that if she kept quiet she might just go on working here and nothing said about dismissal.

'Well, Sarah?' Celia asked sharply.

'I cleans the knives, miss,' she said, 'and does the shoes in there. And the washing, of course.'

'Thank you, Sarah,' the gentleman said kindly and she hoped maybe he was buying the house and she could stay on and work here if Miss Celia went off and left her high and dry.

Sebastian was thinking, Ah yes, washing, I hadn't thought about washing. But the bathroom was more important and the men's clothes would just have to be washed elsewhere. There were laundries nowadays, which didn't exist when this house was built.

He nodded to show that he was finished with this preliminary look at the downstairs rooms and followed Celia upstairs, surreptitiously blowing on his frozen fingers as he went. However did these two women survive?

It was a good staircase, a solid piece of Victorian craftsmanship, the bannisters strong and thick. It wasn't as delicate and graceful as some he'd seen in Georgian and early Victorian houses, but it was the strength that mattered; disabled men would need to lean heavily on them as they went up and down the stairs.

There was a door on the half landing which he surmised gave access to a lavatory, but as Celia walked past it with averted eyes, he decided not to enquire any further.

'This is the biggest bedroom,' she said, showing him into what had been her aunt's bedroom, when they reached the upper floor.

He thought he had never seen a gloomier room. It was decorated in the all pervasive brown paint and thick dark wallpaper, the furniture was heavy and forbidding, the marble washstand had on it some of the most hideous chinaware he had ever seen. Where had they found it? Most washstands have such pretty little pieces on them. His mother's had lots of little jars and pots of blue and white china which he had loved to investigate when, as a little boy, he had been allowed sometimes to play in her bedroom when she was having her breakfast in bed. The Grimsdyke abode seemed to be utterly devoid of any of these pretty feminine things.

Still, it was another good-sized room and might possibly be divided into two, for there were big windows facing south and west.

'That window overlooks the back garden,' Celia said and

he moved politely towards it only to get a view of swirling mist and the dark outlines of leafless trees.

'This is – I mean was – my uncle's room,' Celia said, leading him across the landing and opening a door into a slightly smaller, but equally gloomy bedroom, which faced north. Next to it was a similar room which she described as the guest room, which was covered in dust sheets; he suspected, rightly, that they had never had a guest in it.

'And my room is here—' she began.

'If you would rather I didn't look into it,' he interrupted, 'that will be quite all right. You could perhaps later give me the dimensions.'

She shook her head in dismissal and opened the door to her room. He had expected that this one at least would show signs of being lived in, would have some of her things on a dressing table or washstand. But there was nothing; it was as bare and gloomy as the two bedrooms of the dead.

It contained an iron bedstead with a dark brown and black striped cover, a heavy mahogany wardrobe of the kind which is always bigger outside than in, a chest of drawers and a washstand. Apart from a row of little blue and white dishes on the washstand, there were no knick-knacks here, no little trifles of the kind you might expect to find in a young girl's bedroom. No books.

He murmured a few words of approval, remarked that all the rooms were spacious and well proportioned, which was true, and followed her down a little corridor to the next door.

'This is the maid's room,' she said.

It was smaller and even barer than the others; its furniture consisted of a small iron bed, a hard kitchen chair and a chest of drawers. A hook behind the door on which two or three garments were hanging presumably served as a wardrobe.

After he had gone, taken his hat off the stand in the hall and disappeared out into the mist, Celia went into the kitchen where she made a sandwich for Sarah and herself and, leaving the maid in the kitchen, carried hers into the drawing room, put one more piece of coal on the fire and sat down beside it.

It was clear to her now that they were serious about buying the house and the solicitor had explained to her that the money could be safely invested while she went into lodgings. No doubt, he said, that Nathan and Braithwaite would give her good advice about that. Nobody better. There was really nothing for her to worry about, he said.

Actually the thing that was worrying her most at the moment was how to dispose of her aunt's and uncle's clothes. A lady from church had said she would come back with her one day after church to collect them and give them to the needy. The clothes were all neatly folded under the dust sheets in the guest room but it would be undignified to carry them loose like that. There were one or two trunks, but how would they manage to carry them?

After she had eaten her sandwich and drunk her cup of tea, she carried the tray back into the kitchen where Sarah also, it seemed, had been thinking about clearing the house.

'What's to be done with all the mistress's boxes, miss?' she asked.

'Boxes?'

'The ones she give me to store away in the scullery, miss, when they was taken down from the loft because of them men on the roof.'

'Let me see them.'

Sarah stooped down and opened a large cupboard under the marble slab next to the sink. It was piled high with old dress boxes.

'Oh, that's just what I want, Sarah,' she said, giving the maid one of her rare smiles and together they carried the boxes upstairs to the guest room.

Most of her aunt's clothes presented no problem; there were more of them than she'd expected but then her aunt never threw anything out so her clothes went back to the days before she was married. They fitted easily enough into the boxes. There were three best dresses, though, that she'd hung up in the wardrobe because they were very heavy and she'd thought they would have to be carried separately.

She took them out now. What a weight they were, she

thought as she carried them over to the bed. Of course, it was because the skirts were weighted at the bottom. It was what ladies sometimes did in order that their skirts should not blow up in the wind, in an unseemly manner. It would only be lumps of metal; the dresses would be easier to carry if she took them out. The needy wouldn't mind about unseemliness.

She went for her needlebox and sat in the icy cold room unpicking the hem of her aunt's long black skirt. The stitches were small; it was a tedious business and she was beginning to wonder if it was worth it, when she found she could ease out the first weight with her fingers.

It wasn't a metal weight; it was a gold sovereign.

She stared at the gold coin in amazement and then set about unpicking the rest of the hem.

Nine

'I'm so glad you think the Grimsdyke house is suitable, Sebastian,' Matthew said as he looked at the preliminary sketches, which Sebastian had spread about his room in Mrs Jordan's house. 'I know you'd set your heart on it.'

'You too,' Sebastian pointed out.

'But you're the one who's doing all the work. You've got these sketches done pretty quickly, haven't you?'

'Well, I've nothing much else to do in the evenings.'

He liked working in this room on winter evenings; it was warm and well-lit and quiet.

'What about the doorways?' Matthew asked suddenly, pointing at the ground floor drawings. 'I mean the existing ones. Are they wide enough for a wheelchair?'

'Yes, I'm sure they are, but of course I'll check when I measure up. And the great thing is that there are no steps, the whole ground floor is on the level, including the way into the kitchen. Most houses of that age have a step down into the back quarters and you have to think of putting in a false floor, which all adds to the expense.'

They both looked at the plans in silence for a while and then Sebastian said, 'When things get moving I think we should consult the disabled themselves and let them have a say; they'll be the ones who have to live there, they'll be the ones negotiating their wheelchairs round awkward corners.'

'I agree. My mother says architects ought to consult housewives before they design kitchens.'

'Tell her we do, we do. Even architects have mothers.'

Matthew laughed, then said suddenly, 'I've just thought of something. You know who would be a really useful person to consult? That doctor, what's he called? Bramley, that's it, Dr Bramley, who's doing so much good work with rehab centres. Why don't you talk to him?'

He saw Sebastian's expression change, his eyes darken.

'Don't you agree?' he asked, surprised.

'No, I don't, not really.'

'Why ever not?'

Sebastian hesitated, searching for reasons.

'Well, you see,' he said slowly, 'he deals with severe cases, more like a nursing home in some ways, but we're dealing with men who are back to normal, looking after themselves.'

'But,' Matthew began, thinking this was nonsense because that was what Dr Bramley always aimed at, but then he stopped. Clearly Sebastian's professional pride was hurt at the idea of consulting an expert. These architects could be touchy, even good fellows like Sebastian.

'Well, of course,' he said placatingly, 'all such decisions must be yours.'

'So the next thing is to get a survey done.'

'We usually use Silas Crampton,' Matthew told him, 'but, of course,' he added hastily, 'it's entirely up to you.'

'Oh, Crampton's all right, we've dealt with him quite often and always found his judgement very sound.'

'Yes, a man of few words but sound judgement. A true Yorkshireman, like my good self.'

Sebastian laughed.

'And modest with it,' he said. 'If a mere southerner may voice an opinion.'

Then he sighed and was silent.

'What is it?'

'Oh, Matthew, it's just that I hate to think of that poor young woman having to put up with a surveyor going all over the house, when she's so recently bereaved. And she's no experience of this sort of thing. And you know how critical surveyors can be. I think one of us should go with him, so that she doesn't feel alone with a stranger.'

'I absolutely agree. She should have a man there. You

know her better than I do. Can you spare the time to go?'

'I'll make time. And I can help him with the measuring up, which I need to do for myself anyway.'

When Celia got the letter suggesting a date for the surveyor and Mr Crawley to visit the house, her immediate fear was that they might discover the sovereigns.

It was two weeks since she had unstitched that first one. Then sovereign after sovereign had rolled out of her aunt's skirt, until there was a pile of gold on the purple striped bed-spread. She had sat staring at it, utterly bewildered by it, until she was jolted back to reality by Sarah announcing tea.

She had been terrified the girl would come in, had managed to cover the coins with the dress and gone and stood in the doorway, barring the way, so certainly Sarah had seen nothing.

After tea she had gone back and tackled the other two heavy dresses. The golden pile grew terrifyingly; there must have been hundreds of sovereigns on the bedspread by now. Where to store them? Where to hide them? Thieves might come in the night. Sarah was an honest girl but might be tempted. Besides it was a sin to put temptation in anyone's way.

That was when she'd remembered her uncle's old Gladstone bag. She closed the guest room door behind her and went into his room. She had already put his clothes in his old leather travelling cases, but the bag, where had she put the bag? Of course, up there on top of the wardrobe. She pulled a chair across the room, climbed up and pulled it down. It was blessedly light and empty; for a moment she had feared it might be full of more sovereigns which had become objects of terror to her.

She would count them later, she thought as she stowed them away in the Gladstone bag, scooping them up in handfuls, eager to get them out of sight. She'd meant to hide the bag in the wardrobe but it was too heavy to lift. So she let it down on to the ground and pushed it under the bed. It slid easily across the linoleum, and the dark bedspread covered it nicely.

In the days that followed she thought about the sovereigns day and night, she couldn't sleep for worrying about them. Why had her aunt kept this hoard? There must be some awful secret about them. What should she do with them? She couldn't tell that solicitor man, it might be a crime, at least she felt criminal. And responsible. She had to find a safe hiding place. She must never leave them unattended, never leave the house.

And now this surveyor man was going to come and presumably he'd survey everything, he'd look in cupboards and drawers. He would pry under beds.

Crampton was a gruff fellow, Sebastian thought, as he introduced him to Miss Grimsdyke. He really should have spoken more gently to her, she was obviously in great stress of mind. He didn't want the man to go making hurtful comments about the house, not in her presence anyway.

Crampton opted to go and look at the roof first and asked to be shown the access to the loft. Sebastian went with Celia while she showed him the ladder, then, the surveyor having disappeared into the eaves, he turned to her and said, 'Could I have a word with you, Miss Grimsdyke, when we go downstairs?'

'Of course,' she said. 'We will go into the drawing room.'

She was pale and clearly very nervous.

'It's nothing to worry about,' he assured her, as they sat down, each on a hard-backed chair on either side of the hearth which seemed to contain an even smaller fire than last time.

'It's just that I want to be sure that you understand what the surveyor's job is. He has to look for any possible faults or weaknesses in the structure of the house. It isn't his job, I'm afraid, to make much of its good points.'

'I see,' she said. 'Of course he has to do his duty, doesn't he?'

He smiled at her; there was something so touching in her

simplicity. He wanted to reach out, take her hand, reassure her. But of course he didn't. Instead he asked her if she had any questions, any doubts that he might help her allay.

She hesitated, then she said, 'Does he have to look in all the cupboards and drawers and things?'

'Oh, no, he's only concerned with the house, not its contents.'

'So he wouldn't need to look under the beds?'

How awful, he thought, this poor delicate young creature has been worried about chamber pots.

'No, of course not,' he assured her and was touched at her inordinate relief. He was so glad that he'd come to help her through what must to her seem a terrible ordeal.

'Well,' he said, getting up, 'if you don't mind I'll just take the measurements of the rooms. It will save Mr Crampton having to do so and I need them for myself anyway. If you wish to be in the rooms as I go around, I should quite understand.'

Her face lit up.

'Oh, yes, I can help. You'll need someone to hold the other end of the tape measure.'

He smiled. She was like a child wanting to help the grown-ups.

'There's no need,' he said. 'It might tire you.'

'Oh, no, I don't tire. I've always worked hard, you know, for my aunt and uncle.'

And so they went from room to room together, talking easily. This time he hardly noticed the cold.

Ten

'What are you doing at Christmas?' Matthew asked as he drove Sebastian to the station. 'I'm going with my mother to some cousins who're planning lots of parties. You'd be very welcome, I know.'

'No, I shall be going to my parents, as usual,' Sebastian told him. 'Thanks all the same, but the folks would be very cut up if I didn't spend Christmas with them.'

'Of course, I understand,' Matthew said, then he added, 'I wonder what the Grimsdyke niece will be doing?'

'Staying in that gloomy house, I suppose, with the little maid. She hasn't any relations and one never hears any mention of friends.'

He couldn't put the awful dreariness of that house out of his mind. It wasn't just the cold; it was the utter lifelessness of everything about the place, the lack of any comfort or beauty. He'd found himself contrasting it with Mrs Jordan's home; it too was in a row of solid, detached Victorian houses, smaller but not dissimilar in layout, yet how different!

'It's awful to think of them in that house at Christmas,' he remarked now.

'Perhaps someone from church will invite them for the day,' Matthew said. 'Let's look on the bright side; the survey was very satisfactory, no woodworm, no dry rot. And gloomy old Crampton even praised the roof. First time I've ever known him do that.'

'The original roof too, just one repair job done since.'

'Do you think the Grimsdykes spent all their money on repairing the roof?' Matthew asked, speculating, as they often did nowadays, on what had become of the Grimsdyke savings.

'No, I don't,' Sebastian said, laughing at the very idea. 'It was only a small job, a few slates had to be replaced and the soffit repaired.'

'Oh, well, it was just a thought. They must have spent their money on something and it certainly wasn't on high living.'

'Secret drinking?' Sebastian suggested. 'You can get through a lot of money on alcohol.'

'No, there was never a suspicion of that on Arthur's breath.'

'What about her?'

'I doubt it. Besides I think there would have been a lingering smell in some of the rooms.'

'Gambling?'

'Never! Arthur was an accountant. He'd know the odds.'

'Maybe we shall never find out. But certainly their savings didn't go on that roof; it won't need anything done to it for years, Crampton said. They built to last, the Victorians did. I hope our modern houses will last as long.'

'And another good thing about that house is there's no danger of subsidence on that side of the town, not like the other side where the mine workings are,' Matthew said, stopping while passengers got off the tram in front. 'We're only just going to make it,' he added, glancing at his watch.

It was foggy again and they had been forced to drive very slowly through the evening traffic.

'At times like this,' he went on, 'I think you were right to leave the car down south.'

'Especially since I have a friend to give me a lift to the station now and then,' Sebastian told him, laughing. 'But seriously, it wasn't much use to me up here. It's much quicker to go about the town by tram. And driving home wasn't much fun once winter came. It's much warmer on the train and quicker too.'

Matthew nodded, peering through the thickening mist.

'And now that my father has learned to drive it's more sense for him to have the use of the motor down there.

They live in a little place called Oxenhurst in Surrey, not too far from London, so the car's handy to get up to town and my mother likes to go out for a drive with him around the countryside if the weather's fine. I was surprised he learned to drive. He's in his fifties, after all.'

'Yes, it's quite difficult to learn when you're elderly. He's done well. My father never took to it.'

'Of course he goes very slowly, allows plenty of time.' He laughed and added, 'He's probably just about setting off for King's Cross now.'

'And here we are at the Central Station,' Matthew said, pulling in by the kerb. 'Let me help you out with your case. It's heavy enough, whatever are you taking in it? The crown jewels?'

Sebastian laughed.

'Christmas presents. My mother loves statuary for the garden and I've found two lovely pieces in a little place in the Dales, so I'm taking one now and I'll take the other when I go at Christmas.'

The fog was nearly as dense in London as it had been in Gradby. He could just make out the tall figure of his father, peering anxiously through the mixture of mist, smoke and steam at the station.

'Good to see you, my boy,' he said and then added, 'I'm letting you take the wheel when we drive back. My old eyes get very tired trying to see the road ahead when it's as thick as this.'

Sebastian drove slowly out of the station, manoeuvring the car between trams, motor buses, a few horse-drawn carts and hundreds of pedestrians, his father leaning anxiously forward.

'Sit back and relax,' his son told him. 'Pull the travelling rug up over you.'

His father obediently pulled the rug, which had been lying across his knees, up to his chin.

'Your mother put a hot-water bottle ready,' he said. 'But I forgot it. Was it very cold on the train?'

'No, they use the heat from the engine to warm the carriages.'

'It's a pity they can't do the same for cars.'

'Maybe they will one day.'

His father laughed.

'A heated motor car?' he said, pulling the rug more closely round him. 'That's something that'll never happen, my boy.'

The fog was thinner as they left London behind them and by the time they reached home the sky was clear and brilliant with stars.

His mother came to the door to welcome them.

'Oh, how cold your cheeks are, darling,' she said, as he kissed her. 'Come in by the fire and warm yourself before you go upstairs. We'll have dinner immediately you're ready.'

As the three of them sat round the table an hour later, he thought again how different a home like this was from the Grimsdykes'; so many homely, familiar things around the room, nothing very grand or spectacular but it all added up to a sense of belonging.

'And how are things in Gradby?' his father asked. 'Work going well, is it?'

'Yes, thank you, Father. We've been working on the plans for the new town hall as well as quite a few much smaller jobs. Considering how slow things are in most businesses, we're doing quite well. Of course, it's a very long established firm. Some of the small ones are going under.'

'And Mrs Jordan? Is she still looking after you well?' his mother asked. 'Are you getting enough to eat?'

He laughed.

'Oh, mother, you're always afraid I'll starve, aren't you?'

They were both silent for a minute and he knew that she was remembering, as he was, those parcels of food that she used to send out to him in the trenches. How much they had meant, how much more than mere nourishment they had contained.

And because the mood had become more serious, a little sadder, he found himself telling her about the Grimsdykes, their sad and gloomy house, their lone niece and her frightened little maid. How they would be alone there, the two of them, for Christmas.

'But, darling,' his mother said. 'We can't have that, can we, Father?'

'Have what?' asked his father, who hadn't been paying much attention and was anyway a little deaf nowadays.

'Sebastian has been telling me about this poor orphan girl and her maid, all alone at Christmas. You must bring them here, Sebastian.'

'*Here*, Mother?'

He couldn't believe what she'd said. His mother had always been a bit unconventional, but to invite two strangers from Yorkshire to come down here for Christmas was eccentric even for her.

'Oh, I don't think we could do that,' he said.

'Why not? Isn't that what Christmas is all about? We should share. We should welcome the homeless and—'

'But she's not homeless.'

'Don't quibble, dear. Her home doesn't sound very nice at all, so it amounts to the same thing.'

'But I don't think she'd fit in. I think it might embarrass her to be asked.'

His mother looked at him and smiled.

'I understand, dear. It might seem to put you in a difficult position and I respect you for being so considerate of her good name. That is quite right and proper. So I shall do the inviting. I shall write her a letter this evening. Then you shall see to getting her ticket for the train – and the maid, of course – and she shall then come quite independently of you, as my guest.'

'The maid too?'

'Of course, that is customary.'

He realized that his mother was thinking of those guests who used to come to their London house before the war, those ladies with their smart maids. He thought of little Sarah with her sacking apron and her raw, red hands.

'She isn't a lady's maid, Mother. She would feel out of place.'

'Sebastian. She isn't much more than a child and she has nowhere to go at Christmas. That should be enough for any Christian family.'

Sebastian looked at his father.

His father shook his head.

'Your mother has developed some quite radical notions since the war,' he said. 'You know that she has the right to vote now? Just like a man?' he added, with a slightly puzzled frown. 'Quite right too, of course.'

Mother and son glanced at each other, both remembering how he had railed against 'those dreadful suffragettes' before the war.

'I shall speak to Cook about it,' his mother said decisively. 'She shall take care of her and if the girl would feel happier doing a few odd jobs, then Cook shall see that she is given something suitable to occupy her.'

There was no arguing with his mother in this mood. Besides, part of him knew that she was right.

The subject of their discussions was meanwhile finding her young mistress's behaviour very strange. She never went out now, seemed distracted, often jumped when Sarah came into a room, even though she did take care always to knock and counted up to five before she went in.

She knocked now and waited outside the guest room door. Nobody answered. She went in. Nobody there. She came out, shutting the door behind her. Then she saw Miss Celia coming upstairs.

Celia saw her first and called out, 'Whatever are you doing in the guest room, Sarah?'

There was an edge of hysteria in her voice.

'It's just that the milkman knocked and asked if you could settle the bill tomorrow, miss, and I thought you was in there. I did look downstairs but didn't see you, miss.'

'Very well, if he's still there, tell him I shall see him tomorrow.'

'Yes, miss. Thank you, miss.'

'Well, then, run along, Sarah,' Celia told her impatiently

and stood on the landing until the girl had disappeared down the stairs.

Then she went into the guest room, knelt down and looked under the bed to check that the Gladstone bag was still there. She pushed it a little way to make sure that it was still heavy with the sovereigns. It was.

She had just done this when she heard the doorbell ring and then Sarah crossing the hall to answer it. She got up quickly, brushed down her skirt and went out on to the landing to face whoever was at the door; burglars didn't ring doorbells. But it might be the police.

Sebastian had walked very slowly from the tram stop to the Grimsdykes' house. He carried his mother's letter dutifully in his pocket but had increasingly grave doubts about her decision.

Of course, morally there was no question that his mother was acting as she should, but morality wasn't everything surely in such a matter: social aptness, the need to avoid embarrassment, these considerations might be shallower, but surely they were equally important.

So he had dawdled, as if postponing the evil hour. With every step he took towards the house he had become more certain that the whole thing was a dreadful mistake.

He was sure of it when the anxious little maid opened the door after he'd rung and he saw Celia, clearly very rushed and flustered, coming hurriedly downstairs to greet him.

'I am very sorry to call like this unannounced,' he said. 'Really very sorry,' he ploughed on in his embarrassment. 'I wish I had let you know. I should have done.'

She nodded, said nothing, but led him into the drawing room.

'Miss Grimsdyke,' he began awkwardly. 'Forgive me for calling like this. I should have written to ask your permission first.'

'That's quite all right,' she said, much calmer now. 'You must come whenever you need to look over the house.'

'Yes, thank you. You are very obliging, but the matter on

which I called is not about the house. I have here a letter from my mother to you, I mean *for* you.'

He held out the letter as if some proof were needed.

She took it, puzzled. She held it, unopened.

It's all very well for Mother to talk of what Christian families should do at Christmas, he thought as he stood there, embarrassed, but this isn't actually how people behave. Celia Grimsdyke must think this very odd.

'Do read it,' he said. 'It's an invitation for Christmas.'

She looked at him, startled.

'I'll get a paperknife,' she said and walked over to a table which had on it a paperscale and knife. She stayed over there by the table, opened and read the letter.

The contents horrified her. How could she possibly go away for Christmas and leave the house open to any burglar who chose to come and steal the sovereigns? The sovereigns now obsessed her, they filled her waking thoughts, they had become the main consideration in everything she did. She didn't even view them as wealth; they were just on too big a scale for that; it was as if she had suddenly been told she was responsible for the Bank of England.

She came and stood by him.

'Please,' she said, speaking almost in a whisper she was so nervous. 'Please thank your mother. She is very kind. Please . . .' her voice broke and she couldn't go on.

It was awful to see such distress. This ridiculous invitation had only added to her problems.

'Oh, Miss Grimsdyke, I am so terribly sorry,' he began. 'I did tell my mother that you probably wouldn't feel up to going so far away from home, but—'

'No, no,' she interrupted him. 'It isn't that.'

Confused, quite out of her depth, she who had shed no tears when her aunt died, now burst into a torrent of weeping.

He put an arm around her shoulders to comfort her. She was so slight, so vulnerable, she must have had such a terrible life in this awful house; pity for her overwhelmed him as he held her.

When she seemed a little calmer, he said, 'Can you tell me what it is then?'

'It's the *sovereigns*,' she burst out and the relief of at last telling somebody her awful secret made her start to cry again.

He led her over to the couch, a hard, tightly stuffed piece of furniture, and sat her down.

'Four o'clock and tea's prepared, miss,' Sarah announced, rattling in with the trolley, so intent on being punctual that she quite forgot to knock.

Celia turned her head away and gazed into the fire as Sarah pushed the trolley across the carpet and parked it in its usual place. There was no need for the cake stand today, since all she had managed to find were a few Marie biscuits, visitors not being expected.

Sebastian stood up and placed himself in front of Celia to shield her from view.

He smiled kindly at Sarah, thanked her and said a cup of tea was very nice and he didn't deserve it, coming unannounced like this. He even opened the door for her, something which nobody had ever done before, not in her whole life they hadn't.

Sebastian found himself strangely confident now in the face of Celia's sudden weakness.

'Let me pour you some tea,' he said and she sat there meekly and accepted the cup from him.

'And when you've had that and feel a bit better, tell me about these sovereigns.'

His manner was fatherly; she calmed down and after a little while told him exactly what had happened.

So that was it, Sebastian realized, the old girl was a miser. That explained everything.

Aloud he said, 'But you have no need to worry. The money is yours and we must arrange for you to get it safely to the bank as soon as possible.'

She looked at him in disbelief. Was it really as simple as that?

'If I had my motor here I'd come round and collect it

tomorrow, but I'm sure Mr Braithwaite will help. I gather your aunt and uncle didn't have a bank account.'

'No, the solicitor said he couldn't find a record of one.'

'So one must be opened now for you, the money put safely into it and then you must be advised the best way for it to be invested to give you a secure income.'

As he rose to go he stood looking down at her for a moment; relief about the money had quite transformed her; she had looked so pinched and pale and anxious and now her fair cheeks seemed to glow, her eyes shine with relief.

She had so desperately needed help and he had been the one privileged to provide it; he felt a mixture of pride and gratitude that it was so. Taking her hands in his, he said, 'I'm so glad for you. Truly you have nothing to worry about now. And my mother really does mean it about Christmas.'

Eleven

Christmas with the Crawleys seemed to Sarah a cross between heaven and Fairyland. She had never imagined anything on earth could be like it. There was this big warm kitchen with a room off it called the housekeeper's room but really it was just like a little parlour for Cook, the two housemaids and herself. It had comfortable chairs and a couch and a fire where they burnt coal and logs like nobody's business.

Cook was lovely, ever so kind. She got a bit ratty and flustered at busy times like getting the Christmas dinner, but who wouldn't with all those hot dishes and goodness knows what all bubbling away in saucepans and nearly boiling over the minute your back was turned? And the food! She'd never known anything like it. Mountains of it and they kept putting second helpings of everything on her plate as they sat round the kitchen table and she would eat until her stomach was fit to burst.

The two housemaids were a scream and their funny cockney voices made them seem even funnier. They said they couldn't always make out her Yorkshire accent, which was daft because she didn't have an accent, just spoke normal. Annie was thin and dark, Rosie was fair and plump and a real card. They were frightened of nothing, those two, not even the mistress who talked to them as if they weren't servants at all. They laughed a bit at the master but kindly like because he was a funny old gentleman and never could get their names right.

On Christmas Day they all got presents and she got one too – a little purse with half a sovereign in it. A half sovereign and for doing nothing except be there! 'Half a sovering,' she kept repeating, 'a whole half sovering,' and they laughed at her, the other two did, and said you can't have a *whole* half of anything, but she didn't mind and slept with it under her pillow and dreamed of all the different things she'd spend it on. The purse was so pretty she'd keep it until her dying day.

They shared a big bedroom, the three of them, and it had good furniture – nearly as good as downstairs – and a carpet in the middle. They talked and giggled half the night. They talked a lot in the little parlour too, when they weren't too busy doing tasks. She enjoyed helping. They gave her nice jobs like taking all the silver paper off some things called tangerines, which were like little oranges, but the peel came off lovely and easy.

They sat there by the fire in the parlour unwrapping the tangerines, which came in a big wooden crate. 'They'll never eat all this lot,' she said, but the others just laughed and said she'd be surprised how many tangerines people got through at Christmas. And it was true because next day she ate six. She loved that silver paper and thought it a sin and a shame to throw it out, so they said she could keep it and she smoothed out each sheet very carefully and put it under her mattress to keep flat. She didn't know what she'd do with it, but she did know it looked precious and shouldn't be wasted.

They asked her about her life in the north which they spoke of like it was a foreign land and she told them all about the Grimsdykes and how they'd both died and how she'd seen his feet sticking out behind the couch in the drawing room, just the *feet*.

They'd listened wide-eyed and open-mouthed, knowing that for years to come they'd be able to tell their friends and their friends' friends about those feet that Sarah had seen.

'It must of bin 'orrible,' Rosie said.

'I've never seen a dead body,' Annie said, putting another log on the fire. The way those girls used up fuel – as if it came free, yes, just as if it grew on trees!

'And I don't never want to, neither,' Rosie remarked.

'He wasn't dead,' she explained. 'Not then, not when I saw his feet. They was still alive, 'is feet was.'

She was shocked when they laughed. Death ain't nothing to laugh at, she told them.

'What'll happen now then?' Rosie, the fair one, asked.

'Dunno. I 'spose I'll be dismissed if she sells the 'ouse. I think she's going to – not that I ever listen in, it's just that you pick up things, don't you?'

Oh, yes, they never listened in neither, but sometimes you couldn't help hearing, could you?

'Best thing would be if she married Mr Sebastian,' Annie suggested, 'then you could stay on as a general. Gets more pay, a general does. Or better still all come and live down 'ere.'

'Marry 'im?' she repeated, shocked. 'She won't marry 'im.'

'Course she won't,' Rosie agreed. 'Miss Celia's goin' to be a spinster lady. You can see that plain as plain.'

Celia, upstairs, was much less relaxed than her maid. She found it strange, almost sinful, all this warmth and softness and lavish food. And the way Sebastian's parents behaved together was unnatural, talking so much and laughing and sometimes even holding each other's hands and all that touching. Were they doing it because she was here? Surely they didn't normally behave like this when they were on their own? In all her life she'd never seen her aunt and uncle touch each other.

She knew that all three of them were doing their best to make her feel at home, but they talked of things she didn't understand, of books she hadn't read, of plays she hadn't seen. The only time she felt really at ease was at church on Christmas morning. The prayers, the psalms, the hymns were so familiar, that they seemed to bind her together with the rest of the congregation, including of course her host and hostess from whom she had until now felt herself a thing apart.

Sebastian, standing next to her, listened to her voice; it was a lovely, clear sound, much more exact and confident than her speaking voice. Who knows, he thought, what hidden talents she may have, which have never been brought out, never developed. Her mind was good, but untrained, virtually unused in the life she had led with her aunt and uncle. She was brave too; she had borne so much in the past months. It was a tragedy that so fine a person should have been so neglected.

And, he had to admit, little though he cared about such

things, that her clothes were not what she deserved. She was wearing a brown coat that was too small, old fashioned boots and on her head a kind of bonnet that looked suspiciously like the sort of thing that her aunt might have handed down. She was so delicately formed, her fair skin so fine and clear, if only she was properly dressed she would be beautiful; she still looked pretty, despite all.

He had lain in bed that morning, thinking of her, peacefully planning the day. It looked as if it might be one of those crisp mornings with bright sunshine. It would be good to have a walk after church and maybe games by the fire in the evening. That's what they usually did and, as usual, they were going to have their Christmas dinner at three o'clock so that the staff had the evening all to themselves. So there'd be plenty of time for a walk.

It was only later that he realized that those waking hours had for once not been plagued with thoughts of Diana, with longing and remorse.

'Yes, I think a walk's a splendid idea, Sebastian,' his mother said as they came back into the house after church. 'Which way shall we go?

'How about down the lane, past Bullers' Farm and back by the field path? It'll be quite dry underfoot, the frost isn't thawing yet.'

His mother nodded. 'That'll take about an hour, which is just right.' Then, turning to Celia, she said, 'You'll find it cold, dear. Let me lend you a scarf. 'And she took a pale blue shawl out of the drawer in the hallstand and arranged it over Celia's head and shoulders. It was soft and fell in folds around her face.

She looked lovely, Sebastian thought, as he led the way with her down the drive. He breathed deeply. It was a perfect morning, the air was crisp, the surrounding fields white with frost, the branches of trees etched dark against the clear blue sky.

'It's good to be alive on a day like this, isn't it?' he said, smiling down at her.

She looked up, smiled and nodded, but said nothing.

'Have you always lived in Gradby?' he asked. 'Did you ever live in the country?'

'I used to go visiting in the country sometimes with my parents and brother when I was little,' she told him, 'but it's all very vague and distant. I remember a stream with a pool.'

'It's always like that with early memories, isn't it?' he said. 'There just seem to be impressions, but nothing definite and you try to put them in order and make something rational out of them, but you can't.'

She nodded.

'I remember how it felt,' she said, 'but not exactly where I was or who was with me.'

'That's it,' Sebastian agreed. 'And then of course people in the family tell you things, so you can't sort out what you really remember and what you've been told.'

'It's not like that for me,' she said. 'There wasn't anybody left to tell me.'

It was a matter-of-fact statement, there was no self-pity in her voice; all the same he cursed himself for being tactless. But glancing down at her again he saw that her face was quite composed. How well the shawl suited her, he thought; that blue, which was perfect against her clear skin, brought out the colour of her eyes whose direct gaze was thoughtful but somehow unsophisticated. She might have been the subject of a Renaissance portrait, even a Raphael Madonna.

'It suits her, that old shawl of mine, doesn't it?' Mrs Crawley said quietly to her husband as they followed the younger pair down the lane.

'Better than that bonnet thing she had on before.'

'Sh, dear, she'll hear you.'

'Nonsense,' he said, and tucked her arm into his. 'Don't fuss, Barbara.'

'You just assume that because *you* don't hear well, other people don't either.'

'Nothing wrong with my hearing,' he told her. 'Where are we going?'

'Sebastian thought we might go round by Bullers' Farm and back by the field path.'

'What's that? What did you say about a bull?'

'Such a shame you have to go back to work tomorrow evening, Sebastian,' his mother said, as they sat by the fire that evening. 'I always think Christmas Day on a Wednesday is a little sad. Just the two days. Christmas Day on a Monday is perfect, four lovely days' holiday.'

'Now that you've got the vote, my dear,' her husband said, 'you could insist on a law to make Christmas always fall on a Monday.'

They all laughed. They were always teasing like that; half the time Celia didn't know if they were serious or not.

'You'll have the vote soon, Celia dear.'

'Will I?' She was genuinely surprised.

'Not until you're thirty, and that's a long way off,' Mr Crawley told her.

'Nonsense. Before very long they'll have to bring it down to the same age as for men.'

'So all the kitchen maids will have the vote?'

'And why not? Why shouldn't maids be treated the same as footmen?'

'Because there aren't any footmen left to be treated like, my dear, that's why. They're all working in factories now.'

Sebastian laughed.

'I think Father won that round, Mother. Don't you think so, Celia?'

She smiled, not knowing what to make of any of it.

'I think we'll have some cards,' Barbara Crawley said, observing this and thinking that the girl might find a game easier than conversation. It's always hard for anyone, she reflected, to be thrown into somebody else's family, especially after living as this girl had evidently done.

'What shall we play?' she asked after they'd put up the card table and found the cards. 'Do you have a favourite card game, Celia?'

'I've never played before,' Celia said.

Her aunt and uncle didn't approve of card games, but she didn't say so.

'Then let's play whist; you'll pick it up quite easily, I'm sure.'

She did. In fact she and Sebastian played against the older pair and won again and again.

How pretty she looks, Sebastian thought, watching her as, cheeks glowing from the walk and now the firelight, she kept picking up the tricks from the table, glancing up at him as she did so to make sure she was doing the right thing, needing the reassurance of his approval. And how quickly she learns.

'*You* don't have to go back tomorrow, do you, dear?' Sebastian's mother asked her.

'Oh, I think I should,' she said, frightened of outstaying her welcome.

'Why not stay with us until the weekend? You would be doing us a great favour if you would stay to cheer us up after Sebastian's left. We can put you on the Sunday train.'

'Nothing will happen about the house until Monday, so you might as well stay here,' Sebastian assured her, thinking of the cold house to which she would return.

Celia thought of it too and looked at the fire and then at these kind faces pressing her to stay.

'Yes, please,' she said.

'Oh, innit loverly,' Rosie sang out when she heard that Sarah was to stay until the weekend. 'Our half day's on Friday so we can take you out with us.'

'What do you do on your time off?' Sarah asked.

'Well, in the summer we sometimes stay 'ere. We can use all that garden at the side of the 'ouse, sit in the sun if we want, but mostly we go up town, up the West End, see the sights, go to the pictures. Mind you, we've got pictures local, don't 'ave to go up town.'

'We saw Buster Keeton last Friday. I like 'im best,' Annie put in.

'I like Charlie Chaplin best. 'E don't look so sad. Which do you like best, Sarah?'

'I don't know neither of 'em. Who are they?'

'You *know*, at the pictures.'

'I ain't never bin to pictures.'

'Never bin? Never bin?'

They couldn't believe their ears.

'Well, then,' Rosie said. 'That settles it. We'll take you on Friday.'

Much the same conversation was being carried on upstairs. Celia, it seemed, had never been to a picture house either. Nor had she been to a theatre or a concert.

'When we get back to Gradby, you must let me take you to the theatre,' Sebastian said. 'There are two theatres, the Grand and the Royal, both have very good plays. I'll let you know when there's something interesting coming.'

She demurred, but his mother said, 'Oh, you must go, my dear, it's part of your education,' so she agreed and thanked him.

'And what about finding lodgings for you,' his mother went on, 'when the house is sold? I'm afraid it's all very unsettling for you and you seem to manage everything so well. I hope you'll find a landlady as good as Sebastian's Mrs Jordan.'

The two women talked about lodgings and housekeeping, Arthur Crawley dozed and Sebastian thought of all the good things he could introduce Celia to, how he would lead her towards the arts, which he himself loved. His mother was right to say this was part of her education. She had missed so much that girls of her age took for granted. Never been to a cinema or the theatre! Never been to a concert! Unbelievable. *He* would be the one to show her, he would take her to the City art gallery. How thrilled she would be, she who had seen nothing but those awful grimy pictures in the drawing room. She deserved to be shown finer things. Her life should be transformed now that she was free of that aunt and uncle, with their narrow, miserly ways. Increasingly he saw himself as the one who would bring colour and warmth into a life which had been for too long endured in a loveless atmosphere of coldness and gloom.

Twelve

Cook gave them each a picnic to eat on the train. It didn't seem quite right to Sarah to eat in the same carriage as Miss Celia, but when she'd said this to Rosie and Annie they'd told her not to be so soft and what else could she do anyway? Get out and eat it on the roof?

So she sat there in her corner, munching the turkey and ham sandwiches which Cook had smothered in her home-made chutney and the very taste of it brought back the feel of those magical days, that Christmas dinner, those sandwiches by the fire in the evening, those tales they told in bed. The smell of the tangerine brought back memories too and the feel of it as her thumb pushed under the loose peel, oh she was there again by the fire unwrapping a crateful of them with Rosie and Annie.

And didn't her hands look different? A few more holidays like that and she'd have hands like a lady. Funny that, because she'd always thought that God had created ladies' hands differently from servants' hands but Annie and Rosie said it was just a matter of scrubbing and carbolic soap and nothing to do with God at all.

Celia, in her far corner, was reminiscing too as she looked out at the countryside, now under a gentle layer of snow, but she was glad to be getting home, getting back to normal. None of it had seemed quite real at the Crawleys'. And as the train approached Gradby, where the snow was never white but immediately turned into dirty brown slush, she felt a little rush of pleasure that soon she would be back in a world which she understood.

It was bitterly cold as they waited for the tram. A freezing fog hung in the air, sulphurous and sooty, chilling their lungs with every breath they took. It was hard to see their way as they walked slowly home from the tram stop, for the gaslights gave little guidance, just seemed to light up their patch of fog in a fuzzy glow.

Entering the house was like going into an icy cave. There was a stillness about it which made it seem even colder than the air outside, which at least had some movement in it.

'Get the kitchen fire going, Sarah,' Celia said. 'I'll light the one in the drawing room and then make a cup of tea.'

Sarah came to her in the drawing room a few minutes later.

'I've lit the fire in the range, miss,' she said, 'but there's no water, the pipes must all be frozen.'

Celia went and tried the taps herself. Not a drop.

She remembered her aunt saying you must never leave the house in the winter in case of a freeze up. She often spoke disparagingly of those who did.

'The water met them coming downstairs,' she would say with infinite satisfaction. 'That's what comes of going gallivanting off in mid-winter. I've no sympathy for people like that.'

And Uncle would nod his agreement and say it wasn't right that careless people like that could claim on the insurance.

Even worse was the case of the Jenkinses, who went away for two whole months in the winter and didn't even turn the water off at the main and when they came home the letters were floating across the hall, finding their way out again through the same letter box as they came in.

All these tales came into Celia's mind as she stood in the kitchen with Sarah. She had broken one of her aunt's commandments and was now paying for it. It was all very well for those people down south. They were soft, they didn't have weather like this. Easy for them to tempt her to stay on there, to lead her astray like that; they weren't the ones who would come back to frozen pipes. She shouldn't have listened to them; she should have come home when she'd said she would. Or not gone at all.

'At least,' she said, 'we can make sure we don't have a flood if there's a thaw. We can turn off the stopcock under the sink in the scullery.'

'Shall I do it, Miss Celia?'

'No, I'll do it myself. I want it turned properly.'

When she came back into the kitchen, the fire was blazing up nicely, fuel economy forgotten in the need to unfreeze the pipes. They both stood for a moment looking at it, enjoying the warmth. Then she said, 'This won't do. We must go and put away our things,' and leaving the bright, warm comfort of the fire, she went towards the icy coldness of the rest of the house, Sarah following.

It was then that the explosion happened. With a tremendous roar, the back boiler behind the fire exploded into the room, blowing before it the entire contents of the grate so that flaming wood and burning cinders flew everywhere. The force of the blast lifted the two of them off their feet and hurled them backwards into the hall.

The noise alerted everyone in the street. Strangers came running, police, ambulance and fire brigade arrived. The newspaper reporters also arrived. The timing was just right for next day's news. A cub reporter was the first to get his copy back and a sub-editor got his article finished just in time to go down to the press.

Sebastian, in a hurry to get to the office this Monday morning, didn't look at the paper, which Mrs Jordan brought in as usual with his breakfast, until he had nearly finished. As he helped himself to the last piece of toast, he glanced at the headlines. Then he looked again more carefully. 'Oh, my God,' he said and, toast forgotten, gave himself up to reading the article.

Explosion in Waterloo Road

Yesterday afternoon Miss Celia Grimsdyke and her maid Sarah Higgins returned to their home in Waterloo Road to find the water frozen. They lit a fire in the kitchen range hoping to unfreeze it. But, as our Science Reporter tells us, this is a very dangerous thing to do.

If the water in the back boiler is frozen, the heat will expand the metal until it reaches breaking point when the boiler will explode and, being encased by solid chimney on three sides, the only way it can burst out is through the fireplace and into the room. Fortunately there was little to catch fire in this instance; as the flames flew out into the kitchen, only a light pair of curtains were set alight. Cinders were burning on some matting and the firemen searched carefully in case any were smouldering unremarked.

Miss Grimsdyke and her maid had a lucky escape. They were standing by an open door at the far side of the kitchen and were blown out into the hall and thrown down by the front door. Had the kitchen door been shut they would have taken the full impact of the blast. Had they been standing near the fire they would almost certainly have been killed.

Others may be less fortunate. We would like to take this opportunity of alerting our readers to the danger of lighting fires under a frozen boiler. If in any doubt about what to do, contact your local plumber.

The makers of Trident Kitchen Ranges Ltd., founded in 1876, tell us that their ranges have been tried and tested over the years and are the safest on the market, but no range would withstand the heating of a frozen back boiler.

We are glad to report that both Miss Grimsdyke and her maid were found to be little harmed by their experience. They suffered some cuts and bruises but no bones were broken. They were, however, taken by ambulance to the infirmary where they were found to be suffering from concussion. Dr. Mornington, who treated them at the infirmary, told *The Gradby Chronicle* that his patients were making excellent progress and should be allowed to return home in a day or two.

Mrs Jordan didn't have a telephone, so it was from the office that Sebastian rang the infirmary. Miss Grimsdyke would be staying in until the following afternoon, he was told. Yes, she could see visitors. Visiting hours were from two until four every afternoon.

He was about to ring Matthew, when the telephone rang; it was Matthew who had just read the news himself.

'Well, she seems to have escaped unharmed, that's the main thing,' Matthew said cheerfully.

'Yes, but what worries me is they talk about her going home. She can't possibly go back to the house. It was bad enough before, but it's impossible now.'

'I hope the place was properly insured. It'll cost something to put things right.'

'That doesn't really worry me, because we're going to knock the place about anyway. Certainly that range was coming out.'

'Yes, you said you were going to take it out. It's taken itself out now, saved you the trouble,' Matthew said and laughed.

Sebastian, who didn't feel like laughing, said rather coldly, 'And it could have killed her in the process.'

'Yes, of course. Sorry.'

'Can't you hurry the sale along, Matthew?'

'It would normally have been another six weeks or so, but we'll have to see what can be done. I'll get in touch with the solicitors now, if you like.'

'Would you? We have the funds for the purchase and the grant for the alterations is just about certain. Let's get on with it. At least if there are any more disasters, it'll be our responsibility to deal with them, not hers.'

'One of us should visit her, I suppose,' Matthew said.

'I'll go this afternoon.'

'Oh, would you?' Matthew said, clearly relieved. 'I do so hate hospitals. And it's always so difficult to think of anything to say.'

'I'll have to talk to her about lodgings. Can you help find her some?'

'Of course. And if she needs to be taken anywhere I'll drive – or you can borrow the motor if you like.'

'Thank you. I do now wish I'd kept mine up here.'

'Well, you weren't to know, old chap.'

Celia was up and dressed and sitting in a chair by her bed when he went into the ward.

She was pale but quite composed. One side of her face was bruised and there were scratches on her hands and forehead.

'They're going to give me a final examination tonight,' she told him. 'And if that's all right I can go home tomorrow morning.'

'Celia,' he said very gently, 'you really can't go back there. Please let me help you to find lodgings.'

'No, I've been enough bother to you already. I shall go back home tomorrow. There is so much to see to. And there'll be a lot of clearing up to do.'

He could see that she was adamant. It was no use arguing with her now.

'Then I'll ring the infirmary from the office tomorrow morning and if you are fit to leave I'll come and take you back to the house. Then we can talk things over, but I won't worry you now.'

'Thank you, but we could hire a cab.'

'No, I shall come for you. Matthew has said I can borrow his motor. Besides, I want to see the house myself. Don't forget we are buying it,' he added as an extra bait, 'so I need to see the state of the property.'

At that, she nodded her agreement.

'And how is Sarah?' he asked, as he was getting up to go.

'I think she's still in bed. You might enquire after her as you go.'

On his way out he asked a nurse about Sarah. The nurse smiled.

'Oh, she's a grand little patient, she is. Really happy to be here. Come and see for yourself.'

Sarah was sitting up in bed, looking, as the nurse had said, very happy with her lot.

She smiled when she saw him and then, suddenly embarrassed, pulled the sheet up round her chin.

'How are you, Sarah?'

'I'm very well and they said I could get up if I wanted or stay in bed a bit longer, so I said I'd stay because it's lovely to lie in and I had breakfast in bed on a tray with a teapot all to myself and a milk jug and all. I've never stayed in bed before and it's so warm here, it has to be because of the ill people.'

She stopped to draw breath.

'You need the rest; it was a bad shock that you and Miss Celia had.'

Her expression changed.

'Oh, it was dreadful, that bang. I thought my ear drums had burst and then everything went all swirly and the next thing I knew I was down there on the hall floor and there was Miss Celia with her face bleeding. Oh, is it bad, her face, sir?'

'No, just a few little scratches. It won't show in a day or two.'

'Oh, that's good. I've got a bandage on my leg. They think a bit of cinder caught it, but it doesn't hurt and it don't show neither being high up. When will we be going back?'

'All being well, I shall come and fetch you both tomorrow morning. Miss Celia wants to get back to see to the house.'

'Fetch us? You mean in a motor car?'

'Yes, that's right. Mr Braithwaite's motor. You remember he came with me to the house once?'

'Oh, yes, the day of the funeral it was.'

Remembering that day made her sad, but then she thought of a ride in a motor car and felt happy again.

'Thank you, sir,' she said. 'It'll be much better than the tram.'

The thaw set in that night; as he drove them out of the infirmary the next day a light rain was falling, washing away the last of the brown slush which was all that remained of the snow in the streets.

'If the pipes have burst, there'll be a lot of water leaking out of them now,' Celia remarked, thinking yet again of her aunt's tales of the flooded houses of irresponsible people.

'Don't worry. We'll call in a plumber to see to it. You do have the key, don't you?' he added, wondering why he hadn't thought of that before.

'Yes, the police brought it up to the hospital. They said they'd locked the house up and made everything safe. They were very good.'

She took the key out of her bag as she spoke for they were turning into Waterloo Road now. Sebastian slowed and then parked the car outside the front gate.

All three of them were apprehensive as she turned the key in the lock, Celia fearing that water might be cascading down the stairs, Sebastian afraid that the house might be just habitable and she'd insist on staying in it, Sarah suddenly sure that all the lovely time at the Crawleys' and the spoiling she'd had in the hospital had just been a dream and now she'd woken up.

The house was still cold, but it was a damp coolness now and there was a smell of mildew in the hall. Without consulting each other, they moved to the kitchen.

Dust and ash were everywhere, dead cinders, charred wood and soot had reached every corner. There were burn marks on the table and chairs and one of the windows was cracked.

'But look how clean my grate is!' Sarah exclaimed.

It was true, the explosion had swept all before it, scouring the grate cleaner than any servant had ever managed.

'It's amazing,' Sebastian remarked. 'The force that must have been behind it.'

He felt momentarily ill at the thought of what would have happened to Celia if she had been standing in its path.

'I'll turn on the water again,' Celia was saying. 'Then we'll know if we have any leaks.'

How calm she was, he thought, following her into the scullery. He would rather she'd been distraught, more amenable to going into lodgings. Then he dismissed the idea as unworthy.

The water flowed. They waited to see what would happen. There were no signs of leakage.

'Good,' Celia said. 'Now we have water, we can certainly

manage to stay. We'll set about cleaning the kitchen this afternoon, Sarah.'

He felt himself dismissed.

'But if you can't light the range, you'll have no hot water.'

'That's right, miss,' Sarah agreed. 'We can't boil a kettle.'

'We can boil water on the drawing room fire, Sarah,' Celia said. 'You can go and light it now.'

After Sarah had gone, he turned to Celia and said, 'You really can't stay here, you know that, don't you?'

'No. I am sure we can manage.'

She had that look of acceptance that he had seen on her face before; a look that seemed to say: this is my lot and I am duty-bound to bear it. He knew it was useless to argue. Implacable, that's what she was. Implacable as her aunt.

Reluctantly he left them.

Thirteen

'There's one thing, miss, t'kitchen'll not need spring cleaning this year,' Sarah said, looking with satisfaction around her restored domain.

All afternoon and well into the evening they had toiled. She'd swept up the charred wood and dead cinders and put them apart to use again; waste not want not, the mistress always said. Then she'd filled another sack with soot and dust and ash and dumped it out the back. She'd climbed up on the steps to brush down the ceiling and walls, all greasy and dirty with soot. After that she'd tied a floor cloth round the end of the broom and washed walls and ceiling with it. It looked a bit smeary, the ceiling did, but it was the best she could do.

Meanwhile Miss Celia had cleaned the furniture, not that there was much of it, and the table would never be the same again, that was for sure; there's no amount of cleaning will put right a surface pitted with burn marks, she thought as she set about cleaning the windows, going carefully with the cracked panes.

There was no fire to be lit in the kitchen range until everything was put right with the boiler, but she blackleaded it all the same and polished all the brass knobs till the light bounced off them. Last of all she scrubbed the kitchen floor, chastising the dirt out of every nook and cranny. She worked vigorously; cleaning the kitchen had always been her favourite task. She was nervous in the rest of the house, but felt at home in the kitchen. So she had set about it with enthusiasm, determined to restore it to order before nightfall. And by the time they went to bed, too tired to eat, it *was* back to normal.

And so were her hands, Sarah noticed, as she looked down at them, red and raw, before she fell into a deep sleep.

Water, like the Almighty, moves in a mysterious way its wonders to perform. By devious routes it moves about a house once it has escaped the confines of pipes, cylinders and tanks, seeking ways of finding its own level, of making its way downstream, by hollows and pathways unknown to the householder.

So, as Celia and Sarah slept, water seeped out of a hair crack in the tank and out of tiny orifices in the pipes. As the holes and cracks widened so the trickle increased to a stream which meandered between the timbers of the loft and lay there, before finding various ways down to lower levels.

Sarah's first task the next morning was to light the fire in the drawing room and get a kettle boiling. She'd filled the kettle in the scullery and was carrying it back into the drawing room, when she noticed the puddle. It was just lying there, by the window. Instinctively she looked up at the ceiling; no sign of damp there. And it hadn't come in through the window. The walls were quite dry. However had it got there? Thinking it needed a better brain than hers, she ran up to tell the mistress.

'Roll back the carpet,' Celia told her when she saw the lake on the surrounding floorboards. 'I'll turn off the mains water again and you run round to Mr Bates. And look sharp because he'll be busy and no doubt go off early.'

It was still dark as Sarah ran round to Mr Bates the plumber. She knew the house well and had often seen him when she went on errands to the shops. He was just coming out of his gate now, his bicycle laden with all his equipment.

'Ah've no end o' work on now t'thaw's come,' he told her. 'Enough for weeks on end. But Ah read about t'explosion so I reckon Ah'll come to thee first. T'others 'ave all got a man in t'ouse, so Ah reckon they can wait.'

'Oh, thank you, thank you,' Sarah panted, struggling to

keep up as he pedalled along on his bicycle. 'Mistress'll be right suited.'

When they reached the house, she ran ahead of him and banged on the door.

'Look, Miss Celia, I've bin and gone and got 'im,' she exclaimed triumphantly when Celia opened the door, and she gestured towards Mr Bates like a magician displaying a rabbit he has successfully brought out of a hat.

Mr Bates was used to it: in his experience people were always pleased to see a plumber at this time of year.

'Ah were right sorry to read about t'explosion,' he said, as he stood regarding the lake in the drawing room. 'An' this 'ere is puzzlesome, an' all, ain't it?' He scratched his head, further disrupting his hair which was wiry, sticking up in spikes around his head, like a sweep's brush. That, and his big round eyes, gave his face a look of permanent astonishment.

'Well, Ah like a challenge,' he said at last. 'Ah'll be off upstairs and see what Ah can see,' and he ran out of the room, an agile little man, used to tunnelling his way under floorboards and balancing on the joists of lofts.

They waited anxiously like patients awaiting the doctor's verdict. He didn't keep them waiting long.

'By gum,' he said, 'but t'water's an amazing clever thing. From t'tank, it came down to between t'loft timbers, then it found a way down t'ollow in bedroom walls to just above this 'ere room,' and he pointed dramatically at the ceiling.

'But it hasn't come through the ceiling,' Celia pointed out, indicating the puddle on the floor.

'Nay, I reckon it found a way through t'ole where that curtain rod's fixed.'

'But the wall's dry,' Celia said, wiping her hand down the wall to prove her point.

'It found a better way. Ah've known this before. Look see, it's seeping down behind t'shutters,' he added pulling the shutters away from the wall.

'So what can we do?'

'It'll start coming through t'ceilings soon. It needs men to bucket out t'water lying in t'loft, tek t'weight off t'ceilings like. Or we could mek an 'ole in t'ceiling and let it all through, but it'd mek a mess wi' all t'laths and plaster.'

As he spoke water began to run out of the light which hung, unshaded, in the middle of the drawing room. Down the flex it ran, round the light bulb and plopped on to the floor. Celia stared, Sarah screamed. Mr Bates looked gratified.

'It's found its way down t'hole they made when they put t'electric in,' he said admiringly. 'By, but it's a wonderful thing is t'water. You'd scarce believe what it can get up to.'

The doorbell rang.

'Well, go along, Sarah,' Celia said impatiently, for the maid seemed transfixed, unable to take her eyes off the light which was performing like a tap.

'My aunt didn't want the electric,' Celia told the plumber, 'but my uncle said it would be more economical in the long run than the gas lights. I think she was right because look what's happened.'

'Oh, t'water would've found its way down some 'ow. Mebee even along t'gas pipes. I tell you, it's a wonderful thing is water.'

Sarah brought Sebastian into the room. He hurried anxiously across the room to Celia.

'I promised I'd call,' he said. 'And now Sarah tells me you've more trouble.'

'This is Mr Bates the plumber,' Celia told him. 'I expect he can explain to you what's happened better than I can.'

Mr Bates took Sebastian off with him upstairs. He wanted to show him what the water was up to and he wanted to talk to him without the ladies present. It was a bad do was this, but no good frightening them with too much of the truth.

It was a relief for him to talk to a man. Ladies listened, but then their eyes seemed to glaze over and they nodded politely but they didn't really understand. This Mr Crawley seemed to understand. Oh, an architect, that was it. Not that Mr Bates usually had much use for architects; he'd worked on new houses where the architect had forgotten all about drains and such like, too busy putting pretty touches to fancy drawings, architects were. But this one seemed all right, went up there in the loft with him, agreed they could work with hoses to get the water out before the ceilings came down. It was too big a job for Mr Bates on his own, but his mate Bert Patterson was a plumber by trade and in a bigger way of business having a lad to help him. The three of them could handle it, he reckoned.

'A good man that,' Sebastian said to Celia after the plumber had left and Sarah had gone back to her kitchen. 'I can see we've got to move quickly to save the ceilings.'

Celia nodded.

He took her hands.

'Please,' he said. 'You must see that you can't stay here now? The furniture can be stored and you can go into lodgings. Truly, it's the only sensible thing to do.'

Her spirit was broken. This second calamity defeated her. She had gone away in the winter, broken her aunt's commandment and now she had been chastised with fire and water. She had caused kitchen ranges to explode and ceilings to fall down and there was no health in her.

'Very well,' she acquiesced meekly.

'I want the conveyance signed this week,' Sebastian told the solicitor. 'There is absolutely no reason for any further delay. And it has now become very urgent that we do the repairs to the plumbing immediately.'

'But you can beat them down now. In the circumstances you either pay less or you don't pay until the vendor has carried out the repairs.'

'The vendor *can't* see to the repairs,' Sebastian cut in, exasperated. 'And in view of all the expense we shall be involved in for the conversion, the small sum we shall need to spend on these plumbing repairs is quite insignificant.'

'As your solicitor, I have to point this matter out to you,' the solicitor said coldly, 'and perhaps remind you that it is public funds which you are dealing with.'

He was right of course.

'Very well,' Sebastian said wearily. 'Let us say that we

will deduct the cost of these plumbing repairs from the final price.'

'Good.'

The solicitor smiled. He considered his client a decent man, if a little naive, whom he had brought to see reason.

'Then I think we can safely say that the sale will go through this week.'

Sebastian's second anxiety, after seeing the lawyer, was to find somewhere for Celia to live. In the end, giving up all idea of work, he took the tram back to Mrs Jordan's house and told her the situation.

'Do you know of any respectable boarding house where they might stay?' he asked her. 'And it has to be immediate.'

She considered. She shook her head. She cogitated a little longer. Then she said, 'I think they'd best come here until we can find something better.'

Surprised, he smiled at her.

'Nothing could be better,' he said. 'But surely you don't have the room?'

Mrs Jordan was a practical woman; she saw that there was advantage to herself as well as sacrifice in this arrangement.

'I have a room that Miss Grimsdyke could have,' she said. 'And the girl could have what used to be the maid's room. I don't have a living-in maid now, just a daily woman, so Sarah could have that little room and in return she could help me about the house, because of course there will be more work.'

'Sarah's a good, hard-working girl,' he assured her. It was true, of course, but he would have said anything, told any lie to get some safe haven for Celia, get her out of that house.

'I'll go back and tell her. And I do understand that it would only be temporary. We wouldn't wish to impose on you.'

She smiled and told him it would be no imposition, but when he had gone she went slowly upstairs to the room which she had promised could be Celia's.

It was her son's room, exactly as he had left it last time he came on leave in November 1917. His clothes still hung in the wardrobe, his books were still on the chest of drawers, his photographs on the wall. On a table were the little model aeroplanes he had made when he was still at school, worshipping the aviators, as all schoolboys did. He'd have liked to be one himself and how relieved she'd been when he was put in the army instead, because those daredevil aviators stood little chance of coming out of the war alive. But his friend in the new air force did survive, whereas he lay somewhere in Flanders in an unmarked grave.

There was his photograph on the mantelpiece, taken with his father one holiday in Cornwall. She stood looking at it. She had so often come into this room, intending to tidy away his things, but then stood like this with aching heart unable to alter anything; this was all that was left of him, she couldn't expunge it.

But now it was needed, she told herself firmly. This poor girl was homeless; it was wrong not to put his room to use. Even so she found herself mouthing words that were half apology, half prayer as she began to take his clothes out of the wardrobe and tidy away his books.

Sebastian went straight back to Waterloo Road. He was pleased to see that Mr Bates and his team were already there; the bicycle was outside the front door and Patterson's van parked in the road.

They had rigged up some arrangement for pumping out the water, a hosepipe was emptying itself into the drain at the side of the house. The door was unlocked; he rang and walked in. There seemed to be nobody about downstairs, so he went up to where the men were working.

'When we've cleared this lot, we'll drain the system and repair the tank and the pipes,' Mr Bates told him. 'So at least they'll have water. Then they'll have to decide what to do next.'

'There'll be no need for water, because Miss Celia and her maid will be leaving to find somewhere more comfortable to live. And next week we shall be doing major alterations to the house – in fact, I was hoping that you and Mr Patterson will be able to work for us.'

Mr Bates nodded. It made sense except that bit about not needing water. You could always bring a thermos flask, of course, but a man works better for a nice cup of freshly brewed tea.

Celia was in the kitchen when Sebastian went downstairs. He asked her if she could come and speak to him in the drawing room.

'I am very grateful for all you have done,' she began, but he waved her thanks aside. All he had wanted was to serve her.

'The furniture can go into store,' he said. 'Meanwhile my landlady, Mrs Jordan, who is a very nice respectable woman, will be happy to take you in as her lodger, and Sarah too. There is a room for her and Mrs Jordan suggests that she should in return help her with the housework.'

'Oh!'

She seemed at a loss for words. He had, he realized, just jumped in and arranged everything without consulting her as much as he should.

'I'm sorry,' he said. 'But it seemed the only way.'

He was terrified that she would refuse. He would do anything to convince her.

Still she hesitated.

'What is it, Celia?' he asked.

'It's just that I don't know if it would be right.'

'Why not?'

A blush, cruelly evident on her fair skin, began with two dark spots on her cheeks and spread to cover her whole face. She looked up, but avoided looking into his eyes. It was extraordinary how that look softened her face; she looked so vulnerable, struggling to be brave, to be outspoken about what was worrying her. He realized what it was. Oh, she'd had too much to bear without this extra embarrassment.

'Would it make it all right if we were engaged?' he heard himself say.

'Engaged?'

'To be married, I mean.'

He was almost as surprised to hear himself say the words as she was to hear them. He had only just realized that he must love her, otherwise why all this concern, this caring? This must be what real love is like.

This certainty gave him added confidence.

'I'm asking you to marry me, Celia,' he said firmly. 'Will you?'

This time she looked directly at him.

'Yes,' she said.

He bent down but she did not raise her lips to his, did not put her arms around him as his slipped around her. He kissed her on the forehead, a chaste little kiss. It was just that it had all been too sudden for her, he told himself. It would be different when they had more time together and it would certainly be different when they were married.

Fourteen

'*Marry her?*' his mother repeated. '*Marry her?* Sebastian, you're not serious? You can't possibly mean this!'

Sebastian was amazed. When he had sent a telegram to his parents announcing that he would be coming for the weekend and had news to tell, he had expected surprise at his news; surprise followed by delight. Surprise there certainly was. Followed by dismay.

They were sitting, the three of them, round the fire in the little study. His mother and he were on the couch, his father in his favourite wing chair on the other side of the hearth.

'But, Mother,' Sebastian protested. '*You* were the one who insisted on inviting her down here, *you* were the one who asked her to stay on after I'd left and now you've turned against her for no reason.'

'Of course I haven't. I've nothing against her. But when I asked her here out of goodwill, charity, whatever you like to call it, the idea of your marrying her never entered my head.'

Her husband had been sitting quietly all this time, listening to the conversation, but not taking any part in it. Sebastian now turned to him for support.

'*You* liked her too, didn't you, Father?'

'Oh, yes, a very nice girl. Picked up whist in no time.'

His mother made no comment; her silence made it clear that she did not regard the swift mastery of a card game as an irresistible qualification in a daughter-in-law.

'Of course there is a big difference in your ages,' his father went on, hoping this would constitute some kind of loyal support of his wife.

'Ten years,' Sebastian said. 'But she is old for her years.'

'And then, come to think of it,' his father said, turning towards his wife, 'there's eight years' difference in our ages, my dear.'

When she didn't reply, he added, 'And what about that Dr Bramley? Diana must be twenty years younger than he is and that seems to work all right.'

Sebastian flinched. He said nothing.

His mother saw this and understood.

She had seen her son and Diana dance together when they were not much more than schoolchildren, she had seen them dance together a few years ago at the dinner at which Dr Bramley was guest of honour, seen it and thought nothing of it. But now, this one little sign of pain, this flinching as if he was trying to avoid a blow, alerted her instantly. It never left you, this awareness of pain in your child, she thought, this instinct put in you when they were born. She would not speak of this now to Sebastian, she would bide her time until they were alone.

Usually when Sebastian came home for the weekend, the time passed all too quickly; now the hours seemed to drag. They talked in a desultory fashion for the rest of the evening, couldn't think of much to say at breakfast, avoiding the one subject which was on all their minds, arrived very early at church because hanging around at home was so wearisome. His mother, it seemed to him, hustled him away after church as if she wanted to keep him away from the neighbours lest he made some irrevocable announcement of his engagement.

At lunch they again made laborious conversation; there was none of the usual relaxed banter. Afterwards his father said he would go and have a nap so Sebastian was left alone with his mother in the drawing room.

'I know, darling,' she began carefully, 'that you must feel a little hurt at the way I reacted to what you called your news.'

'Not a little hurt, Mother. A lot.'

'I'm truly sorry. It's just that if I feel you might be doing something that will bring you unhappiness, I simply have to say so. Or blame myself for ever afterwards.'

'But why do you think that marrying Celia would bring me unhappiness?'

She did not speak for a while, just stared into the fire. Then she began slowly, choosing her words with care.

'I think you have quite different temperaments. I think Celia has been brought up with very little love—'

'All the more reason to make it up to her now.'

'And that people brought up without love,' she went on as if he hadn't spoken, 'sometimes are incapable of showing it later on. It's not their fault; it's very sad, but they have developed a hardness to enable them to bear the pain when they were small, and that hardness remains.'

'She is reserved, Mother. That isn't the same as being hard.'

'And you think you can break down that reserve?'

'Yes, I do. With true love, she will blossom, as women do.'

'Not all women. Oh, Sebastian, don't make the mistake of thinking you can change the one you love. People don't change. When you marry you should feel sure that you can accept your wife as she is, love her as she is, not as how you think you can make her.'

'I do accept her as she is. It's you who can't do that. I just feel sure that we can be happy together.'

'But you hardly know her. How can you say you accept her as she is, when you don't yet know *what* she is? You have a romantic nature, Sebastian – why do you smile?'

'I had a good friend in the army, killed in November '18, and we used to talk a lot about the war and he always said that I was an incurable romantic and that he was a cynic. But anyway, what is so dreadful about being romantic?'

'Nothing, unless it makes you delude yourself about people. I mean, Sebastian, can you honestly say that you will live happily from day to day with someone who shares none of your interests, especially in the arts?'

'But, Mother, I love the arts because I was educated to do so. She didn't have my kind of education, but don't you see, Mother, that part of the joy of marrying her will be introducing her to all those good things she's been deprived of. She has a quick mind, she will learn, absorb easily. I'll take her to art galleries, I'll introduce her to literature, take her to the theatre and to concerts and we'll share all these experiences. I shall learn with her. It will be wonderful for both of us.'

His mother sat silently listening and it seemed to her that he was weaving a dream even as he spoke.

'And anyway, I love her,' he concluded defiantly.

'Are you really sure of that? You pity her, certainly, but that isn't the same as love. Compassion has its dangers, it can blind us to other realities.'

'It's no good, is it, Mother? You are quite set against me in this.'

'No, dear, don't say that. I'll never be set against you, but I just want to help you to see this thing clearly.'

She hesitated, hardly daring to raise the subject, then said, 'Last night, your father mentioned Diana.'

Again that sudden alertness, that physical flinching.

'So?' he said.

'I hardly know how to put this, darling, and you must forgive me, it comes only out of deep concern for you.'

'Well?'

'I think perhaps you fell in love with Diana when you were very young. I think that feeling for her survived the war.'

He sat very still, wondering at her awareness, ready to deny it, wondering what she would say next.

'I think,' she said, very gently, 'that it may have been hard for you to see her married to somebody else.'

'These things happen, Mother. A man has to accept them.'

The casual manner in which he spoke didn't deceive her.

'I fear for you, darling. That is all I can say. I fear that you may not find in Celia what you thought you had found in your first love.'

He didn't speak for a while and she knew that he was thinking seriously of what she had said. She was disappointed when he only replied, very formally, 'Don't think I'm not grateful for your concern, Mother. I know it comes from the best and kindest of motives, but I can only tell you that I feel deeply for poor Celia and want her to be my wife.'

'*Poor* Celia,' she repeated. 'Pity, that is exactly what I meant. Pity.'

She bowed her head. It seemed useless to talk any more about it; feelings would only be hurt. And there was just an hour to go before he had to catch the train back to Gradby.

He too was feeling that it was pointless to try to persuade her and was sad that the weekend should end like this, but he couldn't help reproaching her with saying, 'It's only a week since I saw you looking at her with such concern, lending her shawls, wanting her to stay longer, seeming to be fond of her.'

She shook her head.

'Charitableness is one thing,' she said. 'Matrimony is quite another.'

There was nothing more to be said on the subject, they both knew that and talked of other things until it was time to drive him to the station.

Fifteen

All the way back on the train that evening Sebastian relived the scenes with his mother, heard again all the things she had said, regretted his inadequate replies and thought up better ones.

The train swayed, his head throbbed and he felt ashamed that he had put up such a weak defence of his future wife. He should have pointed out that his mother had seen Celia when she was dispirited by the dreadful events of the past weeks in which she had lost both her guardians and all security. He should have said how brave and capable she'd been, how composed. He should have explained that Celia had, as far as he could make out, run that home for her aunt and uncle with such devotion that she had never been able to get away to cultivate other interests. The church and the household, that had been her whole world. What chance had she had? They had used her, those two selfish old relations of hers, and she had never complained.

His eyes were aching and his mouth tasted foul. He dozed a little but the arguments still went round and round in his fevered mind. His Celia was capable of true devotion, she had every virtue; why had he failed to make his mother understand this? He had let her down. And his mother had had no right to speak as she had done about Diana. The memory of what she had said made him hot and angry in a way it had not done at the time.

He dozed intermittently, sometimes lulled by the rocking of the train, sometimes jerked awake when they stopped at a station or the guard came round to look at the tickets. He realized that he had been muttering to himself and was grateful that there was nobody else in the compartment.

His dreams in these brief interludes of sleep were wild; he was being caught up in an immense spider's web, struggling to escape then – half awake – dreamed of a hanging, a body, suspended, swinging in front of him, almost touching his face.

He woke with a start and stared about him, not knowing where he was. Oh, of course, he was on this train. And opposite him was the luggage rack, a string mesh, like a hammock, like a huge spider's web. His case bulged in it; a long strap, which he'd neglected to secure round it, hung loose, swinging, swinging in front of him. These were the last things he had seen before he slept.

His weary mind began again to think of arguments he should have used against his mother. All that stuff about just being charitable, intending nothing more; he should have reminded her that charity *is* love. Let her look at the new Bible translation. It had substituted love for charity. *Caritas*. Even if his mother didn't know Latin, she did know her Bible. 'Faith, Hope and Love and the greatest of these is Love.' He should have said these things then, not just thought of them afterwards, he told himself as the train rocked, and his head lolled. What did the French call it? *Esprit de l'escalier*, the witty response you think of, too late, as you go upstairs to bed. Only this was *esprit de chemin de fer*, he told himself and gave a little laugh which made his head hurt even more dreadfully.

He felt as if he had been on this train for days, weeks even. He couldn't remember getting on it. His father must have driven him to the station. He remembered his father saying, 'Are you all right, my boy? You don't look too bright.' He heard his father say it again now, quite clearly and realized he had dozed off again. He must stay awake, he thought, glancing at his watch. Only another ten minutes.

He got up to reach for his case and nearly fell because there seemed to be something wrong with his knees. They were trembling. He managed to yank the case down on to the seat opposite. Oh, he was so hot, his head felt as if it was bursting. He pressed his head against the glass, then lowered the window and for a moment the cold wind was like a blessing on his face, but suddenly he was seized with a fit of compulsive shivering. He couldn't stop his teeth from chattering or his body from shuddering. He pulled the window closed and fell back on to the seat.

As the train pulled into the station, it at last began to dawn on him that he might be ill. When he got up again, swaying and dizzy, he was sure of it. When the train stopped and the porters came running over to it, he didn't refuse their offers of service, as he usually did, but handed his case to the first to come to his door and muttered, 'Taxicab, please.'

In the cab he closed his eyes and noticed that they were so dry and hot that the lids against them felt rough and painful. All he wanted was to be in bed. He had the key of the house somewhere, but couldn't think where.

It didn't matter; Mrs Jordan was still up.

'I didn't feel easy until I knew you were safely back, Mr Crawley,' she said. Then she looked at him more closely. His eyes were sunken, his face grey.

'You're not well,' she stated.

'A bit tired,' he said. 'Maybe cold coming on. I'll be better in the morning.'

She nodded, knowing that he wouldn't be. And, sure enough, he didn't appear for breakfast and the only response, when she tapped on his bedroom door, was a cough. She took this as a request to enter and went into the bedroom.

The bed was in a fearful muddle, sheets and blankets tangled up as if he'd been thrashing about all night. His eyes were bloodshot and feverish.

'I'll take your temperature,' she said, and when she put the thermometer under his arm, she resolved that if it was over a hundred, she would get the doctor.

It was a hundred and three.

She told him what she intended to do but he seemed past knowing or caring.

'Sarah,' she said, when she went downstairs. 'I want you

to take this note round to Dr Barnes' house. It's Number Six, Farley Square. You turn right out of the house here, then right again and then take the second left which takes you into the square. The house is on the far side directly opposite you so it makes no difference if you go right or left. Hand in the note and wait for an answer.'

Sarah whipped off her apron, took the note and ran to the front door, excited at being yet again at the centre of an emergency. So much was happening nowadays. For months, years even, nothing much had happened. And now all of a sudden, they'd had two deaths, a magical Christmas, a fire and a flood and a moving of house. And now illness. She ran until she was out of breath, then slowed down to a brisk walk.

It was a lovely morning, crisp and sunny. It did you good, a day like this, she thought, as she turned into the square. Oh, and she did love it at Mrs Jordan's. She had a big breakfast every morning and her room had a mat in it which was big enough to call a carpet. And Mrs Jordan had one of those new vacuum cleaners; a demobbed soldier had come selling it at the door, Mrs Jordan said, and she'd bought it out of pity, never really believing it could make such a good job of cleaning a carpet as a stiff brush did. But it worked a treat, you just pushed it around and it roared and sucked up the dirt into its pouch. And not a speck of dust flying around the way there always was with a brush and dustpan.

Sometimes she had a stone bottle in her bed to air it, a bit like those old copper warming pans used to do when they were filled with hot coals and pushed between the sheets. This was different of course, being small and made of stone and filled with hot water instead of coals, still it did the same job and even maids could have one. Warming pans were just for the gentry. Oh, she was really happy to be at Mrs Jordan's and wouldn't mind staying there for ever, she thought, as she pulled at the big brass knob on the doctor's door; she pulled it long and hard because Mr Crawley was ill and this was an emergency.

A maid came to the door and started being polite and then saw it was only a servant on the doorstep so said sharply,

'There's no need to pull the handle off!', took the note from her and told her to wait.

She was back in a moment.

'The doctor says to tell your mistress that he'll be round within the hour,' she said and shut the door.

At first Sarah walked more slowly; there was no point in hurrying, it wouldn't make the doctor come any quicker. Then she thought of Mrs Jordan and Celia anxiously waiting for news, and ran all the way back to the house.

'It's influenza, quite a bad case, I'm afraid,' Dr Barnes told Mrs Jordan and Celia when he joined them in the drawing room.

Influenza, that dreaded word. They both remembered the 25,000 people who had died in the influenza epidemic after the war.

As if reading their thoughts, he said, 'Of course, everyone was very low at the time of the 1919 epidemic. Mr Crawley is a fit young man and I see no reason, if we take good care of him, why he should not make a full recovery.'

His rather slow, deliberate way of speech was reassuring. In fact, everything about Dr Barnes was reassuring, as he stood there with his back to the fireplace, looking benignly down on the two anxious women. A tall, well-built man, portly rather than fat, unhurried in his ways, he inspired confidence. From the toes of his highly polished shoes to the tips of his well-manicured fingers, he exuded well-being; he was a good advertisement for his trade.

'Fortunately,' he went on, 'we now have a powerful drug which is excellent in the treatment of influenza. It is acetyl-salicyclic acid, commonly known as aspirin, and was developed by the Germans but used by us since the war. It not only reduces pain but induces sweating which brings down the fever. For the first few days he should have ten grains to be taken every four hours, which, if he does well, as I am sure he will, we can later reduce to a nightly dose. We strongly advise that anyone who takes an aspirin tablet should lie down for half an hour afterwards, but since he is a bed patient, I need not give that warning.'

The two women nodded, impressed, and gave thanks that this wonder drug had been discovered in time to be of use to Sebastian Crawley.

'Inhalation with Friar's Balsam will be of benefit,' the doctor continued, 'and a linseed poultice will also relieve the tightness in his chest. Sponging down is comforting too. A very light diet, of course, at first mainly liquid. Beef tea is excellent, as I am sure you know,' he added, smiling at Mrs Jordan who had been nodding as if familiar with all these remedies.

'I shall call again tomorrow at the same time,' he concluded, taking a gold watch out of his waistcoat pocket and studying it for a moment, 'that is, at half past ten, but please do not hesitate to send a message to me if he takes a turn for the worse. I don't know if you will want to employ a nurse?'

Mrs Jordan looked at Celia, waiting to see if she would reply. When she didn't speak, Mrs Jordan said, 'I don't think that will be necessary. I can help if Miss Grimsdyke so wishes. I did some nursing in the war, not trained, you know, just as a volunteer.'

'Thank you, Mrs Jordan,' Celia said. 'I'd be very grateful; it wouldn't be right for me to go into his room, but I'll gladly take over your work downstairs if you'll see to nursing him.'

And so it was arranged. Mrs Jordan had always enjoyed looking after a man when he was well; looking after one when he was ill gave her even greater satisfaction. She brewed Sebastian hot drinks, put hot bottles near his feet, sponged those parts of him that wouldn't cause either of them any embarrassment and gave him the tablets every four hours.

She was grateful for Celia's help in the rest of the house. What a correct little thing she was! Of course, it wouldn't be right for her to spend too much time in there with him, but you'd think she might have just popped in to see him now and then, just to give him an encouraging smile, blow him a kiss even. She herself would have been there as a chaperone. And it wasn't as if the poor man could have got up to anything, not in the state he was in, poor soul. Still, it takes all sorts and no doubt the girl had been very strictly brought up. Better than being the other way.

There wasn't much change in her patient after forty-eight hours but when the doctor came again two days later, Sebastian was clearly on the mend, his eyes less bloodshot, his aching body more comfortable and his temperature down to a hundred. By the middle of the following week it was normal.

'I'm sorry I've put you to so much trouble, Mrs Jordan,' he said one morning.

'No trouble at all, it's been a pleasure. And your Miss Grimsdyke is being just wonderful. She's turned to and taken over so much of my housework and cooking. She thinks nothing of hard work. It's a splendid little wife you're going to have, if you'll forgive me for saying so.'

Forgive her? Bless her, he thought and in his weakness his eyes filled with tears. If only his mother could hear Celia's praises being sung!

For the arguments with his mother had been going through his fevered mind throughout his illness. Mrs Jordan had heard him muttering something about charity – or was it chastity? – in those first dreadful days of delirium.

'I feel like getting up for a bit,' he told her now.

'You might get up and sit in a chair,' she allowed, 'and see how you feel.'

He was so weak she had to help him put on his dressing gown and noticed how thin he was, how sharp his shoulder blades.

'You might feel better for a shave,' she suggested. 'I could bring up some hot water and towels for you.'

He smiled at her.

'I expect I look awful,' he said, raising his hand to his face and feeling his beard.

She nodded judiciously.

'Not too awful,' she said, 'but you'll feel better for a shave.'

She brought up the hot water and a bowl, arranged a towel around his neck, put a looking glass and his shaving things on a little table beside him and left.

How weak he was, Sebastian noticed with dismay. Even the razor felt heavy. And what a sight he looked! Like a pirate with all that black stubble. Thank God poor little Celia hadn't seen him looking so beastly.

He ached to see her again. And they had so much to arrange about the wedding, he must remember to get her birth certificate from her and they must agree the wording of the announcement of their engagement. He must get himself back to work, back to normal.

Matthew came to see him that evening.

'You look pretty awful,' he said cheerfully.

Sebastian managed a laugh.

'If you think I look awful now, you should have seen me before I shaved,' he said.

'I did try to see you earlier but Mrs Jordan wouldn't let me. She's pretty firm, your landlady.'

'Yes, she's been wonderful and Celia's been an angel helping her so much around the house.'

He paused for a moment as he thought of Celia and then added, 'And whatever Mrs Jordan says, I'm coming into work tomorrow. Even if it's just for the morning.'

'Look, old fellow, it's Wednesday now. Why not leave it until next Monday? Get a good rest this week. No point in coming back too soon and cracking up again.'

'We'll see. How's the conversion going in Waterloo Road?'

'Great. I've been keeping an eye on things, but the foreman's a good chap, sticking exactly to the drawings and all your instructions. They've made a good start on the kitchen, knocked a doorway into the hall and started on the partition wall, the one with the hatch arrangement. The plumbers have nearly finished installing the new boiler and pipes and altogether you've nothing to worry about.'

He got up. 'You're looking tired,' he said. 'And it's time I was off.'

After he'd gone, Sebastian climbed back into bed. He had thought he might suggest getting up for dinner tonight, but realized he just wanted to lie down again. He couldn't believe that just getting up and sitting in a chair could have been so exhausting. He said so to Mrs Jordan when she brought up his meal on a tray.

'Well, a fever leaves you very weak, Mr Crawley,' she said. 'The doctor did warn you.'

He sighed. 'Yes, I know, but it's a bit disappointing that it takes so long to get some strength back, after all the pampering I've had.'

She smiled. 'May I make a suggestion, Mr Crawley? You have a good rest up here tomorrow and Friday, getting up and sitting in a chair, putting your clothes on if you feel like it, then on Saturday come downstairs and have a celebration dinner with Miss Celia? You've had no celebration of your engagement, have you, being taken ill just when you'd told your parents? I'd like to make you something a bit special.'

His face brightened. 'Oh, could you? And you would join us?'

She shook her head, 'No, there are times when two's company and three's none. I thought perhaps roast chicken with all the trimmings. And something special by way of a pudding. Apple dumpling and custard, perhaps, to build you up?'

'That sounds delicious,' he told her. 'And do you think you could buy a bottle of champagne while you're out shopping, Mrs Jordan?'

'Of course. That's a lovely idea. Nothing like a glass of bubbly for celebrating,' she said, her eyes lighting up.

Oh, it was wonderful the joy she took in his engagement. Unlike his mother.

'I can't thank you enough,' he said, 'for all your kindness to us.'

'Oh, no,' she said. 'You're the kind ones for letting me share in your happiness.'

Why couldn't his mother have felt like that, why couldn't

she have rejoiced in his happiness, instead of spoiling it all with her gloomy predictions?

Mrs Jordan insisted that he stayed resting in his room until it was time for the celebration dinner. So he sat quietly working at his table until after tea, then prepared himself carefully for this first meeting with Celia after what seemed an age.

She was sitting by the drawing room fire when he went in. She stood up to greet him. She looked lovely in the dress which Mrs Jordan had helped her to choose; pale blue, his favourite colour on her. He crossed over, took both her hands in his and drew her to him. She lay, very still, against him, her head on his shoulder, for he was at least ten inches taller than she was. It was so good to hold her there for a while, protectively. Then he put his hand under her chin and raised her lips to his. There was no response as his mouth pressed against hers, no answering pressure, no relaxing of her body against his.

She is still shy of me, he told himself, not wanting to admit disappointment. Then he released her and said with all the enthusiasm he could muster, 'And now for the champagne, my love,' for he had seen that Mrs Jordan had left it ready, with the two champagne glasses, on the sideboard.

She smiled and then was so childishly delighted with the bubbles and the taste of the first glass of any wine she had ever had, that he felt sure that if he took her in his arms again she would react differently. But Mrs Jordan came in to say dinner was ready, so they persuaded her to have a glass with them and then went into the dining room.

It was a festive meal; Mrs Jordan had done everything perfectly, Celia looked radiant, flushed with the unaccustomed champagne. And all he wanted was to make her his wife as soon as possible.

'We must agree a wording for the announcement of our engagement, darling,' he said towards the end of the meal, when he was on his second helping of pudding and feeling stronger by the minute.

'Can we do that before we know the date of the wedding?'

'Yes, we just say a wedding will take place, they don't need a date. We could write to the newspaper tomorrow.'

Just make it a fait accompli. Make it so that his mother would have to acknowledge it.

'And by the way, darling, have you a copy of your birth certificate?'

She shook her head. 'Oh, no, Sebastian. It would surely have been destroyed when my parents' house was bombed. Nothing was saved, nothing at all.'

'I feared as much. In fact, I asked the solicitor to make enquiries for you at Somerset House, but they'd no record of any Celia Grimsdyke.'

'But Sebastian, my aunt and uncle just gave me their surname because I was living with them. I suppose it made it simpler at school and everything.'

'They didn't adopt you officially then, and give you their name legally?'

'No. The birth certificate will be in my parents' name of Arndale.'

'*Arndale*?' he repeated, aghast.

'Yes. Arndale. Does it matter?'

Sixteen

Arndale isn't such a very uncommon name, Sebastian told himself as he lay in bed that night. The 'dale' ending was common up here and lots of names started with 'Arn', like Arncliffe, for example. The chances of Celia being related to Diana's Arndales were really very slight. He'd never heard any reference to Selina having a daughter and, if she had, surely the Arndales would have taken her to live with them at Northrop. They would hardly have agreed to send her so far away, especially if they had known what these Grimsdyke relations of Selina's were like. Why send her to Yorkshire when Gloucestershire was so much nearer to London?

No, the more he thought about it, the less likely it seemed. Of course he should have questioned her immediately last night, but was so taken aback that he'd taken the coward's way out and talked of something else. He knew so little about her: in that, at least, his mother had been right.

He'd talk to her about it tomorrow when she got back from church and they were alone together. He would raise it quite casually and most likely she would tell him that her parents came from Scarborough or some other place that had been bombed, not London. And if it turned out that she was Diana's cousin, well at least he'd know the worst. Having settled that in his mind he at last fell into a fitful sleep.

'I spoke to the vicar about our wedding,' Celia said, immediately she saw him waiting for her by the drawing-room fire. 'I hope that's all right?'

'Of course it is, my darling. And anyway the notice will

be in *The Times* next week so it won't be a secret any longer. But don't I get a kiss from my future wife?'

She was looking so pretty this morning; the sharp air had freshened her cheeks, her fair skin glowed. Her face was cold against his as she accepted his kiss.

'You see,' she went on, drawing away, 'he was asking how I was managing and where I was living, so I felt I had to tell him the truth.'

The truth. Yes, he himself had to be told that too, the truth about her parents.

'Did your aunt and uncle talk to you much about your mother and father?' he asked as casually as he could, as they sat down by the fire.

She shook her head.

'No.' She hesitated and then went on, 'I don't think they approved of them really.'

'Do you know why not?'

'I think they thought that the way that they lived in London was too worldly, too extravagant.'

'I see,' he agreed, thinking it was getting more and more horribly likely that he was marrying one of *his* Arndales.

'They never talked about them to me, I think they felt that they would have been a bad influence.' Her voice and expression were stern as she added, 'And of course they would have been if they were so worldly and enjoyed such a soft life.'

'Yes, of course.'

'Children can be so easily influenced, can't they? I remember once, the only time my aunt mentioned my mother in my presence – I think she had forgotten I was there and was just talking to my uncle – and she said the name Selina. And I, childlike, said, "What a pretty name!"'

So she was Selina's child. Selina who had lied and deceived and stopped him seeing Diana.

'And she was quite angry with me and said it was a silly, fancy name, the sort of name that suited a worldly woman like my mother. She said the best thing I could do was to forget them because they didn't want me anyway.'

'Oh, my poor girl. Didn't that hurt you most dreadfully?'

'I don't remember,' she said and her voice was cold. 'And I was lucky that my Grimsdyke relations took me in and gave me a much better upbringing than my parents would have done, even if they had wanted me.'

The dreadful way she had been hurt as a child made his own anxieties seem paltry. He must face them outright.

'I had a friend in the war who was called Arndale, Teddy Arndale. Does the name mean anything to you? He might possibly have been a relation of yours.'

She shook her head.

'No, I don't remember any relations,' she said.

But you have them nonetheless, he thought. And, oh my God, they'll read the announcement in the paper and expect to be invited to the wedding.

'Celia,' he said, suddenly thinking of an escape route, 'since everyone up here calls you Miss Grimsdyke, would it be simpler to put that name in the announcement? I mean, Arndale won't mean anything to them, will it?'

'Oh, yes, that would be best. I'm sure my aunt and uncle would have preferred it.'

How simple! Why hadn't he thought of that before? Soon she would be Mrs Crawley and then who would care about what her maiden name had been?

So, when he took Celia's hand to lead her into the dining room, he felt like a man reprieved.

His relief was short-lived; the roly-poly pudding had just been put in front of them, when Celia, serving spoon in hand, said, 'I've just thought of something, Sebastian. The banns have to have the same name as the one on my birth certificate and we can't use a different one for the announcement, can we? I mean it has to be one or the other all the way through, so it does have to be Arndale, doesn't it?'

Sebastian nodded.

'Yes, it has to be Arndale,' he agreed, as he accepted his roly-poly pudding with appetite suddenly diminished.

Elspeth Arndale always read the announcements on the front

page of *The Times* first, then the obituaries, then the leader page and letters. She waited to do so until she and Charles were having their second cup of coffee, or rather she was drinking coffee and Charles was wandering about the room, checking that all was in order, returning now and then to have another sip before going off again on his perambulations. She would tell him pieces of news, just as if he could still understand them, and he would nod and smile, have another sip of coffee and go off to check that the window catch was secure or the glass-fronted bookcase locked.

She told him the news steadily and calmly, partly to soothe his anxieties but mainly from force of habit and the need to impart information to somebody because otherwise reading the paper seemed to her a lonely and somewhat selfish occupation.

But this Wednesday morning her reaction to one announcement was anything but calm.

'*Celia, Celia Arndale!*' she exclaimed. 'Selina and William's daughter!'

Her husband was instantly alarmed by her tone of voice and came over to her, his hands working anxiously.

'Not another death?' he asked. 'Oh, not another!'

'Oh, no, my darling. Nothing like that, sit down, be calm. It's good news. Our little Celia, whom we thought we should never see again, is to be married. I'm sure it must be our Celia. Diana will be thrilled. She'll be over in a moment.'

The doorbell rang.

'That will be Diana, but why ever doesn't she walk in? Oh, Charles, have you locked the front door *again*?'

'Oh, yes,' he told her proudly, as she went to let her daughter in, which involved turning a key, undoing two bolts, one of which she could only just reach, and unhitching the chain. 'Oh, yes, I've seen to it. We shall be safe.'

'I've brought you this from the conservatory,' Diana said, kissing her mother and handing her a gloxinia. 'The men have done so well with them this year.'

Her mother took it absently, eager to tell her the news.

'Celia is to be married. It's in *The Times*,' she said. 'And to think we thought she was quite lost to us. All those letters unanswered, I really did think – but, isn't it wonderful?'

'Oh, yes, wonderful. Little Celia. She was younger than Laura, wasn't she, so must be marrying quite young. But who is she marrying?'

'Oh, it does say, but I've forgotten. Nobody we know, anyway. There, you look, dear,' and she handed the paper to her daughter.

Diana read the announcement. She read it again in disbelief. Oh, Sebastian, what have you done? How can you possibly be marrying Celia? It doesn't make sense.

'Anyone you know, dear? You and James know so many more people than I do.'

Diana looked at her, not knowing what to say, then she said at last, 'Yes, Mamma, we have met.'

She knew it was mean not to tell her mother that Sebastian had known Teddy; of course her mother would love to know such a thing, didn't everyone treasure any scrap of information which added to their knowledge of a loved one who was dead? Yet at the moment she couldn't do it, couldn't stay here for questioning.

'I have a lot of work to do today, Mamma,' she said. 'Forgive me for not staying this morning.'

'Oh, won't you have a cup of coffee with us? Well, I do understand how busy you are, so I won't keep you.'

'Give my love to Papa. Where's he got to?'

As they went out into the hall, they heard the sound of a bolt being drawn. They looked at each other, then Diana went and kissed her father, who looked surprised and asked her if she was Celia, while her mother unbolted the door, unleashed the chain, and turned the key in the lock.

Diana didn't go straight back to her office. She needed time to herself, to walk and think. Some of the men were already out in the garden, for it was a lovely spring morning. Adam was coming out of his shed and raised his hand to her. She waved back. Tommy was leaving home to go to school, his satchel on his back. How tall he'd grown, he must be ten now.

Mary-Ann and Nanny were standing in the doorway, waving him off.

Concentrate on these people, Diana, think only of the here and now, not of what might have been.

The Crawleys also were reading the announcement in *The Times*, but they had looked out for it, after having Sebastian's forewarning letter.

'I suppose,' Sebastian's father said hopefully, 'that this makes it all much better, doesn't it?'

'What do you mean?' his wife asked sharply.

'Well, little Celia being an Arndale. Dr Bramley married an Arndale girl, so why not Sebastian?'

She looked at him in exasperation, counted five to herself before replying.

'My anxieties about this marriage,' she began slowly and deliberately, 'have nothing to do with Celia's surname. I think she is an unfortunate choice and it makes not a jot of difference whether she is called Grimsdyke, Arndale, Cobley or Smith.'

Her husband looked bewildered. How many names had this unfortunate girl got herself saddled with? He knew a bookmaker called Cobley, come to think of it. An honest enough fellow, as bookmakers go. And, of course, there were dozens of Smiths. Telephone book full of them.

They'd only just got the telephone installed, newfangled thing he didn't feel at ease with. But the book that came with it was interesting, especially if you liked to study names. There were fewer Joneses than he'd expected, quite a lot of Browns, but columns of Smiths. Descended from the days when blacksmiths were so important for shoeing horses. A lot of them out of work now, everybody moving about in cars instead of on horseback. Still, probably most of the Smiths didn't do anything like that nowadays. Probably worked on the stock exchange. Which reminded him he had to go and speak on the telephone to his stockbroker.

Soon his wife heard him shouting into the instrument, despite the fact that she'd told him many times that it wasn't necessary to raise his voice on the telephone. She tried to block out the sound from her ears as she sat and thought about her son's marriage. This business of Celia being an Arndale did make a difference, despite what she'd said. It was bad enough that he should have chosen such an unsuitable bride, but that the girl should turn out to be Diana's cousin, cousin to his first love, cousin to the woman whom, she suspected, he still wanted, would have married if she'd been free, was appalling. For a moment she wondered if Sebastian had planned this marriage as a way of keeping close to Diana, but she dismissed the idea as absurd. No, now all she could do was to pray that his inexplicable love for Celia would prove strong enough to overcome any lingering passion for his first love.

Should she contact the Arndales? Of course she must, for the families would inevitably see a great deal of each other once they were thrown together by this marriage. What strain would this put on Diana and Sebastian? What did the Arndales make of it? she wondered. Sebastian had said that they had lost touch with Celia and her Grimsdyke relations years ago and that seemed odd for a start.

At last the telephoning in the hall stopped and her husband rejoined her.

'Stock market still falling,' he reported gloomily.

'There was no need to shout so,' she told him. 'You can speak in your normal voice on the telephone.'

'I know you always say that,' he told her. 'And it's probably all right for a local call, but this was to London, much further away.'

Seventeen

'Do you think that I should write to Lady Crawley?' Elspeth Arndale asked her daughter and son-in-law as they sat around the tea table one Sunday afternoon. 'I mean, we'll be related in a way, won't we?'

Diana didn't reply. The whole idea of any relationship with the Crawley family appalled her. Not that she was in love with Sebastian any more, she told herself. It wasn't that. It was just that she knew she could never be at ease with him again. Or his family.

'Why don't you ring them up?' James asked. 'I could take you over to my office now, if you like.'

'That's very kind,' Elspeth said, taken aback, 'but I've never used the telephone before. I'm not sure that I could manage it.'

James stood up.

'Come on, I'll show you,' he said. 'There's nothing to be afraid of and it will be much more satisfactory for you to talk to Lady Crawley than just to write a letter.'

'I'll stay here with Papa,' Diana told them.

'And I'll just see to the locking up,' her father announced.

'No, Papa, wait until they've gone,' Diana told him, taking his hand in hers.

Her father hesitated and then consented to let his wife and son-in-law out of the door before he began turning keys and shooting bolts.

'Do you find it distressing,' James asked his mother-in-law as they walked back to the hall. 'All that locking up that he does?'

She smiled.

'No,' she said. 'I've grown accustomed to it. Besides, it's useless to try to prevent him.'

'You're very wise,' he said.

His admiration for her had grown over the years. Stalwart, that was the word that came into his mind when he thought of her. She accepted circumstances that she couldn't change, didn't complain about them or try to alter them. And she had handed on that quality to Diana; his wife too was sensible, practical and uncomplaining. Stalwart, in fact.

Back in his office he enquired the number for her and spoke to the telephonist on the exchange, who promised to ring the Crawleys for him. When at last it began to ring, he handed her the instrument.

Elspeth took it nervously. She could hear a bell ringing. Then a man's voice said, 'Hello.'

'Hello,' she replied.

'Hello,' the voice said again.

'Hello. I mean . . . ?'

'Is there anyone there?' the voice asked irritably.

'Yes, I'm here.'

'Who are you?'

'I'm Mrs Arndale of Northrop Hall, Celia Arndale's aunt. I was just ringing to introduce myself to Lady Crawley.'

'That's long distance,' the voice suddenly bellowed. 'Better speak up. Can you hear me?'

'Yes, thank you,' she replied, holding the instrument further away from her ear.

'Marvellous invention, the telephone,' the voice roared.

'Indeed yes.'

'So your niece is marrying our son?' the voice boomed down the telephone. She held the instrument even further away.

'Yes, we're all very pleased,' she said, drawing it closer and then moving it away again, ready for the next blast.

'Quite right. So you should be. He's a fine lad. And I'm very pleased too. A nice girl, your niece. Picked up whist in no time.'

'I'm sorry. I don't think I can have heard that properly,' she replied, returning the instrument closely to her.

'That's the trouble with long distance calls,' the voice exploded in her ear. 'Can't expect miracles.'

'No.'

'Look here, I'd better get my wife before it breaks down altogether.'

There was a clatter, the sound of retreating footsteps, a pause, the sound of footsteps returning, then a woman's voice spoke.

'Hello?' it said.

'Hello,' she replied, wishing she'd just written a letter instead.

'I have a suggestion to make,' Mrs Jordan said, as she poured out the coffee. She handed a cup to Celia who was sitting on the couch and another to Sebastian in a wing chair by the side of the fire.

'Come and tell us about it,' Sebastian invited, nodding towards the chair opposite to him. 'Won't you join us for coffee?'

'No, thank you. I never drink it in the evening,' she told him as she settled herself in the chair and went on, 'I was going to suggest that Miss Celia should stay here until the wedding. There seems little point in searching for new lodgings for such a short time.'

Sebastian saw that Celia hesitated about accepting what seemed to him a very sensible idea.

'Thank you, Mrs Jordan,' she said at last, 'but I think it wouldn't be quite proper, would it, for us both to be in the same house together before we're married?'

What a one she is for propriety, Mrs Jordan thought, remembering how horrified the poor little thing had been when Sebastian had shown her the engagement notice he'd prepared for *The Times*, giving them both the same address here. Just in time he had altered it to give his own address at his parents' house.

'It would be perfectly proper,' she said firmly.

'If it really worries you,' Sebastian said, 'I could move into what is going to be our new home in Stanhope Drive. There's a lot to do there and it would mean I would be on the spot to see to things.'

'With no furniture, no carpets, no meals prepared for you?' Mrs Jordan objected.

It wasn't her place to speak so strongly, she knew that, but she couldn't just sit here and see Mr Crawley's comfort and convenience sacrificed on the altar of propriety. This was the twentieth century, for goodness' sake.

Sebastian looked from one to the other, bemused, wanting to agree with them both.

'It's very difficult for Celia,' he told Mrs Jordan, 'having no mother to turn to and with both her guardians so recently lost to her.'

Mrs Jordan softened, but still she persisted. Turning to Celia, she said, 'I shall be here always, as your chaperone.'

Celia hesitated for a moment, then said, 'In that case, yes, I do accept your kind offer to stay.'

'Good,' Mrs Jordan said, 'then that's settled.

She stood up and went to refill the coffee cups, thinking what a lot of fuss it had been about nothing.

'And how are your other plans working out?' she asked Celia. 'Who will give you away?'

'I don't know. I had this letter this morning from Mrs Arndale,' Celia said, taking it out of its envelope.

'Oh, if it's private, please don't—' Mrs Jordan began.

'No, it isn't private,' Celia told her, beginning to read from the letter. 'She says, "Since your dear father is dead, I wonder if you have any close relation on your mother's side to give you away? If not, my husband, your uncle, would normally have been delighted to do so, but I am afraid he is not in the best of health. My son-in-law, Dr Bramley, your cousin Diana's husband, would, I am sure, be pleased to give you away if you should so wish."'

'She sounds a lovely lady, your aunt,' Mrs Jordan remarked.

'I don't remember her. I think that it must have been at her house I went to stay when I was little, but it was all so long ago. I suppose I should agree to what she says about Dr Bramley?'

'It sounds ideal,' Mrs Jordan said.

Sebastian found the idea that his bride should be given away by Diana's husband considerably less than ideal.

'She hasn't asked him yet,' he pointed out. 'He might not even be able to come to the wedding; he's a very busy man.'

'But who else is there?'

Nobody, he knew that. The Grimsdykes had bequeathed her no family friends.

'I don't like the idea of the bride being given away, anyway,' he said.

'Oh, whatever do you mean?' Celia demanded, dismayed.

'It's just, Celia, that it seems so primitive, treating a woman like some chattel that one man can hand to another.'

'But, Sebastian, it's written in the marriage service. In the Solemnization of Matrimony, it says, "Then shall the Minister say, 'Who giveth this Woman to be married to this Man?'" I *must* be given away,' she went on desperately. 'It says so.'

'That was written at a time when women really did belong to their menfolk. It's different now. Women can vote, they own their own property when they're married—'

'But Sebastian,' she interrupted, almost in tears, 'this isn't right. I must do what it says in the prayer book.'

'Yes, of course you must. I'm sorry.'

How different they are, Mrs Jordan thought, as she cleared away the coffee cups, him somehow having a vision of the future, her stuck in the past. Chalk and cheese, they are. Oh, well, perhaps it's what's called the Attraction of Opposites.

'I'll say goodnight then,' she said, as Sebastian opened the door for her. 'And it's early breakfast for you, Mr Crawley?'

'Yes, please, if you can manage it. I've a lot to do tomorrow and want to fit in a visit to Waterloo Road if I can.'

'All's going well there, I hope?'

'Yes, thank you. The men will be moving in any time now. There's one in already, Alf Parker.'

'All on his own?'

'Not exactly, the workmen are still there, I'm afraid.'

'Well, that'll be company for him during the day but it must be a bit lonely at night, him being disabled too.'

'Yes, we'll all be glad when the others move in to join him.'

He smiled, grateful for the way Mrs Jordan took such an interest in his work.

'Further on in her letter,' Celia said, after their landlady had left them, 'my aunt asks if we could go down and stay with them for a weekend at Northrop.'

Sebastian didn't answer. Of course he should have been prepared for this, he knew that they were bound to be invited. He wasn't in love with Diana any more, of course not, but the thought of going there and seeing her with her husband, on her home ground, was unbearable. One day, perhaps, years hence, but not now.

'We do have a lot of things to see to in the next few weeks,' he prevaricated. 'And it might be difficult to get away from work. It's quite a long journey and I'd need to take another Saturday morning off. But of course, if you'd really like to go—'

'Oh, no,' she interrupted. 'I don't want to go at all. I'd much rather stay here and help to get things ready at the house.'

'Good. I don't want to go either,' he told her, smiling.

'Oh, I'm so glad. Of course, I don't mind going down to your parents this weekend because that is my duty as their future daughter-in-law, but I don't feel that kind of duty to Aunt Elspeth.' She hesitated and then went on, 'I really don't like going on visits at all.'

He got up and went over to the couch where she was sitting. He put his arm protectively around her.

'That's because you've been so much alone, so apart from the outside world,' he said, thinking how lonely her life must have been, without the companionship of anyone of her own age, brought up in that gloomy house by two elderly recluses. 'But that's all changed. When we meet people now, you'll always have me by your side.'

'Yes, of course,' she said, smiling up at him, reassured.
He held her close and kissed her.
She moved away.
'Mrs Jordan might come in,' she said.

Alf Parker was the first to move into Ten, Waterloo Road. He was a big man, whose legs had been shattered in the war but whose powerful arm and shoulder muscles enabled him to propel his wheelchair around the ground floor with a speed and abandon that alarmed Sebastian when he came to see him the next day.

'Watch out!' he warned as Alf raced ahead towards the kitchen, narrowly avoiding a length of timber that projected from the door of what was to be the dining room.

'Ah'm quite useful about t'place,' Alf told him, flinging the wheelchair round a large toolbag which one of the men had left spewing out its contents in the hall. 'Even if it's nobbut mekin' t'men's tea.'

'There'll be two more moving in next week,' Sebastian told him. 'You'll be glad of company, I expect.'

'It's a bit quiet of an evening,' Alf conceded. 'But on t'other 'and Ah've gotten used to 'avin' t'kitchen to meself. I can mek you a cup of tea if you want.'

'No, thanks. I've to get off to look at a piece of land. It's on the north side of town, Ugton direction. We've been offered it to build one of our homes on.'

Alf braked and stopped in the doorway.

'Ah know t'place. Where t'Zeppelin come down, weren't it?'

Sebastian nodded.

'Rotten bit o' wasteland,' Alf told him. 'Belongs ter Drugget, t'mine owner.'

Again Sebastian nodded.

'Not surprised 'e wants shot on't.'

'Well, I have to admit I'm not too hopeful but the committee felt I should go and look at it since it'd been offered.'

'I don't know what 'e's askin' forrit, but Ah can tell yer it'll not be worth a quarter on't.'

'You know the area?'

'Ah've a sister lives in Ugton. 'Usband's a miner, well, 'e was but pit fall got 'im two years gone. 'Is legs are no more use than mine now. *And* 'e's coughin' 'is guts out.'

'I'm sorry.'

'Not your fault. They were lucky their lad were just turned fourteen so took 'is dad's place at pit. But they've two girls after that and next lad's nobbut ten so it'll be a while afore 'e gets a wage, and there's two little uns after 'im.'

'How do they manage?'

Alf shrugged.

'They don't,' he said shortly. ''Er man gets a bit o' compensation but not much. And t'pit weren't ever properly repaired. It's cheaper fer t'mineowners to pay compensation than ter mek pits safe, that's the truth on't. It's a death trap is that Ugton pit.'

'But she sends her son down it?'

'Needs must.'

They were silent for a minute, then Alf said, 'None of 'em were in t'war, but they've 'ad it 'arder than me, I reckon, even if I ain't got no legs. Sure about that tea, are yer?'

'Yes, thanks, I'll just go upstairs and have a word with the foreman, then I'll be on my way.'

Upstairs was transformed. He went from room to room, amazed at the difference that light furniture and decoration had made to those gloomy bedrooms. He'd expected it, of course, had planned it, but even so he was astonished at the difference it had made; there wasn't a trace of Grimsdykerie, as he had come to think of their previous state. Here, as in the downstairs rooms, the sun shone through the windows now that the trees had been lopped and a few feet taken off the privet hedge.

Alf was waiting for him at the bottom of the stairs. He was holding an envelope.

'Yer'll be near me sister, where yer goin',' he began.

'You want me to deliver that?'

'Ah were goin' to post it, but it'd be safer by 'and. It'll save me a stamp an' all,' he added. 'Carter, the name is.

Irene Carter and t'address is on't, 302, Queen's Road. It's round t'back, through an archway.'

'I'll see she gets it. And I'm glad you've settled in so well, Alf.'

'Yes, I'm t'lucky one. Tell our Irene that.'

They shook hands, then Alf set his wheels spinning kitchenwards and Sebastian let himself out of the front door.

Ugton lay to the north of Gradby, separated from the town by a mile or so of desolate countryside. Sebastian stared at it out of the bus window. It was strange territory to him. He was used to industrial towns like Gradby, grimy with their blackened buildings and smoke-filled skies. And he knew the countryside, green and open as it was in the Dales or where his parents lived. This was open country too, but it was more soot-begrimed than any industrial town. From pits, coke ovens and chimneys, soot rained down, blackening the landscape and all that struggled to grow in it.

The road ran steeply down into Ugton, which lay in a valley. Here there was not even a pretence of countryside, just a maze of little back-to-back dwellings, built as cheaply as possible to house the men who hacked the coal out of the ground below. In the mean street many of the windows were broken or patched with cardboard, doorways lurched as the earth subsided from the burrowing underneath. And all the time the smoke poured down on them from the works and from every chimney of every wretched little house, that damp and filthy smoke which only the cheapest coal can produce.

There was no name on the street, but the driver had told him that this was as far as the bus went, and that Queen's Road was a turning at the bottom. He seemed to be the only person about at first and then he saw, approaching from the distance, a weary little band of women and children. They had been up on the slag heaps, picking tiny pieces of coal out of the dust, and were now returning with their booty. The women had sacks tied round their waists, shawls over their heads and shoulders, knotted across their chests. Their pale, exhausted faces, pushed forward by the weight of the hard-won coal they carried on their backs, were streaked with coal dust. He looked at these women and thought with horror such were the mothers of the men we sent to fight for us in the war, such are the mothers of the next generation of Englishmen.

The road he turned into was long and dreary, pitted with potholes full of slimy black water. He asked a ragged boy pushing a cart with bits of coal garnered from the slag heap if this was Queen's Road, but out of the two white circles in the grimy face uncomprehending eyes stared back at him, then the lad turned and hurried away, silent, barefooted. Sebastian realized he was not understood in this place, the lad had probably never seen a stranger before.

He found the alleyway at last. It led to several houses, built back-to-back with the ones on the street. He stood for a moment looking at this grim backyard, with its row of ashpits and lavatories. A woman was filling a bucket at the tap.

'Good afternoon,' he said, 'I wonder if you could tell me which is number 302?'

She looked blank, as uncomprehending as the bare-footed boy.

'It's Irene Carter's house,' he explained and she immediately pointed at one of the doors.

The woman who opened the door was very thin, wore a shapeless cotton dress and, although the day was cold, had no stockings and only clogs on her feet. Her face was pinched, her toothless mouth fallen in like an old woman's. A little girl, also wearing only a thin cotton dress and no shoes, clung to her skirt. The woman looked at him with suspicion. Strangers meant trouble, officials, narks.

'I've come from your brother Alfred,' he began.

Suspicion changed to alarm.

'Our Alfie? Is summat up wi' Alfie?'

'Oh no, he's just moved into a nice room in a home and he asked me to deliver this letter to you.'

'You'd best come in,' she said, reassured.

The room was very dark, the one window being covered

with cardboard. It was damp and stuffy too from the steam which rose from the clothes around the fire. From upstairs came the sound of coughing and every now and then a baby whimpered.

'Do open your letter,' he said. 'If you want to send a message back, I'll deliver it for you.'

She hesitated, then pushed her way through the wet clothes to pick up a little kitchen knife from the hearth.

The child stayed where she was, staring at Sebastian, eyes huge in her peaky little face.

'What's your name?' he asked partly to distract her but also to make her mother more at ease as she opened the letter.

It was not a letter but a ten shilling note.

Irene Carter stared at it in disbelief, then made a little choking sound and her eyes filled with tears.

The child stopped staring at Sebastian, turned and stared at her mother instead.

For her mother seemed transformed, lively, almost joyful and suddenly talkative.

'Just when I didn't know 'ow we'd mek out till end o' week,' she said. 'Oh, 'e's good, is our Alfie. Allus was a good lad.'

She reached up and took a cracked mug off a shelf, tipped out a few pence and replaced them with the note.

'Now Edie,' she said, counting the coins out into the little girl's hand, 'tek this five pence to t'shop and bring back a tin o' milk, a screw o' tea and a happuth o' broken biscuits. Look sharp now.'

'Ah can give you a cup o' tea now, if you'll bide while she gets back,' she said to Sebastian, as she smoothed out the envelope with great care. Clearly not a scrap of anything was wasted here, even after such a windfall as Alfie's ten shilling note.

'It would be quite out of the question to build on that land,' Sebastian told Matthew when he got back, weary and disheartened, that evening. 'It's low-lying, unhealthy, away from all entertainment and, oh I don't know, it's everything that a disabled soldier doesn't want.'

'I'm sorry, old chap. I shouldn't have let you go there. Just a wild goose chase.'

'Oh, I'm glad I went. I didn't know that places like Ugton existed,' Sebastian said, and told him about how he had visited the Carters before going to look at the land.

'Such utter, grinding poverty,' he ended. 'There's nothing like that down south where I was brought up. Yes, there are poor people in the country, labourers on low wages, but the air they breathe is pure and they have fresh vegetables they grow themselves. There's nothing like the poverty I've seen today.'

'I know. Drugget pays starvation wages. The mine's small and inefficient, like so many others. There are some fifteen hundred owners altogether, you know, and scarcely any of the mines are well run or profitable. That's why the government took them over during the war. Pity they ever handed them back.'

'I thought they were going to keep them. Didn't the Sankey Commission recommend it?'

'Yes, and the government agreed, but then handed them back to the mineowners in 1921. Hence the strike that year.'

'I didn't realize that.'

How much he hadn't realized, he thought guiltily, absorbed as he had been in his own problems after the war. All the same.

'I should have done,' he said.

'Why?'

'*You* did.'

'But it's part of our world up here, you know. And the Yorkshire mines aren't as hard hit as the ones in South Wales. Ours sell to local industry, but they depended on exports and now their markets are filled with cheap reparation coal from Germany. Unfortunately we didn't think of that when we decided to squeeze Germany until the pips squeaked. And of course going back on the gold standard has made our coal too expensive to sell abroad anyway.'

'Oh, what a world, Matthew!' Sebastian exclaimed, getting up and beginning to walk restlessly about the room. 'It's so unfair that people have no say in these things. Think how the generals made decisions in the war and thousands of men died. And this is just as bad. Politicians make coal expensive, mineowners run inefficient mines. And who starves, who gets maimed? Not the statesmen, not the mineowners.'

He was silent for a moment, remembering the exhausted faces of the women who picked coal on the slag heaps and carried it back in sacks on their thin shoulders.

Then, 'Alfie said he was better off than they were,' he began slowly, 'even though he'd no legs. And I didn't believe him. Not until I saw how they live in Ugton. It's not enough, Sebastian, is it, for us to try to provide decent housing for the war-wounded. We've got to do something about those awful back-to-back slums, give the miners decent houses too.'

Matthew shook his head, thinking what an admirable chap Sebastian was, idealistic, quixotic even. But it might all end in bitter disillusion; he feared for him.

'There's a limit to what any one person can do,' he said gently. 'You can't fight all the dragons.'

'But, Matthew, you know as well as I do that all the wealth of this country, the steel works, the mills, the factories, all depended on coal. Without the miners there'd have been no industrial revolution, no great wealth, no Empire. And we treat them like this! They should be treated like heroes, not worse than animals.'

'I know. It's more shocking for you because you've come into it suddenly. I've grown up amongst it. I can remember as a lad, with my first bicycle cycling over to that area before you get to Ugton. It was in the spring and there were green blades of grass and green shoots on the shrubs and it looked so jolly. Then I came back two weeks later and they were all black, like the rest.'

'And didn't that make you want to do something about it? What about the children growing up in all that smoke and filth?'

'Of course I thought about it. I've seen coal-pickers too, you know, and the little girls going step-cleaning.'

Seeing his friend looking puzzled, he went on, 'They walk to one of the better-off suburbs, not the grander houses where they'd have plenty of servants, but the little places who can't afford servants, and they knock on the door and ask if they can clean the steps and edge them with stepstone. They can earn about tuppence a house. They look like little old women, crouched there in a thin dress with a sack tied round them and their hands blue with cold.'

It seemed to Sebastian, as he walked back to Mrs Jordan's, that there was a whole world up here which he hadn't known about and that Matthew was much older in experience than he was.

He knew he must try to put all this misery out of his mind; he owed it to Celia to present a cheerful face this evening, talk happily of their plans for the wedding, prepare to go down to his parents next weekend. Yet even as he walked through the pleasant suburban streets towards Mrs Jordan's house, he thought of that other landscape, which was pockmarked with pools of slimy water, whose spring shoots were black before the summer came, as if even the hedgerows knew it was useless to struggle against the forces of darkness and there was no hope for any living thing.

Celia enjoyed that weekend with his parents much more than the earlier one, he could see that. And his mother was kind and welcoming. Of course she always was; it was just that this time he was conscious that she was making an effort to be so.

He showed them the plans of the house in Stanhope Drive, which his father was buying for them.

'It's very kind of you, Mr Crawley,' Celia said.

'Glad to do it. My father did the same for me when I was married. Besides, it would come to you in the long run. Now let's have a look at those plans.'

Sebastian produced an architect's drawing that he had done of the front elevation of the house.

'It's in a cul de sac, so very quiet,' he said.

'And safe, when you have children,' his mother pointed out.

Sebastian, seeing that this remark had embarrassed Celia, went on quickly, 'And there's quite a good garden at the back too, bigger than you usually get in these suburban streets.'

'And how many rooms do you have?' his mother asked.

He spread the ground floor plan out on the table.

'A big drawing room, which goes right through the house, so is very light. That's to the right of the door as you go in. Then on the left, the front room for my study, behind that the dining room and then the kitchen quarters at the back.'

They looked, they nodded, they approved.

'Then upstairs,' he went on, unfurling the first-floor plan, 'there are two large bedrooms, two smaller ones, but each of a good size, and a smaller one for a maid's bedroom. And there's the bathroom.'

'And in store I have enough furniture for the whole house,' Celia said.

His heart sank at the thought of that furniture, those awful iron beds, those dung-coloured striped bedspreads, but he said, 'Yes, we're lucky to have that to start with and then later of course we'll get some of our own as and when we can afford it.'

'It looks a good house, my boy,' his father said. 'You've chosen well.'

'We're very grateful to you, sir,' Sebastian told him, 'Celia and I.'

'Pleasure, my boy, pleasure. Now how about some cards?'

They taught her to play bridge and again she won his approval.

'A lot of women can't grasp it, you know. Don't have mathematical minds. My mother was like that. Lovely woman but no grasp of numbers. Dead now, of course.'

At church she was introduced to all their friends; his mother, seeing her son's pride in his future wife, began to think that perhaps her fears for the marriage were groundless. Perhaps he would bring her out, introduce her to books and the arts so that she would be a companion to him as well as a wife. She prayed hard that it should be so.

'I've been thinking,' she said to them as they walked back, 'that you might like to take a few pieces of silver back with you. There are one or two things that rightly belong to you, Sebastian.'

'Are there?'

'You've forgotten, but I have always told you that there are some christening presents given to you when you were a baby. There's a pair of christening mugs, some napkin rings, and a sugar dredger.'

'You might take some of the rest of the silver while you're about it,' his father put in. 'It's only a nuisance to clean now that we don't have the staff.'

'We do use most of it,' his wife demurred.

'We never use those great fish servers your aunt Bella gave us.'

He insisted on going to the butler's pantry and adding the fish servers to the more delicate pieces that his wife was arranging in a carton for Sebastian to take away.

'They're enormous,' Sebastian said, lifting them out of their velvet-lined box. 'They must be at least eighteen inches long and look at the engraving on them! And feel the weight of them! Did anybody ever use them?'

'You have to remember, dear, that people had much larger families in those days.'

'Must have had much larger fish as well,' his father pointed out.

Eighteen

There were noticeably more people on Sebastian's side than on his bride's, Diana noticed as she made her way, with her parents, up the aisle of St Bartholomew's church. She longed to hide away at the back, but inevitably the usher led them into the front pew on the left.

Her mother, too, would have preferred to be somewhere less conspicuous; Charles was normally calm in church at home, but this was a strange building and anything unfamiliar had a way of unsettling him. He had already tried to close the heavy church door behind him as he came in. It had taken two ushers and a curate to prevent him.

She was worried too about Rupert. Of course it was lovely that he was back in England – she'd been overjoyed when his letter arrived – but after that first brief visit to Northrop he'd gone away up north to instruct these men in their flying machines. He said it was the best place to go but surely if men must train to go up in the air they could just as well do it somewhere in the south, like Gloucestershire?

Of course his grandparents, Charles' father and mother, came from the north so perhaps it was in his blood. In Laura's too, of course. She was worried about Laura. Fancy not being able to get away from work until this morning, catching a milk train from Edinburgh of all things! What a way to get to a cousin's wedding! She and Rupert were so casual about everything. It's simple, they'd said, Rupert would meet Laura at the station, take her to the hotel to change and bring her along to church.

It was a very pleasant hotel where they were all staying, not that she knew much about hotels, never having had the necessity of staying in such places. The servants seemed a little uncouth but then they probably didn't have the training they would have had in a private establishment. And, after all, they were Yorkshire. Still, they'd been very helpful, ringing up the station to find out if the train was delayed.

It was, of course. So neither of them had arrived when it was time for the rest of the family to leave for the church. She'd said all along that the train might be late, but they'd just told her not to worry. Well, if Rupert and Laura were late they'd just have to sit somewhere at the back; they couldn't possibly come and sit in the front with family. But that's where they should be and she never would understand the casual ways of young people nowadays. She must try not to worry. She must pray for the gift of serenity.

Across the aisle she could see the two young men: that must be Sebastian, the dark-haired one nearest to her, and the fair one must be his best man. She glanced across at them and smiled before kneeling down.

Diana was already on her knees, eyes shut so that she couldn't see him. Mustn't look at him, mustn't remember, she told herself. Is he conscious of me, does *he* remember? Stop it, Diana; he is waiting for his bride, for goodness' sake, my little cousin Celia. Will he remember how we were kept apart by the lies and deceit of her mother? Beautiful, scheming, treacherous Selina. Why had she done what she did? What did she think to gain by it? Some motiveless pleasure in wrecking other people's lives? No good speculating, but I can't help it. Stop it. Try to pray.

She's been down there a long time, her mother thought, watching her as she herself sat back in her pew and took Charles' hand. Of course, it's right to kneel and say a little prayer like that when you come into church, but there is a customary limit to its length. She'd been worried about her daughter recently; Diana seemed tense, not as excited about her cousin's wedding as she might have been. And now this prolonged praying.

She was relieved when Wagner's bridal march rang forth and Diana stood up with the rest of them.

However much she had prepared herself, Diana still felt a tremor of shock at the sight of Celia, veiled, walking up the aisle on James' arm. She was wearing a very plain, ivory dress, long-sleeved, high-necked and had no bridesmaid. She seemed remote, a thing apart. She didn't look up at Sebastian when he stepped into the aisle to join her and stood, smiling down at her. Instead she looked directly ahead, eyes fixed on the vicar as he spoke solemn words about the honourable estate of matrimony.

As he pronounced the causes for which it was ordained, Diana felt the stab of pain she always felt when she went to her friends' weddings. If the prime cause was for the procreation of children, then her marriage had failed. It had not done that for which it was ordained.

Her mother, alongside her, was thinking similarly and wondering if it was some sort of punishment meted out to poor Diana for being married in a registry office.

Rupert, ever argumentative, who wrestled with himself now as much as he had ever done with Nanny Stone, pondered the meaning of the second cause – about marriage being a remedy against sin and to avoid fornication. Actually what it did was to enable adultery since you couldn't commit adultery *unless* you were married.

And it was all very well to say that people without the gift of continency could marry and so keep themselves undefiled. Jolly decent of seventeenth-century churchmen to say so – except that if everyone had their precious gift of continency the human race would have come to an end long ago. In fact it would never have started. Just as well for the rest of us that Adam hadn't had the gift of continency.

Laura, next to her brother near the back of the church, was thinking about the old days, catching remembered glimpses of Celia visiting them and of playing in the garden and by the stream. It always seemed to be warm then. She remembered sunlit games of croquet and being hot and sticky on the tennis court as she lobbed easy shots towards little Celia, which her cousin invariably missed. She couldn't see anything of the child Celia in the young woman standing there, looking somehow remote, even from Sebastian, as they made their vows.

On the other side of the aisle Sebastian's mother was thinking how beautiful the words were as she heard her son vowing to love and cherish this girl whom he had so unwisely chosen. No, she must no longer even think such thoughts. The die was cast. Concentrate instead on the meaning of the vows the bride is making. Her voice was clear and firm as she spoke the words, looking directly ahead, even though the priest had placed her hand on Sebastian's. From where she was sitting his mother could see Sebastian's profile as he looked down at his bride, but she could only see the back of Celia's veiled head. It seemed a bad omen. Don't be so silly and superstitious, she told herself.

Her husband, alongside, didn't catch everything that was being said. People mumble so much nowadays, he thought, don't speak up loud and clear the way they used to. Of course it didn't help that they were standing with their backs to the audience, as it were, though maybe it didn't make much difference because the padre chappie was difficult to make out too. Still, he heard Sebastian promising to endow Celia with all his worldly goods. That would include the fish servers, of course. And evidently he was now free to worship her with his body. Funny choice of words that. Very ancient of course. Goes back for centuries.

The padre was easier to hear once he got into the pulpit. Not that he had much new to say. Mind you, to be fair, there isn't a lot new to be said about matrimony. Must be quite difficult thinking up something different each sermon. Poor devil can't repeat himself in case the same people turn up in another congregation. Our new padre in Oxenhurst was caught out like that not long ago. Not that it was any better second time round. I was going to tell him but Barbara banned it. Probably wouldn't have done any good, poor little so-and-so wasn't a patch on the old padre. Once you'd heard the old padre preaching about hellfire, you never forgot it.

Time to go now and sign the register. Amazing how stiff you get sitting on these pews. Other lot over on the other side getting up too. Old fellow looks a bit lost. Come along, Barbara.

The two families stood in the vestry and watched as the newly married couple signed the register, then they each did so in turn. Celia allowed her mother-in-law to draw the veil back from her face and accepted their kisses as calmly and unenthusiastically as she accepted their good wishes. Sebastian seemed so delighted, his mother observed, his bride so reserved and aloof. She was distracted from these thoughts by Elspeth Arndale requesting a quiet word.

'My husband is not in the best of health, Lady Crawley,' she whispered. 'I wonder if you would mind if I walked with him just to make sure he is all right?'

'Of course, my dear. I shall walk with my husband behind you.'

What a nice family the Arndales were, she thought, so friendly and warm and Dr Bramley was quite charming. How was it that Celia was so different from her relations, she wondered as, guided by the vicar, they left the vestry, the younger ones following.

The anthem was over. The congregation had begun to chatter, Sebastian's father noticed as they emerged from the vestry. Probably because the vicar had been out with them, leaving just that little curate in charge. Didn't look as if he'd be much good at keeping order. The old padre they'd had in Oxenhurst would only have had to give them one of his ferocious glares and they'd all have shut up. People shouldn't be allowed to talk in church even if they are bored and rather young. He was bored himself sometimes at these weddings. The bit he always liked best was when the padre cast a defiant look at the congregation and said *Whom God has joined Together Let no Man put Asunder*. He looked down at his wife. She looked up at him and he saw that her eyes were full of tears. He squeezed her hand and smiled reassuringly down at her. Nobody was ever going to put him and Barbara asunder. Just let the buggers try.

It wasn't far to walk to the reception, over at St Bartholomew's church hall. The sun was making tentative efforts to creep out from behind the clouds as Sebastian and Celia led the procession down the path between the tombstones. It lit up the sooty leaves of bushes and touched the grimy stones of the building with a gentler light.

Mrs Jordan had organized everything so well that she had managed to get to the service, sit at the back and come quickly out before the wedding party to make sure that the waiters had a glass of champagne ready for them when they all arrived.

'Mrs Jordan has been wonderful,' Sebastian told his mother. 'She's seen to everything, organized the catering and the waiting at table, done the flowers, ordered the wine—'

'Oh, Mrs Jordan, I would have been very happy to have helped you,' his mother interrupted. 'You've obviously taken so much trouble.'

'It's been no trouble,' Mrs Jordan said. 'In fact I've really enjoyed it, just telling other people what we wanted done. I have connections in the trade and then of course I've had the experience of arranging my own daughter's wedding.'

'She's been like a mother to Celia,' Sebastian said. 'Hasn't she, darling?'

Celia nodded and smiled.

'Miss Celia's done her share,' Mrs Jordan told him, 'and worked so hard on the house. She's been going up there with Sarah every day.'

'I'm sure you've all worked very hard,' Barbara Crawley said. 'Oh, look, I see the Arndales have arrived.'

'Celia, dear, it is so good to see you again,' Elspeth said, embracing her niece. 'I really despaired when there was no reply to my letters for all those years.'

'Letters, Aunt Elspeth? I received no letters.'

'There was a confusion about addresses, I'm afraid, and then with your uncle not being in the best of health our records weren't very well kept, address books and so on.'

Diana listened and wondered. Maybe those dead relations of Selina's had also destroyed letters. Perhaps it ran in the family. She tried not to think about it as she embraced her cousin and was relieved when Laura bounced up and began reminding Celia of the times they had played together when they were young.

'You remember much more than I do,' Celia said.

'Well, I was three years older, which makes a lot of difference at that age. But don't you remember the time you fell over in the pool and nearly dragged us all under, including Mary-Ann? And Tom jumped in and saved her? Then he sat in the custard pie and that night war broke out?'

'What a jumble of memories!' Rupert told her, laughing. 'What I remember most about that day is building the dam. Oh, and Tom having to wear Teddy's trousers which were much too big for him. Where's Father off to?'

He hadn't got used to seeing his father like this and stared at him helplessly now.

'I'll see to him,' Diana said. 'You go and talk to the other guests.'

Her father had gone over to the door and clearly intended, when the last guests had arrived, to bolt and bar it. She went across to him, glad of the chance to get away from the family with their talk of that day when Teddy and Tom were still alive. If only the war hadn't happened how different everything would have been: Tom and Teddy still here, her father unbroken, Celia not orphaned. James' wife and children wouldn't have been killed by that bomb, he would still have been living with them, working as a doctor in London. And surely, if times had been normal, Sebastian would have found her and this strange marriage would never have happened?

Because it *was* strange; it wasn't just her imagining, she was sure of that. Sebastian was obviously elated but Celia seemed so cold and distant and there were none of those little conspiratorial glances between them, that lovers give, no rapture. Her own strange marriage was begotten of the war, but what had brought about Sebastian's?

She had persuaded her father away from the door and was walking arm-in-arm with him towards the dining room when she noticed two elderly women who had been the last to arrive. They were standing alone, so she went across to introduce herself and her father.

They were friends of the Grimsdyke family, they said, the Misses Beale of the congregation of St Bartholomew's and had known Celia since she was a small child, had taught her in Sunday school. Miss Gertrude Beale was long and thin and dressed in gunmetal grey. Everything about her was grey, her face, what little could be seen of her hair under her grey hat, her coat, her stockings, all grey. Miss Agatha Beale was pink-cheeked and fat, her face dewlapped with many chins, her body encased in a kind of purple tent. Her hair was white and on it she wore a navy blue straw hat with cherries.

'You must come and have a glass of champagne before we all go in for lunch,' Diana invited.

They looked at her with horror.

'We do not imbibe the demon drink,' Miss Agatha Beale said.

'Oh, then you must have some fruit drink.'

'Water will suffice.'

'This is my brother, Rupert,' Diana said, taking her brother by the arm as he walked past. 'This is Miss Gertrude Beale and this is Miss Agatha Beale, Rupert. Could you see that they get a glass of water, please, while I take Father into the dining room?'

'Wouldn't you rather have champagne?' Rupert asked. Diana gave him a look which was meant to convey 'Just get the water and don't argue with them'. He failed to interpret it so she left them having what she hoped was a friendly discussion about alcohol and led her father away.

He liked to wander, so she went with him from group to group catching snatches of conversation.

'It's amazing what children can do nowadays,' one proud father was saying to another. 'Our boy's fixed up a wireless at school. Used the bedpost as an aerial and an old gaspipe for an earth, crystal set's hidden under the bed and he lies there with his headphones on listening to anything from the Savoy Orpheans to boxing matches.'

'Our lad's just the same. Wants to set one up at home,

using the clothes prop for an aerial, never stops talking about earths and cat's-whiskers and suchlike. We don't understand half of it. In the old days a father could explain science to his sons, now the children know more than their parents about all these new inventions.'

'It's progress, I suppose.'

All around her Diana could hear people greeting each other, working out how long it was since they'd met, exclaiming that they hadn't changed a bit in all these years, catching up on news of mutual friends of long ago.

'Patsy Fosdyke, you remember Patsy at school? Lovely girl, debutante of the year. Then she married a chiropodist and went to live in Wigan.'

'No! I'd quite lost touch with her. But I did see Rosalie not long ago. She had this fearful pain last year and was rushed into the nursing home with suspected appendicitis and, my dear, she had twins *within the hour*. She swears she'd no idea. Premature, of course.'

'Goodness! and I remember her as a wee little thing in Miss Timming's class at the Academy.'

She saw, to her relief, that Rupert had arranged for the Miss Beales to be provided with glasses of water. She was less pleased when she heard him saying, 'But if alcohol is so bad surely Christ would never have turned water into it? It would have been more logical for Him to turn wine into water whenever He saw it.'

'I have it on good authority, Mr Arndale, that New Testament wine was non-alcoholic. The grapes of the Holy Land were of a different variety from our modern ones.'

'But it's not the grapes, it's a question of how they're processed and . . .'

She didn't hear the rest, but moved away before Rupert could involve her in the argument. Nearby two old men were discussing flying.

'They're talking of taking passengers in these damned flying machines,' one was saying. 'A man must be mad to go up in one of them.'

'Their shares are going up.'

'What goes up must come down.'

'Shares or flying machines?'

'Both.'

'You must meet my brother who was an aviator and now teaches men to fly,' Diana said and beckoned to Rupert. Then, congratulating herself on providing entertainment for the two old gentlemen and at the same time preventing open warfare between her brother and the Miss Beales, she moved, with her father, towards the dining room.

In front of her Sebastian's father was having a loud conversation with someone she assumed must be his brother or cousin, they were so alike.

'I do wonder about these gatherings, don't you?' he was saying at the top of his voice. 'Not very enjoyable with everyone talking at once, can't make half of 'em out.'

'But you have to have 'em. The only time you get all the family together is at weddings or funerals. Christenings too, though there don't seem to be so many of them nowadays.'

'We still have 'em where we live.'

'I just meant they're smaller affairs than weddings and funerals. Quieter too.'

'Ours aren't very quiet now we've got this new padre. He lets the babies cry like billy-oh. Old padre just had to look at a baby and it shut up. New padre's got no discipline. And the babies sense it, you know. Like dogs and horses.'

'How's Barbara?'

'Champion. Hope she's not straining her voice in all this hubbub. It's the women I feel sorry for, you can see their little mouths working away, quite inaudible, of course, on account of not having an Adam's apple.'

'And have you noticed how everyone mutters nowadays?'

'Just what I'm always telling Barbara. You might point it out to her when you get the chance. Back me up, you know.'

'Isn't that old Geoffrey Peabody over there?'

'Where? Oh, yes, Geoffrey. Cousin of Barbara's. Funny chap, writes for the newspapers.'

'I've read his stuff. Atheist, isn't he?'

'Really? Doesn't look a day over sixty-five.'

The reception was simple, as the service had also been, but they were all agreed that the best man's speech was one of the best they had ever heard. He spoke of how the couple had met, was very funny about how he had watched Sebastian bringing about the destruction of Celia's home by fire and water in order to bring her under his own roof. Everyone laughed, Sebastian took it in good part, Celia looked horrified, as if she believed it might be true. 'It's just a joke, darling,' Sebastian assured her but she was disinclined to think it funny. James spoke too, but appeared to forget that this was a wedding and talked almost entirely about Sebastian and his work for the disabled. It was only at the end that, having received a little note from his mother-in-law, he remembered to mention the bride and propose her health. Sebastian, thanking him on her behalf, also thanked his parents for all they had done for him and especially for providing this reception.

'Oh, dear,' Elspeth whispered to Laura, who was sitting next to her, 'that's something *we* would normally have done.'

'You could still talk to him, Mother, offer to contribute,' Laura suggested.

Her mother was shocked.

'Unthinkable,' she said. 'If your father had been in better health, he would certainly have discussed it with Sebastian's father. The gentlemen would have settled it between them but it is not for a lady to talk about such matters.'

Yet she worries about it, Laura thought. Why do women have to feel responsible for things when they don't have the power to put them right?

Most of the young people came to the station to wave them off, their elders staying behind to drink tea. Celia had changed into a soft blue costume with a neat little flower hat. She looked ravishing, Sebastian thought, and much more approachable than she'd seemed when she sat next to him in her bridal finery at the reception, smiling and making polite conversation, playing her role but somehow not deeply involved, as if she might have been at somebody else's wedding.

He leant out of the window, waving until the train rounded the corner and the wedding guests were no longer in sight.

'I expect I'm covered in smuts,' he said, yanking up the window with the leather strap, and turning towards her.

'Yes,' she told him, 'there are quite a few on your face.'

'You wipe them off for me,' he suggested, offering her his handkerchief and glad that they had the compartment to themselves.

But she only smiled and nodded towards the looking glass opposite, a long mirror under a picture of a station they would see somewhere on this L.M.S. line.

So he got up and dealt with the sooty smears himself.

She is still the same bride, cool and aloof, he thought as he wiped his face. Separate from me, shrinking from any intimacy. How different it will be after tonight. He longed to awaken and arouse her, to give her delight. Oh yes, after tonight it would be quite different, meanwhile they would sit here companionably, their new luggage on the rack opposite, occasionally taking her gloved hand in his. Oh, but tonight we two alone will sing like birds i' the cage.

The train had moved out of Gradby, past the sidings, over railway lines which crossed and recrossed each other in a giant cat's cradle of steel, past the jumble of warehouses, past rows of houses and back gardens with lines of washing hanging out, braving the soot from all the trains passing close by.

Then they were out in open country, for Gradby was one of those northern towns that people paid the doubtful compliment of calling easy to get out of. The rows of houses were soon replaced by green fields criss-crossed with drystone walls that lay like a net over the undulating countryside. The fields were dotted with sheep and boulders and sometimes a farmhouse nestled in a sheltered spot, as if it had grown there.

'I do love the Dales,' he said, watching the green and grey

countryside slip by. 'I expect you know them much better than I do, having been brought up here.'

She shook her head.

'No,' she said. 'I've never been here before. We never went out of Gradby. At least Aunt and Uncle did sometimes, but I stayed at home to mind the house.'

'Alone?'

'There was Sarah.'

She said it so simply, without any resentment, but he nearly exclaimed at the injustice of the way they'd treated her. All that money and they'd been too mean even to take her on holiday, not so much as a day's outing into this lovely countryside which was almost on their doorstep.

He knew better than to say so; she wouldn't accept criticism of them; their ways had become too much part of her life. Besides, they were dead.

Anyway, he told himself, it's all in the past now and I, Sebastian Crawley, will devote myself to showing her all the beauty she's been so wickedly deprived of until now.

'Look, darling,' he said. 'Isn't it lovely?'

In the watery sunshine, the clouds cast swiftly moving shadows on the hillside and seemed to race along beside the train.

Then, looking at her, he added, 'And you are lovely too, my darling. That soft blue suits you perfectly.'

'Mrs Jordan helped me to choose it.'

Dear Mrs Jordan, she's been like a mother to her, he thought, the first motherly soul she's ever known, because Selina had been no kind of a mother and the very thought of Ethel Grimsdyke, dead or alive, made him shiver. Mrs Jordan must have been the first person ever to take an interest in her as a girl, in how she looked and what she wore.

'When we're in our own house,' he said, 'Mrs Jordan must be our first guest.'

She nodded.

'She's been very kind,' she said.

'And she's very fond of you.'

'Only because I was marrying you.'

'Oh, no,' he said, shocked at the casual way she had spoken. 'Think of the time and thought she gave to shopping with you. That was for your own sake alone.'

'She likes shopping.'

She paused and went on, 'Mrs Jordan has quite a frivolous, worldly side. And all frivolous people like shopping.'

He wanted to speak in defence of Mrs Jordan, but didn't want to disagree too strongly with anything his bride said.

'But of course,' Celia conceded, 'she is very kind too.'

And frivolous people are sometimes kinder than solemn ones, Sebastian thought but didn't say. There are no rules.

'Let me tell you about where we're going, darling,' he said instead. 'I'm sure you'll love it. It's on the edge of the village of Lowsham and used to be the manor house of the squire but was converted into a hotel after the war. It's more wooded than most villages in the Dales. It's so peaceful. My parents took me up there a couple of years after the war and I remember my mother saying what a lovely place it would be to have a honeymoon.'

She smiled up at him and said, 'So you had to get married to find out?'

He laughed and, happy that she was at last relaxed enough to tease him, put his arm around her and drew her close.

He felt her body tense, stiffen against him.

'The ticket collector might come in,' she said.

Nineteen

'The station's about a mile from the village, Sebastian told her as he reached up for their cases off the rack. 'When it was being built about eighty years ago, people were still very afraid that trains would frighten the sheep and cattle to death so they petitioned that it shouldn't be allowed any nearer than that.'

'I expect they regretted it later.'

He laughed.

'I'm sure they did, but it's good for the village taximan now. I've asked him to meet us. Barton, he's called.'

It was raining steadily as they drove up from the station.

'T'rain's been 'ard at it these two days past,' Mr Barton told them.

'Oh, it was quite sunny most of the way up from Gradby.'

'That's as maybe,' Mr Barton said. 'Any rain 'ereabouts falls on Lowsham.'

Lowsham Hall Hotel was much more forbidding than he remembered from the time he had spent three glorious summer days here with his parents six years ago. Then the trees gave welcome shade and the old granite building sparkled in the sun. Now, as the cab drove them along the wooded road which narrowed into not much more than a lane, the dripping foliage that surrounded them was dank and depressing. The hotel too looked gloomy; the grey stone which had reflected the light during those three sunny days looked, under leaden skies, cold and dreary.

There was nobody about to help with the luggage, so Sebastian carried it into the hall where a tall angular receptionist stood behind a desk. She had a long, lugubrious face, wore her hair skewered into two earphones and didn't look particularly pleased to see them.

'Mr and Mrs Crawley,' Sebastian said. 'We have a double room booked for a week.'

She put on her pince-nez and peered at a diary which seemed remarkably empty given the season. Despite this it took her a long time to find their name. She rang a handbell and a porter appeared.

He was a heavily built man and they had evidently interrupted his meal because he was chewing as he came and looked resentful at being disturbed.

'It seems very quiet,' Sebastian remarked conversationally, as they followed him up two flights of stairs. 'It was much busier when I came with my parents five or six years ago.'

'New management since then,' the porter told him. 'And foot-and-mouth disease at a nearby farm.'

He shrugged as if there wasn't much to choose between the two afflictions.

'This is the bathroom,' he told them, indicating a door as they passed.

'And this is your room,' opening another and handing Sebastian the key.

He waited while Sebastian searched his pockets and found a florin, which he took without thanks and left them.

It was a large, chilly room with stone mullion windows looking out over the grounds. A fire was laid but not lit in the grate, in front of which stood a small electric fire attached to a meter. There were two armchairs and a small sofa, a pair of mahogany wardrobes and, Sebastian saw to his dismay, two single beds, one at each side of the room.

But at last they were alone and free from interruption. He put his arms round her. She moved away.

'Shouldn't we unpack?' she asked. 'We'll be late for dinner.'

'No, don't unpack,' he told her. 'I'm going to go and ask them to change the room for one with a double bed.'

'Oh, you can't do that,' she said, dismayed.

'Why not?'

'It would seem so, so, well, *rude*.'

'Don't worry about that,' he told her. 'And it's cold in here as well,' he added, leaving before she could protest further.

The receptionist heard him out before saying, 'None of our rooms have double beds.'

'I remember when we stayed here before that my parents had a four-poster in their room.'

'We replaced all the double beds with twin beds when we modernized,' she told him. 'Our advisers said they were more fashionable.'

'And it's very cold. I should like a fire to be lit.'

'The boy is off duty now. He can see to it tomorrow.'

'I'll light it myself,' he said, beginning to get really angry now.

'The coal can't be brought up until tomorrow.'

She had the implacability of the determinedly unhelpful. He left her and returned to the room.

Celia had started to unpack.

'It's no good,' he said, 'but at least we can have a fire tomorrow. You choose which bed you'd like to share.'

'No, you choose,' she said and went on unpacking. 'I thought I'd use the three bottom drawers and you can have the higher ones. And I've hung up my dresses in the left-hand wardrobe. Then shall I go along first to the bathroom?'

'Right. I'll follow on after.'

They unpacked methodically, not speaking much, then she took her sponge bag and went along to the bathroom. When she returned he went to wash and shave.

The bathroom was colder even than the bedroom, but she hadn't complained. Presumably nothing felt really cold after the Grimsdykes' abode in Waterloo Road. He shaved carefully in the chilly bathroom, wanting his skin to be as smooth as possible against hers.

When he returned she had already changed into a dress for dinner. She jumped and looked startled when he opened the door.

'Oh, I'd thought you'd knock,' she said. 'I'm sorry. I'd forgotten we're married.'

She looked so young standing there in her long dress, hair loose on her shoulders. He felt guilty, as if he'd intruded on her privacy. Perhaps he should have knocked. No, that was ridiculous. Of course he shouldn't. It would be better after tonight.

A few minutes later, a distant gong sounded.

He opened the door for her, noticing, as he crossed the room, that she'd put his pyjamas on one bed and her night-dress on the other.

There was only one other couple in the dining room, an elderly pair, who scarcely spoke to each other. An ancient waiter hovered between the two tables. He's evidently not part of the modernization scheme, Sebastian thought as he ordered wine. Celia refused any, saying that she had drunk wine at the reception.

'It's not rationed,' he told her, laughing. 'You're allowed two glasses on your wedding day.'

'It's not good, though,' she told him. 'Miss Agatha Beale gave us a very interesting talk on the evil consequences of alcoholic liquors.'

'Well, of course, darling, it's bad to drink to excess, but a little wine is good for you, helps you to relax.'

'But the devil starts by tempting us in little ways,' she told him.

The remark shocked him; he tried to diminish it by laughing and saying, 'Well, it means I shall have to drink your share, so the devil will get me instead of you.'

The meal was surprisingly good, but Celia ate very little and talked even less.

Coffee, the waiter told them, could be served here or in the lounge.

'That's the room we passed on the way in here? The one with the fire?'

The man nodded.

'We'll go in there, shall we, darling? It looked quite cosy.'

He took her hand and led her into the lounge. There was

a good fire with armchairs on either side. The elderly couple were already seated in them.

The choice was to join them or go and sit in a far corner. He would have preferred the latter, but Celia moved to join the others, who introduced themselves as Mr and Mrs Hannington-Jones.

On closer inspection they didn't look any more attractive than they had done at a distance. He was a potbellied little man whose pale blue eyes and down-turned mouth gave him, Sebastian observed, the look of an aggrieved haddock. The wife reminded him horribly of Ethel Grimsdyke, but at the moment they had both contorted their features in an attempt to look welcoming.

'Just arrived today, have you?' she who looked like Ethel Grimsdyke remarked. 'We've been here a week already.'

'And we always sit here in the evening,' her husband announced, an edge of belligerence in his voice, as if warning them off.

'And when do you leave?' Sebastian asked, hoping that it might be tomorrow.

'We have another week.'

Sebastian glanced apologetically across at Celia but she was talking to Mrs Hannington-Jones.

'It's fortunate that you've come to join us,' the latter was telling her. 'Only yesterday we were saying how we'd like others to come to make up a four at bridge in the evenings. Do you play?'

'Oh, yes. I've only just learned, but I'd very much like to get better.'

'Then you shall get some practice with us,' Mrs Hannington-Jones told her, as if doing them a favour.

'That will be lovely, won't it, Sebastian?' Celia agreed, glancing across at him.

'But not tonight,' Sebastian said firmly. 'We've had a busy day and are very tired.'

He couldn't bring himself to tell them that he and Celia were on their honeymoon. And Celia didn't volunteer the information.

Later when, coffee consumed, they were making their way upstairs, Celia said, 'You don't think we've been a little rude, leaving them alone like that?'

'No, I don't. I'm sorry you were lumbered with them.'

'Oh, I don't mind. I thought they were rather nice. She reminded me a bit of Aunt Ethel.'

So I didn't imagine it, Sebastian thought, inwardly groaning as he opened the bedroom door.

The chambermaid had been in, drawn the curtains and turned down both beds.

'I think I'd like a bath,' Celia told him. 'I didn't have time for one before.'

'We could share one,' he suggested, putting his arms around her.

'What?' she exclaimed, startled. 'You mean get into the bath together?'

'Yes, wouldn't it be a nice friendly thing to do?'

'Oh, no,' she said, backing away from him. 'It wouldn't be right.'

'Why not? We're married now.'

'And there wouldn't be enough room. I'll go first and you can follow.'

She turned away abruptly and began undoing her dress.

'I'll help you,' he offered as she struggled with the back fastening.

'No, thank you. I can manage.'

'It's a lovely dress.'

'Mrs Jordan's choice.'

'She knows what suits you.'

He knew she didn't like being watched, so turned away, but not before he had glimpsed the thick knitted vest and dark serge knickers that the dress had concealed. Evidently Mrs Jordan's guidance hadn't been sought as to underwear.

After she had gone, he undressed, put on his dressing gown and sat down on the couch. He had a premonition of disaster. He wasn't a particularly confident man, he knew that. What if all those little rejections, which he'd put down to her modesty, her strong sense of propriety, were actually her instinctive reaction? The women he'd known had all been warm and responsive and he'd naively assumed they were all like that. Perhaps Celia wasn't?

He told himself not to be absurd. She was young and had lived a very lonely life. It was natural that she should be shy with him at first. Patience and gentleness were what she needed and deserved. And that was what he would give her.

She was away a long time. True to his resolution, he waited patiently and, when she returned, gave her a gentle little kiss and then went to have a quick bath himself.

When he returned, she was sitting up in bed brushing her hair. She was wearing a high-necked, long-sleeved nightgown of some thick grey material.

'I love your hair,' he said, gently taking the brush from her. 'Let me do it for you.'

She sat very still as he brushed her fair hair with long smooth strokes, playing with it in his fingers at the same time. Then after a while he laid the brush aside and, still fondling her hair, eased himself into bed beside her.

'I love you,' he told her, taking her in his arms and wishing that the bed was a few feet wider.

She didn't reply, but lay impassive as he kissed her. He twined his fingers in her hair as he kissed her head, her lips, covered her face with little kisses. He stroked her neck, kissed her throat and all the while she lay very still, until he laid his hand on the part of the nightdress which covered her breast, when her body stiffened and she edged away from him, as if to say, thus far and no further.

He moved his hand away and stroked her back instead. Oh Celia, he thought, if only you would give one little sign, one gesture of affection, one loving touch. That's all I long for; never mind passion, just show a little warmth towards me, a little tenderness.

The nightdress material was quite rough against his hand. Knowing that the skin underneath it would be soft and silky and lovely to touch only added to his frustration.

He took her hand and kissed it and held its palm against

his cheek moving it gently across his face, but still she did not caress him.

'Happy?' he enquired.

'Yes,' she said. 'But I think I'm rather tired and would like to go to sleep now.'

'All right, darling, you'll feel brighter in the morning,' he said, settling to sleep alongside her, his arm over her, his body curved around hers.

'I'll go to the other bed,' she said and had slipped away from him before he had time to demur.

He was surprised, when he awoke the next morning, to see that she was already up and dressed.

'You're a very early bird,' he said. 'I had thought we'd have breakfast in bed.'

'It's such a sunny morning,' she said, smiling at him from where she stood by the window. 'It seemed a shame to lie in bed.'

She seemed much happier this morning and looked so fresh and girlish, he thought as he lay and watched her. He'd been silly to have such dark and gloomy thoughts last night. They'd both been tired out and needed a good night's sleep. They loved each other and were married, that was all that mattered; it was enough.

But it wasn't enough, as he discovered in the days that followed. In the daytime all was well; the weather improved and they walked together on the hills, the air fresh on their faces, the April sun strengthening day by day. They looked around Lowsham, went into its beautiful old church, admired its mediaeval stained glass, deciphered the words inscribed on the effigy of Sir Thomas Gassington's 'dutyfulle wyf of greate pietie' who lay on her back, amid the marble folds of her robe, hands modestly clasped across her breast.

They explored other villages too and little market towns, they climbed the surrounding hills, they studied maps and admired the same views and he learned that it is one thing to be alone together as you walk, which is companionable, and another thing to be alone together in bed, which can be the loneliest thing on earth.

For in the evening she seemed to change, to become wary of him. The expression on her face when he approached her seemed to say, I am the sacrificial lamb facing slaughter, which made her look vulnerable, which there was no need for her to be and made him feel guilty, which he wasn't. She submitted to his love-making, but didn't share in it, didn't respond or reciprocate. She lay as still as Sir Thomas Gassington's dutiful wife.

'I must send a postcard to the Misses Beale,' Celia said one day towards the end of their honeymoon, as they walked across the fields to the neighbouring village of Netherby. 'They were very kind to me.'

'Yes? Tell me,' he prompted when she didn't go on.

'They, well especially Miss Agatha, helped me to understand.'

'Understand what?'

She hesitated, then said, 'You see my parents didn't really trouble themselves much about me. They were too busy, I suppose. Then my aunt and uncle took me in and they were very good to me, to give me a home, I mean, but naturally they couldn't be expected to love a child who wasn't their own, so it was all the more admirable that they gave me a home and did their duty.'

'You mean loveless duty is admirable?'

'Oh, yes. Virtue is its own reward.'

They had reached a drystone wall. Some nearby sheep stopped cropping the grass and watched with round, glassy eyes as they climbed the stile.

'Go on,' Sebastian said, helping Celia down on the other side.

'But perhaps, being a child, I didn't understand as well as I do now. And then I met the Misses Beale and they explained the love of God to me and how Jesus loves little children. Not like my mother, who disliked all children. Especially little ones.'

Oh, yes, he recognized Selina.

'Of course, it doesn't matter now, but at the time it was a great help to me to understand that heavenly love is different from earthly love and more reliable and that God loved me even if nobody else did, so I needn't worry about anything except loving Him in return, and that as for the others I must just do my duty by them. Miss Agatha told me she found it much easier to love God than her fellow human beings.'

'But don't you remember the question of how can you love God whom you've never seen if you can't love your neighbours whom you have seen?'

She smiled.

'It's obvious,' she said. 'God is entirely good but people are full of the sinful lusts of the flesh. I mean I know that God's love for me is pure, yours is carnal.'

'No, Celia, no.'

He was shocked, silenced for a moment and then went on, 'I want to love everything about you, including your body. You shouldn't spurn total love, shouldn't fear it. It will strengthen you too.'

'Women are made differently,' she said with a kind of childish obstinacy.

'No.'

'I've been thinking and praying about this,' she went on, speaking as if she was reciting a lesson learned by heart, 'and it seems to me that in a marriage we both have to be prepared to sacrifice something. I have to do my duty and surrender my body to you more than I might wish and you have to curb your carnal desires and make fewer demands on me than you might wish.'

'But, Celia,' he said, horrified at this view of marriage. 'You can't split love up like that. Love of the body is just a part of the whole love, indivisible from it. If you try to make it a separate thing it becomes warped and twisted. Just a thing apart to be called up and used now and then, not a part of the whole.'

'But I've told you, I shall do my duty as your wife.'

'I don't want you to make love out of duty, Celia. It's a horrible notion.'

'It's what I promised in the marriage service.'

'No, it isn't. Oh, Celia, don't you see, whole love, mutual love strengthens us, unites us against the world – or for the world – and makes us stronger and safer together than the two of us would be separately?'

She shook her head, but didn't reply and they walked on in a silence which he feared to break in case he provoked their first quarrel.

They reached Netherby sooner than they'd expected and decided to return by a longer route, climbing up the lane and over the hill which lay between the two villages.

Near the top they heard water and, looking up at the hillside above them, saw a few gnarled trees and an outcrop of stones, among which a spring bubbled up, rippled over pebbles and descended, gradually widening, down the hillside.

'A good place to picnic,' Sebastian said. 'Come on, it's a bit steep,' and he held out his hand and she let herself be pulled up towards the crag.

At the top, he took off the knapsack and spread his jacket out for her to sit on, while she unpacked sandwiches, fruit, cake and orange juice. He liked to watch her doing this simple task, so neatly, with a kind of childlike concentration. She is so young, he thought, years younger than I am in her ways and in her knowledge of the world. I must never forget that.

Afterwards, they lay down to rest; he put the knapsack under her head as a pillow and lay back beside her. It was very still. The only sounds which broke the silence were the occasional throaty bleating of sheep and the answering high-pitched call of their new-born lambs. The sun sparkled on the stony scree of the distant hills and warmed his body as he lay beside her. He remembered how Mrs Jordan had said what a good little wife Celia would make him and the memory of those words of approval warmed him too.

He turned towards her, looked down at her as she lay there, leaned over to kiss her, but even as he did so he caught the wary look that came into her eyes, felt the slight movement as if she would have backed away from him if she could.

He hesitated and then turned away from her. How still she lies, he thought, like an effigy in church; he shivered, fearing for a moment that if he touched her he might feel only stone. All the warmth he had just felt drained from him, replaced with a fear that it would be ever thus. And he remembered his mother saying that people who haven't been loved find it hard to give love. Then he cursed Celia's mother, her aunt and the Miss Beales. He cursed them equally, not sure which was the most to blame.

It was suddenly cold as a dark cloud obliterated the sun, a reminder that the year was still young, had not yet had time to warm the air. A curlew wheeled overhead, uttering its desolate, lonely cry.

'Time to make a move,' Sebastian said.

Celia got up, handed him the knapsack and they set off along the top of the hill. At the highest point was a cairn built by previous climbers who had each added to it one of the stones which lay scattered about on the ground.

Sebastian found a stone to put on the top of the cairn. With a smaller one he inscribed their names: Celia and Sebastian Crawley, 22nd April 1926.

Twenty

The wedding had been so magical that Sarah expected the new Mrs Crawley and her husband to come back from their honeymoon quite transformed from the people they had been before the ceremony.

She had worked hard with Mrs Jordan to get the new home ready. The furniture had all arrived from the storeroom last week and everything had been put in its place; Miss Celia had written down on a piece of paper exactly where it was all to go. Only the master's study was empty because he was going to choose his own things in there, so it looked a bit bare and creepy. The other alarming thing was the telephone instrument attached to the wall near the front door. Mrs Jordan said only Mr and Mrs Crawley would use it, so she needn't worry. All the same she didn't like the idea of being left in the house alone with it when it might go off.

Sebastian saw at once that the two women had done their best to make the house welcoming; he noticed the flowers in the hall, the fires in the drawing room and bedroom, the meal laid ready on the dining-room table, but these warm little touches didn't stand a chance against the Grimsdyke furniture, the Grimsdyke curtains, the Grimsdyke bedspreads and the Grimsdyke pictures. They were no more effective than glimmering little candles in the encircling gloom of a cave.

He glanced apprehensively at Celia.

'It'll all look much better when we've got our own furniture in it,' he began.

She looked at him, surprised. 'But it's perfect as it is,' she said. 'Everything fits so well,' and she went from room to room delighted with her new home, so wonderfully like her old one, the one she had grown up in and felt at ease in.

'I've told Sarah she can come and see me as often as she likes on her free afternoons,' Mrs Jordan said as she was leaving.

'That's very kind of you.'

'Oh, she's a good girl, Mr Crawley, and it will be nice for me to have the company,' she told him and hurried off to catch the bus which would take her to her empty house where no welcoming voice would greet her.

Meanwhile Sebastian and Celia sat by the fire, looking at the letters which Sarah had brought in with the tea. There were bills for Sebastian and cards addressed to both of them from his parents and one from her aunt Elspeth Arndale and another from Matthew asking Sebastian to make sure to call in on him tomorrow.

Sebastian looked at it and realized – guiltily – that he was looking forward to getting back to work.

Matthew's office was very different from his own, Sebastian reflected as he made his way there towards the end of the following morning. Whereas his was modern, foursquare and boring, Matthew's occupied two floors in a rambling old building which, as Sebastian often told him, should have been knocked down and rebuilt years ago. It was a warren of narrow little rooms, winding corridors, odd corners, unexpected little steps and steep stairs.

Heaven knows what would happen if they had a fire here, he thought, as he always did when he climbed the stairs.

Matthew greeted him warmly.

'Oh, my dear chap, it's good to see you back. How's Celia? Was it all wonderful?'

Sebastian assured him that yes, Celia was well, and yes, it had all been wonderful and then quickly went on to ask how things had been here in Gradby.

Matthew's face clouded.

'Not so good,' he said, 'but I expect you'll know all about the industrial trouble we're in?'

'No, I'm afraid I . . .'

Matthew gave him an old-fashioned, indulgent look.

'Oh, Sebastian, forgive me. As if a fellow goes on his honeymoon to read the newspapers! You had far better things to do. Come on, we'll go and have lunch and I'll tell you all about it.'

Doing his best to look like a man who has just returned from an ecstatic honeymoon, Sebastian allowed himself to be patted on the back by his friend and led off to lunch.

Here, in the little restaurant which was as quaint and rambling as his office, Matthew became serious again.

'Things are coming to a head,' he said after they'd ordered. 'You remember that last July the government gave a subsidy for nine months so a Royal Commission could investigate conditions in the mines?'

'Vaguely, yes.'

'And that when the commission reported, it recommended that all these little mines should be amalgamated, voluntarily at first but later the government should use compulsion if the mineowners wouldn't agree?'

Sebastian nodded.

'They said a few other things too, like the owners having to provide pit-head baths, a profit-sharing scheme and family allowances.'

'All very favourable to the miners.'

'Yes, but they were things which would take time, no date was given for them. But they also said that in return the miners should *immediately* accept lower wages as a temporary measure and that the subsidy should not be renewed at the end of the nine months.'

'And when is the nine months up?'

'Next Friday.'

Sebastian didn't reply. They both sat quietly subdued, until two plates of steak and kidney pie steamed into view and were placed in front of them by a burly waitress.

'So what do you think will happen?' Sebastian said at last.

Matthew shrugged.

'Who knows? There are plentiful supplies of coal but if the owners are as obstinate as they've been before, the railwaymen and dockers could refuse to shift it.'

'And other industries might join in?'

'Possibly. But there's never been the kind of ill will against mill owners and factory owners up here that there has been for the mineowners.' He paused and putting down his knife and fork, went on, 'You see, Sebastian, people up here recognize the hard work the mill owners put in to create their industry, but there's not that kind of respect for the mineowners. They just happened to own the land on which coal was found. And exploited it. That's the difference. And they didn't put their profits back into making mines safer. Conditions are awful. Two out of every hundred miners die within twenty years of working in the pit and a quarter of them are badly injured or disabled by illness. And now they've been told to take a cut in wages.'

As Sebastian listened he saw again those ragged, barefoot children he'd seen at Ugton, the exhausted women coming down from the slag heaps carrying their sacks of rubbishy coal and, most vividly of all, Irene Carter with her precious pence in the cracked mug.

'But how can they accept less money when they're on starvation wages already?' he demanded.

'The owners say that prices will fall so that *in the end* the miners' wages will be worth the same amount,' Matthew told him.

'It must all seem a bit theoretical if you're starving.'

'Exactly.'

'So what can we do about it?'

'Oh, we're just observers. We can only try to keep our own businesses going and follow the news as best we can. There are so many rumours flying around and it'll be hard to get at the truth if the printers join in the strike.'

'Then I'd better get myself a wireless,' Sebastian said, knowing that there was nothing of that sort among the Grimsdyke furniture. 'I'd no idea things were so serious.'

'Well, you've been living in a different world,' Matthew

told him, smiling indulgently as they got up. 'We'll have to let you down gently, so lunch is on me.'

'That's the last I've got,' the shopkeeper told Sebastian as he showed him the wireless set. 'Everyone seems to be going mad for wirelesses. All the standard Fellowes models have gone, I'm afraid, but it's a nice job, is this 'un. Can't beat a Fellowes cabinet. It's a three valve model at nine pounds eighteen shillings. But we do instalments: twenty shillings down and ten monthly payments of twenty shillings.'

Sebastian did a quick calculation and said he'd pay for it outright.

'Yes, we've been cleared out these last few days. And it's not just the expensive models neither. We've sold out of all the parts too. They've been coming in for valves and batteries and loudspeakers, aerials, receivers, extension wire, you name it, they've bought it. Everyone's getting their old crystal sets going, setting up the cat's-whiskers.'

'Then I've been lucky,' Sebastian told him.

Celia didn't think so. She thought he had been recklessly extravagant.

'We'll need to keep up with the news,' he explained and told her what Matthew had said.

'There's newspapers,' she pointed out.

'There may not be if the strike spreads to the printers.'

'They'd never dare!' she exclaimed.

But they did dare and it was from the elegant new Fellowes wireless set that they got most of their news in the following weeks. As they sat facing it they heard that on Saturday at midnight the owners had put up lock-out notices, telling the men that if they didn't agree to having their pay reduced they would be locked out of the pits. They heard too that the government had decided to stop negotiating with the trades unions to try to find a solution and had instead declared a state of emergency, whereupon the unions voted for strike action in support of the miners to start the following Tuesday.

After that Celia no longer mentioned the extravagance of his purchase.

Since their return from honeymoon he had noticed that she had taken to wearing the old dresses she'd worn at Waterloo Road.

'What's happened to all the pretty clothes you bought before the wedding?' he asked her after they had turned off their wireless one evening.

'I've put them away for special.'

'Aren't I special?'

'You know what I mean. It's a waste to use them for everyday.'

Twenty-One

'I'll set off early tomorrow morning,' Sebastian told Celia on Monday night. 'There may not be as many trams as usual and some of the bus drivers might not turn up for work either.'

The avenue was quiet at seven o'clock in the morning, but then it always was. The astonishing thing was that when he reached the main road, that also was very still. He waited for a while at the bus stop, but no bus came. He walked to the tram terminus. That too was deserted. No trams clanked and clattered along the middle of the road, no electric rod set off sparks on the overhead wires. Nothing of trams was to be seen; only the deserted parallel lines of steel in the quiet, empty street.

Soon he was walking through the industrial area on the edge of the city but saw no queues of workers outside Atkinson's steelworks, nobody waited by the gates of Draycott's Engineering, nobody was clocking in at the railway foundry. The air was sweet outside Laud's Tannery, where people usually held their noses as they hurried past. The factory boilers were unlit. So it wasn't just the transport workers who had come out; everyone seemed to be supporting the miners.

He had walked nearly as far as the city centre when the town seemed to erupt into life – not with trams or buses, but with pedestrians and hundreds of bicycles. They all seemed very cheerful, these people, as if enjoying the challenge. They called greetings to strangers, they smiled at each other. A man on a tandem offered passers-by a lift.

The air was unusually clear; no smoke belched out of factory chimneys, no pall of smoke hung over the city. It was as if people had taken back their town. Shopgirls and office workers walked arm-in-arm in the road. Nobody seemed to be hurrying; they knew their employers would be grateful to them for turning up at all, never mind when.

'We live in interesting times, eh?' a familiar voice called to him.

'Matthew! So you set off early too?'

'Not as early as you, I expect. I don't have so far to tramp from my lodgings as you do out in the sticks. I must admit it is rather jolly, isn't it?'

A pony and trap, driven by a very old man, clip-clopped along the road, with four girls, in cloaks and bonnets, up on the back.

'Don't get your wheels stuck in the tramlines,' Matthew called out as they passed and the girls waved and laughed.

Even as they watched, the road seemed to fill up with more and more people making their way to shops and offices on foot or bike, in carts, in pony and traps, on anything that had wheels. Very old cars crawled slowly along, their drivers unused to coming into town. These were Sunday cars, that normally spent the week in the garage.

'That's Humphrey Squires, KC, on his way to the Law Courts,' Sebastian remarked as a portly gentleman rode magisterially past on horseback.

Sebastian was the first to arrive at the office. An hour later two draughtsmen turned up, brothers called Sydney and Joe Coles.

He heard them laughing as they came up the stairs.

'We've made it,' they told him cheerfully, as they came into the room, without the usual courtesy knock.

'We had a lift in a neighbour's car,' Joe said. 'It broke down the minute it saw the main road. Blessedly he's joined that association for automobile owners and they have these men who ride about on motorbikes with side-cars to rescue their members.'

'Yes, I've seen them.'

'Well, one happened to be passing and saw us stuck there on the kerbside. A great chap, we left them sorting things out and we walked the rest of the way. Is there any tea? Where's Elsie?'

'Not in yet.'

'Better make it ourselves.'

In the little room known as Elsie's bunk hole, they found a gas ring on a tin tray, a tea caddy, sugar and a box of biscuits.

'No milk.'

'She usually brings it in with her.'

'I'll go and get some at Fosters round the corner.'

'Thanks Syd,' Sebastian said. 'Can you come with me, Joe? I'd like you to see these drawings for the railway sheds extension.'

Syd was away a long time.

'Whatever have you been doing?' his brother asked. 'Milking the cow?'

'No, I stopped to listen to the news on the wireless. I saw this crowd of people round the shop. He sold his last set on Friday—'

'To me,' Sebastian put in.

'Lucky devil. We've just got the cat's-whisker and does one get tired of those earphones! Anyway he's letting everyone listen in the shop and he's got a loudspeaker out on the pavement. So I stopped to listen.'

'So what is the news?'

'London's jammed up with private cars. No underground, no trams, no omnibuses or trolley buses. I think the unions are surprised at how total it all is.'

'It all seems so unreal.'

'And they're organizing volunteers to do the work.'

'What, blacklegs?'

'No, though I expect there'll be a few. It's mostly students and such. It's different in London. You won't get volunteers up here because people know what the miners' lives are like.'

'I'm not so sure. I've always wanted to have a go at driving a tram.'

'You wouldn't?'

Syd hesitated.

'No, I suppose not,' he said reluctantly at last.

They were interrupted by the arrival of Elsie, a strapping girl, pink cheeked and with a lot of unruly red hair.

'By gum,' she said. 'But I 'aven't 'alf 'ad a time gettin' 'ere today. Our dad borrowed our uncle's old car to get us in, me and Nancy from the 'aberdashery and Edie from the shoe factory, and we couldn't get it started. Our dad was swingin' away at the startin' 'andle and then 'e 'ad us girls swingin' at it while 'e were at wheel and suddenly it got goin' and Edie still in t'road, but 'e wouldn't stop. So she's runnin' be'ind, poor lass, but I nearly bust meself laughin' all t'same.'

'So you left her?'

Elsie shook her head.

'Nay, we were goin' that slow that she caught up on us. Then after a bit we 'ad to stop for summat – a cart got in t'way; one of them lile governess carts – and our dad couldn't get us started again. 'E wanted us to stay, like, and do t'crankin' up again but we said no, ta, we'd rather walk. So 'ere I am and I'd better mek tea. I've got t'milk on t'way.'

She left but returned almost immediately to demand, 'And who's been messin' in my cubby 'ole? Dirty cups all over, a wet spoon in t'sugar and biscuit-tin left open and crumbs all over t'shop.'

She was always quick to anger.

'I'm sorry,' Sebastian said. 'We tried to make our own.'

'It wasn't nearly as good as you make,' said Syd, who was generally acknowledged as being the best at dealing with her, 'and Elsie, dear, you sounded just like Mother Bear when you said, "Who's been in my cubby hole?".'

Mollified, she returned to her bunk hole and began noisily washing up cups, muttering the while about how men shouldn't be allowed in kitchens.

The rest of the staff drifted in during the remainder of the morning, but not much work got done. Other offices they needed to contact were closed either through the strike or because their people hadn't managed to get in, so in the end Sebastian decided it would be better to go home early, knowing that everyone's journey back would be more difficult with so many people trying to get out of Gradby at the same time.

He enjoyed the walk back in air that was so unusually clear and fresh. He walked briskly out of the town and into the suburbs, now bright with spring blossom. But out there in Ugton, he thought, they will be lighting their fires with coal picked off the slag heaps and the chimneys will be pouring out filth into air already thick with smoke. There won't be much excitement there, no talk of eventful journeys, no challenge except that of desperation. He thought of the children without shoes, of the women in rags with sacks tied around their thin bodies. And he felt ashamed of the way he had enjoyed the day, as he thought of their deprivation.

'I think it's disgraceful,' Celia said, almost immediately he got in. 'They say milk is going to be more expensive and food might not be unloaded at the docks. I sent Sarah down to the shops to get supplies, while I did her cleaning. What a start to my new housekeeping! I've spent half already and it's only Tuesday.'

'It doesn't matter, darling,' he said, putting his arm around her shoulders. 'These are very unusual times. You must just get what you need.'

'I'd put all the strikers in prison,' she said. 'Anyway the government's going to get all these volunteers to take their place and that'll show them.'

'But Celia, my dear, I know it's worrying for you, but the unions have already said they will safeguard food supplies and hospitals and so on.'

'It's very selfish of them all the same.'

'No, Celia, what they're doing is very *un*selfish. They're not striking for themselves but for the miners. Most of them will be worse off.'

'I hope they are – *much* worse off.'

He was shocked by the bitterness with which she spoke; he had never known her be so vehement about anything. It seemed so strange that she, who had been brought up here and surely knew something of the lives of the workers involved in the strike, could be so harsh.

'If the miners hadn't gone on strike in the first place none of this would have happened,' she was saying.

'It wasn't a strike, it was a lock-out, Celia,' he told her. 'When the men refused a cut in wages – a savage cut of 13% for men already on starvation wages – and longer hours, they were locked out by the owners.'

'I'm surprised at you, Sebastian, taking their side like this.'

'If you saw the way they live, saw the hardships their wives and children have to bear, Celia, you would feel some compassion, I know.'

'I've had a hard life,' she said, surprisingly. 'And I've always done my duty. The miners should do theirs. And so should these strikers.'

He realized there was no point in discussing it. He tried to talk of other things, of what she had done with her day, but their meal was a silent affair and afterwards they sat and listened to the news bulletins on the wireless. Evidently it wasn't just here and in London that public transport had disappeared from the streets. In all the other industrial towns, tramcars, trolley buses and trains had vanished. It seemed that not just the government but also the unions were surprised by the response to the strike.

They listened together, but did not talk about it afterwards. Still hardly speaking to each other, they went early to bed.

The next day followed much the same pattern except that, knowing there would be no public transport, he found short cuts into work and arrived in town earlier than he had on Tuesday. There were even more bicycles and carts on the streets now and more cars offering lifts. Some had placards tied to the door handles saying, 'Give us a wave if you want a hitch' or 'Stop me and tell me where you want to go.' Others just drove slowly, offering lifts by shouting through open windows.

Boys who had never ridden in a car before and thought they

never would, now got lifts to school in Lagondas, Citroëns, Packhards, Lanchesters and thought that the general strike was the best thing that had ever happened.

So there was still a festive air, everyone friendly, everyone cooperative. There were plenty of policemen about but they were a benign presence.

'They're our mates, the police are,' he heard a man in a crowd of strikers say. 'We fought together in the trenches, they'd never turn against us, whatever the government said.'

Later that day, when he saw a lunchtime football match between strikers and police, both sides being bored with hanging about with nothing to do, he was reminded of those matches in the war when men on both sides had refused orders to try to kill each other on Christmas Day.

On Thursday morning he realized, as soon as he got near the town centre, that there were many more volunteers on the streets now. Lorries appeared with three men on board; one to drive, one to navigate, and a policeman. Volunteers, mainly students, were driving a few buses and trams through the town. Appealing for their help, the government had told them, 'If you can drive a car, you can drive a bus or a tram and even a train,' but passengers, thrown about as vehicles jerked erratically and took wrong turnings, were not so sure. Strikers gathered to watch their progress with interest.

As he left the office that evening, Sebastian found himself among a little crowd on the pavement. A bus had stalled, the volunteer, evidently used to having a self-starter in his own car, struggled with the starting handle. Bystanders cheered as he made repeated attempts to swing the handle until eventually the engine backfired and he was thrown down on the road.

'Poor young gentleman,' one of the strikers in the crowd remarked. 'No idea, 'as 'e? Almost meks yer feel yer should go and give 'im an 'and. Oh, and look at 'is lovely plus-fours, all greasy and torn.'

Sebastian, listening, wasn't sure if the words were spoken sardonically or not.

By Friday the mood seemed to be changing.

'It's these damned Special Constables,' Matthew told him. 'They've been volunteering for weeks in case there's a strike. They don't understand the working man the way the police do. They come of a different class.'

'You think it's a class matter?'

'Yes, I do. And the government's stirring things up. Look at this *British Gazette*, you know the paper the government's putting out? It says that the strikers want to take over the government, smash the constitution and bring the country to ruin. It's such nonsense, but there are people who'll believe it, you'll see.'

'I suppose,' Sebastian said slowly, 'there are always people who want to believe such things. And have you noticed how young all the volunteers are? These students were still in short trousers during the war. They didn't fight alongside working men as we did, never got to know them. And they seem to relish the prospect of a fight.'

'Young men do – unless they've been in a real one, as we were.'

They were quiet for a while.

'I don't know how it can end,' Sebastian said. 'The truth is that it's an industrial dispute and has nothing to do with politics.' He paused, then went on, 'But all the same non-strikers have to be taken to work, goods have to be kept moving, children have to get to school.'

Matthew laughed suddenly.

'Have you heard what some of the boys are doing? They get a lift in the grandest car they can and when the driver asks where they live, they say somewhere miles away, even if they live just round the corner.'

'Then walk all the way back?'

'They try to find another kind volunteer to take them home in another car. And even if they don't, they're happy to walk a few miles back. It's probably the only chance they'll ever get to ride in a car. So someone's getting a bit of fun out of the strike.'

'A lot of the volunteers are too, I'm afraid. And if I'm honest I must admit it would be great fun to drive a tram.'

Matthew nodded.

'I feel so divided,' he said. 'I sympathize with the miners and the strike, but on the other hand it's a real worry for the wives and mothers trying to keep their families fed and not knowing if there'll be enough food or if it'll all get expensive, like milk. I expect you've talked it over with Celia. What does she think?'

Sebastian hesitated. Loyalty forbade him to say it was quite impossible to talk about it with his wife, that they never discussed things as he and Matthew did.

'Oh, she's managing,' was all he said.

But that evening as they sat by their new wireless set, they heard the bulletin from the Home Secretary asking for fifty thousand more Special Constables to volunteer by Monday. Celia was jubilant.

'That will put the strikers in their place,' she said. 'And not before time. They're nothing but traitors and the government should have cracked down on them from the start.'

He knew it was hopeless, but in all conscience couldn't let her say these things unchallenged.

'They're not traitors, Celia. You shouldn't say that. Most of them fought in the war, all of them lost relatives. We owe them so much. The last thing they want is to overthrow a country they fought to save. It's an industrial dispute and it's the government – or rather a section of it – that's trying to make it political.'

'Well, I wish you were out there driving a tram like Mrs Sandford's husband,' was all she said.

He couldn't help thinking that she sounded remarkably like one of those ladies who handed out white feathers in the war.

At the weekend he showed her the archbishop's appeal for peace.

'Look,' he said, showing her *The Times*, reduced now to four pages, since the government had commandeered much of its stock of newsprint in order to have enough to produce many more copies of the *British Gazette* than they could sell. 'He is asking the mineowners to withdraw the wage cuts and the government to renew the subsidy for a while to allow things to be settled. That's reasonable and it's what half the cabinet wants, but a few firebrands are trying to make it seem like some kind of civil war. Surely you'll take a little notice of what the archbishop says?'

'It's not printed in the *British Gazette*,' she said, as if that somehow impugned its credibility.

It was true, it did not appear in the official government newspaper, nor was the British Broadcasting Company allowed to quote the archbishop's words on the news bulletins.

Sebastian looked at her. He didn't want this division between them. Perhaps, if she wouldn't listen to reasonable words from living people, she might be moved by the voices of the dead, he thought, thinking of Teddy, about whom he had never spoken to her.

'Celia,' he began. 'In the war, I got to know your cousin, Teddy Arndale. He was a very fine and intelligent man and I remember how he said to me that most officers like himself had a great deal to fight for. They were defending their acres of English soil. But the men, he said, what did they have that was worth defending? A miserable slum, yet they fought like tigers. What for? For their country, nothing else, for there was nothing in it for them.'

He paused, appealing to her. 'So surely you see that you should not call them traitors?'

'Maybe,' she said, 'but to tell the truth I've never had any time for the Arndales. It was my aunt who brought me up and did her duty by me and I know what *she* would have thought of these strikers.'

He gave up.

At church on Sunday the vicar prayed for both sides to be charitable towards each other and said that special services of intercession would be held each morning for half an hour as long as the industrial crisis lasted.

'I shan't go to them,' Celia said. 'And anyway somebody said the vicar had a brother who was a communist.'

On Monday he was surprised to see a tram making its way into town. Grateful, because he was later than usual this morning, he got on it. The cheerful conductor, wearing plus-fours and a college scarf, refused his money, said it was a pleasure and told him to hang on tight because the driver liked going fast. 'I volunteered to drive in the High Speed Motor Patrol,' he said. 'But its cars have to be able to do sixty miles per hour and mine won't go beyond the usual fifty-one.' He was quiet for a moment and then suddenly said, 'Don't you worry, we'll soon have these strikers wishing they'd never been born. What I'd really like to drive is a tank and smash my way through one of those mining villages.'

Sebastian, enraged, got off at the next stop and walked the rest of the way.

'But last week,' Matthew objected when he told him the story later, 'you said that the volunteers were doing a necessary job. I suppose that's what your conductor thought he was doing.'

'But not with such *relish*, Matthew, not with such relish.'

By evening there were many more trams and buses in the town, Matthew and Sebastian noticed as they came away from the city centre, sharing the first part of the walk home, neither of them wanting to use a volunteer-driven tram.

'Oh, how's it all going to end?' Sebastian asked suddenly.

'Badly for the strikers, I think,' Matthew told him and then went on, 'I had a telephone call from a cousin in Cambridge last night. He'd just done a forty-hour stretch at the docks in London, hundreds of volunteers went by river from Westminster Pier to King George V Dock. Took the pickets, who were guarding the gates, by surprise, of course. He said the military force was tremendous, Grenadier Guards at the buildings, then the convoy of lorries was escorted by armoured cars. There was nothing the strikers could do, they'd have been mown down, he said, if they'd tried to interfere with the lorries. So it seems to me that if the government is going to use that kind of force, the strikers can't win. The government's got all the propaganda on its side, all the machinery and organization. And the money. Union funds are running out, bound to. And rumour has it that the government's going to seize union funds anyway.'

'But they're still enthusiastic up here,' Sebastian protested. 'And in all the other industrial centres as far as one can make out.'

'Yes, but it's not up here that things will be decided.'

Matthew was right. Two days later the strike was declared at an end by the General Council because, 'through the magnificent support of the Trade Union Movement' a settlement of the mining problem had been secured.

Cheers broke out in the streets of Gradby at the news and plans were made for celebrations in the evening. But in the evening the Prime Minister made it clear that the strike had ended without any conditions being agreed by the government and next day the *British Gazette* reported triumphantly that the Prime Minister had received the surrender and the *Daily Mail* said the 'revolutionaries' had surrendered.

Celia was delighted.

'I don't expect they'll try anything like that again,' she exclaimed triumphantly after they had heard the news bulletin and turned off the Fellowes radio.

He said nothing for a moment. Part of him knew already, even after only three weeks, that it was hopeless to try to discuss anything that was important to him with his new wife; the strike had simply revealed the truth about the great differences between them. But he couldn't admit it to himself, couldn't give up, couldn't face the loneliness of life with a woman with whom he could never share his thoughts. But he loved and pitied one whose life had been hard so he said nothing and it was another three weeks before they talked again of the strike.

He had been out to Ugton again, ostensibly to look at some more land, actually to see if he could do anything for the Carters, having been entrusted with another envelope from Joe. It was not very well stuck down; he managed to slide in another ten shilling note, confident that Irene Carter would not be able to write a reply.

It was a hot day and there was a powerful stench from the earth closets in the backyard. Irene looked even thinner and paler than before and once again was overwhelmed with the contents of the envelope.

'I'll thank him for you,' he told her.

'Oh, would yer? Ah'd be that grateful. I'll mek yer a cup.'

She put the kettle to boil on the fire and found two cups. The room was grillingly hot. How did they survive? he wondered, looking at this one room in which the whole family lived, ate, cooked, washed. In the other room they all slept.

'How are you managing?' he asked, awkwardly.

'Our lad's goin' back next week. 'E's not the only one. Others 'ave gone back too. Needs must, folk understand. We was starving,' she said simply. 'Ah'd no milk for babby.'

'Do you get any help from outsiders?'

'There's some women come from t'church and bring soup for t'strikers' families, so we've bin goin' for that.'

He didn't stay long. The despair here was almost tangible. The bright sunshine did nothing to alleviate it; indeed the sun seemed, by its very harshness, to show up the stark poverty of the place.

As he went back home, he thought of what she had said about the women from the church and resolved to talk to Celia about it.

'I know you feel very strongly about the strikers, darling,' he said. 'But you must see that these men have no way of righting dreadful wrongs. The miners will struggle on alone but in the end they'll have to go back. Their despair is dreadful.'

'It's no excuse for trying to have a revolution,' she said.

'They weren't. Don't you see, they only have one weapon? The strike weapon. And they shouldn't have been forced to use it. They should have been allowed to negotiate, shouldn't have been locked out. It's not tolerable that the men who provide the wealth of this country should be treated like this. And be forced to live in such dreadful, abject poverty.'

He paused and then said, 'There seems to be some organization of the women of the churches to help the strikers' families. I wonder if you would like to find out more about it and perhaps offer to help?'

He knew as he spoke that it wasn't a very wise suggestion, but still part of him hoped that she might get involved in some charitable work, as his mother was.

'I think not, Sebastian,' she said. 'Besides I must take care of myself. I am expecting a baby.'

He stared at her, amazed not only at what she had said, but at the way she had said it, so coldly, as if this was some kind of weapon she was using against him.

'Celia, oh, Celia, my darling,' he said, going across and embracing her. 'It's wonderful. Of course we must take great care of you. Have you felt ill?'

'I was a little unwell this morning. I think it might be wiser if I slept by myself until the baby is born.'

Twenty-Two

'Oh, such news,' Elspeth Arndale said as she let her daughter into the house. 'Come along in, dear, and I'll show you. I've just this very moment been reading it to your father.'

Bemused, Diana followed her mother into the breakfast room of the dower house. Her father rose to greet her and then moved towards the door, clearly intent on barricading them all in.

'It's Celia, Diana,' Elspeth said, picking up *The Times* and pointing. 'Our dear Celia is a mother. So soon, isn't it? It must have been – well, never mind. But the great news is that she's had twins, a boy and a girl.'

Diana tried to keep calm, drink the coffee which she'd poured out for herself. She had no right to feel this pain.

'Does it give their names?' she made herself ask. 'Or perhaps they haven't decided yet.'

'Oh, yes. Listen. The girl is to be called Victoria Ethel. That will be after the late Queen, of course. It's so lovely that people can call their daughters Victoria now; nobody would have done so in the great queen's lifetime. It would have been taking a great liberty, but of course it's all right now. Victoria is a wonderful name.'

She paused and then said rather less enthusiastically, 'I don't care much for Ethel. Rather a servant's name, isn't it? But I imagine there must have been someone of that name on Selina's side. Selina is a much prettier name and her mother was such a heroine. A pity Celia didn't remember her in her daughter's name, don't you think?'

I'd rather the poor little thing was given a servant's name

than one of a liar and a cheat like Selina, Diana thought but didn't, of course, say.

'And the boy?' she asked instead.

'Arthur James. Arthur will be after dear Sebastian's father, of course.'

She took a sip of coffee, then put the cup down suddenly.

'Just think, Barbara and Arthur will be grandparents. Won't they be delighted? And I shall be, well, I shall be a great aunt.' She smiled bravely. 'Better than nothing, I suppose.'

Diana flinched.

'Oh, dear, I only meant, well, I mean . . .'

'I know what you meant, Mother.'

'I mean I'm not suggesting in any way that . . . of course, it's entirely up to you.'

Diana sat very still. A part of her wanted to cry out, '*But it's not up to me*'. A part of her wanted to give in to grief, fall on her mother's shoulder and cry all the unshed tears, weep for the disappointment until she was exhausted and then lie there and be comforted. But that was only a part of her. The other part was made of sterner stuff.

'I must go, Mother,' she said, getting up. 'There's a pile of correspondence to deal with for James.'

'I wonder if they chose the second name, James, after *our* James?' her mother suggested.

'Why should they?'

'Well, everyone has such admiration for James, my dear. And Sebastian was also helping soldiers, was he not? So they have something in common.'

They have nothing in common, she thought, though once perhaps they might have had me in common.

'Oh, Diana, I wonder if they might have the christening down here? It's such a long time since we had a family celebration at Northrop, isn't it? Your father and I were married here and so were Selina and William, because your grandmama wished it, and then all the children were christened here. I'd so like to think that the next generation might be so too.'

'I imagine that Celia would prefer to have the christening at her own church, where they were married.'

'Yes, perhaps you're right. It's odd perhaps that they didn't tell us that they were expecting a baby, but we have been rather out of touch since your father's illness in the autumn and then of course they may have had anxieties over Celia's health.'

She is so good, her daughter thought, at finding alternative reasons whenever the real one might be hurtful. Celia simply does not want to know us.

'Now the next thing we must think of is christening presents for the twins. A little mug each, do you think? With their names inscribed?'

'Whatever you think suitable, Mother.'

'Of course we don't want to give the same as Sebastian's parents, do we? Perhaps I should consult them before I decide what to give.'

Sebastian's parents also saw the announcement in *The Times* though, having been forewarned, they read it more calmly.

'If they'd called the lad Albert, they'd have been V and A,' Arthur remarked, feeling that Barbara would like him to make some comment.

Perhaps it was the wrong comment, because his wife ignored it.

'I'm so pleased,' she said, 'that Sebastian has called his son after you.'

'Can't remember why we called him Sebastian. Anything to do with the saint chappie that got himself spiked with arrows?'

'No, it was after your uncle Sebastian, the Admiral.'

'So it was. Old Uncle Seb, sailor chappie. Bit pompous but heart of gold. Came up trumps and gave a generous christening present, I remember.'

'Oh, presents! We must think what to get for the twins. What did you say your uncle gave Sebastian?'

'A thousand pounds.'

'Goodness me, that *was* generous.'

'Well, admirals are never short of a bob or two. Can't equal that, I'm afraid, not after getting them the house.'

'No, of course not. They wouldn't expect it. Besides, I think a silver present is much more suitable for a baby.'

'Good,' her husband said, getting up suddenly. 'I'll go and see what's surplus to requirements in the butler's pantry.'

'No, dear,' she said firmly. 'I've seen just the thing in Johnstone the Jewellers. Lovely spoon-and-pusher sets in little velvet-lined boxes. Very pretty and very useful.'

'Spoon-and-pusher? What do you intend they should spoon and push?'

'Their food, of course, Arthur! They're wonderfully designed to make it easier for children to feed themselves. The spoon has a very short handle so it's easier for babies to get it into their mouths and the pusher is like a little hoe, which they hold in their other hand to push the food on to the spoon.'

Her husband was hovering by the door.

'It seems such a waste not to use up some of the stuff we've already got,' he pointed out.

'No,' she told him firmly. 'Come back and sit down. You really cannot dump old fish servers and such things on these poor little mites.'

'They've got the fish servers already. But there's that small bore shooting goblet, all manner of cups and at least a dozen silver napkin rings nobody uses.'

'Give them cups with inscriptions about small bores? Really, Arthur!'

'Jewellers can soon gouge out inscriptions and scratch something else on instead. That's what burglars have done for years.'

Sister Vera Tomkin settled the second twin down in his cradle.

'There now, Master Arthur,' she said. 'You just go off to sleep like your sister. And we'll give your mother a nice cup of tea so that she can have a nice sleep.'

Three decades of working as a monthly nurse had done nothing to suppress Sister Vera's natural garrulity. Sebastian sometimes wondered if she left behind her a trail of demented young parents as she went from client to client. At other times he was sure of it. She was capable and tireless, but oh how he longed for her to go. She was one of those people, he had quickly realized, that are so willing, so determined to please that they make you feel guilty for not loving them as they deserve. She must surely be the original of the lady who had every virtue and only one fault: she was intolerable.

'There now, Mr Crawley,' she said now as she met him on the landing. 'I've put both the babies down and Mrs Crawley is going to have a nice little sleep. So I shall go to my room, such a nice room, I must say and I am very grateful for it, because some are much less so, though of course I never complain. Then, if that is acceptable to you, I shall have a nice little rest myself in order to get strength for the night.'

'Of course you must rest. I'm afraid you must get very tired after all these disturbed nights.'

'Oh, Mr Crawley, you must never think that, kind though it is of you. It is my duty and my pleasure to lift the babies when they cry at two o'clock in the morning and take them to Mrs Crawley to be nursed.'

'Perhaps I could do that for you one night?'

'Oh, dear me, no! That would never do. The master of the house must have his rest.'

Sebastian, who didn't feel as if he was master of anything, least of all this household, reflected that he would really love to get up in the blessed silence of the night and lift his little son and daughter.

'Oh, no,' Sister Vera was saying, 'the breadwinner cannot have his rest disturbed. Oh, dear me, no. I am attuned to it, it is part of my job. Sometimes I feel a little sad to have to wake Mrs Crawley when she is sleeping soundly but she always awakens quickly to nurse the babies. She is a lovely mother, she will always do her duty by your children. There is no mistake about that.'

'Yes, I'm sure. And we're very grateful to you. Do go and rest.'

'Yes, I shall, immediately I have seen to Mrs Crawley,'

and she bustled off in the direction of what had now become Celia's bedroom.

He waited until she was out of sight before going quietly into the nursery though he knew it was ridiculous to feel she might disapprove of his going to look at his own children.

Once inside, he forgot all about her in the wonder he always felt when he gazed at these sleeping babies. They were so perfect, so tiny, so composed, their skin so delicate, their eyelids so translucent. Their lips still made little sucking movements as if in their dreamworld they were still at their mother's breast.

He thought of Celia. How stoically she had borne it all! Fourteen pounds the two of them together, what a weight to carry. How bravely she had faced the trauma of the double birth. She had looked so pale and fragile when he had been allowed in to see her afterwards, so childlike. He felt a great rush of tenderness for her, all his old protective love seemed to flood back and, as he took her hand, bent over her and kissed her brow, he was suddenly quite sure that all would be well between them now that they had so much that was precious to share.

But it hadn't been like that since, not with Sister Vera in the house. She and Celia were in charge of the babies. Well, that was understandable. But they were in their closed world and he was shut out. He sometimes felt as if, having performed his function of begetting, he was no longer of any significance in the family, except as the breadwinner. That was how Sister Vera viewed fathers, maybe that was how Victorian fathers used to be, but he longed to be a real father, not some remote figure uninvolved in the minutiae of their little lives. That is what he would be when Sister Vera left, then he and Celia would share responsibility and all would be well between them.

Looking back afterwards, it seemed to Sebastian that the graph of his marriage was a series of little rises and dips, marking the times of hope and of subsequent disillusion, but that, for all these intermediate ups and downs, the curve was irreversibly downwards.

Yet how real had been the moments of hope! How glad he had been when Sister Vera had packed her bags after doing her month's duty, how full of hope as he drove her to the station on a bright sunny morning that felt more like May than February. She had talked all the way, explaining how she had established the babies' routine and how she had shortened them, as she put it rather to his surprise until he realized that it was their baby robes that were shortened and not the twins themselves.

After he had seen her on to the train, he had driven home light-hearted with relief that now they were a proper family, a family of four, on their own at last.

'Oh, it's so good to be on our own again,' he said as he joined Celia in the drawing room, taking both her hands in his.

'It's all very well for you,' she told him, 'but I shall miss her help.'

'I'll help you, darling. I want to help in any way I can.'

She made a dismissive little gesture with her hand.

'Men don't understand these things,' she said.

Sarah knocked at the door.

'One of 'em's cryin', m'm. I think it's Miss Victoria.'

Celia looked at her watch.

'It's thirty-five minutes until feedtime is due,' she said. 'So we shall ignore the crying.'

The cries were more audible now that the door was open.

'Shall I go and pick her up, darling, just carry her about a little until you're ready?'

'No, we must keep to the timetable. You may go, Sarah.'

After the maid had gone, she got up and took a book off the table.

'This is the book Sister Vera recommended,' she said. 'It's by Dr Truby King. He advocates internal discipline. It's all very scientific, Sister Vera says. They must learn to keep to a strict timetable. And there is this other mothercraft manual by

Mabel Liddiard, which says the same of potty training. That too must be disciplined.'

'Potty training? Good heavens!'

'There is no need to swear and if you don't believe me I can show you what she writes.'

'Of course I believe you, but—'

'Here on page 26: "Strict potty training results in self-control, obedience, the recognition of authority and, later, respect for elders."'

'They'll respect us because they've been strictly potty trained? Celia, that's absurd.'

'Sebastian, these people are experts, Sister Vera is an expert. You know nothing about babies.'

He wanted to tell her that instinct had guided parents for generations, wanted to tell her that they should be free to love their children, he wanted to tell her – oh, what did he want to tell her? He didn't want a whole lot of experts and Sister Veras to get between him and his children.

'I'll go up and sit with them,' he said, getting up and making for the door.

'Don't pick them up,' she warned, 'or you'll upset their routine.'

'No,' he replied with unaccustomed coldness, 'I'll just tell them they'll be fed in twenty minutes, or maybe it's eighteen by now,' he added and went upstairs.

Sarah was right; it was Victoria who was crying. He pulled a chair up alongside her cot and gave her his little finger to suck.

'I'm sorry, little one,' he told her. 'It's just a temporary measure, but the best I can offer.'

She latched on to it gratefully, sucked and was silent. He sat crouched beside her, watching her, but now and then glancing around at the nursery. He had decorated it himself and there was nothing of Grimsdykerie in it. With its white paintwork, its wallpaper brightly patterned with flowers and animals, its colourful curtains, it was easily the most cheerful room in the house. He had been determined that the twins' first view of the world should be a cheerful one. In the rest of the house he had failed.

'Why buy new when we have perfectly good furniture and curtains already?' Celia had asked. 'How can you be so extravagant?' The paintwork she had determinedly kept dark. 'Brown doesn't show the dirt like cream or white, Sebastian,' she'd said. 'It is much more *practical.*'

It seemed absurd that he, who spent so much of his time planning to make homes that were agreeable for other people, should have so little say about the character of his own home.

Their tastes were so different, he reflected as he sat quietly in the nursery. And it wasn't just about furnishing and decorating their home that he and Celia differed, but about practically everything. At first he couldn't accept that it was so. He had taken her to the City art gallery, one of the best outside London, as he had so often dreamed of doing, but the great paintings left her unmoved. Apart from a few crucifixions, she bestowed on each picture a look of incomprehension unless they displayed any nudity or even a baby Jesus at his mother's breast, in which case she hurried past after a cursory and disapproving glance and then opined that she preferred the ones at home.

It was the same with books; he had dreamed of evenings together reading by the fire. When she was pregnant he would make her sit down, her feet on a stool, and read aloud to her. Everyone likes to be read to, he'd thought; he would read the classics and then maybe current favourites, like H. G. Wells. But she had made it plain that she regarded this as a waste of time and, if she must rest, she would rather play patience. So in the end he took to spending his evenings in the study working, as he had done in the days when he lived with Mrs Jordan.

It was as if they were both reverting to the way they had lived before they were married. With that sense of fairness which had always weakened him, he tried to see it from her point of view: she had married a man whose views were strange to her, who was trying to push unfamiliar and unpalatable ideas at her, things she didn't want or care for. And after all, it was he who had insisted on marrying her. Left alone she would probably have eventually married someone much more suitable. He was older and should have been wiser. The least he could do now was to try to make amends by going gently with her, especially now that she had borne his children.

It hurt him all the same that she didn't value beauty: poetry, music, art left her unmoved, there was no spark of recognition, nothing in it aroused her. And not only did she not value beauty in her surroundings, she neglected it in herself. She still insisted on not wearing her 'best', so that his vision of her ceased to be attractive and became simply dowdy. He bought her little gifts of jewellery, which she did not wear, of scarves that she put away in a drawer.

All these thoughts, a mixture of guilt, sorrow and resentment, were in his mind as he sat in the nursery and watched his daughter sucking at his little finger. Then, at last realizing that it was not what she wanted, grievance filled her eyes, her mouth pulled away and puckered, her expression clouded ready for the storm and, ten minutes before the time allotted for her feed, she began to yell, being too young to appreciate the benefits of the Truby King method.

Twenty-Three

Sebastian came home early on their first wedding anniversary. He had brought her flowers, chocolates and a little make-up box and gave them to her as they sat by the fire, he with a glass of sherry, she with a glass of vitax, a non-alcoholic drink recommended by Sister Vera.

'Here's to our second year,' he said, raising his glass to her and praying that it might be happier than the first, telling himself that the first year must be a time of adjustment and that it behoved him to make this marriage work, for it had been his idea in the first place.

She had put the flowers in a vase already and now opened the chocolates.

'We'll keep them for after dinner, shall we?' she said. 'Thank you, Sebastian,' and she gave him such a sweet smile that he wanted to get up and kiss her, but knew all too well that it would only make her turn from him.

Then she unwrapped the second little parcel.

She looked at the contents with horror.

'Powder!' she exclaimed. 'Lipstick! Stuff which prostitutes use to paint their faces!'

Her face was contorted with rage and disgust, unrecognizable as the face which had looked at him so sweetly just now.

'Do you want me to be a harlot?' she demanded. 'Is that what you want your wife to be? A woman of the streets?' and she threw the little box into the fire.

Taken aback by this outburst of fury, he could only stare at her aghast.

'I don't know what my aunt would have said,' she raged

on, 'that you should have wanted to turn her niece into a painted woman.'

'No, no, Celia. It's not like that at all. You mustn't say such dreadful things. Lots of respectable women wear a little make-up now. I know Mrs Jordan does and—'

'So you want me to behave like a landlady now? When am I supposed to start taking in lodgers?'

'Please, Celia, don't talk nonsense. I only wanted you to make the best of yourself.'

'I shall go upstairs. I need some time on my own before we go out.'

After she had gone, he sat very still by the fire, his head in his hands, given up to despair as his little present flared and melted in the flames. Then he told himself that she was overtired, she would be better, more reasonable, when she stopped breast feeding; women have so much to bear that it must take its toll emotionally. But he dreaded the evening ahead.

She was more composed when she came down and the evening passed pleasantly, she praised the food in the restaurant and was even persuaded to have a glass of wine. The episode of the make-up box, he told himself, had just been one of those dips in the graph of their marriage, quickly followed by this peak when all was well between them.

When they came home she almost apologized.

'What you did was wrong, Sebastian,' she told him, 'but I should not have reacted as I did. I should simply have handed it back to you. For that I am sorry.'

He smiled and felt strangely relieved at being forgiven for what he had never envisaged as a sin.

They went up to the nursery together to give the twins their ten o'clock feed although normally she didn't let him watch. He held little Arthur while Victoria was fed and then was allowed to take his baby daughter, gorged and full of wind, and hold her against his shoulder, patting her back. In return his daughter posseted copiously over his jacket and they both laughed and Celia smiled and handed him a nappy to mop himself. Then together they tucked the babies up in their cradles and stayed, watching them as they slept and he took Celia's hand and, still holding hands, they walked along the corridor to Celia's room where she let him into her bed.

'Goodness me,' Elspeth exclaimed. 'Another baby! Poor little Celia, three babies in two years. Rather too soon, don't you think, Diana?'

Diana nodded, thinking what a passionate marriage theirs must be. How unlike her own.

'And this time, I gather, the christening will be at the Crawleys' house. They have invited us to go for the day and stay overnight. I think we should go, don't you, James?'

Her son-in-law nodded.

'It would give me a chance for a good talk with young Crawley,' he said. 'Once or twice recently I've thought to myself that I'd like to have his advice about houses for the disabled. Yes, certainly let's go.'

'And I'll stay behind and look after Father,' Diana volunteered.

'Oh, no, dear. Your papa will come with us. The little change will do him good.'

'But you know he hates change, Mamma.'

'Well, there are changes and changes,' her mother told her enigmatically.

James laughed.

'And this will be the right sort of change, will it? It's no use, Diana, she has made up her mind to go, so you might as well give in gracefully. I have a very determined mother-in-law.'

He took Elspeth's hand in his for a moment, and she shook her head at him and told him he was dreadful. And Diana thought how well they got on together now, despite an inauspicious start. It struck her, as she looked at them, that James was nearer in age to her mother than he was to herself and that a stranger, coming in on the three of them sitting together like this, might take them for a married couple and their grown-up daughter.

'Then I shall accept Barbara's kind invitation to stay. I shall see to it immediately.'

'You could come across and use our telephone,' James suggested.

'No, I don't care for the instrument. Besides, it would be discourteous not to write a written reply to a written invitation,' she told him firmly.

'I think you were very clever, Arthur dear, to persuade them to come down here for the christening,' Barbara Crawley said as she went with her husband into the conservatory from where they would get a good view of the front drive when their family drove up. 'I mean considering how adamant they were last time about having it up there.'

'Powers of persuasion, my dear, powers of persuasion. Never underestimate my powers of persuasion.'

He didn't tell her that, knowing how much she wanted the christening to be held here, he had somewhat exaggerated the minor illness she had had at Christmas, thereby contriving to suggest to Sebastian that it was almost his mother's dying wish.

'The garden's looking pretty good,' he said instead, putting his arm round his wife's waist. 'That drop of rain this morning has freshened it up. Speaking of which, I wouldn't mind a drop of something myself.'

'It's a bit early, isn't it?' she demurred, glancing at her watch.

'As soon as the sun goes down over the yardarm, as Uncle Seb used to say. And an admiral should know,' he added, picking up the whisky decanter. 'You?'

'No, thank you, dear. They may arrive any time now. Oh, it will be so lovely to have a houseful of young people again.'

'Got enough room, have we? Bedrooms and so on?'

'Goodness, I never thought of that! Is there time to put up a tent in the vegetable garden?'

For a moment he was deceived, then he laughed and putting down his drink, put his arms around her.

'You still tease like a sixteen-year-old,' he told her.

'I'll tell you what I've arranged,' she said, when he'd released her. 'Celia and Sebastian have the choice of the pink bedroom with the double bed, or the blue bedroom with the twin beds. The Arndales can have the other one when they arrive tomorrow. And I've put James and Diana in the double room on the second floor; being younger and free of children the extra flight of stairs won't trouble them. Sarah will go in with Annie and Rosie as before. Then I've put the twins' cots in the dressing room between the other two double bedrooms on the first floor and the cradle in with Sebastian and Celia. I'm so glad we hoarded all our baby things.'

'You're a great hoarder, my dear. Think of all that silver hoarded in the butler's pantry! It might be a good idea to give the new baby something from it. There's a silver cocktail swizzler in there and one of those gadgets the Victorians used for slicing off the top of a boiled egg. And much more, enough to keep us in christening presents for years. Just as well, with them breeding like rabbits. Can't keep up with 'em. Remind me what this one's called?'

'Deborah, such a pretty name. I expect she'll get shortened to Debbie, but that's pretty too. Deborah Gertrude.'

'Good Lord! *Gertrude*, what a name! Wherever did they get it from? We don't have any Gertrudes, do we?'

'No. Apparently it's a friend of Celia's who is going to be godmother. She can't come to the christening, but when that happens the parents just take the vows for her.'

'With a name like Gertrude I'm not surprised she didn't want to show up.'

'Don't go saying things like that in front of Celia. She is evidently a close friend, but I am a little surprised that they didn't ask Celia's cousin Diana to be godmother, especially since she's no children of her own.'

She stopped. She'd been about to say that it would have been kind to give Diana a share in Celia's blessings, but then, remembering her earlier unease about Sebastian's feelings for Diana, said instead, 'Well, I just hope the three of them don't cry all the way through the service.'

'What Celia, Elspeth and Diana?'

'Of course not. I meant the babies. Women cry at weddings, babies at baptisms. And that reminds me, Arthur. The christening will be at the end of morning prayer. Do you think you could make it less obvious that you're reading throughout the sermon?'

'I can't hear a word the chappie says, Barbara. I have to read. And dammit, I do read the Bible and the prayer book. It's not as if I'm taking some lurid thriller in with me.'

'I'm not suggesting that you are, just that you should read more discreetly. And not make any noise about it. I mean it must be very disconcerting for the vicar to hear you laugh when he hasn't said anything funny.'

'Well, some of the things one reads really are extraordinary and people should be alerted to them. Did you know that the church doesn't allow me to marry my grandfather's widow?'

'Did you ever want to?'

'No, but it's the principle of the thing.'

'I suppose the rules were laid down to prevent too much interbreeding.'

'Maybe. But then the prayer book says I can't marry my deceased wife's sister either. And she's not a blood relation. Furthermore I came across an old law – can't remember where, Leviticus possibly – which said that a man has to take unto himself his dead brother's wife and lie with her.'

'That would be to give her children to care for her in her old age.'

'Well, yes, it was a bit before the time of old age pensions. But you get my point. Front end says you've got to get into bed with your brother's widow who doesn't have an old age pension and the back end forbids it.'

'What nonsense you talk! Front end and back end indeed! These rules were laid down for different societies in different ages.'

'It needs clarifying all the same. People just don't realize. I mean you wouldn't want me to impregnate your widowed sister, would you, Barbara?'

'I haven't got a sister.'

'Good Lord, nor you have. But a chap who takes his religion seriously should think twice before marrying a woman with three or four sisters. It's a bit of a responsibility.'

'I should try to forget about it, if it upsets you so, dear. Just think about our new granddaughter instead.'

'You know what I think? I think we should give Deborah

Gertrude that silver cocktail swizzle stick for her christening present. In a few years she'll be going to these cocktail parties the way all the young people do and she'll be very glad of it. You mark my words. You're not listening.'

'I think I heard a car.'

'I can't hear anything.'

'Because you're deaf, dear,' she said as the sound of car wheels on gravel grew louder.

'No, I'm not. Just a bit hard of hearing. I'd manage well enough if people didn't keep mumbling. Good Lord, here they are. What a car, eh!'

The Lagonda was packed with babies and their trappings. Celia sat in the front with Deborah on her knee. The twins were in the back with Sarah, who sat with her legs balanced on cases on the floor and an arm round each small, wriggling child.

Sebastian got out, stretched and then embraced his mother, who had run down to welcome them. Then he held her away from him, looking anxiously into her face.

'How are you, Mother? I hope this isn't going to be too much for you after your illness?'

'Illness?'

'Yes, at Christmas.'

'It was just a cold. I'm very well.'

'You certainly look it,' he said, turning to shake hands with his father while Barbara went round to help Celia.

'She puts a brave face on it, my boy,' his father told him. 'Probably doesn't realize how ill she was. Better now, of course, and all the better for seeing you all. Now what can I carry? I'll get Parker to take the cases in.'

There was a flurry as they all emerged from the car; the two maids came and helped Sarah with the twins, Parker took the cases out of the boot, Barbara explained that Cook had boiled a marrow bone and made gravy and seived carrots and potatoes all ready for the twins' tea and Celia could come and choose where to sleep and everyone must be longing for a cup of tea, mustn't they.

Celia chose the twin-bedded room and prepared to feed the

baby there, while the twins sat on high chairs in the breakfast room and splashed their silver spoons and pushers into their mess of gravied vegetables, getting a little of it into their mouths and a lot on to their faces and into their hair, watched by Sarah who could hardly contain her pride in them when Rosie and Annie stole in briefly as they ran about the house, taking tea up to Celia, laying up the dining-room table and helping Cook in the kitchen.

Meanwhile Sebastian sat with his father in the drawing room, where Elspeth soon joined them.

'It's amazing how young people manage with so little help nowadays,' she said. 'You tell me Celia just has Sarah and a daily woman. No nanny, no cook, goodness when I think of the staff we had!'

'Houses are smaller now, Mother, and much easier to run with all these modern devices. And we're lucky in the help we do have. Mrs Lettuce comes in every day and sees to the cleaning and helps with the cooking and Sarah has grown into somebody we can really rely on and she adores the children, but is quite firm with them.'

'But, darling, she's only a *maid*, not a nanny.'

'The babes don't seem to know the difference.'

'But they will.'

'It's the way you young people get about that amazes me,' Arthur put in. 'And you seem to do it all yourself, my boy. When we went away the coachman saw to it all, didn't he, Barbara?'

'And the footmen looked after the luggage, packed it all in and unloaded everything when we arrived. Ah, come along in, Celia, dear. Are the twins settled?'

'Yes, thank you.'

'Then we'll dine early, for you must both be very tired and we've a busy day tomorrow. It's a shame the Arndales can't join us tonight, but James has an important meeting, so they'll leave home early in the morning and arrive in time for the service.'

'It's a long way from Gloucestershire. What sort of car has he got, Mother?'

Barbara laughed.

'My dear boy, what an extraordinary question. I've no idea what kind of car James has and I shouldn't dream of asking him such a personal question.'

'People do ask such things nowadays, Mother.'

'Oh, some people might, but it isn't the sort of thing a well-bred person would enquire into,' she told him as she led the way into the dining room.

Meanwhile Sarah settled herself in the kitchen, helping Cook to dish up while Rosie and Annie journeyed to and fro to the dining room, where they reported that young Mrs Crawley wasn't saying much and had brought some funny stuff of her own to drink which looked a bit like medicine but the rest of them were enjoying their wine and talking ten to the dozen, the master not always talking about the same thing as the others but then that was just to be expected with him not hearing as much as he should. Mr Sebastian was looking older, but then he'd got a wife and three children now and that was enough to make anybody go grey.

Afterwards they sat down to their own supper in the kitchen and Sarah told them all about the house in Gradby and the twins. And how lovely the nursery was, oh, if only they could see it. Mr Crawley had seen to it himself and there were lots of pictures for the twins to look at and interesting toys to play with and he'd got books for them already although Mrs Crawley said they were too young for books. She didn't think her master and mistress always saw eye to eye, but the master was such a kind person and loyalty forbade her to say more.

The objects of their discussions had by now finished their coffee, settled arrangements for the morrow and were preparing for the night. As he went upstairs, Sebastian reflected on how good it felt to be home again, for this still seemed like home to him, warm, cheerful and welcoming and he realized that he had subconsciously been trying to recreate this atmosphere in his own home with Celia, just as much as she, poor girl, had been trying to recreate the familiar atmosphere of Ten, Waterloo Road.

Twenty-Four

They all agreed that the christening had gone off very happily. In the absence of the godparents, her parents had promised on Deborah's behalf to renounce the devil and all his works, the vain pomp and glory of the world and the carnal desires of the flesh. As the water was poured over her head, Deborah had cried just once, loudly and briefly, which was, the vicar told them afterwards, a good sign; it showed that the devil was coming out of the child.

'Mind you,' Arthur Crawley remarked to his wife as they walked home. 'Without those carnal desires of the flesh, there wouldn't have been any baby to baptize.'

Diana, alongside them, laughed.

'That's just the sort of thing my brother Rupert would say,' she told them.

'Oh, hello, my dear, didn't see you there. Probably wouldn't have spoken like that if I had.'

'But aren't the words beautiful in the Edward VI prayer book?' his wife put in. '"The Vain Pomp and Glory of the World." Isn't it wonderful? So simple and strong. We don't write prose like that any more.'

'No, that's true, Barbara. Prose isn't what it was. Writer chappies aren't so good as they were. Though,' he added as an afterthought, 'I must say I enjoy Edgar Wallace.'

Diana stayed with them. She loved the way they talked, and anyway clung to them in an effort not to be with Sebastian and Celia. At lunchtime she was placed on Arthur Crawley's right, Celia on his left with Sebastian next to his wife. He looked, she thought, much older than he had at the wedding; not surprising after becoming the father of three babies so soon.

And yet there was always that remoteness between him and Celia, who still looked aloof, not in a proud kind of way, just cold and withdrawn. They were so unlike Sebastian's parents whose constant chat, bickering and *closeness*, she found enchanting. Arthur was now criticizing the lesson in church.

'All that stuff, on and on, about Uriah the Hittite. What was poor little Deborah to make of all that about a commander sending a chap to his death so he could sleep with his wife? What a thing to have brought to your attention before you're dunked.'

'She wasn't *dunked*, darling. The water was just splashed gently on to her face. And the vicar can't choose suitable lessons. He has to read whatever is ordained to be read on that particular Sunday.'

'All the same, principle of the thing. And you know, during the sermon I was reading Leviticus, as I often do, and came across the laws about animals being legally punished for their crimes.'

'No!'

'Oh, yes, he's quite right,' James put in. 'And animals went on being tried until quite recent times. Pigs especially. I suppose because they lived so close to people in bygone days. A pig was hanged for sacrilege in the fourteenth century for going into a church and eating a consecrated wafer.'

'You're making this up, James,' his mother-in-law put in.

'No, I promise you it's true. And it was all done very correctly. The animals had the same rights as human beings. Evidence was taken, witnesses called, a lawyer was appointed to defend them. When a mad bull gored a man to death, the bull's defence lawyer argued that the bull, being a mad bull, couldn't be held responsible for its actions. So it was found not guilty.'

'Fascinating, fascinating,' Arthur murmured. 'Mind you, I've always agreed with the chap who said the law was an ass.'

'Speaking of which,' James went on, now thoroughly

launched, 'there was the case of the man who was accused of bestiality—'

'That's frowned on in Leviticus,' Arthur put in.

'He was put on trial. The donkey also was accused and both were to be hanged. But the donkey was lucky. It had worked for a convent and the nuns came to court and gave evidence that he was a very hard-working donkey of excellent moral character. So the donkey was reprieved.'

Arthur guffawed, Sebastian and Diana laughed, Celia looked shocked. Elspeth thought it a very unsuitable tale and wondered if her son-in-law had partaken of rather too much champagne, and Barbara changed the conversation by saying how much the law had been improved in this enlightened century, particularly as far as women were concerned, and soon they were reminiscing about the suffragettes. She didn't mind what they talked about, really, so long as it didn't concern bestiality and donkeys.

Towards the end of the meal, James, to Diana's horror, leaned towards Sebastian and said, 'How about coming back with us to Northrop for a day, Crawley? I'd like to show you around our place and talk over a few plans with you. It's a pity not to come when you're down south.'

Sebastian hesitated.

'It's very kind of you and I should be very interested to see what you're doing, but I think I should perhaps stay and help—'

'Oh, no, Sebastian,' Celia cut in. 'Do go. I can manage perfectly well with Sarah. There's really nothing you can do to help.'

It was true; he knew it. He was useful as a chauffeur, no more, no less.

'You certainly won't be short of volunteers to look after the lovely twins, Celia dear,' Barbara Crawley put in. 'Apart from us doting grandparents, Rosie and Annie can't wait to be asked to help. They're both absolutely besotted with Victoria and Arthur.'

He could think of no way out of it. He glanced at Diana but she was looking determinedly out of the window.

So he accepted as gracefully as he could.

'Why don't you take Diana in your car?' James suggested as they set off the next day. 'Be a bit of company for you and she can put you right about which roads to take if you lose track of me. Charles and Elspeth will be happy with me.'

Charles was always surprisingly relaxed in cars. He seemed to lose his restlessness and, once having made sure that the doors were locked, sat back and gazed out at the surrounding countryside with evident enjoyment of the beauty that was being unreeled for his entertainment.

The rest of the house party stood on the steps and watched as the two cars set off. Diana and Sebastian, in the second car, waved briefly before disappearing down the drive.

They did not speak for a while, then they both started at once.

'How did you get on in the strike?' Diana began.

'Do you mix much with the men, socially, I mean?' Sebastian asked at the same time. They both stopped and laughed.

'Your question first,' Sebastian said. 'Well, as you can imagine it was pretty tense up there, as it was in all the industrial towns. People were very divided. Some swallowed the government propaganda that it was a conspiracy to bring down the constitution and loved the idea of a fight, but most knew that it was a desperate effort to save the miners from starvation. It left a lot of bitterness. I suppose down here you were hardly aware of it?'

'It scarcely touched us at all. I think that was true in all the towns and villages in South West England. There were no newspapers of course, the government news sheet didn't get to Northrop, nor did the workers' paper. The ex-soldiers here were very interested. To a man they supported the miners. I think most of the men who'd fought in the war did. I know Teddy would have done.'

They were quiet for a moment, both remembering her brother, and he thought how different her reaction to the strike had been from Celia's with her endless condemnation while it was going on and her triumph when it failed.

'Yes, it was the young chaps who hadn't been in the war who were most belligerent,' he said at last. 'And of course they loved driving trams and buses. What young man wouldn't? But go on about how it was down here.'

'We had the wireless and James got me to take the news bulletins down in shorthand and then type them up with six or seven copies to distribute. He couldn't resist adding a little editorial of his own, giving both sides' points of view because we were all sickened by the government propaganda and the way they controlled all the information that went out.'

'So you can type?'

'Oh, yes. James made sure that I got my full nursing qualifications *and* did a Pitman's shorthand and typing course so that I'd be a really useful wife.'

There was an edge in her voice when she spoke the words. He glanced at her, but there was no bitterness in the face she turned towards him.

'You were asking about how much I mixed with the men. Well, of course I know them all well and we're good friends. James often has a meal with them, but I feel they'd find the presence of a wife a bit inhibiting, so I don't intrude.'

'And have they all been there since the war?'

'Almost all, but a lot have left, you know. Some were able to go home to their parents, some married. I do admire the women who take them. We explain to them what is involved and how hard it will be, but they seem to manage and be very happy as far as we can tell. Some live nearby and we see them often, but they all keep in touch. Of course it's so much better for the men, a much more natural life than all living together here. James hopes that by the time he retires there won't be any more need for the centre as it is now.'

They talked more easily after that and the silences, when they came, were companionable. It's going to be all right, Sebastian thought, relaxing at the wheel. Diana, alongside him, was thinking the same.

That evening James took Sebastian to share the men's meal, while Diana went back to the dower house with her parents. She was back home and asleep before they returned.

James devoted the next day to showing Sebastian around; he watched the men in the gym, saw what was being done in the garden, visited the few who had rented flats or cottages on the outskirts of the former estate, had lunch with the men and only saw Diana in the evening.

'I have to go over to Cheltenham,' James said as they had dinner. 'Sorry to abandon you, Sebastian, but Diana will keep you amused, won't you, my dear?'

'Of course, but I thought you'd miss the meeting, with Sebastian here.'

'Afraid I can't do that. Important board. You understand, don't you, Sebastian?'

'Yes, of course. I'm very grateful for the time you gave me today.'

'Oh, that was a pleasure. There's nothing I like better than showing off what we do at Northrop, is there, Diana?'

She nodded and he pecked her on the cheek, said he'd see them both in the morning and left them.

She made more coffee and they settled down on the sofa by the fire, for the evening had turned chilly.

'So how did you enjoy today?' she asked. 'Was it as you expected?'

He sighed.

'Sadder,' he said. 'All the men here are more badly hurt than the ones we've rehoused and goodness knows they're damaged enough.'

'Well, obviously we're here to help the ones who most need help.'

'Quite.'

He paused and then went on, 'I was amazed at what they can do in the gym – and in the garden. But I think visiting the married ones was the most touching of all. The wives were so cheerful, so incredibly brave. It's going to be a lifetime of caring and they must know it won't get easier. And no marriage is easy anyway,' he added.

She looked at him and nodded.

There was something so sad, so resigned in her expression

that he could only look back at her in wonder. Then, 'You're not happy,' he heard himself say.

She didn't turn away, but said nothing.

'Any help to talk about it? To an old friend?'

Oh, yes. What a relief it would be to share with somebody all that had grieved her since she married James. But loyalty forbade it.

She shook her head.

'It's all right,' she said. 'I mean *I'm* all right,' she added defiantly. 'And lucky.'

'You mean lucky to have James to work with?'

Again she nodded.

'And children? You miss having children? Oh, I'm sorry, Diana, I shouldn't have asked that.'

'No, it's all right, Yes, of course I do. But the work we do here – well, that James does here – is so important, so good. I think after the war we all wanted to do something useful, didn't we?'

He had seen James neglect her – no, that was too strong a word. But he was casual with her. He remembered how at the dance James had just walked away from her, left her there on the dance floor. He found himself getting angry as he remembered.

'It's James, isn't it?'

She nodded.

'Please, Sebastian, don't think I'm complaining. I'm not and it's all much more complicated than you might imagine. You see, his wife and two young children were killed in the war. He'd sent them up to Scarborough to relations, thinking they'd be safer there than at their home in London. His wife was a lovely person. I met her once at Selina's and she was so kind to me. The loss must have been unbearable and of course he felt guilty for sending them away to a place where they were killed. But there it was. His whole family killed. So he toiled and toiled in the war, took no rest, operated day and night. I saw him doing it. We worked together and afterwards he asked me to join him in this great project he'd been thinking about. And it *is* great, Sebastian, and he is too.'

But that gives him no right to treat you as he does, Sebastian thought but didn't say.

'It's as if,' Diana went on more slowly, choosing her words with care, 'as if he had lived one whole life, completed it, as husband and father. He doesn't want to think of anything like that, much less repeat it. Perhaps it's too painful to contemplate. Please don't think I'm blaming him in any way. I'm not. He is as he is, as that awful war has made him. And, of course, I too was thinking in terms of the war, thinking only of what we could do for the wounded. The war excluded all else, all other considerations, it narrowed our judgement.'

She leaned back in her corner of the sofa, as if tired with trying to find the words.

After a while he said, 'Have you talked to him about this?'

She shook her head. 'It's no good. I did try at first, yes, tried to let him think we could have something together, obviously not like his first marriage, but approaching it, but it was no good. He can't miraculously change. I can't change him. At first I thought I could, but I'm wiser now. You can't change people to suit your needs, have them made to measure,' she added with a smile.

It was the smile that did it. There were tears in her eyes as she struggled to smile. It was such a sad smile, such a bereft look, like a child struggling not to cry at parting, fighting back tears and looking the more vulnerable for trying to be brave.

'Oh, Diana, I am *so* sorry,' he said as he put his arms around her. 'So sorry.'

He held her close, trying to comfort her, murmuring into her hair, rubbing his cheek against hers which was wet with tears, blaming himself that he had ever been parted from her.

'It wasn't your fault,' she said, raising her head at last.

He didn't reply, his lips on hers, a lover's kiss that lasts and lasts until one kiss isn't enough and there must be more kisses, hundreds of them on forehead, cheeks, neck, fierce little kisses, hungry little kisses. Then they separated, and looked into each other's eyes before returning lips to lips. And the more they kissed the more they needed to kiss, appetite growing with what it feeds on. This was not the compassion he had known for Celia, this was not the respect she had had for James; this was love, simple love, love which embraces so many feelings, compassion and respect among them, but can exist without any of them, just of itself, a thing apart.

They stayed there on the sofa until the fire burned low and they heard a car on the gravel, and if they seemed in any way different when James came in he didn't notice it as he told them about the satisfactory outcome of his committee meeting in Cheltenham.

At breakfast the next morning he plied Sebastian with questions about houses and fitments for the disabled and the chances of building more suitable accommodation around Northrop when the centre was eventually able to close, its work done. It could perhaps be converted into a sports and recreation centre for the disabled who could live independently nearby. They could build something much smaller for the few remaining men who would never be able to live in the outside world.

Sebastian made an effort to apply himself to what his host was saying and answered as best he could while thinking all the time about Diana, who spoke hardly a word.

'It's been very useful, all that you've told me,' James said, holding out his hand in farewell. 'Forgive me for dashing off. You stay and have another cup of coffee with Diana.'

'No, I'll be on my way,' Sebastian told him, getting up from the table. 'I'll just pack up my things and be off. Thank you for showing me everything here. It's been . . . a great experience.'

So James left and Sebastian went to his bedroom to pack his case.

A few minutes later he stood alone with Diana in the hall. He took her hands in his.

'I love you,' he said. 'I always did and I always shall.'

She didn't move, just said, 'But Sebastian, I don't understand you. I've been thinking about it all night. You seem to have a happy marriage. You have children. There must have been love, passion between you.'

He didn't reply for a while; how could he explain? To detail his marriage would be so dishonourable, so disloyal to the woman he had made his wife.

'It is not as it seems,' he said at last. 'You must believe that. Any more than your marriage is as it seems.'

She nodded, she accepted what he said, completely trusting. And he loved her even more for that.

'I love you,' he said again. 'Somehow we shall be together in the end.'

She said the same and they kissed, not in the frenzied way of last night, but solemnly, almost formally, as if sealing a vow. Then she stood in the doorway and waved him off, as any polite hostess might speed the parting guest.

He felt elated as he drove through the Gloucestershire countryside; she loved him still, that was all that mattered; somehow, sometime, they would be together, unravel their past mistakes. It felt inevitable. But as the distance between them grew, it began to seem less real, more dreamlike. As he drove towards Oxenhurst he became less and less Diana's avowed lover, more and more Celia's husband, her useful chauffeur, begetter of her children.

All the same, as he approached his parents' house he still felt the warm glow of knowing that he was loved by the woman he loved and for the rest of their stay he kept well away from his mother, fearing her discerning eye.

Twenty-Five

Having been a placid baby, Debbie took to crying when she was two. She screamed loudly during the day and wept pitifully at night. Unlike the twins who slept soundly, she awoke at the slightest noise. She would look up, startled, her eyes wary, her mouth beginning to quiver and then the thin, sad lament would begin. The only thing which soothed her was sucking the bottle, which Dr Truby King forbade after the second birthday, though Sebastian knew that sometimes Celia resorted to it in desperation.

Afraid that even the twins might be woken by her, Celia took her into her own bedroom, though he suspected that this was partly to safeguard her own privacy from any intrusion he might have in mind. He thought of his unhappy daughter as he walked back from the office to the tram stop one evening and saw a little girl of about her age happily sucking a dummy as she was being pushed along in her pram. On an impulse he went into the chemist and bought one for Deborah.

The twins were in bed when he got home, their sister screaming in her cot. Celia was sitting by the drawing-room fire, looking very tired.

'Bad day with her?' he asked, giving the usual peck on the proffered cheek.

'She's cried a lot.'

'I don't know if this would be any help,' he said, producing the chemist's package, 'but I thought it might be worth trying. It's a dummy.'

'A *dummy*,' she repeated outraged. 'A *dummy*. They're filthy things. Only sluttish mothers use them and they let them fall on the ground and then push them into the babies' mouths to keep them quiet. It's disgusting.'

'But you wouldn't do that—'

'This is what Dr Truby King says,' she interrupted, going to the bookcase and taking out what had become her bible. 'Here on page 172 it says, "A dummy deforms the jaws, interferes with the digestion and causes adenoids." Is that what you want to do to your daughter? Is it? They shouldn't be allowed. I don't know what you're thinking of.'

'I thought it might be worth trying,' he said again.

'Well, it isn't,' she said and threw it in the fire.

For once he didn't make excuses for her, didn't tell himself she was overtired, had disturbed nights. For once he lost his temper.

'You are totally unreasonable, Celia,' he told her with quiet ferocity. 'We've tried everything to get her to settle and nothing's worked. She can't be happy and this might have comforted her so why not try it? But you won't discuss anything rationally. I *want* to help. I always have, but you won't let me. You dismiss anything I try to do as useless, yet you complain all the time. It's just hopeless trying to get anywhere with you.'

It seemed he was blurting out a truth which he'd only just recognized, but of course, he realized later, it wasn't really like that. It wasn't a spontaneous outburst; it had been forming over the past months and years.

'Hopeless,' she repeated.

'Yes, that's how I feel. Hopeless.'

'You mean you want a divorce?'

He was dumbfounded. It wasn't what he'd meant, not what he'd ever imagined she would say, but suddenly it seemed to offer hope, an escape from all this wretchedness, all this pretending.

'Yes,' he said. 'I do.'

They looked at each other, both surprised at what they had said. The rubber teat of the dummy bubbled, flared up and melted in the flames.

'Yes, I do,' he said again.

Last time he'd said those words it had been standing at the altar with Celia. He said them again now with equal conviction.

'You look all in, old chap,' Matthew said when they met at lunchtime the next day. 'All right, are you?'

'Oh, just a bad night.'

Matthew was easily reassured for he had other things on his mind having just got engaged to the most wonderful girl in the world. He, who was generally regarded as a confirmed bachelor, found himself no longer confirmed in his bachelordom and engaged to Paula Harrison.

'You will be my best man, won't you?' he said now.

'Of course. I'd be honoured.'

They seemed well matched, his friend and this cheerful, warm-hearted farmer's daughter from the Dales. But of course you never know how people will change until it's happened. He realized how much less trusting he'd become, not quite cynical, but something approaching it. For hadn't he seen Celia change from a vulnerable girl in need of a knight errant into a single-minded, obdurate woman in five years? He had witnessed her rages, her hurling of harmless objects into the fire, her censoriousness and violent prejudices. Even physically she had changed, her pretty face hardened, her expression suspicious.

'Penny for them?' Matthew said.

He laughed, shaking off these doomladen thoughts. He was glad for his friend, of course he was. It was just that a part of him wanted to issue warnings. He made himself chat about everyday things.

'Don't overwork,' Matthew said as they parted. 'And I hope you have a better night.'

He had lain awake most of last night, shocked and excited by what had happened. Hope and fear warred within him: hope that his dream of spending the rest of his life with Diana could be a real possibility now that one obstacle might be so unexpectedly removed. But fear for his children.

At four o'clock he'd got up and gone along to the nursery,

walking very quietly past Celia's room where Deborah seemed to be sleeping peacefully.

It was almost the longest day of the year; the pale glow of early dawn, filtering through a fine veil of clouds, filled the nursery with a tender, opalescent light as he looked at his sleeping children. Arthur lay, as he always did, on his stomach, his bottom stuck up in the air, head on one side. However did he sleep like that? his father wondered. However often he was turned on to his side, he always managed to wriggle back on to his stomach to the accompaniment of various little grunts and moans.

Victoria lay tranquil, on her back, arms outstretched above her head. In sleep she seemed more babylike than she was during the day, her little fingers curled up, her long eyelashes dark against her pink cheeks. They were so unalike, these two, despite being twins. Arthur was restless, even in his sleep, and crashed about during the day, constantly falling over but always cheerful and good natured. She was such a composed little person. And a beauty, unquestionably a beauty, already able to cast a spell on all beholders.

He looked from one to the other, touched their little hands. How could he abandon them? Because that is what it would be. Celia would keep the children, hers would be the prevailing influence, he would be cast as the wicked father. She would care for them physically, he had no doubt of that, she would spend sensibly and see they were well fed and clothed. But what of food for their minds? What of warmth and affection, of understanding and love? Could he surrender them to a home without such nourishment?

He stayed with his children in the nursery until bright sunshine played on their faces and they began to stir, when he left them and went quietly back to his room, knowing that he could not do it.

They didn't speak of it until after dinner that night, when she came and sat by him, holding her housekeeping book. It was bound in black with red boards and filled with columns of neat figures.

'I have prepared a list of essential expenses,' she told him.

'It doesn't include the main bills which will go direct to you, nor the cost of household repairs, but it does include wages for Sarah and Mrs Lettuce and £4 a week for food and household necessities.'

The relentless accounting went on.

'If you have any objections, we can of course discuss them,' she said in conclusion.

It was all calmness and logic. About household accounts she could be reasonable. Was this the same woman who threw presents in the fire and screamed at him, with mad accusations?

He waited until she paused for breath and then told her he had decided to refuse her kind offer of a divorce.

Her face lit up. Malice and triumph vied with each other in the look she gave him. She had known he would say this.

'Can't leave the children, is that it?' she said. 'Oh, you are so *weak*, aren't you?'

She spoke with contempt; he knew that she regarded all compassion, affection, all such feelings as weakness.

He didn't reply for a moment and then began quietly, 'Celia, we're responsible for the children, we both want their happiness, we both know that a happy home is the best thing for them, so please can't we try to give them that? Whatever our feelings, can't we find some way of living together so that they don't grow up in a tense and unhappy atmosphere? After all, they're the innocent victims in all this.'

'You don't know much about children if you think they're innocent,' she put in.

'I mean they're not to blame for what's wrong in our marriage. I mean that it's our duty to give them a secure childhood.'

'Duty? Don't talk to me about duty. I know my duty. I always have done my duty and kept my marriage vows. And I shall always do my duty as your wife.'

She got up abruptly and left him.

He sat by the fire, watching as the coals shifted and reformed themselves. His mind too seemed to be shifting and reforming between relief and despair. It had seemed briefly that he might be free of her; that hope was now gone. But he had last night felt the horror of what might happen to his children and that fear was also gone. Hope and fear both gone. What was left seemed a great empty weariness. He must throw himself into work, he resolved as he got up and went into his study, and he must keep the atmosphere at home as calm as possible, refusing to quarrel with his wife whatever the provocation and striving always to see what was good in her. He felt like a man with a long and dreary road to be travelled, who hasn't the heart for the journey, yet knows it must be undertaken. Silently he prayed for strength.

Twenty-Six

'The King's life is moving peacefully to its close.'

Arthur and Barbara Crawley listened intently to the solemn announcement.

'Poor old chap,' Arthur said, when slow music replaced the announcer's voice. 'I wonder what's wrong with him?'

'He is seventy-one, dear. That's a great age.'

'Not nowadays. And even kings have to die of *something*.'

'I feel sorry for the poor Queen,' Barbara said after they'd sat quietly worrying about the royal family for a few minutes. 'I'm sure we all do. They are *our* royal family after all.'

'We shan't have a queen when Edward succeeds, shall we, since he's not married?'

'No, it will seem quite strange. The Queen will become the Queen Mother, I suppose.'

She smiled.

'It probably isn't the time to think of such things, but Meg, who was a lady-in-waiting, you know, told me that it was quite embarrassing the way the Queen, who was a great collector of silver, would go into people's houses and if she saw they had some interesting piece of silver, she'd stare at it, admire it, say she didn't have such a thing in her own collection until finally the poor owner felt obliged to offer it to her as a gift. In the end people used to hide their most precious pieces away when they knew she was coming to see them.'

'I wouldn't hide anything. She's welcome to come and have a poke around our butler's pantry any time she chooses.'

'Really, Arthur, you are obsessed about that silver!'

'Well, just look at it, not kept the way it used to be. I don't know what poor Forbes would have thought.'

'He'd have realized that Cook and the maids and Parker have enough to do cleaning the silver we *do* use without worrying about all the silver that we don't.'

'I can't see the point of keeping things we don't use. Come to think of it I don't know why you keep Mrs Partridge. You don't use her either.'

'Mrs Partridge has made our clothes for years.'

'Not mine she hasn't. And you seem to buy yours in shops nowadays. Times have changed. Anyway as far as I'm concerned the Queen Mother can have the lot.'

'Sh, dear, you mustn't call her that. She is still the Queen. The poor King isn't dead yet.'

'All right, the Queen Mother To Be.'

'I'm not sure that that's much better either,' she told him.

Diana and James listened to the same announcement.

'He's done well to last so long,' James commented. 'Heart and lungs in a poor way for the last six years. That pleural abscess very nearly got him; always a tricky business when they're hidden behind the diaphragm, difficult to locate. Dawson did a good job on him, I'm told.'

Diana nodded.

'So it will soon be Edward VIII,' she said.

'I wonder if we could get the men up for the coronation?'

She smiled. His first reaction to any piece of news was always to think what might be in it for the men.

'He's very popular with them, you know, Diana. They liked the way he spoke up for the miners during the strike. He really seems to care. We could hire Roper's omnibus to take the abler men and our two converted ambulances should take the rest. We'd need plenty of help, a nurse or two and then of course you and I'll be there. Yes, yes, it could be done.'

'There'll be huge crowds, James,' she pointed out. 'And maybe vehicles will have to be parked at some distance.'

'Oh, come, my dear, I'm sure that can be arranged. A word with the authorities should do it. Think what these men sacrificed for King and country. They deserve to join in the coronation of the next one. Thank God men won't be asked to give their lives for the next king.'

'He isn't king yet.'

'Soon will be. Doesn't sound as if the present one will last the night.'

In Gradby little Felicity Crawley sat under the mahogany table while the man talked on the wireless. It was evidently sad. Her parents were listening in silence. She didn't understand it but felt the solemnity of it and knew that she must keep quiet and anyway liked sitting here under the table which was like her own little house. She had her wooden Betty with her and a tiny toy dog with a blue lead.

The wireless stopped. Suddenly she thought of somewhere nicer than under the table so crawled out and made for the door, which was slightly ajar. Then she walked down the corridor to the kitchen. The kitchen door was shut but Sarah heard her, opened it and picked her up.

'How's my little Felicity?' Sarah asked, swinging her up in the air.

She'd loved the other three children, of course, but Felicity was special. She felt more like her big sister, or her auntie or her nanny. She didn't feel like the maid of all work, as she held Felicity aloft and gazed up at her bright little face. She loved her with her whole soul.

Felicity looked down at the big face, the bright red cheeks, the mouth laughing and open. She put her fingers into it and Sarah pretended to bite them while Felicity giggled and squealed. Then they settled down by the kitchen fire, Felicity comfortable on her knee.

It was a good fire, all glowing and full of funny shapes that Felicity liked to stare into and imagine stories about. And Sarah was comfortable to sit on, being soft and warm.

Sarah took her hand now. 'This little piggy went to market,' she began, tweaking the pink little finger, 'this little piggy stayed at home, this little piggy had roast beef and this little piggy had none. And this little piggy went wee wee wee all the way home.'

Before she had got the words out Felicity was already squealing and giggling in advance of being tickled under her arm. They rocked and laughed and Sarah knew that they were the two happiest beings on this earth.

'Again,' Felicity commanded.

'This little piggy . . .' Sarah began.

The door opened.

'Whatever are you thinking of, Sarah?' her mistress demanded. 'Have you no work to be doing? I thought I told you to polish the kitchen brasses.'

'Yes, m'm. Sorry, m'm. I'll see to it, m'm.'

She put Felicity down and took up the abandoned polishing rags.

'Come along,' Celia instructed the child who had been born nine months after she and Sebastian had decided not to get divorced. 'Back with you into the drawing room.'

In the hall the telephone rang; Sarah heard it from the safety of the kitchen. Celia unhooked the instrument, spoke briefly and went to find Sebastian.

'It's your mother,' she said. 'I expect she'd rather speak to you than me.'

At the other end of the line, Barbara sighed. It was ever thus: however hard she tried, her daughter-in-law responded with hostility. It was true that before the marriage she had told Sebastian that she thought he was making the wrong choice, but once he was married she had given them both her absolute support, she had nothing but goodwill towards Celia. She wanted to welcome her, love her as the daughter she had never had, but Celia did not want her love.

Why her daughter-in-law viewed her with suspicion, she could not understand; nobody else had ever rejected her friendship in this way. She couldn't talk to Sebastian about it because it would seem like a criticism of Celia and clearly he must owe his first loyalty to his wife. She would never wish it to be otherwise. She told herself that they seemed to be getting along all right and that was all that mattered, but still she could not help feeling hurt and bewildered by Celia's obvious antagonism. She only had to approach her to see the wariness in her eyes, as if a shutter had come down. She only had to telephone them for Celia to be curt and abrupt as if she regarded the call as an intrusion. Could it be that Celia resented the easy way she and Arthur got on with their son, felt left out? Could she be so immature as to be jealous? But then surely she would have got over that when she had children of her own? Could she not realize that Arthur and she were anxious to help and support the whole family?

She put these thoughts out of her mind when Sebastian came to the telephone.

After the usual exchange of news and greetings, she said, 'I'm really ringing, dear, on Elspeth Arndale's behalf, to ask what you feel about visiting Northrop? I don't mean now, next year.'

Suddenly alert, he thought carefully before replying, rather guardedly, 'What should I feel?'

'Well, it's just that Charles is to be celebrating his seventy-fifth birthday next year. Elspeth is quite determined he should have a special one, despite his unfortunate illness, a real gathering of the clan. She has already spoken to us and invited your father and me and said she was wondering if you and Celia might bring the children.'

'It's quite difficult, you know, Mother, with all four of them.'

'Yes, she knows it's a long way, but you see yours are the only children in the family. Laura and Rupert hope to come, but of course neither of them is married, and Elspeth fears they never will be because Laura is wedded to her work and Rupert never seems to stay in the same place for two minutes on end. So you see, dear, it's really up to you to come. Poor Charles seems to get on well with little children. Elspeth feels it would make him very happy.'

'Yes, well, I'll have to speak to Celia about it.'

'Of course.'

Silence. They both knew that Celia didn't approve of her

Arndale relations. They didn't know why and the simple explanation – that she had been brought up to disapprove of them – didn't occur to them.

To his surprise, Celia seemed quite amenable, only remarking that it was a long way off and too soon to make arrangements.

'I expect your aunt just likes to plan ahead,' he told her. 'I don't quite know how they'll fit us all in.'

'If they can't accommodate us, they shouldn't invite us,' Celia told him.

Elspeth was already making plans.

'What do you think, Diana?' she asked her daughter over coffee that evening. 'Laura and Rupert can stay here, of course, and we could have all of Celia's family here in the dower house as well, then the senior Crawleys could stay with you.'

'Won't you find four children rather a lot to manage, Mother? I mean, you're used to being so quiet here.'

'Well, there isn't room for them all in your flat, dear. You only have two spare bedrooms.'

Diana thought of being surrounded by Sebastian's wife and children, including the latest one conceived since his visit here, so soon, it seemed to her, after that avowal in the hall on the day he left.

'No, that would be impossible,' she said. Then she went on, 'But have you thought of putting them in one of the cottages? You know there's a pair being totally renovated later this year? I'm sure James wouldn't mind letting us use one of them – or even both – just for a few days before the men move in.'

'What a good idea! They'll feel so much freer that way.'

'Then the senior Crawleys could stay with you, which would be much more suitable, and Rupert and Laura can stay with us. Isn't Nanny going to enjoy it all? I saw her yesterday walking with Tommy. She looks so well. She doesn't seem to have changed at all since we were in the nursery.'

'Rather an exaggeration, dear, considering she's now in her eighties.'

'Is she? Are you sure? She doesn't look a day over, well, sixty-five.'

'We can easily work it out. She came here when she was thirteen as an undernurse to old Nanny Bradshaw, who died years ago. Your father was a baby when she came. So that must have been in 1862, which would mean she was born in, er . . . Have you a pencil, dear?'

'Well, if she's thirteen years older than Father, she must be eighty-eight next year.'

'Oh, what a quick mind you have. I suppose it's all the practice you get working for James, accounts and so on.'

Diana laughed.

'The trust does have an accountant, Mother. Doing the sums isn't really my job.'

'You never know what jobs women will be doing nowadays. They've quite taken over from the clerks in offices and they're in factories too and working the telephone exchanges. It's all wrong. I don't know what your grandmama would have said if she'd lived to see it. Now don't argue with me,' she said quickly, seeing that her daughter was about to object. 'I know you think it's progress but I'm too old to change my views.'

Diana looked at her and then said gently, 'Don't worry. I shan't try to badger you into changing. Besides, I think you've adjusted very well to all the changes here at Northrop.'

Her mother looked at her, surprised. It was not their habit to exchange compliments. Perhaps she *had* adjusted better than she realized: her lovely home had become an institution, its master lost to this world, its heir killed. It wasn't that she'd been brave about it; she'd had no choice. It wasn't as if God said, 'Bear this if you can. And if you can't, I'll think of something else for you.' It wasn't like that. You had to bear any load that was put upon you and then get on with life. And what she was going to get on with now was planning Charles' birthday celebrations.

Twenty-Seven

'What an enormous house you live in,' Victoria said. 'It's even bigger than Granny Crawley's.'

'Bigger than Granny Crawley's,' Felicity agreed. She had a way of repeating what her elder sisters said in a way which they found irritating. Victoria told her to shut up and stop being a copy-cat.

'I don't live in all of it,' Diana told them. 'Just a little bit. But when I was a girl we did live in it all.'

'It was our family home,' Elspeth put in sadly.

'It must have taken ages to dust it,' Debbie said.

'We did have people to see to such things,' Elspeth told her.

Debbie gazed anxiously at the many-windowed façade and thought of all the window ledges there must be and all the corners that would gather the dust, all the rugs to beat and the floorboards to polish, to say nothing of the linoleum and the skirting boards, and the curtains to shake. And the light bulbs, imagine the number of light bulbs! And the walls and ceilings to wipe down at spring cleaning. Spring cleaning would take all year in a house like that.

'I don't think Sarah would manage,' she said.

She saw at once that she'd said something silly because Victoria gave one of her looks, Great-aunt Elspeth's mouth wobbled as if she wanted to laugh and Aunt Diana said rather too quickly, 'Come along, let's go and find tea.'

'I'll be in the dower house with your grandparents,' Great-aunt Elspeth said. 'I expect I'll see you there after you've had your tea at the cottage. Nanny Stone will be there to look after you.'

She sounded quite normal; perhaps she hadn't been trying not to laugh.

'I think it's too big for a cottage. It's a proper house,' Felicity remarked as they made their way across the grounds with Diana.

'No, it's not. It's a cottage because it's thatched,' Victoria told her.

'What's thatched?'

'All that hairy stuff on its roof.'

'Who's that standing in the garden, Auntie Diana?'

'That's Mary-Ann, Debbie. She lives with Nanny Stone. I expect she's come to help in the kitchen.'

'Couldn't Sarah come and help?'

'No, Felicity. She's helping your Mummy unpack your things ready for tonight.'

'Is Nanny Stone Mary-Ann's mother?'

'No, Victoria. Nanny Stone isn't married.'

'Is Mary-Ann married?'

'No, she's a widow. She has a son called Tommy.'

'What's this slopey thing for?' Felicity asked as they approached the front door.

'It's not a slopey thing, silly,' Victoria said. 'It's a ramp.'

'Why?'

Victoria shrugged. She never liked to admit she didn't know.

'It's so that men in wheelchairs can get up it,' Diana explained. 'They couldn't get up steps.'

'Why?'

'Why what?'

'Why wheelchairs?'

'Because the men who live here were injured in the war.'

'What war?' Debbie asked.

'The Great War, silly,' Victoria cut in. 'Don't you remember Daddy telling us about it?'

'Of course I do, but it was years and years ago, before we were born and I don't see why they have wheelchairs now. That's all I meant.'

Diana brought their argument to an end by hurrying them all inside.

Nanny Stone had prepared tea around the dining-room table. There were sandwiches, marmite on toast, bread and butter, two sorts of jam, summer pudding and custard.

The children were momentarily subdued by their strange surroundings and by Nanny Stone in her old-fashioned black dress nearly down to the ground with a long white apron on top and stiff little cuffs at her wrists and her white hair drawn back into a plait which wound round her head. They hadn't seen anybody quite like her before, except perhaps the Miss Beales. They longed for Sarah and were glad when Auntie Diana decided to stay with them.

'You're not really our aunt, are you?' Arthur said. 'I mean, you're not our father or mother's sister, are you?'

'No, you call me your aunt because it's easier, but I'm your mother's cousin, so I'm your second cousin – or is it cousin once removed? – I'm never sure which.'

'Cousin once removed!' Arthur laughed loudly. 'It sounds as if you're furniture.'

'That's not very polite, is it, Master Arthur?' Nanny Stone reprimanded.

'It's all right, Nanny,' Diana said. 'He didn't mean any harm.'

'All the same, we must mind our manners. And no jam, Miss Victoria, until you've had a plain piece of bread and butter.'

Victoria blushed and, to her siblings' amazement, tried to return the jam to the pot until Nanny told her there was no need.

'We haven't seen any of the soldiers,' Arthur said, wanting to sound grown up and make conversation, to make up for his previous lapse.

'No, they're not in this part of the estate at the moment. And of course they're not in uniform so you might not realize they are soldiers.'

'And if you do see any of them on crutches or in wheel-chairs, you mustn't stare,' Nanny Stone put in.

'Why not?'

'Because it's rude to stare. Eat up your crusts, Miss Felicity.'

Felicity smiled. She didn't like crusts, but she did like being called Miss.

'You must remember what we all owe these men,' Nanny Stone went on.

'Why? I mean what did they lend us?'

'They didn't lend us anything, Master Arthur. They fought for us against the horrid Germans who wanted to kill us.'

'Why?'

'Because they were bad and asked too many questions. You still haven't eaten your crusts, Miss Felicity. Eating crusts makes your hair curl.'

'But Felicity's hair is curly already,' Arthur objected.

'Then if she doesn't eat her crusts it will grow straight,' Nanny told him imperturbably.

'I think they're ready for their pudding now,' Diana suggested.

'The fruit is from the garden,' Nanny Stone told them as she handed round the bowls. 'There are raspberries and strawberries and blackcurrants bottled from last year. And Cook made them into a summer pudding specially for you because it's always a children's favourite.'

'And still is apparently,' Diana said quietly to her as the children sat silent now, absorbed in eating.

'I don't like the skin on custard,' Debbie said, pushing it round her bowl.

'Eat it up,' Nanny told her. 'It's the best part.'

'Why? Why is it the best part?'

'Because goodness rises. Like the cream does on milk.'

'I see,' Debbie said and gulped it down somehow, though they could all see it made her want to be sick.

'But scum rises to the top too,' her brother pointed out.

'That's what we call the exception that proves the rule,' Nanny told him. 'And it's bad manners to answer back.'

'Oh, I wasn't answering back,' he told her. 'Just explaining.'

'That's as maybe,' Nanny said, reflecting that he was as argumentative as Rupert used to be. 'Now, what do we all say before we get down?'

Meanwhile their great-aunt Elspeth had gone back to the dower house.

The children were enchanting and she loved them dearly and had enjoyed every minute she'd spent with them since they arrived, but there was no getting away from the fact, she admitted to herself as she returned to the peace and quiet of her own home, that she did find them very tiring. Modern children are so constantly on the go, she reflected; they never seem to stop dashing about and asking questions. Perhaps children had always been like that but of course one didn't see so much of them in the old days. Or perhaps it was just that she was getting old herself.

Whatever the reason it was good to be back in the dower house with dear Barbara and Arthur Crawley.

They talked, of course, of the royal family.

'Three kings in one year!' she exclaimed offering Madeira cake. 'Who would ever have believed it?'

'Three kings of orient are?' Charles suggested.

'No, dear. George V died in January last year, then Edward became king and abdicated in December, so then we had Geoge VI as our third king in one year. Look, we have King Edward's coronation mug. I bought a lot and gave them to the children round here,' she explained to Barbara Crawley. 'But then, of course, he was never crowned.'

Barbara Crawley duly admired it and thought how much more she admired Elspeth for the calm way she managed her poor Charles, so matter-of-factly, so totally without embarrassment.

'An awful waste of mugs,' Arthur put in. 'Pity they couldn't have used them for George VI. Their faces are quite similar. They'd have had to alter the lettering of course and fitted the queen in somewhere.'

'Nonsense, dear. Of course they couldn't let the poor Yorks have Edward's cast-off mugs.'

'I'm so sorry for the Yorks,' Elspeth said. 'Though I suppose I shouldn't call them that any more, now that they're king and queen, but you know how it is, the habit of years.'

'Yes, this isn't at all what they expected when they got married. And they say he has a very bad stammer, poor man.'

'And all because Edward got led astray by that dreadful divorced woman. I mean the very idea! What was he thinking of? Divorcees aren't allowed into Royal Ascot. Imagine, the queen of England not being admitted to Ascot!'

'All the same, Elspeth, when he spoke about not being able to reign without the woman that he loved at his side, it was deeply moving. There is something very romantic about giving up a throne for your loved one.'

'I can't agree, Barbara. In my opinion, no woman is worth the throne of England.'

'Barbara is,' Arthur told her, helping himself to another piece of cake.

The children were up early the next morning and after breakfast presented themselves, as instructed, at the dower house.

Elspeth Crawley had also been up betimes.

'As you know, your great-uncle Charles' birthday is today. He is having breakfast in bed for a treat and to get plenty of rest. You children will be having a picnic lunch –' she paused to allow time for their oohs and ahs of pleasure to subside before continuing – 'by a stream, a favourite place for picnics in the old days. Mary-Ann and Sarah will go with you and your aunt Diana. Your father is going to do some work with Dr Bramley and your mother says she will help me with preparations for your great-uncle's tea party.'

'Please, will we go in our car?'

'No, Diana will drive you to the picnic. But we have overhauled bicycles in case you older ones want to cycle there, as our children used to do.'

'Are we going now?'

'Not yet, the picnic has to be made. We've put the croquet

hoops up on the lawn so you can play there for an hour or so and then be off.'

'Can we swim in the stream?'

'Yes, though I don't think it's very deep. Oh, I forgot to tell you. Nanny Stone has put ready some swim things for you.'

'Goodness, you've thought of everything!' exclaimed Barbara Crawley, who had just joined them and was standing listening in the doorway. 'Are we allowed to watch the croquet?'

'Of course. What is it, dear?'

This last question was addressed to young Arthur who was trying to attract her attention.

'These photographs, on the top of the desk there, who are they of?'

'This is your grandmother, Selina,' Elspeth said, going over with him to the desk and picking up the photograph, 'taken when she was getting married to your grandfather William Arndale. She was very beautiful, as you can see. Your sister Victoria is very like her. In fact, when I saw her yesterday I said to your aunt Diana, "There's a little girl who is going to be a great beauty like her grandmother," didn't I, Diana?'

Diana nodded; so long as Victoria doesn't grow up to be like her grandmother in character, she thought but didn't say. She glanced across at Sebastian who had just come in. She saw that he was looking intently at her. They both looked quickly away.

Arthur was still looking closely at the photograph of Selina.

'Is she dead?' he asked.

'Yes, I'm afraid so. And this is your grandfather William. He's my husband's brother.'

'Is he dead?'

'Yes, dear, both dead.'

How sad it was, she thought, that Celia had no photographs of her own family to show her children. They didn't even know what their relations looked like.

'I shall find some for you to take home,' she said. 'We used to have Philpotts the photographer come up and take pictures quite often and then Charles used to take some too.'

'And who's the young one?'

'That's your uncle Tom, your mother's brother.'

'Uncle? I didn't know I had an uncle.'

Again he looked closely at this picture of a fair young man in uniform, open-faced and laughing. Then he said in a resigned kind of way, 'Dead, I suppose?'

'Yes, dear. I'm afraid so.'

Diana waited until Sebastian had left to go and join James before she began rounding up the children. 'Time for croquet,' she told them and led the way out of the house. 'It's ages since anyone played. Your aunt Laura was very good, so was Mamma.'

'Where's Aunt Laura now?'

'She couldn't come, Victoria. She had exams.'

'Why?'

'Because she's studying to be a doctor, Felicity.'

'She couldn't come to Debbie's christening because she had exams, could she?'

'That's right, Arthur. Fancy your remembering that! You were quite small then. You must have a very good memory.'

Felicity beamed. She loved to hear her big brother being praised.

'And Uncle Rupert, where's he?'

'In America.'

'*America!*'

'Why?'

'He's helping some men to learn to fly aeroplanes.'

'Why?'

'Oh, do shut up, Felicity. You're always asking why. Let's start playing.'

'But, Victoria, we don't know *how* to play,' Debbie pointed out anxiously.

'Don't worry, dear. You'll soon learn,' Diana reassured her and, taking up a mallet, showed them how to hold it and knock a ball through a hoop or hit another ball and put them together and hit them again.

'Felicity won't be able to manage,' Victoria said. 'She'd better just watch.'

'I can do it,' Felicity said and hit a ball with surprising accuracy through a hoop.

'That was just luck,' her sister told her.

'No, it wasn't. I aimed like she said,' Felicity replied and did it again.

'It's rude to say *she*,' Victoria told her.

Somehow Victoria always had the last word.

'You can play partners or just each one for yourself,' Diana told them, 'I think that might be better because playing partners takes longer and we don't want to be late with the picnic.'

They managed to play two games before it was time to go, and were reluctant to stop until they were told the bicycles were ready, whereupon they dropped their mallets and ran to the shed.

'Croquet, swimming, bicycle rides, we don't have anything like this at home, you know,' Debbie told Diana.

'Well, you live in a town and have other things like the pantomime you were telling me about yesterday.'

'And we do swim in the pool at school,' Victoria said.

'But it's not the same, an indoor pool isn't,' Debbie insisted. 'It smells of chlorine and veruccas.'

'*Smells of veruccas*,' her sister repeated with one of her dismissive little laughs. 'You really do say the stupidest things.'

Blushing, Debbie ran quickly into the shed, desperate to hide her face in its comforting darkness.

'Oh, we don't know where we're going,' Arthur said suddenly as he got on his bike.

Diana smiled.

'I was wondering when you'd realize that. It's straight down this road and there's only one turning. You go left at the fork. It's quite easy because you can see the willows by the stream from there. I'll set off a bit later and keep behind you because the car raises such a lot of dust.'

'Dust roads? We have proper macadamized roads in the town.'

'Don't show off, Arthur.'
'Oh, shut up, Victoria. I wasn't showing off, just informing.'
'It's rude to say shut up.'
'Then why do you say it so often?'
Still arguing, they set off, bumping over the ruts, dust flying, all three of them wishing they could live in the country for ever.
Felicity began to bemoan the fact that she hadn't been allowed to go on a bicycle with the others but Sarah pointed out that she was going with the grown-ups and therefore rather special. Thus mollified, she consented to get into the car.
The dam the boys had built all those years ago was still there, though breached in several places, Diana noticed, when they arrived. So the pool was shallower. She hadn't been here since that last picnic on the last day of peace before the war which had taken Teddy and Tom, the dam builders. She was quiet as she handed the children their swimming things and unloaded the picnic from the car.
Mary-Ann too was quiet. She hadn't been here since she'd tried to drown herself in this very pool. She could hardly recognize her former self. Had they really lain together, she and Tom, under that tree? And had she come back here Sunday after Sunday to be alone with the memory of it? She, Mary-Ann, aged thirty-eight and with a nearly grown-up son, was she the girl who had waited and hoped, always praying that he wasn't really killed, that it was all a mistake, that he was just missing or a prisoner of war? It did happen to some soldiers. But it didn't happen to Tom.
At the beginning she used to dream about how it would have been if he had come home to her, how they would have been married and gone away and lived together with little Tommy. And Tom would have worked building dams, which he'd always wanted to do, and they would have had lots of children, which she'd always wanted to have. She had made herself stop dreaming. She was the Arndales' maid and Nanny Stone was her only family. And she had to be grateful that it was so and that fate had not dealt her any more blows.

She pondered these things as she looked at the tree beneath which she'd lain with Tom and at the pool where she had so nearly drowned.

Not finding either Diana or Mary-Ann very communicative, Sarah played with the children. The three older ones splashed in the pool which was only big enough to take three strokes, so they were always kicking and bumping into each other. Felicity paddled in the shallow water at the edge and occasionally pretended to swim, keeping her hands on the bottom of the stream, letting her legs trail behind her.

'Don't go in the deep water,' Sarah warned. 'Wait till I come in,' and, tucking her skirt into her knicker legs, she waded in alongside, not trusting the others to look after their little sister.

Mary-Ann watched and remembered, remembered how the girl she once was had done the same all those years ago, holding on to Celia and Laura and how Tom had jumped in to save her. He was Master Thomas to her then, of course; Master Thomas Arndale.

'Mary-Ann,' Diana said, as if reading her thoughts, 'how's Tommy getting on at college?'

'Wonderful well, thank you, Mrs Bramley. They think real highly of him.'

'Good. I'm so glad. Shall we call them in for the picnic now? We mustn't be late for Father's tea party and they'll all need baths first.'

Elspeth and Nanny Stone were waiting for them at the side gate when they cycled back up the lane, the car following slowly behind.

'Now children,' Elspeth said, 'off with you to change ready for tea. There's plenty of hot water.'

It still sometimes surprised her that so much hot water could go on coming out of taps, used as she had been for years to having footmen carry it in jugs around the house in such tiny quantities compared with today.

'And here's Tommy,' Nanny Stone exclaimed as a fair-haired youth cycled up the drive.

He dismounted and joined them.

'Now, Tommy,' Nanny Stone told him, 'come and be introduced. This is Miss Victoria and Miss Deborah Crawley and Felicity. And this is Master Arthur.'

They were shaking hands when Arthur suddenly said, 'He's just like that photograph of my uncle Tom you showed me this morning, Aunt Elspeth. I mean without the uniform.'

Elspeth laughed and shook her head, thinking how funny the boy was. She glanced across at Nanny Stone and Mary-Ann to share her amusement. Then she saw it: the nanny and the maid glanced at each other and there was something strange, conspiratorial in that brief look, not exactly guilty but certainly secretive, and then Mary-Ann seemed to be struggling not to smile as if there was some joy hidden in Arthur's words. She looked at Diana but her daughter either hadn't heard or was pretending she hadn't.

Of course, of course, it would explain everything.

'Perhaps there is a passing resemblance, dear,' she said calmly. 'Now hurry everybody and get ready for tea.'

'I'm starving,' Arthur remarked as they stood outside the dining room in the dower house, waiting for their elders to appear. 'All that fuss to get us back on time and now the grown-ups aren't even ready.'

'Sh, they're coming,' Victoria told him and they watched as their parents and grandparents came down with James and Diana.

'Isn't Great-uncle Charles a bit old for birthday parties?' Debbie asked.

'I don't know. He's sort of young in a way, isn't he?'

'I asked Great-aunt Elspeth and she just said he was not quite himself.'

'Well, if he's not himself, who is he?'

At that moment Charles came in with Elspeth and they all sang happy birthday to him. He looked very happy and thanked them all and they all clapped. After that there was a great deal of eating, a bigger tea than any of them could remember, and a huge cake with seventy-five candles, which gave out so much heat that the icing began to melt and Uncle Charles had to be helped to put them out. And Debbie said should they get the fire brigade and everyone laughed, except Deborah who blushed and wondered what she'd said wrong. There were crackers too, with fancy hats. But best of all a magician came and did tricks, wonderful tricks that the children knew had to be magic because how else could you explain the goldfish that came out of Uncle's ear or how he knew that Aunt Elspeth had looked at the ace of spades, just looked at it and put it back in the pack while they were all watching and knew that the magician couldn't possibly have seen which card she'd picked?

They sat enthralled and could see that Uncle Charles was too. Just like them he was amazed and delighted, lost in the magic of it all.

'It's wonderful to see him so relaxed and happy, isn't it, darling?' Elspeth remarked to her daughter, as they were leaving the table. Seeing the tears in her eyes, Diana bent over and kissed her. They looked at each other, both grateful that, if he had to endure this time of second childhood, at least it included some moments of childish joy and wonder as compensation for all the rest.

'What do you want to do now until bedtime?' Elspeth asked the children.

'Croquet,' they answered with one voice.

So they went back to the lawn, the children playing partners this time, helped by Diana while the grown-ups watched and commented. Charles sat with Elspeth under the beech tree and she could see that, although he wasn't sure who all these nice people were, he was happy to hear once again the thwack of croquet mallet against ball and the sound of children laughing.

James and Sebastian went back to the hall after tea to finish looking at the plans they had been discussing for most of the day. James seemed capable of talking about them most of the night too, Sebastian thought, suppressing a yawn; he is indefatigable, this man who has given his life to helping the wounded, this man whom I admire and whose wife I love, although we have spent a day and a half avoiding each other.

'I've tired you,' James said. 'Let's have a whisky.'

They took their tumblers over to the window. The study was on the first floor and gave them a good view over the grounds; they could see the men gathering up gardening tools, putting away sports equipment, preparing to come in for the night.

'It's been a glorious day for them,' James remarked. 'It's so much easier to keep physically busy in the summer than in the winter, though we do our best, of course.'

He turned to Sebastian.

'Well, here's to your very good health,' he said. 'You've seen something of my plans, so now tell me what your plans are up there in the north.'

'Well, it's difficult to plan when the future is so uncertain. If war comes—'

'*War?* you don't really believe that, do you?'

Sebastian looked at him.

'I'm afraid it's almost a certainty,' he said.

He was going to say more, but stopped, taken aback by the look of horror on the older man's face.

'How can people talk of war?' James Bramley demanded. 'Have they learned nothing, seen nothing? Look, look.'

He took Sebastian's arm and almost dragged him back to the window, from which they'd turned.

'There now, look,' he said again, still gripping his arm. 'Look at Philips there. Lost both legs and an arm. And Charlesworth, almost blind, and there goes young Sadler in the wheelchair, double amputee and balls blown off. Think of that happening to a lad of eighteen. He'd have chosen death if he could, but we insisted on saving him and patching him up. That's three of them that happen to be in front of our eyes. And it's repeated over and over again. Years and years we've spent patching up their bodies, chopping bits off, sewing bits on. *These are bodies*, for God's sake, *flesh and blood bodies*. Young bodies we've shot to bits. And then the ones that took days to die, days of hell. Crucifixion was a merciful death by comparison. But we don't crucify people any more. Oh no, we're far too civilized. But once we've got a war going, there's no holding the barbarian in us. Who cares about being civilized when we've invented another weapon of torture?'

He stopped, almost choking with rage and misery.

Then more calmly he said, 'Nothing is worth it, Sebastian. I tell you, nothing is worth it. Do we never learn? Must we fill this place again with tortured bodies, with the remnants of what were once healthy young men? And next time it will be women and children too. No, nothing is worth it, no cause on earth is worth it.'

Sebastian stood in silence. He could have said freedom was worth it, he could have talked of Fascism and anti-Semitism, he could have said war would be a justifiable police action against Nazism, he could have said that to abandon Czechoslovakia to the wolves would be as shameful as deserting a friend, but he said none of these things, silenced by the older man's despair.

Twenty-Eight

They usually stopped work at one o'clock on Saturdays, but today Matthew had come round to Sebastian's office to discuss details of a tender to build a block of flats for the council and talk about another house conversion for the disabled.

'If you come home with me, I'll let you have some background about this,' he told Sebastian at the end of the afternoon's work. 'I kept newspaper cuttings about the scheme which are worth looking at.'

If they did any work together away from the office, it was always at Matthew's house, ostensibly because it was nearer than Sebastian's but also because Sebastian knew that Celia didn't welcome unexpected visitors in the way that Matthew's Paula did.

'Just getting them off to bed,' she said, kissing Matthew over an armful of washing when they arrived, 'but I'll bring you in some tea.'

'I'll do it, love,' Matthew told her, lifting up his son who was holding on to his mother's skirt and giving him a hug. 'Where's your baby sister then?'

'She's up there already. Come on, sonny boy. There's some cake in the old toffee tin, Matthew, and some biscuits I've just made, on the airing tray by the cooker. Help yourselves. Oh, and you might bring the nappies in off the line.'

It was so unlike his own home; sometimes Sebastian wondered if Matthew knew how lucky he was. He seemed to take for granted this welcoming warmth, this homeliness, this sharing in every part of his children's lives.

They carried the tray into the sitting room, which was

strewn with books and toys, moved the children's belongings off two chairs and discussed work as they had tea.

'It looks a good bet, that property,' Sebastian said. 'But it's hard to make decisions just now. When war comes it may be requisitioned or flattened by bombs, but how do we explain that when the vast majority of our fellow citizens are celebrating the outbreak of peace?'

'Paula and I saw one of the Pathé newsreels last week and the crowds greeting Chamberlain were just unbelievable. I wouldn't have thought there were so many people in the whole of London. They were filmed at the airport and outside Downing Street, cheering and clapping as he waved his bit of paper at them. It was awful.'

'I've only seen the pictures in the newspapers and that was bad enough. It makes you so ashamed. Anything Hitler demands, our wretched prime minister rushes to give him.'

They'd had this kind of conversation several times since Chamberlain had returned waving his Munich agreement. And it never got them anywhere.

'Does it ever strike you as odd, Matthew,' Sebastian said now, 'that in the Great War people were so eager, so enthusiastic to go off and fight – remember the women with their white feathers? – and this time, when there is so much more reason to fight, they just want to run away from it?'

'Like Travers who never stops saying that he wouldn't go and fight for a country that he can't even spell and then laughs his stupid laugh. Once more and I'll hit him.'

'But then there are other people, men of conscience, like James Bramley, for example, who simply cannot bear to think there might have to be another war, but you can't put them in the same category as the Traverses of this world,' and he told his friend how passionately James had spoken to him last year at Northrop.

They were silent for a while, then Matthew said, 'Do you remember in the general strike when we hated the way some of the volunteers really enjoyed strike-breaking, really gloated, yet we knew that there had to be volunteers to get people to work, children to school and so on? And you said, "Yes, it has to be done, *but not with relish*."? I always remembered that phrase. And I think now that this war is going to have to be fought against the Fascists, we'll do it as a horrible duty, not something we relish at all.'

'Except that once a war starts, hatred flourishes.'

'Yes, and this time it will be fought in the air and involve everyone, women and children.'

'What will you do about your family?'

'They'll go to Paula's parents on the farm. I suppose you and I will just have to wait and see what we're told to do either in the army or organizing things here. These industrial cities will obviously be targets. What about your family?'

'I've been thinking on the same lines. I'd like to go and look for somewhere in the country fairly soon. There'll be a lot of people moving out of Gradby next year.'

'You're both looking very serious,' Paula said, coming in and taking off her apron at the same time. 'The children want a goodnight story, Matthew, but I'll do it if you're still busy.'

They both got up.

'No, we've finished,' Matthew told her.

'And I must be on my way,' Sebastian said. 'I'm sorry if I've delayed you, Paula.'

'Of course you haven't. It's always good to see you. Stay as long as you like.'

'Thank you, but I must be off,' Sebastian said, making for the hall. 'Felicity isn't at all well. She's in bed and gets bored and needs a story.'

'Matthew told me you were worried about her and you weren't sure what was wrong.'

'She's very feverish. At first we thought it was flu but now it seems it might be swollen glands.'

'Give her our love and tell her we hope she'll be better soon,' Paula said, opening the front door for him.

He went straight upstairs when he got home.

'How's my favourite patient this evening?' he asked as he opened the bedroom door.

Then he stopped and gazed in amazement at the scene

before him: Miss Agatha Beale prone across the bed, his daughter sitting up, deathly pale and terrified, her eyes fixed on the recumbent figure of her godmother.

He strode over to the bed and put his arms around her. She fell against him and began to cry.

'Is she dead?' she sobbed. 'I think she's dead. Debbie's mouse looked just like that.'

'It's all right, darling. You just lie back. There, let's make the pillows comfy. Now shut your eyes and try to sleep. Leave it to Daddy.'

She did as she was told, except that she did just peep out of one eye so saw him take Miss Agatha by the arm and give her a shake. She wasn't dead. Her eyes came open and she smiled at him in a loopy kind of way.

'Up you get,' he said. 'And out you go.' And he yanked her up and steered her out of the door and down the stairs.

She heard him calling for her mother, evidently leaving the visitor with her, then he came back.

He sat on the edge of the bed, thanking God, not for the first time, that he had stayed with his children, tempting though Celia's offer of divorce had been. Who would have protected them if he had gone?

'So what was it all about?' he asked.

'She came to visit me and I thought she was praying, then she seemed to die and fall across my bed. And, and . . .'

'Go on.'

'Please don't make me go to Sunday school, *please*, Daddy.'

'Of course nobody will make you go if you don't want to, but I thought you always wanted to go.'

'I did, but I didn't know about the blood.'

'The *blood*?'

She nodded.

'Come on, little one, tell me.'

'She said I'll be washed in the blood of the lamb.'

He shook his head, hugged her and tried to explain about metaphors, which she didn't really understand, but that didn't matter because he made her quite sure that there definitely wouldn't be any blood. He could see that she believed him. He sat on the edge of the bed for a while, gently stroking her head until he saw her eyelids flutter and knew that she would soon be asleep. Then he left her and went downstairs.

He found Celia in the drawing room doing her mending.

'So you've got rid of her?' he said.

'If you mean has Felicity's godmother left, yes she has,' Celia replied without looking up from the neat darn she was doing on the heel of a sock.

'We can't let her be alone with the children, Celia. To come and frighten a sick child is intolerable.'

'If that child is frightened of a harmless adult falling asleep, then she's too highly strung,' came the sharp rejoinder.

'Felicity is not highly strung and Agatha Beale is not harmless. And she was drunk this afternoon.'

'Of course she wasn't.'

'Celia, I could smell it on her breath.'

'She'd probably been to Holy Communion.'

'You know that's nonsense.'

There was a pause; Celia cut the end of the wool, moved the wooden mushroom into the other sock, rethreaded her needle.

'Agatha is teetotal, like her sister,' she said. 'But she is sometimes obliged to take a little brandy for medicinal purposes.'

'Celia, why try to blind yourself to the truth? She doesn't just drink a *little* and I'm sure her doctor knows nothing about it.'

'You've no right to say that,' Celia told him. 'The truth is that you've never liked Agatha although she has been my best friend since I was a child.'

It was no good. She could tolerate no criticism of the Beales. Like Ethel Grimsdyke they could do no wrong. It had puzzled him over the years: she had loved her uncle, yet it was her aunt whom she emulated. There was no sense in it but then we human beings are not logical, he thought, and there is no point in pursuing this with her.

Instead he broached the subject which had been worrying him for some time.

'I think we should be prepared for you to take the children out of Gradby into the country in case of war,' he said.

'There won't be a war. Mr Chamberlain has seen to that. Everyone except you seems to rejoice that he brought back peace from Munich.'

'Appeasement isn't peace, Celia. Please, for the children's sake, listen to what I'm saying. Schools will evacuate their children into the country en masse when war comes. Some will be separated from their brothers and sisters. I think we should find somewhere for you to go with the children, somewhere in the Dales perhaps, where you'd be safe.'

'And what would you do?'

'I shall go where I'm sent. Maybe into the army, maybe doing war work here. You see, the industrial towns will be the first to be bombed so we shall need to build air-raid shelters, probably move munitions production out of the town, see to the protection of transport. All these things are already being discussed, Celia.'

'Well, men always like to talk, don't they?'

'I'm sorry we can't agree about this, Celia, but I am going to insist that the first weekend after Felicity is better we go and look for somewhere suitable for you to stay for the duration of the war.'

At suppertime that night, Debbie suddenly asked, 'Daddy, what's a warmonger?'

'It's somebody who likes fighting for its own sake, I suppose. Why do you ask?'

'The girls at school said you were one.'

'Yes,' Victoria said. 'Debbie and I were changing our shoes in the cloakroom, and they started saying it.'

'They said you'd written to *The Times* that we shouldn't have peace with Hitler.'

'And then they pointed at us and said, "Your daddy's a warmonger," and it was horrible the way they said it. They kept sort of chanting it. It's not true, is it?'

Celia shot him a look of malignant triumph.

'Now who's upsetting the children?' she asked.

Twenty-Nine

'You can almost feel the mood of the country changing,' Sebastian remarked to Matthew as they stood waiting for the tram to take them across town to a meeting. A ferocious wind, laced with hailstones, cut through them as they stood at the tram stop. Locals called it a lazy wind because it didn't bother to go round you, just took a short cut straight through you.

'Yes, you can sense it among people, can't you, even if they're strangers and nothing is said. Oh, here's the tram, thank goodness.'

A few weeks ago Hitler had ordered his army into Prague and taken what remained of Czechoslovakia. On this bitterly cold March day people were no longer rejoicing as they had done in sunny September. Apparently giving Hitler what he wanted hadn't guaranteed that he'd be a well-behaved ally from now on.

'Even young Travers has stopped talking about not wanting to fight for a country he can't spell,' Matthew said, as they settled into their seats.

'Especially since that country no longer exists, thanks to people like him.'

'It'll be Poland next,' Sebastian prophesied. 'And even Travers won't have the excuse that he can't spell it.'

They looked gloomily out at the blizzard through the grimy windows as the tram rattled and shook and the hailstones melted on their heavy overcoats. The crowded tram had its usual winter smell of damp cloth and steaming humanity. It was all so normal that it was hard to imagine how different everything could soon become.

'And then what? Austria, Holland, Belgium, France?'

'Then Britain' was in both their minds, but neither of them spoke the words.

'How are your plans for moving the family out of Gradby?' Matthew asked instead.

'Oh, didn't I tell you? We've decided to take the house we saw in Netherby. It's a rambling old place, but charming – at least I think so. It's too big really, far bigger than our present house and has more garden, including a paddock. It belonged to an old man who lived there alone for years and hasn't done much to it, thank goodness. At least we're spared so-called "improvements". There are three beneficiaries who have to agree to everything about the sale which always slows things and the fact that one of them lives in South America doesn't help. But we can't go anyway until the end of July when the schools break up.'

Matthew nodded.

'It's much easier for us. Paula and the children can move in with her parents whenever we feel we should make the move. What will you do?'

'I haven't decided yet, but Mrs Jordan sent a message with Sarah that she's going to take in lodgers again because there are going to be so many men left on their own when the women and children move out. Obviously most of the young ones will be in the services but there'll be others who have to stay in Gradby. I think I'll probably go back to her pro tem.'

'Would she have me too? Paula doesn't think I'm capable of looking after myself.'

'I'll certainly ask her.'

'What a weird bachelor life it'll be! Isn't it odd to think how we used to plan our lives, be in control of them and now we don't know who'll send us where.'

'Yes, it's a strange feeling. Good lord, are we there already,' he added as Matthew got up. 'We're very early, aren't we?'

'Let's drop into the News cinema. We've got time.'

They sat in the stuffy darkness and watched pictures of

refugees leaving Spain. They were becoming familiar figures, these refugees. From Austria, Germany and Czechoslavakia they had come, all with that shocked look, the look that said so plainly that they'd never thought it could possibly happen to them, their homes destroyed, livelihood lost. The two men watched and pitied. And wondered if it could ever happen here.

At least the children have settled well into their new home, Sebastian reflected as he drove up to Netherby one Saturday in early September. He missed them dreadfully, the house was achingly quiet without them, for he hadn't yet arranged to move to Mrs Jordan's. Here in the Dales they would be safe, that was all that mattered.

As he rounded the corner he saw them waiting, perched on the five-barred gate at the bottom of the drive eagerly watching the road for the first sight of him. It warmed his heart to see them and he thanked God for them as he hugged each in turn, even Arthur who had been moving into the handshaking age when they left Gradby but now hurled himself at his father, as wildly excited as the girls. He knew it was partly the tension of these days, even the children felt it, every emotion was heightened.

He tried to keep things normal for their sake; soon he was cutting the lawns and they were playing croquet and after tea he tried to speak as calmly as possible when he explained that Hitler had invaded Poland yesterday and that meant that there would probably be a war, so tomorrow morning he would listen to the radio because if Hitler didn't get out of Poland by eleven o'clock we had said we would fight him. He realized it meant little to them; part of him wanted them to grasp how serious it was, but part of him was glad that they didn't.

Immediately they had left to go to church with Celia the next day, he turned on the wireless, tuning with difficulty into the new and unfamiliar wavelength which two days ago the BBC had announced would in future carry the only programme to be broadcast. It would start at seven in the morning and go on until just after midnight with news bulletins and music throughout the day; somehow this, more than anything, made it seem that war really was imminent.

He already knew what had happened in the House of Commons last night; Matthew had telephoned him very early this morning to let him know that Chamberlain had actually told the House of Commons that he was still prepared to negotiate with Hitler but that when the Labour leader, Arthur Greenwood, rose to reply, demanding the end of appeasement, even some on the Conservative benches cheered him. 'Speak for England, Arthur,' they called. He did, he said there must be no more appeasement and temporizing, 'at a time when Britain and human civilization are in peril'. All this Matthew had relayed to him, having heard it from a friend who was a Member of Parliament; Sebastian, as he sat waiting for the news, thanked God that he had chosen to live in one of the three houses in Netherby that possessed a telephone.

At eleven fifteen the announcement that he was waiting for was made. Chamberlain's tired, unemotional old voice informed the world that this nation was at war with Germany.

Sebastian sat very still, feeling a strange mixture of relief and anxiety, relief that the uncertainty was over at last, anxiety about the family. Celia had everything under control, he knew that. She would see to the blackout, she would make sure the children always carried their gasmasks with them. The twins and Debbie were to start school in Pendlebury, Arthur at the Boys' Grammar, Victoria and Debbie at the Girls' High School. Felicity would go to the village school.

He was worried too because Sarah was looking so unwell. She was coughing and her voice was hoarse. He had spoken to Celia about it but she'd just said that the girl was healthy enough and probably looked like that because of all the fumes she'd caused in the kitchen. The silly girl had taken it into her head to blacklead the hot plates of the electric cooker, so that when she, Celia, had turned one on, the kitchen had been filled with filthy black smoke. Sarah had had to stay up late to clean up the mess, so if the girl was looking tired, it was her own fault for being so stupid.

He looked at his watch now; he must pack and be ready to leave after lunch. The children would be disappointed, expect him to stay all day as usual, but apart from the need to get back to Gradby as soon as possible, he didn't want to drive in the dark, not since cars were no longer allowed to drive with their lights on.

As he crossed the hall, he saw Sarah standing on the stairs. She was leaning against the bannister and seemed to be struggling for breath.

'What is it, Sarah?' he asked, going quickly up to join her. 'What's the matter?'

He was shocked by the sight of the face she turned to him. Her eyes were sunken, her cheeks putty-coloured.

'Oh, I do feel funny,' she whispered.

'You're ill. Get along into bed,' he told her.

'Oh, I can't. I've done the pots but haven't made a start on the vegetables and—'

'Sarah, you can scarcely stand. Please, go to bed.'

She didn't argue this time, but walked slowly down the corridor to her room.

Clearly she has a high fever, Sebastian thought, making his way to his room and beginning to pack. But what? Possibly influenza; she certainly looked like he'd felt when he had it so badly at Mrs Jordan's house years ago. But then it might be diphtheria or scarlet fever. Had she been vaccinated against smallpox? The children had been safe-guarded against it, but against the other two there was no protection. Pity for the maid and fear for his children gave him no peace.

He went and tapped on Sarah's door. The only answer was a gasping cough.

'I'm coming in, Sarah,' he warned, fearful of embarrassing her.

But she seemed beyond caring as she looked at him with feverish eyes, yet trustingly too, like a child believing that a grown-up can make things better.

'I'm going to take your temperature, Sarah,' he said, resolving, as he went to fetch the thermometer, that he would call the doctor if it was over a hundred and two.

'I'm sorry,' she managed to whisper as he put the thermometer under her tongue.

'Don't worry, we just want you better,' he told her and he went and stood by the window, which overlooked the field where the cows munched placidly in the morning sunshine oblivious of wars and fevers.

Her temperature was a hundred and three.

'You're quite ill, I'm afraid, Sarah,' he said. 'I'm going to call the doctor.'

She didn't respond, but lay still, eyes shut.

He heard the family returning. The children seemed to be staying out in the garden, Celia coming indoors. As he walked down the corridor she was coming upstairs.

'Where ever has that girl got to?' she demanded. 'She's not in the kitchen and half her work's not done.'

'She's ill, I'm afraid, Celia. Very ill. I've taken her temperature and—'

'You have been into her room,' Celia almost hissed with rage. 'How dare you go into the girl's bedroom?'

'Because she is ill. That's all that matters,' he told her, taken aback by this unexpected onslaught.

'The minute my back's turned you creep into a maid's bedroom. I take the children to church and you stay here and I find—'

Something snapped.

'Be quiet, Celia,' he ordered. 'I'm going to ring the doctor.'

'She doesn't need a doctor. She's a strong working girl, she'll weather it.'

'And pass it on to the children, who may not,' he told her and went downstairs to ring the doctor, giving thanks once again that the house had a telephone.

Within two hours he was explaining to the children that Sarah had diphtheria and had to go into an isolation hospital so that nobody else would catch it from her. They watched miserably through the window as the ambulance bore her away. They all waved, and Felicity wept because poor Sarah wouldn't be able to see them because there were no windows in the ambulance. He took her on his knee and explained how Sarah's bedroom had been fumigated to disinfect it and strips of brown paper had been stuck round the door so that the infection couldn't get out, which intriguing details distracted them from their grief.

'So all that infection is locked in her room?' Debbie asked, awestruck.

'Yes, but all the same you must promise not to go down the corridor to her room.

They nodded and promised.

'And you must help your mother as much as you can because she'll be very busy without Sarah.'

Again they nodded and promised.

'I'll do the garden and heavy things and the girls can help with the meals,' Arthur said, suddenly very grown up.

'Good, now I have to go and I may not be able to get up to see you so often,' Sebastian told them.

They looked puzzled and he realized that, in all the worry about Sarah, he had quite forgotten to tell them about the other crisis: there was a war on.

Evening was coming by the time he got away, so he drove slowly along the darkening roads. Driving without lights was going to be like wearing a blindfold, he thought. Not a glimmer showed in any of the houses and cottages he passed, nor were there any street lights in the towns. He wondered how his parents were faring in the blackout; he would ring them when he got back.

Alone at last, he relived the day. He heard again Celia's shrill, accusing voice as she ranted at him on the landing about going into Sarah's room. He felt again the wonder that anyone so prudish could be so foul-minded. Whatever the reason, he knew beyond a scintilla of doubt that he never wanted to hear that harsh, censorious voice again.

The sudden strength of this conviction took him aback. He passionately wanted to be free of it, of her, of the whole situation. He thought about the children. Well, they were growing up. The day was not far off when they would understand, he told himself, wanting to be convinced. When this wretched war was over – and unlike most people, he thought it might last for years – that would be the time to act. Perhaps by then Diana would be free. After all, she was twenty years younger than her husband, so in the nature of things . . . no, he wouldn't think anything so dishonourable. James Bramley was an admirable, even a saintly, man and a trusting husband. Determinedly he put such a thought out of his mind as he drove back to Gradby.

'Thank goodness for Mrs Partridge,' Barbara Crawley said to her husband as they finished breakfast. 'I just don't know how I'd have managed without her. I never realized how many windows we had.'

'Widows? What widows?'

'*Windows*, Arthur.'

'What about them?'

'They're all to be blacked out. We have sixty-two.'

'Simplest thing would be to take out the light bulbs of all except a couple of rooms and lock the doors.'

'Darling, don't be absurd, though we could close the top floor, I suppose, when Rosie and Annie leave to go into munitions. But even then the light might show from the rooms below. Just the merest chink and you can end up in prison.'

'I wonder how they blackout the prisons? Lucky to have such small windows, I suppose. Easier than this place.'

'Blessedly the drawing room has shutters, which are the best of all, and I did buy a lot of that government black-out material, you know, that heavy sateen at two shillings a yard?'

'That's cheap enough.'

'Not when you need as many yards as we do! Do you know it took Mrs Partridge, Annie and me four hours just to measure all the windows in the house?'

'I'd have given you ladies a hand, if you'd asked.'

'I did mention it, dear, but you were so wrapped up in making plans for the Anderson shelter you didn't even hear. Anyway, we've made about half and now the shop's run out of the material. So we may just have to dye some sheets. You mix up size and lamp black and stir it up with gallons of boiling water. So that's what I am going to help Cook to see to after breakfast. They have to be our best sheets too, the light would show through any worn patches.'

'And I'm off to make preparations,' Arthur said, getting up from the table. 'The first thing is to get all the iron railings uprooted. Tear them all out. The government will want all the metal they can get for munitions. They've plans for taking out all the railings in the towns.'

'But, Arthur, if we take the railings down, Mr Buller's cows will get in.'

'Can't be helped. Bigger issues at stake than a few cows munching their way round our garden. But if it worries you,' he added hastily seeing she was about to object strongly, 'we'll put up wooden fences. Come to that, we could do with keeping the odd cow.'

'Why?'

'Milk supplies. Everything will run short. Best to have our own.'

He looked thoughtful for a moment as he mentally surrounded his land with wooden fences and populated it with cattle.

'Oxen at Oxenhurst Manor,' he said with satisfaction. 'Very appropriate.'

'Arthur, you know perfectly well that the name has nothing to do with cows. It derives from the oaks that once grew here on the hillside. We looked it up years ago.'

'Oh, well, that's all speculation, guesswork, don't you know? And we'll get a goat or two to crop the lawn. Can't waste time cutting it. Better still, dig it up and plant potatoes.'

'Wouldn't it be easier to plant potatoes in the flower borders and leave the lawn alone?'

'Well, yes and of course part of the top lawn will be over the Anderson shelter. It's a good design you know but quite a task to put it up. I've got the directions somewhere. Don't know where I put 'em.'

'There, by your plate, you were reading them just now.'

'Yes, well you start by digging a hole seven foot six inches long, six foot wide and four foot deep.'

'That's quite a big hole, Arthur. It'll take some digging.'

'I've seen to that, asked Dankers, the grave digger. A bit wider than he's used to, but that makes it easier really. More room to move about as you go down.'

'Then what do you do?'

'You put in six of these great curved steel plates and bolt them together at the top. Makes an arch, you see. Look, shall I draw it for you?'

'No, I can imagine it. Go on.'

'At each end you put flat steel plates, one with a hole at ground level through which you can climb down into the shelter. Outside you cover it with at least fifteen inches of earth. Then pop the lawn back on top.'

'So it will look a bit like an igloo?'

'That's right, that's the ticket.'

'It must be a bit cramped inside?'

'Oh, it holds two lying down or six sitting or standing. I think we could make it quite cosy. I'd like to think you were safely tucked away in a shelter when I'm out there fighting.'

'Out *where*? You surely can't imagine they'll take you in the army at your age?'

'Local army. ARP or we could raise one of our own. D'you know, I heard a rumour that the old padre might be back?'

'Really?'

'Yes. Idea is that new padre will go off into the forces and old one come back on duty here. It'll happen in everything. The young men will go off and do the fighting and their places will be taken by old men and women. You'll see, in schools, factories everywhere.'

'You'd be glad to have old Mr Godfrey back.'

'Oh, yes, he'll get to grips with things. A great fighter, the old padre. He'll help me train up the men.'

'Which men, Arthur?'

'Well, there's Parker for a start and both Forrest and Maitland fought in the Great War, so they know how to do things. And there'll be some young lads. A bit of initial training before they're conscripted won't come amiss. And there's Tomlinson—'

'Arthur, Tomlinson is *ninety*.'

'That's right. Born before the Crimean war, fought in the Boer war, so a man of vast experience. Very knowledgeable about explosives. I know a bit about 'em myself, don't you know? Between us we could lay a mine or two.'

'I hope you'll tell us where.'

'Of course. It'll all be done professionally. Mostly in the lanes, catch the Germans as they're marching along 'em.'

His wife shook her head.

'I just can't imagine it's possible,' she said.

He looked at her. He took her hand.

'Then don't try, my dear. Just leave the war to me.'

It seemed to Diana that James had aged ten years in the first few months of the war. Although there had been no fighting in this strange waiting time of what people called the *phoney* war, despair seemed to sap his energy. He slept little, reverting to catnapping as he had done in the Great War when he never had the chance of undisturbed sleep.

He was sitting over breakfast now, evidently in no hurry to prepare for the address he was to give at an armistice day service this morning. Once he would have rushed off, fired by some new idea, to add to his notes, revise his speech.

'All these years we've worked,' he said in the hopeless voice that was increasingly his, 'all these post-war years, to mend men and make their lives tolerable, even happy. We have toiled to heal the wounded, honour the dead, help and support the widows. For twenty years we have striven to do this. And now it seems we're to be told that they weren't the post-war years after all: they were the pre-war years of stoking up another war.'

She ached for him but had no words of comfort. To see all the good that he had done to these war-wounded men about to be completely overwhelmed by new armies of damaged bodies, of the blind and maimed, was more than he could bear. 'It's criminal,' he said. 'I suppose they'll call it the *Second* Great War. Do you know, I heard someone say the other day that future generations will look back and say it was just *one* war?'

'I suppose they just mean that the Treaty of Versailles reduced Germany to such a state that she'd turn to any dictator?'

'Yes, that's all they mean. So people will think that these years of hope and toil when we've tried to rebuild our country, were really just years of a truce, waiting to get our breath back for the next round? But we who lived through it know it wasn't like that. We all believed, everybody believed, we'd fought the war to end all wars. The world had learned its lesson, we thought. Or at least Europe had.'

The clock over in the tower chimed ten o'clock.

'Time we were getting ready,' she said. 'It's still right, my dear, to honour the dead of the last war, whatever is happening now.'

The church was crowded with old soldiers and their families, with newly conscripted men, with men and women from all the services. Sitting among them, Diana sensed they were waiting for some rousing call to arms, wanted to be inspired for the fight.

If so they were disappointed. James spoke, as always, from the heart but this time with little hope. If there must be war, his bleak message seemed to be, do not delude yourselves that war is glorious. If you take glory as your guide, then your road will lead to disillusionment and bitterness. Instead I will offer you the truth which, though unpalatable, will be a safer companion. He ended by quoting the words spoken by Arthur Quiller-Couch at an armistice day service not long after the war:

> *There are few households in this land that this war has left without a domestic sorrow far more real, more natural, more abiding than any exultation over victory. All the old statues of Victory have wings; but grief has no wings. She is the unwelcome lodger that squats on the hearth-stone between us and the fire, and will not move, or be dislodged.*

These were the last words she heard him speak. He went back and sat in his place by her side, smiled at her and shut his eyes. He looked so calm and peaceful that for a little while she thought he had fallen asleep. But then his head fell forward and, looking up into his face, she saw that he was still smiling as if glad at last to have earned that long sleep which nothing can disturb.

Thirty

The day of James' funeral was one of those rare November days of perfect stillness. The winter sun was low in the sky but shone brightly, lighting up the bare branches of the trees, melting the frost on the grass. It warmed the men as they waited patiently outside the church to be helped to their pews. They came on crutches, they came in wheelchairs and the blind were led in by their friends.

It was Diana's determination that had brought them there; she knew how much these men wanted to say a last thank you to the one who had battled ceaselessly on their behalf. She had insisted that any of the men who wanted to come – even if they had long ago left James' care – should be helped to do so. She'd organized cars and ambulances and helpers, knowing that the presence of these men would matter much more to James than any number of brass hats.

It's the last service I can do for him, she thought as she followed his coffin up the aisle and, as she took her place next to her parents, she was aware of feeling deeply grateful that she had been able to help this man who had worked to mend so many broken lives.

Sebastian, sitting with his parents near the back of the church, found the simple service almost unbearably sad. He remembered how James had raged against war the last time they had spoken to each other; he himself felt the older man's rage now as he looked at these casualties of war and wondered why men continued to do this to each other, century after century, when the results were so awful, why after several millennia they had not found a better way.

Diana stood in the porch after the service talking to

everyone as they left. He was reminded, as he stood with his parents in the queue, of that other occasion fifteen years ago when he had waited in the line where she was standing with James at the reception. How different it had been. How deeper now his feelings. When he reached her he found that he could talk honestly to her of his regard for James, could talk without his love for her getting in the way.

He did not linger, sensing that she wanted to give all her attention to the men whom James had served. So he left her and walked quickly away to catch up with his parents.

Even his father was subdued as they sat on the train in the early evening.

'Great chappie, that James,' he said. 'Pity there aren't more like him.'

The train was packed, every seat taken, the corridor crammed with soldiers and their baggage. There was no light on the train, so he felt rather than saw that his mother was weeping, that his father was holding her hand.

'No idea how we're supposed to know when we've arrived,' his father said, breaking the silence in an effort to be cheerful, 'now they've painted out all the station names. Not that you'd be able to see them anyway.'

The only light they saw on the entire journey was a faint glimmer from the guard's lamp as he pushed his way down the crowded corridor.

'So you've laid up the car, Father?' Sebastian asked, knowing that car talk always distracted his father and that if his father began to talk, his mother would join in, if only to contradict him.

'Yes, put it up on wooden blocks for the duration. They say petrol's going to be even scarcer. Anyway this pool petrol probably wouldn't do the engine any good. D'you know these black market scoundrels are charging six shillings and sixpence for a gallon of the stuff instead of the legal one and six on the ration?'

'Where do they get it?'

'It's commercial petrol.'

'But it's dyed red.'

'Ah, but these clever johnnies have found a way of getting rid of the dye by pouring it through a gas mask filter. Just an ordinary one like this,' he added tapping his gas mask box.

'Good lord! The things people get up to in wartime.'

'Well, can you blame them? People are forever running out of petrol and having to abandon their cars miles away from home. The hearse ran out of petrol at Joe Simonds' funeral. You know, old Joe the smithy chappie?'

'What did they do?'

'Went and got a horse to pull the old boy. Quite suitable when you think how many of them he's shod over the years. Still, it's a bit much if you can't go on your last journey without running out of petrol. Bloody Huns. Sorry, Barbara.'

'That's all right, dear. Have you told Sebastian about the shelter?'

'You'll have to look at it before you leave tomorrow morning, my boy. It keeps very dry. Some people have six inches of water in theirs.'

'Jenny Sawyer told me that when she and Bill went into theirs one night they were kept awake by frogs splashing about in the water,' his wife told him. 'She says she'd rather die in her own comfortable bed than survive in a frogs' pond.'

'She always was a silly woman. What's the harm in a few frogs? The French eat them, though that's no recommendation. I've put a mattress on the board, Sebastian, and we've made up a proper double bed and we keep supplies ready, put a bottle of water in fresh every day, biscuits and so on. Barbara will be quite comfortable down there.'

'I shan't go unless you do too.'

'Well, I shall have my duty to do, so we'll talk about that when the time comes. But I can tell you, Sebastian, it's a pretty splendid air-raid shelter.'

'What kind is it?'

His father raised his watch and squinted at the luminous dial.

'Half past six,' he said.

* * *

It was several months before they put the shelter to any use. On a clear August night, German airmen jettisoned their bombs on their way back home after bombing London. The bombs landed in a field a mile away and killed a cow.

By that time, Arthur Crawley had ushered his wife into the shelter, seen her comfortably settled.

'You're to stay here as well,' she told him.

'Don't you worry about me. I'm just going up to get a rifle out of the store in the barn.'

'What do you need a rifle for?'

'In case any of them bails out.'

There was no sign of a parachute in the clear, starlit sky, but he went in search of a rifle all the same. It was pitch black in the barn and before his eyes had accustomed themselves to the darkness, he had tripped over a plank of wood and broken his leg. His wife found him lying on the floor when the all clear sounded.

'He was very lucky,' she told Elspeth on the phone two days later. 'It could have been much worse, just a fractured leg and a few cracked ribs, but really, it is exasperating. All that preparing of the shelter and then when he should go into it, he goes wandering off and breaks his leg. The hospital's done a splendid job on him but obviously they don't want to keep civilian casualties in unnecessarily but heaven knows how we'll manage at home.'

'You must come here,' Elspeth told her. 'You must stay here until the war's over. It's far safer here than where you are.'

'Oh, my dear, I couldn't think of imposing on you.'

'Barbara, all over this country people are moving in with other families, everyone is sharing what accommodation they have. And we have plenty of room. And I should be glad, so glad, of your company. Diana is here; she will speak to you.'

Diana took the phone from her mother.

'I think I've got the gist of that,' she told Barbara. 'I suggest I come over in the small ambulance, pick you up and we'll go on to the hospital and collect our patient. I'll talk to the sister in charge of him first, if you could let me have the hospital number.'

'But will they allow him to leave?'

'Oh, yes, I'm sure they'll be glad to agree. We have all the equipment here that he can possibly need. And, as I heard Mamma say, you'll both be much safer here. And she'll just love having you to stay.'

'Then I must accept very gratefully.'

'Good. Don't forget to bring your ration cards.'

'I shan't. They're beyond price. They say that when burglars break into houses nowadays, they don't bother with the silver, just take the ration cards.'

How well it has worked out, Elspeth thought as she stood at the dining-room window and watched Arthur walking slowly on his crutches, Charles alongside. He seemed to have a soothing effect on Charles. Perhaps he had needed to have a man's company, she thought, watching as they took their morning constitutional in the grounds. Of course their conversations were rather curious with Arthur not hearing much of what Charles had to say and Charles not understanding much of what Arthur said. But, though it might sound odd to an outsider, it didn't seem to worry either of them as they walked companionably together towards the lake.

'I was thinking how lucky we are to have you both here,' she remarked to Barbara who had joined her at the window.

'I think *we* are the lucky ones.'

'And you're both looking so much better,' Elspeth told her, remembering how dreadful they'd looked when they arrived, Arthur obviously in pain and Barbara exhausted, bringing with them their gas masks and ration cards and not much else.

'Diana was wondering if you would like her to go and bring anything you need from home?'

'Oh, I'd be so grateful!' Barbara exclaimed.

She had been quietly worrying about clothes. She didn't like to go off home for a day and leave Arthur to be looked after by Elspeth who already had enough to do looking after Charles. Besides the thought of the train journey there and then struggling back with cases of clothes appalled her. Yet she hadn't liked even to raise such a trivial worry when this dreadful war was raging.

'Diana says she could finish work by midday on Saturday. If you give her a list she'll bring back anything you want. My only worry is that she'll have to drive back in the dark and really to drive on our narrow roads without lights is so dangerous.'

'She must stay the night and drive back the next morning. Our bed is aired and the last thing I did was to change the sheets.'

It was the first time Diana had been away from Northrop since James had died. She was glad of the break, even if she did feel slight guilt at using supplementary petrol for an outing which wasn't, strictly speaking, to do with nursing. She'd spent the intervening months, after answering thousands of letters, trying to complete all the many projects James had been involved in, grateful for the fact that she had been so involved herself that she knew what needed to be done.

In fact the profound gratitude for sharing in his work which she had felt so strongly at his funeral had remained with her, but now she felt that she was doing some kind of final rounding off of her life with James. It was as if, as she saw to the business of concluding his work at Northrop, tying up all the loose ends, preparing the hall for whatever other use the nation might require of it, she was writing the last chapter in the book of her marriage. It must, of course, be in the style of the rest, but it was a concluding chapter all the same.

A new life was soon to start, but she had no idea what sort of life it would be or where she would be sent to help in the war effort. Neither did anyone else, of course, in wartime, she reflected as she drove up the gravel drive to Oxenhurst Manor.

Even though she had been given the key, even though she had a list of all the things she was to collect, she still felt like a thief as she entered the silent house. The owners' absence reproved her and her footsteps sounded unnaturally loud as she crossed the hall.

There was a damp smell in the house, probably increased by the bowls of dead flowers in every room. She carried them into the kitchen, lifted the soft slimy stalks out of the putrid green water and dumped them into a bucket. She wasn't sure what to do with them; dustbin men didn't call as they used to do, everything that wasn't eaten was burnt as fuel to eke out the coal ration or disposed of in the garden. That was it; there was bound to be a compost heap in the vegetable garden.

The last time she'd walked in this garden had been at Debbie's christening some ten or eleven years ago. Was it really so long since she'd driven back to Northrop with Sebastian and he'd stayed the night with them? Better not to think about Sebastian, she told herself as she went back into the house and found the boxroom where Elspeth had told her the cases were kept.

Filling a case with Arthur's clothes was easy. She had done this for James often enough and men's clothes seemed to be arranged to a similar pattern. There were the familiar piles of vests and underpants, the drawer of socks, the shelf with the handkerchiefs, the shoes stretched on shoe trees on a rail at the bottom of the cupboard.

It was different with Barbara's things. How much more *personal* women's clothes are, she thought, looking at the skirts, dresses and blouses hanging in the wardrobe, at the drawerfuls of underwear. She'd been asked to do it, mustn't be squeamish, she told herself firmly, as she set about finding twin sets and tweed skirts, but she found herself apologizing to their absent owner all the same.

By the time she had filled the two cases, carried them out to the car and collected an assortment of hats, gloves and walking sticks from the hallstand because they had a useful, much used look, it was almost dark.

She was hungry, she realized as she went back into the kitchen. Elspeth had said she should help herself to any food in the larder. There was the remains of a knuckle of ham on the marble slab, some cheese in the meatsafe. She sat at the big kitchen table, sliced some of the loaf of bread she'd brought with her, made herself a sandwich, which she ate off the breadboard, something which, she reflected, no self-respecting servant would ever have done in this kitchen.

It was a big kitchen, almost as big as the one at Northrop, with a truly Victorian *batterie de cuisine*. All those copper saucepans and frying pans, skillets and griddles; would anyone ever use them again? There was a capacious old armchair by the fire just like the one at Northrop which only Cook was allowed to use. She wondered if Sebastian used to come in here when he was a little boy, did he beg for scones and tarts from the cook as they used to do at Northrop from their grumpy cook with her unpredictable moods, vast girth and astonishingly light hand with pastry? Better not think about Sebastian. But it was hard not to when she was in his house.

Her mother had, of course, plied Barbara with questions in the last few days, about Sebastian, about Celia, about the children. Barbara spoke mostly about the children, it was fairly obvious that she and Celia weren't at all close, which was strange because nobody could be easier to get on with than Barbara Crawley. Perhaps Celia didn't get close to anyone. To Sebastian? She must have been close to him at least three times. Better not to think of him and Celia, she told herself again as she washed up her few dishes. Better get off to bed before it was quite dark. She didn't want to worry about the blackout, would make do with the little torch, thin as a pencil, which gave out only the regulation glimmer of light.

It was as she was crossing to the dresser where she'd left the torch, that she heard the footsteps. They were overhead. She stood very still, every nerve strained to catch the sound. She knew she'd locked the front door and she'd checked that all the windows were bolted. But somebody was in the house. Somebody was coming down the uncarpeted back stairs. She could hear them clearly now, a man's tread. So there might have been a parachutist after all, hiding in one of the many unused rooms, even in the walk-in cupboards. With no lights on, with the windows not blacked out, they would think the house had been abandoned. The footsteps were in the lobby now, approaching the kitchen. As the door opened she snatched one of the pans from the wall.

The man came in cautiously, she could just make him out in the semi-darkness, peering round the door, so that his back was towards her. It was her one chance to take him by surprise. She brought down the frying pan on to the side of his head as hard as she could. He turned, lost his balance and fell on the floor.

She hesitated as he lay there, knowing that she had the advantage, but not sure how to use it. She was still holding her weapon but, as she hesitated, he suddenly jumped into a crouching position and lunged at her. So he was only pretending he was knocked out, she had time to realize, as she stepped back, her hands raised, instinctively trying to ward off the expected blow.

But he stopped. He was looking at her feet, then his eyes travelled up her body until they were face to face. It was Sebastian.

She fell against him, laughing hysterically with relief.

'Oh, God, Diana! I thought it was a man, I was going to give him the rugby tackle of his life, and then I saw those feet. Even then I never thought it would be you. Oh, I am so sorry.'

'I'm the one who should be sorry. How's your head?'

'Oh, it wasn't much.'

He looked at the pan; a small omelette pan.

'You should have taken one of those heavy copper ones. That really would have knocked me out.'

'I just grabbed the nearest. Just as well I did. But, Sebastian,' she asked, pulling a little away from him and looking up into his face, 'why are you here? Nobody said you'd be coming.'

'Let's sit down and I'll tell you,' he said.

'But first – are you hungry?'

'No.'

'Cup of tea?'

'Not if making it takes you away from me.'

He meant it; he was terrified that somehow she'd escape him once again.

She laughed, took his hand and led him over to the sink where, his arm around her, she filled the kettle and put it on to boil. He knew where the candles were kept in a box by the stove, lit one and put it on a saucer on the ground, well away from any window.

'There's only one comfortable chair,' he told her. 'We'll have to share it.'

So she sat on his knee in the cook's armchair, as they drank tea by candlelight.

'Now tell me why you're here,' she said.

'It was a snap decision. I knew the parents were safely in Northrop – Mother rang me the day before yesterday – and when I found I was free tomorrow I suddenly thought I should come and check that they'd left everything in order. I've always had the keys of the house and I just never thought for one moment that there would be anyone here. Of course in normal times I'd have seen lights on, but these aren't normal times.'

'I decided not to struggle with the blackout, just creep to bed by torchlight.'

'I didn't see your car.'

'I parked it round the back.'

'If only I'd seen it, I'd have rung the doorbell and not given you such an awful fright.'

'And I wouldn't have biffed you with the omelette pan.'

'I'll forgive you,' he said, laughing and kissing her. 'But how are things at Northrop? It was wonderful of your mother to take my parents in.'

'Oh, she loves having them. It really has given her a new lease of life. Your father's making good progress, managing his crutches, and your mother's fine. We just don't plan too far ahead nowadays. We don't even know what will happen at the hall.'

'You mean now that James has gone?'

'Well, not only that. The numbers were being run down anyway. The government might take it over for a maternity home—'

'Maternity home! That's a real change of use.'

'Yes, but they must get expectant mothers out of the towns to safe places to have their babies now the bombing's started. Laura's involved with other gynaecologists in schemes in the north. She says they're always looking for places like Northrop, safely in the country but not too remote.'

'Perhaps she'll come down and run it?'

'It could happen. Then she'd be my boss.'

'Would you mind that?'

She laughed.

'No, of course not, but it's more likely I'd be on the admin side, though obviously I'd help out in a crisis.'

They talked on, they talked of the past, she told him about Rupert and Laura, they gave news of each other's families, talked of Teddy, of the last war, even of the time before that war, a time which might have been a century ago, so different was life then. And he thought how comforting it was, how easy to talk like this, without having to weigh his words, just let it all come out, knowing that she would understand.

'What are you thinking?' she asked suddenly, taking his face between her hands.

'I was just remembering something I once read about friendship, about how you needn't measure your words with someone you love, just offer it all, chaff and grain together, knowing that they will sift it out, keep what is worth keeping—'

'"And with the breath of kindness blow the rest away,"' she completed for him.

'Oh, Diana, my darling,' he said, holding her tightly in his arms. 'Oh, thank God I found you here.'

They clung together for a while, not speaking, no sound except the loud ticking of the kitchen clock.

Then at last he spoke. Taking both her hands in his and suddenly very serious, he said, 'I know that what you've just said, that nobody can make plans nowadays, is true, but can't we at least try to think about *our* future, Diana? Is it too soon for *us* to make plans?'

She looked up at him, startled.

'I won't say another word if you don't want me to, Diana.'

'It's all right. Go on.'

'Would you marry me if I was free? If I was divorced?'

Divorced! The dreadful word seemed to cut into their safe, candlelit world. The voice of conscience told her that it was all wrong, that it would be bad enough to come between man and wife even if the wife was a stranger but to do so when the wife was your cousin surely added treachery to the sin? Because it was a sin to come between man and wife. She had been brought up to believe that those whom God has joined together no man should put asunder. She had seen and heard Sebastian make his vows.

But another voice told her that his marriage was unhappy, that she was not coming between them. He had told her there was nothing between him and his wife and she believed him. She wouldn't be breaking up their marriage. It was broken already.

He watched her closely. He saw, in the flickering light of the candle, the conflict in her face, understood the argument that was going on in her head.

Then she looked at him and said quite simply, 'Yes, Sebastian, I would if you were free to ask me.'

'Oh, my darling,' he said and she could hear the relief in his voice as he took her again in his arms and held her close. After a while he said, 'It's so different from how it was when we were young. How easy it would have been then, how carefree. I am so sorry that it will all be so difficult now, so unlike what you deserve.'

'Sh, Sebastian don't think like that.'

They sat for what seemed a long time, not speaking, then Sebastian broke the silence, saying, 'I have decided that after the war, I shall ask Celia for a divorce. She did once suggest it—'

'Oh, Sebastian, I didn't know! I mean I didn't know it was so bad between you. But you didn't . . . ?'

'No, I couldn't then – the children were so small, so vulnerable. But in a few years they'll be old enough to understand. Even now, I think the older ones know that all is not well between us.'

'And if the war is over sooner than any of us expect?'

'It won't be. I think four years minimum.'

'She might not agree to divorce you. She might change her mind.'

'That's true. And as the law stands I can do nothing about it.'

'Yes. I know people who're caught like that. The only alternative is to live as man and wife although you're not married.'

He shook his head.

'I could never ask the woman I loved to do that,' he told her.

Of course not, she should have known. He was far too decent, too honourable to bring such shame on any woman, least of all herself.

They were quiet for a while, both thinking of what might have been.

'Have you had any moments of happiness?' he asked suddenly.

She thought and then said carefully, 'I don't really know if it counts as happiness but there is something about being useful, you know, a kind of deep satisfaction, a sense of something achieved. And you?'

'Yes, I recognize what you mean. But for me the children, despite all, have brought moments of great joy; they're so full of surprises.'

'Yes, I can imagine. I've missed that.'

Her voice broke. 'It's awful, the hope and disappointment, Sebastian.'

'But you once said—'

'Oh yes, I know we talked about it that time after Debbie's christening and I glossed over it as usual, said I had so much else that really I didn't mind, or something like that. Oh, I got so good at pretending. And all the time it hurt so much and I felt such a failure.'

'No, no, Diana,' he murmured, rocking her in his arms as she wept. 'Never that.'

'Yes,' she contradicted bitterly.

She had never talked about it to anyone before, never admitted the pain, least of all to James. They'd worked together, but never talked together as man and wife. Her mother's questions she had parried. Even to Sebastian she had pretended. Now she couldn't stop talking and through her tears went on, 'Everyone else was having babies, or so it seemed. Friends and relations begin to look at you after you've been married about eighteen months and their eyes question you even if their tongues don't. The word *barren* finds a place to lodge itself in the mind.'

It's so unfair, he thought. Mother nature is so unfair, so cruel.

'So you see I felt a failure *as a woman.* However successfully I did anything else, I had still failed at being a woman.'

'But, darling,' he said, wiping her cheeks against his own to dry them, 'quite hopeless women have babies, stupid women, any sort of woman and it doesn't mean they're successful.'

'It does, yes it does. They've performed their function as women. Fulfilled it. Anway that's how it *felt.*'

'And James? You talked to James?'

She shook her head and he realized that just as he had never been able to talk, really talk, to Celia, so she had never been able to talk to James. He held her close and after a minute, she grew calm and said, 'I'm sorry, it's probably something only women can understand. It's different for men; they don't fail as men, even if they fail at work or anything else.'

But they do, he thought. I always felt I'd failed as a man because I'd failed to arouse and satisfy my wife. That was partly what lay behind those black moments, those days of depression. It was nothing compared with Diana's pain, but it was a primitive sense of failure all the same.

He took a handkerchief out of his pocket and gently wiped her eyes. She looked weary, this woman he had loved for so many years. The years had marked her face with lines around her eyes and with strands of grey in her hair, and he loved her the more tenderly for it.

'You must be very tired, my darling,' he said. 'We'd better go up.'

'You too. We're both exhausted.'

'You're all right now?'

'Oh yes,' she said, kissing him. 'I think it was just that I'd never spoken of it to anyone before. I'm sorry.'

'No, never say that to me. Your sorrows are my sorrows. I *want* to share them. Promise?'

'I promise. And will you promise me something?'

'Anything.'

'I know how dangerous it's going to be in London. Please don't be killed. I couldn't bear to lose you *twice*.'

'I promise to do my best to survive.'

'Thank you.'

They spoke lightly but they both knew how fragile life is in wartime. They both feared that they might have found each other only to lose each other again.

'Speaking of survival, if there's any trouble from Hitler tonight, we make a dive for Father's shelter.'

'Oh, but those bombs your parents had were just a fluke, weren't they? Planes jettisoning their bombs they'd failed to drop on London.'

'Well, yes, but if they launch a major attack on London this summer, we'd be in the flight path. Anyway Father would like to think it got some use after all his efforts putting it up.'

He eased her gently off his knee and stood up.

'Now let's be practical,' he said. 'It's gone midnight and we're both very tired.'

'There's hot water if you want a bath. I turned on the immersion heater on your mother's instructions.'

'Bless you. And she always leaves my bed made up. You take your torch, I've got the candle.'

He followed her upstairs, one pinpoint of light behind the

other in the darkness. On the landing they said an awkward goodnight.

'Diana?'

'Yes?'

'Nothing.'

And he walked resolutely away. She washed quickly, climbed into his parents' bed and thought how good he was, how self-controlled, how honourable. Part of her wished that he wasn't. She suppressed the thought and, exhausted, instantly fell asleep.

She woke up with a start. The bed seemed to be shaking and she heard what she thought was thunder rumbling and crashing. Suddenly there was a loud banging on the bedroom door and Sebastian rushed in, shouting, 'Get up quickly, it's a raid, come to the shelter,' and he was wrapping a coat around her and pulling her along the corridor, down the stairs, out into the moonlit garden. She had pushed on some slippers, but one fell off so she kicked off the other and ran barefoot across the damp grass.

They could hear bombs crashing down close by, machine guns rattling as anti-aircraft guns crackled and exploded, followed by a muffled rumbling. The very air seemed to reverberate. Then a tremendous crash behind them told them that the house had been hit. Suddenly there seemed to be lights everywhere, as fires broke out and searchlights criss-crossed each other in the sky. She ran frantically behind Sebastian, as exposed and vulnerable as a hare caught in the headlights of a car. Then he was pulling her down into the shelter, down into the earth, into the darkness and the quiet.

They stood panting in their little sanctuary, which had a dank and earthy smell. Then, 'We can have lights on down here,' he said, probing the darkness with his torch. 'Oh, look, there's a Tilley lamp and matches, Father's thought of everything.'

He lit the lamp and its light showed that the space was almost entirely occupied by a double bed, except for a corner stacked with all the provisions his father had laid on, including a carafe of water. 'Not very fresh, I'm afraid,' Sebastian said, 'but we shan't die of thirst. And there are some biscuits and a few tins and a tin opener and – are you all right?'

'Yes,' she said, but she was shaking. 'I think it was hearing the bombs. You know it brought back those awful months in Etaples when we thought the Germans were going to come.'

'I know, I know,' he murmured holding her close, 'but you're safe now, safe now in Mother Earth.'

She was still trembling.

'There's about a foot and a half of soil over our heads, topped with turf,' he told her. 'So we're as safe as houses – no, I don't mean that, much safer than that.'

If Sebastian hadn't been here, she thought, I might have been buried under the house, as Selina was.

'No, I should have said that we're as safe in this shelter as rabbits in their burrows, as foxes in their holes,' Sebastian corrected himself.

He remembered how in the war the men used to try to dig their way into the earth during a bombardment. It was instinctive; with their bare hands they'd try to claw themselves into the ground. Sometimes, when their bodies were brought in, you could see clods of soil deep under their fingernails.

The bombs were still falling, but the sound was muffled now and seemed far away. Outside shrapnel would be flying, fires breaking out, buildings shaking and juddering. Down here it was very still. Tomorrow they would have to go back into the world, face its dangers, but for tonight they could forget it; down here they were safe, the two of them gone to earth.

She had stopped trembling. She was relaxed in his arms.

'Come to bed,' he said.

And really there was nowhere else to go.